The Desert Plant

by

Candio Willene

DORRANCE PUBLISHING CO., INC.
PITTSBURGH, PENNSYLVANIA 15222

ISBN # 0-8059-6252-2
Printed in the United States of America

First Printing

For information or to order additional books, please write:
Dorrance Publishing Co., Inc.
701 Smithfield Street
Third Floor
Pittsburgh, Pennsylvania 15222-3906
U.S.A.
1-800-788-7654
Or visit our web site and on-line catalog at www.dorrancepublishing.com

This book is dedicated with love to my husband Joseph and my son and daughter.

I also dedicate my work to my dear mother and father, and thank them for my education.

I want to thank my sisters and my niece for their inspirations, and especially my husband for his support and contribution.

Contents

Chapter One

The Search

Good! The plane had landed. Everybody was rushing to get out. The sun was glaringly hot. She pulled her sunglasses out of her bag and perched them on her nose as she stepped outside the plane. Taking a deep breath, she exhaled and thought, *The beginning of a new life.* As she walked down the stairs, she heard a familiar voice.

"Julie!"

She looked straight ahead and there he stood, tall and handsome in his jeans. She smiled as they came closer. He embraced her and kissed her on her cheeks. She hugged him back. "How are you, Jacque? I am so excited to be here!"

After clearing Customs and Immigration, her luggage was stored in the Jeep. Opening the passenger door, he helped her in, then he got in the driver's side, saying, "*C'est l'heure d'embouteillage du trafique. Il y a beaucoup de monde dans la station* (It's the rush hour traffic time, and there's a lot of people in the street. I'm sorry, I forget that your French language is not that fluent)."

Smilingly she replied, "That's okay, I need to practice. The earlier I start, the better it will be for me. So from now on I'll try to talk in French as much as I can."

Rolling down the window so that she could feel the breeze through her hair and on her skin, she said, "Port-au-Prince is hot. I need to cool down. Oh, Jacque, I can't wait to see the rest of the family!"

The traffic was not so bad. In less than two hours they arrived at the Bassine's mansion (Jacques's home that he shared with his sisters Carine,

Nicole, and Maxine and also his younger brother, Jean). He drove up the driveway to the front door and stopped, helping Julie get out. The butler opened the door as Jacque took Julie's hand and walked inside with her. There were three female and four male servants standing to greet her. Jacque introduced her around.

They bowed their heads and all addressed her, "Madame!"

She looked around in admiration at the beauty of the mansion, tastefully decorated in light colours to match the marble floor and high ceilings. The crystal chandeliers and curving balustrade went all the way up to the upper floors. The windows were covered in sixteenth-century drapes that reached from the ceiling to the floor that would give it a closed-in look in the evenings but an airy, light look during the day.

Maxine ran down the stairs to greet Julie. Hugs and kisses were exchanged between the two friends. Maxine stepped back to get a better look at her friend and said, "Look at you, you're as beautiful as ever. Jacque did not sleep at all last night. He couldn't wait for you to arrive."

Julie looked at him and smiled. Jacque took her arm, saying, "Let me show you your room."

As they turned to go up the stairs, Julie, smiling indulgently, said, "Impatient man! Excuse us, Maxine."

Maxine said, "All right! Julie, see you later. Oh! By the way, welcome home, sister."

At the top of the stairs, Jacque opened the door to the bedroom that was going to be hers. She walked in and looked around the room, which was extravagant. It was overlooking the front of the yard with its beautiful manicured lawns and rows upon rows of flowering trees and plants. The carpet was piled so high you actually sank in it. In the middle stood a king-sized bed draped with a pale pink satin spread to match the curtains at the windows. The dresser was the highest grade of mahogany ever produced. On it stood an enormous vase of fresh-cut flowers. There was even a private balcony outside the windows. It was a bedroom that one can only dream about. There was nothing missing that would prevent someone from being comfortable. Still she felt something was missing.

Seeing her expression Jacque asked, "Is everything to your satisfaction, Julie? If not, tell me now, so I may change it. We want your stay here to be a happy and comfortable one."

Fearing that he might think her ungrateful, she quickly said, "Oh don't worry, Jacque, everything is fine. I'm just a little tired, that's all."

There was a knock on the door by the butler, Roy. Jacque called, "*Rentrez donc* (Come in), Roy!"

He had brought her luggage and also one of the maids, "Your luggage, madame."

Turning to the maid, Jacque said, "Will you help madame with her clothes and anything else she might need?"

To Julie he said, "She will be your personal maid while you are staying with us."

Bowing, the maid said, "*Bonsoir, madame. Je suis Marie* (Good afternoon, madame. I am Marie)."

And she picked up one of the suitcases and placed it on the bed to start unpacking. She made short work of hanging Julie's clothing. Then she asked, "*Puis-je préparer votre bain* (Can I prepare you a warm bath), Madame?"

Julie turned from the window where she was admiring the garden with a smile and replied, "Please, very warm!"

Jacque smiled and said, "Can I join you, Julie?"

She replied, "I will see you in three hours."

"Three hours," he responded as he walked out of the room.

Laughing and shaking her head, Julie said, "Close the door behind you. Marie, help me please."

Removing her clothes, Julie laid in the tub of scented bubble bath water. She closed her eyes and wondered, *Did I make the right decision?*

She must have drifted off, for the next thing she knew, three hours was almost gone. Looking at the clock, she jumped up and called, "Marie!"

Marie came running. "*Oui, Madame.*"

"Look at the time. My robe, please! . . . Thank you!"

Shrugging on her robe, Julie walked to the closet to pick out something to wear as she continued to talk. "I haven't been in Haiti for quite sometime. Is there any new sight for me to see and new things for me to do while I'm here in Haiti, Marie?"

The maid helped her to put her clothes on. "Oh, Madame, there are many things to do here. Monsieur Jacque will show you."

"Really, Marie!"

She nodded. "He has a lot of friends and tonight I'm sure he'll surprise you."

Julie finished putting on her clothes, and Marie helped her to style her hair. Turning around she asked Marie, "Voilà! How do I look?"

With a wide, admiring smile Marie said, "Beautiful, Madame. You have a beautiful figure."

There was a knock at the door, and a voice said, "*C'est moi* (It's me), Julie. May I come in?"

Turning to take a final look at herself in the dressing table mirror, she called, "One moment, Jacque."

She put on very light lipstick, picked up her bag, took a deep breath, and opened the door. Jacque looked at her. She took his breath away. He looked at her as if he'd never seen her before. "You're beautiful, Julie."

Taking her hand, he tucked it under his arm and walked down the stairs and to the family room, where Maxine and the others, Carine, Jean, and Nicole, were waiting.

"Hello, Julie."

They all came forward and hugged her and kissed her on her cheeks.

Maxine hugged her tightly and whispered, "Girl! We have a lot to talk about, and I want details."

Jean pulled her away from Julie. "Pay her no mind. She's so nosy."

Nicole embraced her warmly. "Julie, welcome to Haiti."

While they were talking the butler came in and announced, "Dinner is ready."

Jacque crooked his elbow to Julie and with a flourish, said, "Shall we?"

Together they all walked to the dining room where an exquisite dinner was prepared for them to eat. Jacque sat Julie close to him on his right, Carine sat on his left, and the others took their places. In the middle of the second course the butler came in and handed Jacque a paper. Jacque looked at it and gave it back to Roy.

Suddenly Jacque stood up and cleared his throat. Everyone fell silent as he announced, "I'd like to make a toast. Welcome again, Julie, to Haiti and to my home. My family and I will do our utmost to make your stay an enjoyable and unforgettable one. Also, I want everyone to know what you really mean to me and how much I love you." He raised his drink. "To you, *ma chérie* (my darling)."

Jacque's words as well as his actions surprised Julie as he lowered his head and kissed her. She looked around at everyone and smiled coldly. The butler signaled Jacque with his eye, and Jacque said, "Will you excuse me, my love, someone came to see me. I'll be back. Have dessert without me."

As he walked away, Julie called to the butler, "Roy, can I have a martini, please?"

"Yes, madame."

Julie looked at Carine and asked, "What have you been doing with your life, Carine?"

Seeing that Julie needed to get away from the table and from all the eyes looking at her, Carine replied, "Let's go to the balcony so we can talk away from this nosy bunch."

The butler gave Julie her drink as they all got up from the table. She took it from him, thanked him, and together she and Carine walked down the hallway toward the balcony. She passed the library room, which was slightly open. Julie gave a quick glance through the library door and saw the back of a man sitting on a chair. His legs were crossed, and his hair looked bronzed from the light shining upon it. His legs were long. She could not hear anything, but Jacque's green eyes caught hers as she walked by.

Julie was wondering who was this person in black? But she continued to walk with Carine. Then she noticed that Carine was unusually quiet, which was not the norm for her.

Concerned that Carine might be upset she asked, "Carine, you seemed kind of quiet this evening. Is there something wrong?"

Suddenly someone spoke up behind them. Maxine and the others had followed them out to the balcony.

Maxine said, "Lately, strange things have been happening here, spooky things that can not be explained."

Carine rounded on her. "Yeah, right! Your own lusty desire, that's the only spooky thing, Maxine. If only you would stop lusting after Louis, then the spook would vanish."

Julie was curious. "Who is Louis?"

Nicole responded, "He's the richest man in Haiti. Young, tall, good-looking, smart–you name it, he's got it."

Julie laughed and said, "Sure he's not gay?"

Carine said, "Oh no! He's as straight as they come!"

Jean said, "I heard he's the devil. 'Louis Janvier, *le diable* (the devil), that's what people around here call him."

Maxine said, "To some he is *le diable. Il est méchant. Il n'a pas de pitié, surtout pour ceux qui sont contre lui* (the devil. He's ruthless. He has no pity, especially to those who go against him)."

Carine supplied, "He is Jacque's good friend. They do business together on certain occasions. You know he's a doctor."

Julie was more intrigued. "What kind?"

Carine looked at her as if she wasn't living in the twentieth century. "He's a surgeon, a neurologist. As a matter of fact, he has invited me to fly with him in his four-seater sports plane tomorrow. Julie, would you like to come with us?"

"*Merci* (thank you), but I have to say no."

Maxine asked hopefully, "Can I come instead?"

Nicole shushed her, "I thought he was the devil, Maxine. You know, I dreamed about Louis? He held me in his arms," Grabbing Jean, she started to twirl him around with her in a funny dance. "He danced with me, and then when he was about to kiss me, Carine came in my room and disturbed me," pointing her finger at Carine.

Jean struggled, trying to loosen himself from Nicole's grip, saying, "Nicole, let me go."

Everyone started to laugh. Jacque walked in and said, "Can someone fill me in on the joke?"

Everyone became quiet. Julie leaned over the balcony to see the tall stranger walking toward his car. As he opened the door to climb in, he stopped and looked up as if sensing that she was looking at him. Quickly Julie stepped back so he could not see her face. Carine whispered to Julie, "*C'est lui. Le célèbre Louis* (That's him. That's the famous Louis)." Turning to Jacque, "What brings Louis here tonight, Jacque?" she asked.

Jacque answered with a question of his own. "Are you going flying with him tomorrow, Carine?"

Nodding her head in affirmative, she chirped, "Bright and early. I wouldn't miss an opportunity like that."

Glancing at her, he said, "I want to talk to you about that." He looked at his watch. "I am sorry, Julie. I need a few more minutes in private, to talk to Carine. Excuse me. Come, Carine."

Jacque started to walk ahead, not looking back at Carine to see whether she was following. Carine looked apprehensive, but she followed him to the library. Everyone was quiet till they were no longer visible. Maxine spoke softly to Julie, "I smell trouble. Well, Julie, I'm glad you're here. Welcome back. Maybe your presence will bring some happiness so we can all have some peace and happiness."

Julie thought Maxine did not sound like someone who was thrilled. There was definitely something in the air.

She said quietly, "Let me disappear before he returns."

Nicole and Jean agreed, "The same here! See you tomorrow, Julie."

Nicole walked up the stairs like a lost young girl who didn't know where she was going. Jean walked behind her and put his arm on her shoulder. They both looked back and threw a kiss to Julie and waved good night. Julie turned back just in time to see Maxine running to the terrace of the mansion in the opposite direction of her bedroom. She stopped cautiously and looked around to see if anyone was watching. Julie stood there wondering, *What's she up to? I hope she's not in any trouble.*

She thought to herself, *Maybe I should follow her to make sure she's okay.* But she decided not to follow her tonight.

She stood there all by herself, lost in her own memories, wondering where she should go from here and what she was to do with herself now. Looking up at the stars, she began questioning and reasoning to herself. *Is there someone out there for me? Is it worth ruining my marriage for a new relationship? I care for Saul, I know I love him, but what is wrong with me? What happened to the loving woman he married? What did I do to make him so distraught? I do not understand his jealousy. What did I do to make him feel that way? Why did he blame Bill, our sweet baby? And where did he disappear to? I needed to get away to think!*

She shook her head, trying to dispel the bad memories and rekindle some good times Saul and she shared. She reflected back on the first time he kissed her, when he first made love to her, how gentle he was, and how he was concerned about her needs. And the time she was pregnant. How he used to put his head on her stomach, kissing it and listening to the sound of the baby's movements. She thought about her son, whom she left with her mother in New York. She missed him so much. A tear ran down her face as she embraced the wind against her face. She whispered, "Bill my love, my innocent."

She heard footsteps coming close toward her. She did not turn around. She looked up to the sky. There were many stars in the sky tonight. Then she felt someone warm enfold her and a whispered, "*Faites un souhait* (Make a wish)."

The feather of a kiss on her neck, and the voice came closer to her. Again a whispered, "*Faites un souhait, mon amour* (Make a wish, my love)."

It felt so good to be touched. For a moment she forgot her sadness, drifting between reality and fantasy. She wanted more of what she was getting, a feeling of such intense love and protection, as if it was real. But she knew it couldn't be, because she was alone. A soft moan exhaled out of her, and she almost lost control. In the distance she heard a voice call, "Are you all right, Julie?" The voice repeated, "Julie! Are you all right?"

She turned, but there was no one behind her except Jacque coming toward her. As he came closer, he repeated, "Are you all right, Julie?"

She answered, "*Bien! Très bien* (Fine! Real fine)!" Wondering what just happened to her, she asked, "Jacque, did you see someone else here?"

"No, and what happened to everyone?"

"They all left," she said.

"Were you here all alone?"

"Yes, but not that long," she said and looked away.

He continued, "Look, Julie! I know you've traveled a long way to come here. I'm going to do everything in my power to make you happy."

While he was talking, the butler came and asked them if they wanted some tea or a drink. She said she wanted another martini and Jacque wanted brandy.

"Julie, I want to see you happy."

He touched her face. She looked away.

"Look at me when I'm talking to you." Julie was still wondering what could have happened to her a few minutes ago.

Before she could reply, the butler brought their drinks. "Excuse me, madame, sir."

Julie took her drink. "Thank you, Roy. Where is Marie?"

Roy said, "Marie is in the back. I'll call her for you."

"No need to. Tell her to prepare a warm bath for me. I'll be up for bed soon."

"Yes, madame." The butler went off to deliver her message.

Jacque was disappointed. "You're going to bed so early? Why don't you spend the night with me? I want to spend the night talking to you."

She looked at him and smiled indulgently. "All right!"

They walked inside. She saw Marie going up the stairs. She called out, "Marie, I'm coming up now. Wait for me."

Jacque was startled at her sudden change of direction. "But, Julie, I thought. . . ."

"Later, Jacque," she interrupted. "Now I am going to take a bath. After I'm finished I'll let you know."

She grabbed Marie's hand and ran up the stairs, both of them laughing like two naughty children. She flung open the bedroom doors and Marie closed them behind her. Removing her shoes from her feet, she fell back on her bed. "Tell me, Marie, how long since you've been working for Jacque?"

"Almost two years now, madame."

"Almost two year? Then you must know a lot."

The maid remained silent. Julie opened her eyes widely, yawned, and pleaded, "Tell me one or two secrets about Jacque."

Bustling about the room picking up stuff and preparing Julie's bath, Marie felt there was not much to tell about Jacque. "Oh, madame, not much at all," she replied in a way that she didn't want Julie to know that she was nosy. "*Rien du tout* (Nothing at all)! Monsieur was very sad. Now that you are around, he seems to be very happy. Monsieur wants you also to be happy. Monsieur carried on about you day and night, how beautiful and how kind you are. Monsieur was right. You are kind and beautiful."

"Sit down," Julie invited. "Not there! Here." She tapped her hand on the bed.

Marie hesitated, because it was not a custom where the servant was allowed to sit or associate with the mistress of the house. "Your bed, madame?"

"Yes, don't be afraid. Tell me, what else did he say?"

Gingerly, sitting on the edge of the bed, Marie continued, "Monsieur said you are his princess and if anyone doesn't like it, they all could go to Hell."

Julie laughed and asked, "Oh, Marie, who was the tall man in the library?"

"What tall man, madame?"

"The tall man who came while we were eating; the tall man in black, with bronze hair."

Startled by the question, Marie said, "That tall man? Oh, madame, he's bad news. Everyone is afraid of him, but lately Monsieur Bassine . . . et, monsieur has a lot of exchange between them and I also heard that Monsieur Janvier is very mysterious and has many women. Young women can never resist his charms."

Smiling at her teasingly, Julie said, "Even you, Marie?"

"I'm too old, madame!"

They both laughed and Marie got up to finish preparing Julie's bath. "Madame, the water is getting cold."

She removed the rest of her clothes and put on her robe and walked to the bathroom. Marie started the jacuzzi as Julie called, "Make it very warm."

Marie said, "*Oui* (yes), madame. Do you want me to rub you down, madame?"

Julie declined her offer. "It's okay, Marie! Close the door behind you. Let me stay here for a while. Don't let anyone in. I want to be alone for a few moments."

She slid into the water up to her neck, closed her eyes, and wondered what had happened to her while she was on the balcony.

She was puzzled about what she had felt and heard. Was it real or was the island air getting to her?

But one thing she knew, something touched her and she wanted more of it. Marie knocked. Julie called, "Yes!"

"Monsieur wants to know if he can come in," Marie informed her, coming into the room.

"No," Julie replied. "Tell him to wait outside. I'll be out soon."

In a few minutes Julie was out of the tub. She combed her hair down and put on her pajamas and robe. She dabbed on some of her favorite perfume and walked out of the bathroom.

"Where's Monsieur?"

Marie indicated the door. "He's outside, madame!"

"Good." Julie smiled. "Okay, Marie, that will be all."

She walked out as Jacque appeared through the open door. He stood by the door with a bottle of wine in one hand and two wineglasses in the other. He stared at her and was hoping he could have seen her silhouetted figure through her sleeping clothes, but there was nothing to see because she was all covered up. She slowly turned around and held out her hand to him. "Come in, Jacque."

He walked closer to where she was standing and set the wine bottle and the wineglasses on the table. Still he didn't say anything. "Jacque, pour me some wine."

Jacque stood as if hypnotized by her beauty. He shook his head as if waking up from a dream and confusedly replied. "Oh, yes!" He poured the wine and handed it to her.

"Thank you!" She took the drink from his hand and took a sip. "Now, why do you want to spend the night talking to me?"

"Because I want to catch up with what you've been doing with your life. I have not seen you in years. I miss you."

Out of nowhere she heard the whispering voice in her mind that caused her to startle. She became afraid and she didn't want to let Jacque know what was startling her. She thought she had an ear infection. She sat by Jacque for a moment without saying a word, then she asked, "Jacque, how are you and your girlfriend doing? And when are you two going to get married?"

She sat quietly with her glass in her hand, listening to what Jacque was telling her.

Carine was in her room talking on the telephone with Louis, pleading to him, "Why can't I be with you, Louis, *pourquoi* (why)? You know I love you."

He softly explained to her why she should be listening to her big brother. "Between you and I, a relation can never be, because I do not feel the same way you do, Carine. I feel no love for you. I don't want to hurt you. I wish I could find a gentler way to tell you this, and for you to understand why."

Carine became distressed. She couldn't understand why Louis wouldn't want her. "Is there someone else, Louis? Do I know her? I want to give myself to you, Louis. I'll do anything you want me to do, darling."

"Then forget about me! Good night, Carine!"

Carine spent her whole night sobbing and wondering who Louis was with. Was it Maxine or was it Nicole or someone else? She wondered where Maxine was. She was not in her room when she checked earlier. Was Maxine with Louis? With these slashing thoughts going around her head, she fell asleep.

Julie fell asleep while she was listening to Jacque's life story on the comfy chair. He got up from his chair. Gently picking her up, Jacque carried her to her bed and laid her on it. As he moved away from her, he kissed her gently on her cheek. He smiled as he walked to the balcony outside her room. Walking out, he removed his shirt to get some breeze against his chest because it was a hot night. Jacque was well built and quite distinguished. He was wondering how he should help Julie and what he should have her do.

"Later we should see a counselor," he whispered to himself. "I'm going to make sure she got her divorce from that man."

Out of the corner of his eyes he saw Maxine on the terrace, trying to climb up the tree that was next to her bedroom. Jacque could not believe what he was seeing. He shook his head in disbelief, thinking how he was going to kill her. But before he did, he wanted to find out who she was with. This girl was trouble. How many nights had she been doing this?

Walking back inside, Jacque put his shirt back on and very quietly left the room so as not to awaken Julie. He walked down the hallway and went to the east wing of the mansion to Maxine's room. He opened the door and without switching on the lights, he walked over and sat on an armchair by her bed.

It was dark inside so Maxine could not see him sitting there. She breathed in relief, "I made it! Oh, I made it."

She was dancing, and singing quietly, "Ease on down, ease on down the road."

She turned the night lamp on and let out a little scream as she noticed Jacque sitting with a furious look on his face. Sidling to the other side of the bed out of his reach, she stammered, "I can explain, Jacque. You see, you were talking and I did not want to disturb you. I went over to Louis's place and I forgot my key. I did not want to disturb anyone so I climbed up the tree to come in my room."

Jacque stood up. Slowly he walked toward her, shouting, "Did you say Louis?"

"Yes."

"What were you doing there?"

The sound of Jacque's voice woke up Carine because her room was next to Maxine's. She got out of bed, pulled on her robe that was lying at the edge of her bed, and went to see what was going on. Going into Maxine's bedroom, she saw Jacque and Maxine arguing. Jacque was so furious at Maxine, he did not notice Carine had come into the room. He grabbed Maxine and was still shouting, "I don't want you to see Louis anymore. You will not be able to handle him. He will hurt you. You know his reputation!"

Carine hastily stepped between them. "What's going on here? Jacque, Maxine?"

Jacque turned in surprise to Carine. "You're awake? I did not mean to wake you up. I'm sorry." To Maxine, "We'll finish this later."

Brushing his apology aside, Carine asked, "I heard Louis's name. What did he do now?"

Maxine replied hotly, "None of your business!"

Jacque warned, "Maxine, you're already in deep trouble. Don't make it worse for yourself."

Taking Carine's arm, he pulled her into the hallway. Carine insisted, "What's going on? Why won't you tell me?"

"We'll talk later! I promise."

Jacque went his room. He removed his clothes and made ready for bed. While lying down he was thinking about what Maxine said: "*I was with Louis.*"

He nodded his head and thought, *That girl is crazy.* He was shocked to know that Maxine was now involved with Louis, and thought, *No wonder Louis is so nice to me and has become quite friendly.* Now he understood why. He felt a whole line of opportunity was about to open to him.

As he was drifting to sleep, he thought how distant Julie looked tonight. Her mind seemed troubled. Jacque wished he could enter her mind to find out what was she thinking. And what did she whisper when she fell asleep while they were talking? Something that sound like "loin," but he could not make it out.

11

Chapter Two

The Mysterious Ones

At seven o'clock in the morning, Jacque woke up. When he went to check on Julie, she was not in bed or in her bedroom. He went back to his bedroom.

Roy was in his room preparing the clothes he would be wearing for the day. Jacque did not say good morning when he walked in, but the butler greeted him, "Good morning, Monsieur Bassine!"

"I'm sorry, Roy," he hastened to apologize. "I seem to be absent this morning. Good morning. I'm supposed to be having a wonderful time, but my family is making it impossible for me."

Walking into the bathroom, he took a shower, brushed his teeth, shaved and put on his clothes, then combed his hair. Roy brushed him down and made sure nothing was on his suit. He surveyed himself in front of the mirror on his closet door.

As Roy opened the door for him, Carine was coming out of her bedroom. She looked him up and down and complimented, "My brother looks good, a woman killer."

She took his arm and together they walked down to the lobby. "You're early."

"What was all that between you and Maxine last night?"

"I saw her sneaking inside her room. She climbed the tree like a cat. I'm going to have that tree cut down."

Shaking her head, she looked at him skeptically. "You think cutting the tree down will solve the problem? Nonsense, brother! Who was she with?"

"With Louis," Jacque answered. He glanced at her to see her reaction, but she stayed calm, although Jacque knew she was enraged. He put his arm around her shoulders as they walked to the dining room. Nicole and Jean were already there.

In unison they called out, "Good morning, Jacque, Carine."

"Are you still going flying, Carine?" Nicole wanted to know.

"Nope, but I'm going shopping. Do you want to come?"

Nicole nodded. "Yes, why not. Jacque, I want to dine out tonight."

He looked at her indulgently. "Where do you want to eat?"

She shrugged. "I don't know."

The telephone rang. Roy brought it to Jacque.

"Monsieur . . . "

"*Merci*, Roy. Hello! *C'est lui. Pas plus tard que onze heures. Okay, à bientôt* (Thank you, Roy. Hello? This is I. No later than eleven. Okay, see you then)."

It was about nine o'clock when Julie came down for breakfast. She had gone jogging. Entering the room, she called, "Good morning, everyone."

"Did you sleep well last night?" Jacque asked.

"Yes, I did and I had a wonderful time running this morning."

Jean interrupted, "Be careful when you go jogging."

She smiled. "I'll keep that in mind. Oh, Jacque, I'm going riding today."

He looked at his watch ruefully. "Can we do that later? I want you to meet someone this morning, a good friend of mine."

"All right, at what time?"

"Can you be ready in about one hour?"

Julie had a big breakfast of grapefruit, a boiled egg, two nice-sized sausages, buttered toast with jelly, and a tall glass of orange juice. As she was leaving, she bumped into Maxine, who was coming in for breakfast. Julie said, "See you later, Max," which was Maxine's nickname.

Carefully avoiding Jacque's eyes, Maxine sat to eat her breakfast and the heat was turned on. Jacque sarcastically said, "Since you do not do anything in secret and you have no respect for anyone. I find myself very disappointed in you, Maxine. Why did you go to this man's house in the middle of the night? Do you know how dangerously you play? Here I am telling Carine, who is older than you, not to go anywhere alone with that man, and you dare! If something were to happen to you, what should we say or do on your behalf?"

Maxine did not say anything because she knew she was guilty. She looked at Carine and smiled weakly but Carine did not smile back. She continued eating her breakfast.

Finishing her breakfast, Carine left the room and went to her bedroom to call Louis. He answered.

"I see now why you do not want me. You want my sister. You spent the night with my sister! Why do you prey on young, vulnerable women, Louis?"

She didn't wait for a reply, but abruptly hung up the phone. Louis did not call her back, not even to explain himself. She sat by the telephone crying, hoping that he would call her back. "Louis, why?"

Someone knocked and the voice behind the door called softly, "Carine! *C'est moi* (It's me), Julie!"

"Wait a minute."

She quickly dried her eyes, took a deep breath, and opened the door. Julie asked concernedly, "Carine, are you all right?"

"Yes!"

Julie could see she wasn't okay, even though she tried to hide it. She had known Carine too long. Her voice sounded sad and angry as she said, "When we were children, we used to talk about everything, no matter how embarrassing the conversation was, no matter how sad it was. We always found time and ways to talk about it. Are you in love, Carine? Is someone hurting you? Your eyes say so."

Stepping away from Julie, Carine walked away toward the window and replied, "I'm in love with a man, but he does not love me. I'm afraid he is involved with my sister Maxine. She spent the night with him and it hurts. I found myself wanting him more. I hate myself for that. What is special about this man! Julie, why do I want him so much, I'm even willing to share him, as long he wants me and loves me. What is wrong with me? I find myself jealous of my baby sister. I even think of hurting her for this man. I hate her! I feel she's the cause of my problem! My pain! If she was not in the picture, would he want me and love me too? I sound sick! Don't I, Julie?"

Wiping Carine's tears with her handkerchief, Julie consoled, "Does Maxine know how you feel or how much this man means to you?"

Carine suddenly replied, "I don't know, and even if she does, I don't think she would care!"

"Then ask her," said Julie. "You may be surprised by her answer. You know Maxine likes to tease you and when was the last time you prayed, Carine?"

"Do you pray, Julie?"

"Oh yes, I do pray, and praying is what has kept me going. I have strange dreams. Scary dreams. Sometimes I thought I wasn't going to wake up; some mornings, I woke up crying that things are never going to work out the way I want. God knows I'm trying. I'm trying hard to do the right things. Carine, do yourself a favor. Never bundle up too much inside you. It may cause you do things you don't want to do and later you may regret them. Many times I found myself thinking about doing the wrong thing. Then I thought, *Is it worth ruining my life over?* Then I get on my knees and pray for every good thing I can think of, especially for my marriage and to appreciate my husband and be thankful for what God has given me. I pray for love to continue growing in my heart. Who knows, maybe Maxine is asking for your attention and she doesn't know how. This is her way of asking. Nicole told me you two are going shopping, so why don't you ask her to go along? She might say yes."

The telephone rang. Carine picked it up. "Hello? . . . She's here. . . . Okay, I'll tell her. Jacque is waiting for you downstairs."

"All right. But, Carine, we will talk later."

Kissing her on the forehead, Julie turned and walked away. She was wearing a two-piece suit. Her hair, combed up, revealed her innocent features. She walked elegantly and slowly across the floor.

As she appeared on the first step, Jacque moved closer toward the bottom steps and watched as she walked down. She put her purse under her arm and gave her hand to Jacque.

He kissed it and said, "My lady, shall we?"

Retrieving her sunglasses from her purse, she perched them on her nose as they went outside into the brilliant sunshine. Jacque took her to see his lawyer. His name was Constant Edouard. He explained to her the proceedings of a divorce, even though Julie had not discussed divorce with Jacque. Then Jacque drove her to downtown Port-au-Prince.

There were people everywhere, and cars as much as people. He stopped at a boulevard called Bicentenaire in front of a restaurant. He jumped out and ran around to her side, opening the car door for her. She stepped out and placed her hand in his. They walked in the restaurant. The maitre d' greeted them, dressed in perfect black and white. "Monsieur Jacque. Bonsoir, mademoiselle."

She looked around the place. It looked cozy. The man said: "Your table is ready, monsieur and mademoiselle. Follow me, please!"

The table was placed in a secluded corner with a single red rose in the vase on the table. Everything was arranged very tastefully. Jacque held her chair to seat her, and she sat. The waiter came forward to take their drink order. "Mademoiselle, what would you like to drink?"

"Martini."

"Monsieur, your usual?"

"*Oui* (Yes)!"

Taking her hand across the table, he asked, "Are you comfortable?"

Annoyed, she replied, "Yes! But I'm hungry. Can we order now please, Jacque?"

Jacque smiled and let go of her hands. "Oh, *oui, mon coeur* (certainly, my heart)."

He signaled the maitre d' with a wave of his hand to bring the menu.

"I want something light. I'll take the shrimp salad," she ordered.

The waiter returned with their drinks and Jacque placed the orders. "Two shrimp salads."

Moments later two plates of delicious-looking shrimp salads were placed in front of them. Julie was halfway through her salad when she noticed the man from the house was in a private corner. With him were two women and another man. As before, all she could see was the back of his head. Pretending she hadn't noticed him, she turned to Jacque. "Do you know everyone in here?"

"Almost."

"Who are those people in the back?" she indicated.

Turning his head, he replied, "Oh that's Louis Janvier."

Hearing Jacque mentioning his name, Louis slowly turned halfway and glanced at Julie. She caught a raised eyebrow before he turned back to his guests. The man across from him looked at Julie and smiled but she did not smile back. One of the ladies got up from her seat. Louis and the man stood and allowed her to leave the table. Now Julie was looking at the profile of his shoulders. Upward and downward, he was tall. There wasn't any other man taller than him in the restaurant. He looked handsome from the back, she thought.

They resumed their seats as the lady walked toward Julie and Jacque's table.

Extending her hand, she greeted them with a warm smile. "Hello! Jacque!"

Jacque stood and kissed her on her cheek. "Hello, Nadine! How are you?" Turning to Julie, he introduced her. "This is Julie."

"Hello." Julie smiled and extended her hand.

With a curious look on her face, Nadine took her hand, saying, "You're new in town. It's so good to see a new face."

Turning back to Jacque, she offered, "Oh! Jacque, tomorrow night I'm having a few friends over at my place. I would like you and Julie to come. Please say yes. It will be an honor for me." Nadine looked at Julie and smiled. "Nothing fancy, casual wear. Jeans or short pants. We'll be playing games and so on. Please say you'll come."

Julie nodded her head to say yes and Jacque accepted the invitation. "Yes, fine with me."

Nadine said, "Great, see you at eight."

She walked back to her seat. Louis and the man stood and he held her chair as she sat back down. Curiously Julie inquired, "Who is the other lady on his left?"

Jacque glanced over his shoulder and shrugged. "She is his secretary. Sofia's her name, and Nadine is his cousin. The man is Henry Claude. He works for Louis. Sometimes he sends this man to do business deals for him."

"What businesses is he in, besides being a brain surgeon?"

"How do you know he is a doctor?"

"Your sisters told me."

Jacque looked at her funnily but continued his explanation, "Well, he's in real estate. He owns many ships, plantations, and he has the largest ranch in town. When it comes to the business world in Haiti, he is a powerful man. Are you ready to go, Julie?"

"Yes."

Signaling the waiter for the check, he got up and held her chair for her. As they were leaving the restaurant, Nadine turned and whispered as she waved, "See you tomorrow."

They continued their conversation in the car. Julie questioned him again, "How did this man come to be so rich?"

"Well, he inherited his parents' wealth as an only child and I heard a few years ago when he returned from America, his relatives turned over the family business to him, everything they possessed. That's the mysterious thing about him. Nobody knows why. Many people say he's ruthless. So far, I cannot complain. Ever since this man became my partner, business could not be better. He advised me but he does not tell me what to do."

Julie smothered a quiet laugh. "Maybe he's making you feel comfortable for the big kill. You know I heard that the meat is more tender when fatter." Reaching over, she gave his arm a little squeeze.

With a mocking expression, Jacque exclaimed, "Julie! I did not know you had it in you. You look so innocent." He smiled. "I'm not ready to be slaughtered. I think he's a man who plays fair. What are you going to do tonight? You still want to go riding?"

She rested her head back against the seat, closed her eyes, and smothered a yawn. "Yes, then I think I'll go for a swim after my afternoon ride. Then take a little rest. Maybe tonight I can walk up the mountain to look at the stars."

"I thought you had grown out of that." Jacque smiled. "You don't look at things like that anymore, now that you are a married woman."

"That is something I never want to stop enjoying, looking at the stars in the heavens." She smiled. "What can be more pleasurable than looking at the stars?"

Jacque laughed. "Making love."

"Oh yes," Julie said. "And I think making love under the stars can be very pleasant."

"Yes, I must agree!"

When they arrived she did not wait for him to open the door. She quickly jumped out of the car and dashed inside, bumping into the butler as he swung the front door open.

"I'm sorry, Roy! Marie!" she shouted. She was all excited, running up the stairs.

Marie came running, saying, "Yes, madame!"

"Marie, I want you to call the beautician for me and tell her to be here tomorrow by five to do my hair. I'm going out tomorrow night."

Entering her room, Julie flopped down on the bed while Marie made the phone call to the beautician.

17

Jacque stood by the door looking at her. He asked, "Are you still going swimming?"

"No! I need to rest for my walk tonight. I need to sleep."

"Madame, do you want something to eat?" inquired Marie, laying a pair of jeans on the back of the armchair.

"No," she replied.

"At what time are you leaving for the party tomorrow?" Marie asked Jacque.

Jacque replied, "Eight." He didn't stay long as he had to take a little rest himself before he headed back out.

Julie had a good three hours of sleep. It was around four when she got up.

Marie said, "I have a warm bath prepared for you. You'll enjoy it, madame."

Julie did enjoy her bath. She put on her jeans then left the mansion without anyone noticing. She took a long walk that night up into the mountain. During her walk she saw someone watching her further up on the hills, but she couldn't make the person's face out. The person was sitting on a horse, and from the shape she assumed it was a man. She wondered who that man was on her lands. Maybe one of the workers. She wondered why was he standing there looking down at her, or was he looking at something else? Then she saw another person ride up beside him who also stopped to look down at her. She thought they were looking at her through binoculars, then they rode off. She wished she had brought her binoculars with her, because she was not able to make out their faces.

Made nervous by the sight, she didn't continue, but headed back home. Later that evening Maxine dropped by her room to see how she was doing. She stayed for awhile, talking, and told Julie she was going to Louis Janvier's place to see him. That night Jacque had to work late so Julie didn't see him, nor did she see the rest of the family.

The following morning Jacque dropped by her room to see her, but she was gone for the day. Marie wasn't able to tell him where she went. She wasn't around the mansion. Julie went by the orphanage that was in Delmas, visiting a few friends she had not seen in years. She had helped established this institution to help the children in need. The place was improving. She could see that they had put the donations to good use. The children were well-taken care of. They looked healthy and fresh and the place was clean. She gave her friend a personal check for a donation, and told her she had shipped blankets and clothes for the children and they should arrive by the end of the week. They walked on the balcony to look at the view. There again she saw the back of the man called Louis Janvier walking toward his car. For a moment she thought he was Saul, her husband. She was about to wave to call out his name but caught herself from doing so.

He opened the car door then stopped because he felt that he was being watched. He turned and looked up in her direction. She was watching how the wind was blowing his hair. He removed his shades from his shirt pocket and perched them on his nose. He pushed his hair back away from his face, staring in her direction. He stood there for a minute looking back at her before he got in the car to drive away. Julie felt a little lightheaded. She held on to the lady's hand. For a moment she thought she was going to fall and thought she heard the whispering voice on her mind calling her name. The lady next to her held her hand and thought she was unusually cold and asked her if she was okay. But she told the lady she was feeling fine; it was a brief spell that just came out of nowhere, but everything was well. Then Julie asked her who that man was and why he was there.

The lady explained the man was Louis Janvier, a well-known tycoon who came twice a week to spend time with the children and made some generous donation to the institution. And he was there today inviting a few of the children to his ranch for the weekend.

Julie thought that was mighty nice for a man they claimed to be the devil. She stayed for a little while longer to play with the children, then left the orphanage. She visited a couple of old friends who were living in her neighborhood. It was around one when she returned home. She quickly washed herself then had her lunch. She thought the family was home, but no one was there. She had her lunch alone, then went to her room to catch up on her reading.

Jacque was home early because it was the night of Nadine's hang-out. When he arrived, Julie was resting. She wanted to look fresh for tonight. Marie was going through the closets to look for an outfit. Holding up a pair of jeans and a silk halter top, Marie asked, "Would these do . . . or would you prefer something a bit more glamorous?"

"Something modest," Julie waved.

The door opened and Jacque walked in. He looked at Julie lying down on the bed and asked, "Are you ready for the night?"

Julie, who was halfway asleep, smiled when she heard his voice and said, "Jacque, how are you, brother?"

He gave her kiss on her cheek. "I hope we have a wonderful time tonight."

He knelt beside her bed, looking at her like a puppy that needs a master. While he was talking to her, she fell asleep from lack of interest. It was around four-thirty when she woke up.

The beautician was sitting in the lounge waiting to be called up stairs.

"Marie," she called.

Marie walked out of the closet where she had been searching for a pair of sandals to match Julie's outfit. "Madame, did I wake you up?"

"No, Marie, you didn't. Where is Jacque?"

"Monsieur left when you fell asleep, but he said he'll see you at seven-thirty."

Rolling off the bed, she stretched herself gracefully. "Oh! I feel so good. Now I'm ready to party all night long."

Carine returned home. She knocked on the door while Julie was in the tub. When Julie didn't reply, she walked in to tell her about the wonderful time they had while shopping today and to ask if she wanted to go out to a movie. Julie informed her that she was already invited to Nadine Janvier's hang-out.

Carine tried to hide her frustration at not being invited to Nadine's, shrugged her shoulders, and said, "Well, then, there will be other times." She explained to Julie, "Tonight will be a good night to see Louis, because Jacque is not going to be around here."

She thanked Julie, but Julie couldn't quite understand what she was being thanked for. Walking to the door, she said to Julie, "Well, see you tomorrow."

After she left, Julie got out of the tub, pulled on her robe, and sat down and waited while Marie brought the beautician lady up to wash and set her hair. After she finished washing and blow drying her hair, she wanted to know what style Julie would like. "Nothing fancy, just one tail, please."

The lady smiled and put her hair in one as instructed, stepped back, and said, "Voilà, madame!"

"Thank you." She paid the beautician and she left. Julie finished dressing, put on some lipstick, and dabbed on some of her favorite perfume. She looked at herself in the mirror and thought, *I'm ready.*

Marie smiled as she walked out and said to herself, "You have a big future ahead of you, child."

Chapter Three

At Nadine's Place

It was 8:15 P.M., and half of Nadine's guests were already there. Louis and his cousins, Brian and Patrick Bravé, were away from the crowd playing chess in Nadine's study room. As Julie and Jacque walked in, Nadine hurried to greet them with a warm smile. "Welcome to my home, Julie. Jacque, you are no stranger. So help Julie make herself comfortable."

Taking Julie by the hand, she walked around with her and introduced her to her friends. Among them was Henry Claude, whom she saw at the restaurant. When she finished introducing her to those in the room, she indicated the study room and said, "Later I'll introduce you to my cousins. They're in the back room playing chess. . . ."

Before she could finish her sentence, Brian and Patrick walked out. She introduced them to Julie. Then she went to the back room, where he was sitting. Pausing in the doorway, Nadine called, "Fuji."

He turned to look, rose slowly from his chair, and walked toward them. Nadine pulled Julie forward. "I'd like to introduce you to Julie."

Extending his hand, in a voice like warm velvet, he said, "*Je suis Louis Janvier* (I am Louis Janvier)."

She put out her hand to shake his, but was surprised when he brought it to his lips to kiss it.

Trembling inwardly she replied, "Julie Philip."

"*Heureux de faire ta connaissance* (A pleasure to meet you), Mademoiselle Philip."

Julie corrected: "Madame, but you can call me Julie, Monsieur Janvier."

"Please, Fuji," Louis replied. "My friends call me Fuji."

She looked at the chess table and said, "Okay, Fuji."

Noticing the way her eyes strayed to the chessboard, he asked, "You play chess?"

She said, "A little. . . . Well, Nadine, I'm here. What's your program?"

Looking at her with passion (which he tried to hide) Louis made an attempt to touch her. He wanted to touch her so badly that he had to stick his hands into his pockets to prevent them from reaching out on their own accord. Then Patrick came in with a glass of cognac and handed it to Louis.

"Thank you." Louis accepted the glass eagerly to give his hands something to do so he wouldn't embarrass himself.

Above the noise, Nadine shouted, "I would like to play a game called 'Question'."

"'Question'." Julie turned and said, "Sounds interesting." Looking at Louis she said, "See you in the next room."

She walked away. The lingering resonance of his voice was sending shivers down her spine as he replied, "See you then."

"You look beautiful." Jacque came toward her and took her hand. He kissed her on her cheek.

Suddenly Julie could sense a pair of eyes boring into her back. Turning, she saw Jacque's girlfriend sitting in the opposite corner looking at them. Her name was Debbie Dubois. Louis came out from the back. He walked directly over to Julie and Jacque and extending his hand, said, "Hello, Jacque."

Jacque was about to introduce Julie, but she forestalled him. "We've already met."

Louis responded with a smile. He wanted to touch her again. "A second introduction is usually better."

Debbie saw an opportunity to say hello. She got up and walked toward them with a forced smile. "Oh! Jacque, it is you!"

But her eyes were on Julie when she said, "Monsieur Janvier."

Bowing slightly, he replied, "Miss Dubois. Excuse me ladies, Jacque."

Louis walked away to the bar. Debbie inched closer to Jacque and slid her arm through his as she continued talking, "I haven't seen you for a while. How's everything," indicating Julie, "and who's this little girl?"

With a smile Julie fluttered her lashes. "Oh my! I look like a little girl! I'm flattered by your remark!"

Losing interest in Debbie and her superficial attempt at friendliness, she looked toward the bar where Louis was standing sipping his drink and talking to Henry. Louis turned around as if someone was calling out to him. He looked straight at her. She heard the same voice, the same whisper she had heard last night on the balcony. This time the sensation she felt was even stronger.

Seeing that Julie didn't have a drink in her hand, Louis ordered her one. He walked over to her and handed her a martini. Accepting the drink, she thought, *How did he know?* "Thank you."

Taking a sip, she looked at him, then she looked at Jacque and Debbie still clinging to Jacque" arm. Debbie asked Julie, "Would you mind if I talk to Jacque in private?"

"Not at all." She smiled.

Jacque was nervous. He didn't know what Debbie wanted to talk about. He looked at Louis, who was already standing beside Julie as if to claim his territory. He said, "I will not be long, Julie."

Nadine showed them into the back room where they could talk without being disturbed.

Crooking his elbow, Louis asked Julie, "Care to walk with me on the patio?"

She hesitated for a moment, then took a deep breath, and taking his arm, accepted gracefully. "Why not!"

She walked beside him as he steered a path for them. They walked out through the French doors leading to the side garden. They were both silent. Julie looked at the sky. The stars seemed so close she felt she could reach out and touch them. She lifted her hands to the sky. He asked, "What are you doing?"

"I feel like I could reach and take a star from the heavens."

She didn't know he had moved till his voice whispered like a feather on her ears, "*C'est-ce-que tu demandes.* (Is this what you are wishing for), Julie?"

She slowly turned and looked at him. It was the same voice that had whispered to her the night before: "*Make a wish, my love.*"

She hugged herself to stop the shivers running up and down her spine. "*Je ne crois pas au souhait. La bénédiction est ma foi* (I don't believe in wishing. I believe in blessings)."

"What's the difference?"

Turning her back, she looked up at the sky again and answered, "Wishes are temporary, but blessings are forever, because they come from the Almighty God."

She walked further down the patio steps into the garden.

As he followed her, he said, "You remind me of a flower, Julie."

"What kind of flower?"

Picking one of Nadine's prize red roses, he held it out to her. "A rose."

She laughed, took the rose out of his hand, and brought it to her nose, inhaling the poignant fragrance. "A rose! Please, Mr. Janvier, flattery will not get you everywhere."

"Hopefully, and please call me Fuji."

She looked at him and said, "Fuji, you see, a rose may look strong because of it thorns. Because of its beauty, it stands out among others. But

23

when the sun fully sets, it withers. As a woman, I am not flattered by your insolent compliment. No thank you, Fuji."

For the first time Louis did not know what to say, but "Pardon! *Excusez-moi* (Excuse me)."

Before he could ask her for an explanation, Nadine put her head out the door and called, "Louis, Julie, we're going to start the game now."

Inside her living room everyone was sitting down, some on the sofa and some on the floor (anywhere they could find a seat) around her coffee table. Nadine patted the cushion beside her on the floor. "Sit by me, Julie!"

Louis sat by the bar with Henry, Patrick, and Brian. Jacque was still talking in private with Debbie. Nadine looked around at everyone and announced, "Tonight, we're going to do something different, and Brian, I will like you to go first. The game is 'Question'."

Brian held up his hands. "Oh no! Not me. Let someone else go first."

"Come on, Brian, don't be a chicken," the girls said as they were laughing and teasing him.

Then Louis spoke up from the bar. "I know, let me."

Which made everyone stare in shock. He took a sip of his cognac and looked around at everyone in the room and with his eyes centered on Julie, he asked, "This question is for the women in the room. What kind of flower are you?"

One of the girls named Michelle jumped on her seat and said, "I am a rose," which made Louis smile.

Another girl said, "I'm a rose."

And so they all started to name what flower they were, and most were roses. Nadine said, "Everyone cannot be roses, so I'm a carnation."

Patrick asked, "Why carnation?"

Slowly lowering one eyelid in a wink, she replied, "Because men like to wear them, silly."

Everyone laughed.

The girls named every single flower they could think of, except for Julie, who still said nothing. Henry, who understood Louis more than anyone else in the room, knew he wouldn't have asked such a question without a reason and a good one. He turned and looked at Louis, trying to figure out what game he was playing, then he looked at Julie and said, "I heard everyone, but you, mademoiselle. You haven't answered the question."

Smiling, she looked at him. "Please call me Julie."

"Well, Julie, what about you?"

Everyone chorused, "Yes *et vous*, (what about you), Julie."

Julie made a face. "Well, can't I remain the unnamed flower?"

There was laughter as everyone said, "*Non* (No)!"

Seeing that she was outvoted, Julie conceded defeat. "Let me put it this way, I'm not any of the flowers you all mentioned. But I would like to tell you this little poem I know."

The room became very quiet as they all waited expectantly.

> *I am standing in the corner of my mind.*
> *I looked at everything that I can see.*
> *People picked on me and they would not stop.*
> *I could not cry.*
> *But I could feel every single thing that was happening to me.*
> (She glanced at Louis as she continued talking)
> *Summer kept me warm,*
> (She hugged herself)
> *Autumn stripped me off.*
> (She spread her hands.)
> *And winter put me in my grave."*
> (She softly spoke and closed her eyes.)
> *"I kept my faith high above,*
> *So when spring comes,*
> *That I should rise.*

Opening her eyes, she asked, "Who am I?"

Nadine said, "Loneliness."

Henry said, "No, hope!"

She got up and walked to the bar and asked for a drink, lifting her glass to the faces all looking at her. She took a sip and said, "When you figure it, you let me know."

Louis said, "Can you tell us another one, Mrs. Philip?"

Looking at him over the rim of her glass, she said, "Please call me Julie."

Brian said, "Are you always this mysterious, Julie?"

"Oh no! That is one thing I don't want to be, is mysterious. People think badly of you. I am a survivor."

Patrick replied, "Your poetry was beautiful, but sad, even though it has a happy ending. I listened but I don't understand it and I don't like to wonder. Would you like to explain it to me, please."

She turned to the group of people and asked, "Did everyone understand my words?"

Michelle said, "I did!"

And the others all nodded.

Michelle continued, "The beginning gave it away. You were talking about yourself, how much you've been hurt, and now you are doing better."

Louis cut in, "No, let Julie explain it. I'm eager to hear her explanation."

Julie said, "All right. It's not about me, it's about a tree, a unique tree."

Nadine said, "Yes! I see, the four seasons!"

Brian cut in, "But what about the corner! How can a tree stand at a corner?"

Patrick snickered at him, "Easy—no matter where a tree stands, it cannot move."

Julie looked at him warmly. "You're getting somewhere. What else?"

Michelle said, "My mind—how can a tree stand at its mind?"

"Well," Julie replied, "the trees clean the air and give us oxygen and trees do many other things, but what do they get back in return? We use them for furniture. Children carve their names on them. We use them to cook or for the fireplace and during hot summer days we have them to cool us, for shade, etc.! During autumn their leaves fall, winter puts them into a coma, and what happens in spring? They start to blossom so. . . ."

They all chorused, "They rise!"

Everyone applauded just as Jacque and Debbie emerged from their discussion. Jacque said, "What did I miss?"

Louis looked at him, but Julie did not give him a second glance. Nadine said, "Give us another one, Julie."

Louis looked at her and said, "If you not a rose or any other flower, then what are you, Julie?"

"You really want to know, Fuji?"

Jacque was surprised by the name she called Louis. He knew only Louis's close friends were allowed to use that name. Even he wasn't privileged to do so. He looked at Louis and smiled coldly then walked over to the bar and asked for a drink. "Brandy, please."

Julie said, "I'm a desert plant."

Michelle started to laugh. "A desert plant? What kind?"

"A cactus!" replied Julie.

Brian looked at her as if she was crazy. "Be quiet. A cactus? Why not a Lord, Lady Baltimore, or a rose?"

"They are too vulnerable."

Patrick, too, wanted to know, "What makes them too vulnerable?"

"Because of their beauty. They think it's all they need."

Henry was looking at her with admiration and interest. "Give us an example."

She responded, "Take the rose for example. Truly her thorns are sharp, and her beauty stands out as long as she's not in the heat. She does not hide her claws. Because of that, one can always know where to hold her and take what she has. She holds no surprises."

"What about a carnation?" Nadine asked.

Julie put down her drink. "I think I talk too much."

"Come on," Nadine cajoled. "This sounds interesting."

Louis put his hands on his pockets and leaned back against the bar as he crossed his legs at the ankle. "You still didn't tell us why a desert plant, Julie . . . Ms. Cactus?"

Listening to the way Louis spoke softly and warmly to Julie and emphasized the name he called her, Michelle took a sip of her drink and jealously gave a cold smile. "I know what she means. She likes scorpions, snakes, and all kinds of desert animals. She likes them rough and dangerous. Don't you, Julie?"

Julie looked at Michelle with a smile. She knew exactly why Michelle had said what she did. "If that's the way you see it."

Eagerly Patrick picked up the conversation, "There's got to be more to it than hardship. Don't leave my thirsty, woman, I want to know more."

What Patrick is saying is true. Louis thought to himself. *You're right, Patrick; she is making me thirsty. I want more. I want to know. I need to quench my thirst to the full. She has me interested. What am I thinking?* He came back to reality with a jolt. *This cannot be, I never thought about any woman that way before.* He looked at the door to the room where he was playing chess earlier with his cousins, thinking, *I want her. She seems so innocent.*

He studied her features, how well she was shaped, how small her waist was. He looked at her from her head to her feet. He thought, *Just right.* He stared at her face. Almost a perfect circle. She looked oriental with her slanted eyes. He wondered if she came from an Asian family. Her full, soft lips were calling him. Her eyes were seducing him. He was lost. *Wake up, Louis Janvier . . . hands off! She is dangerous-goods. You don't want to become entangled.*

He meditated on her and thought his work was cut out for him. *The woman is a parang! She's a phenomenon. . . .I like that.*

He thought to himself, *She is like an exotic fruit that is rare. There's a challenge. I wonder if her bite is as deep as mine?* He swilled his drink as he closed his eyes.

Henry asked, "What did you say, Louis?"

Startled, he looked at Henry. He didn't know he was thinking out loud. "Nothing."

Louis could actually smell and taste her. He held on tight to the glass and imagined it was Julie he was touching.

Julie had gone back and sat down by Nadine with her drink. She slowly looked around at everyone. She was thankful that they were so busy talking. She didn't want anyone to realize what was happening to her. She clasped her stomach to still the deep ache and wobbling feeling she had inside her and continued looking around. Surreptitiously she watched how Louis was holding on to his glass.

She closed her eyes, took a deep breath, opened them, and looked right at him, wanting him to look at her yet afraid of how she would feel if he did look at her.

As if drawn by an invisible bond, he finally lifted his head and revealed his eyes to her. His eyes looked unusual. She couldn't make out what color they really were. From this far they looked gothic. His face was well coordinated. His lips she couldn't avoid, they were well pronounced. He pushed his hair back away from his face. His color was golden bronze, roasted cashew, she thought. *I actually felt his touch. It is impossible; it can't be.*

27

Sensing that Julie was uncomfortable, Nadine looked in the direction Julie was focusing and saw Louis intently staring at her and thought, *Oh no, not Julie!*

She put her arm lightly around Julie's shoulders and gave her a hug and asked, "Are you all right, Miss Cactus?"

Sighing, Julie made to get up. "I need some fresh air."

Jacque came closer to her and asked concernedly, "Is everything all right?"

"I need some fresh air. I'm going outside for a minute or two."

Without asking, Jacque took Julie's arm to walk with her outside, leaving Debbie to wonder what was going on. Julie's hands were ice cold. As they walked out, Jacque started rubbing her hands.

"Your hands are so cold."

She stopped and stood at the same place where Louis and she had stood earlier. Jacque wrapped his arms around Julie and asked, "Do you want to go home?"

"No, I'm all right."

While they were outside, Louis brought her a glass of water. "I thought you might like this, Julie. Here, drink."

Putting the glass to her mouth, she looked up at him and took a sip of the ice cold water. He smiled and said, "Good girl."

Putting the glass away from her mouth, back into his hands, she said, "Enough! Thank you."

She opened her eyes widely. As he wiped her lips with his fingers, he said, "Voilà!"

Jacque was speechless, with a furious look on his face. Julie thought, *It can't be! His touch felt good against my lips. The same sensation, the same feelings I had two nights before.*

Controlling herself, she said, "Well, excuse me. Where were your fingers before you touched my lips? I don't appreciate anyone touching me without knowing where their hands were or without my permission."

"You should worry where I got the water." Louis smiled as he walked away, saying over his shoulders, "Hands and fingers can always be washed."

Fuming at the gall of the man, Julie thought, *The arrogance of that man.*

Debbie was by the door, looking at the way Jacque was hugging Julie. She thought that Jacque was a character, and he was stupid if he didn't notice who just served her water.

Ignoring Louis's last comment, Julie turned and called, "Hello again, Debbie."

Debbie moved closer to where they were standing. Jacque tightened his hold on Julie. She tried to loosen his arms, "Jacque, I need to breathe."

He loosened his arms, apologizing, "I'm sorry."

Debbie walked over to them and tried to make conversation. "How long do you plan to stay in Haiti?"

28

Julie shrugged. "I don't know. I need some time here."

She walked away from Jacque and toward Debbie. Jacque stood wondering what Debbie was up to. Julie asked Jacque, "Can I have something to drink, Jacque. Make it club soda."

Jacque went in to get Julie her drink as Debbie continued her line of questioning. "I heard you were married."

Julie looked at her, wondering if she was trying to find out how serious she was about her marriage. "You heard wrong. I'm still married, and I have a five-month-old baby. What else did you hear so I can correct it?"

Debbie asked, "What did Nadine mean by calling you 'Miss Cactus'?"

Julie smiled and looked up at the sky. "Miss Cactus, huh! For you to understand, you would have to come from where I came from and even then you may or may never understand."

Debbie looked at her with reluctant admiration. "You look so young and yet you talk so old."

She sounded so sad and hurt. Julie really took a good look at her this time. She looked as if she, too, was searching for something.

Softening her expression, she asked, "Is something troubling you, Debbie? You look full. I am not a psychiatrist, but I do have two good listening ears."

Looking down so Julie wouldn't see the tears forming in her eyes, she replied, "I used to go out with Jacque, you know."

"I know. Jacque told me."

"Did Jacque also tell you. . . ."

Before Debbie could continue, Jacque returned with Julie's drink. "I heard my name."

Julie scolded, "Can't a woman talk about what's on her mind, Jacque?"

Julie was looking at Debbie and didn't notice the look that Jacque gave Debbie. It was enough to kill her. Debbie turned and walked away and Julie called to her, "We'll talk some other time. . . . Hmm! This tastes good. I feel much better. I'm ready to go back in."

Nadine came out and said, "If you stay one more minute out here, everyone is coming out to get you."

She laughed and turned to go in. "I'm coming in."

"Good!" Sofia exclaimed. "Here is Julie. Since you picked the strangest plant to be, I chose to be a dandelion."

Sofia was Louis's secretary, whom she had seen yesterday in the restaurant.

Julie smothered a laugh while pulling on her right ear lobe. "What! A dandelion!"

Sofia continued, "Yes, the yellow flowers that grow on people's lawn. They grow everywhere."

"I know them. They're also good for medicine and many other things for the body," Julie enlightened her.

Sofia looked perplexed. "I didn't know that. Then I chose well. I'm good for many things."

Louis looked at Sofia as though she was crazy.

Julie said under her breath, "Yeah, I'm sure you are."

Putting her arm around Sofia, Michelle responded, "You look at her and make her sound as if she was out of her mind to choose dandelions." She agreed with Sofia, "It's true, dandelions do grow in unexpected places, Julie!"

Nodding her head, Julie answered, "You're quite right, Michelle, but what usually happens a dandelion? Can you explain it to her?"

Not knowing an answer to give, Michelle went back to where she was sitting and kept silent. No one knew what to say or how to give an explanation to what Julie was asking.

Julie realized she had put everyone on the spot, so she sought to make amends.

"Then I'll tell you a little story about dandelions."

> *As the grass grows green,*
> *The master of the field is happy.*
> *So, he let his dog run free on the green grass.*
> *You know how it is.*
> *No matter what it's doing,*
> *When it's time for it to go,*
> *No master can hold it back.*
> *So it urinates and does the other thing on the grass.*

Brian piped up, "What other thing?"

Michelle looked at him as if he was born yesterday. "Feces, of course! That's the other thing on the green grass, right, Julie?"

She nodded her head in agreement.

"Continued," Patrick encouraged.

> *This is when dandelion comes up.*
> *And this is when its service is mostly appreciated,*
> *Because it covers up the feces.*
> *But once the sun dries it away,*
> *Dandelion's services are no longer needed.*
> *So the master of the field started to be annoyed*
> *By these yellow scavengers.*
> *He said, "This yellow son of so-and-so*
> *Is destroying my beautiful green grass."*
> *Furiously, he called his executioner,*
> *Meaning the gardener, pointed his fingers, and said,*
> *"I want you to cut the heads*

Off these yellow sons of so-and-so. . . ."
They got their heads cut off.
But the amazing part was
That dandelions were called
All kinds of names except
Its name. . . .

"So you see, Sofia, no matter how hard they work, they can never sit back to enjoy their success. Some big feet will either crush their skulls or cut off their heads."

Sadly Sofia said, "Are there any positive things about flowers Julie?"

"Oh yes," Julie said, "there are. As long they never grow to maturity."

Michelle said, "So does cactus. They get old, too."

Julie conceded, "How true, but with wisdom. My time is up. Miss Cactus needs to go home. Thank you, Nadine, for a wonderful evening."

"Don't quit on us now," Michelle said. "The night is young. You know what kind of a plant I really am? It is a mistletoe."

Julie quickly placed her glass over her mouth to cover her grin so no one would see that she was laughing at Michelle as she was giving the meaning of what she was, "This prig of a plant, hung as Christmas decoration. . . ."

While she was explaining to Julie of her mistletoe, Louis was attentively looking at Julie, which caused Michelle to get upset. She looked at Louis and asked, "Isn't a mistletoe a romantic plant, Louis?"

He didn't reply. To cover her embarrassment, Michelle looked at Julie and said, "I think it is, because men by custom kiss women standing under it. So you see if any man or woman stand under it they would have to give each other a kiss. I think that is very romantic."

"If they are a loving couple," Julie responded.

Louis questioned, "Have you ever stood under one, Miss Cactus?"

"No!"

"Why not!" Louis asked.

"I avoid that kind of a plant," Julie said, "and I'm careful not to stand under one during the time of Christmas season, because men would use this tradition to put their lips on me. I would hate for that to happen to me."

Louis smiled because he felt she was referring to him because of the way he had just touched her lips. He also felt Julie was holding back the real truth about the plant Michelle claimed to be. So she dished that plate to them and he was not about to buy it completely. He said, "Is there something you're not telling us about that plant?"

"There is nothing to say," Julie replied, tasting her drink.

"Well then, Miss Cactus," Louis complied, "why did you laugh at the mistletoe woman?"

Nadine laughed, trying to cover up what Louis did, then everyone else followed with laughter. Julie couldn't believe Louis put her on a spot. After the moment of laughter, everyone became quiet, waiting for her explanation. Looking at him she said, "It's a vampire plant."

Shocked, Henry repeated, looking at Michelle, "A vampire plant!"

Everyone murmured, "Vampire plant."

"Yes," Julie explained. "They drink other tree's life forces to keep themselves healthy."

They all were surprised to hear that. No one knew it was that kind of a plant. Julie looked at everyone who was listening very carefully to her description of the yellowish-green leaves and yellowish flowers of the mistletoe. "Even their shiny white berries are poisonous. . . . A strangler they are, like passion vine."

Brian laughed, "Other words are parasite, free loaders, that fit Michelle perfectly."

Everyone was laughing. Michelle threw a napkin at him. Nadine said, "But you never explained to us the meaning of a desert cactus."

Debbie spoke up, "She told me."

Everyone asked, "What is it?"

Debbie replied, "She said the only way for me to understand is to come from where she came from, and still I may or may never understand."

Louis thought that Debbie was as disturbed as Sofia and Michelle were. He shook his head and thought, *Women!*

Michelle looked at Debbie in disdain. "She told you nothing. Is this another riddle you've given us, Julie?"

Julie looked at Michelle. "No! Please don't let my words trouble you, Michelle."

Patrick asked, "What surprise would you give me if I or anyone else found out the definition of your cactus?"

She closed her eyes, inhaled, exhaled, and said, "If you find out, you'll have your surprise. . . . You'll never be hungry or thirsty again!"

When she finished her statement, Louis looked at her with amusement. He thought to himself, *She already gave them the answer but they were too busy looking down at the tips of their noses. They missed it. I must say she's something else. Does she know she's unique? I wonder if she felt the voltage that I felt. I feel like she could see right through me.*

She walked by the bar with Jacque and shook the hands of those who were sitting there. When she got to Louis, he held her hand in his. "Your hands are cold. Can I drop in tomorrow to see how you are doing?" He turned to Jacque. "Of course, if you don't mind, Jacque."

Jacque took her other hand in his. "She does feel cold. I'll be happy if you would."

Julie pulled her hands away. "I'll be fine. I need no doctor."

Jacque ignored her. "Please do drop by. What time should I expect you?"

Louis looked at him. "Well, Jacque, why don't you invite me for lunch?" He never took his eyes off Julie.

Irritated, Jacque issued the invitation. "Okay! Then see you at twelve."

Nadine walked them to their car. She was so pleased she had made a new friend in Julie. "When can I see you again, Julie? I had so much fun tonight. I usually have a few friends over every weekend or so. We talk but there is never anything interesting to say. Always the same, old, boring business. But tonight, you really made it fun and interesting. Thank for dropping by. I've never seen my cousin Louis talk as much as he did tonight. Thank you again."

She kissed them on their cheeks as they got in the car and drove away.

Chapter Four

Interesting Lunch

The next morning, Julie did not get out of bed till ten. She stayed in her room. She placed a phone call to her mother to see how her son was doing. Her mother assured her everything was fine, her son was in good hands. Saying goodbye to her mother, she hung up the phone. Marie knocked and came in her room bringing her breakfast on a tray. She looked at the time. "This is a late breakfast, I'll have coffee only. Marie, last night I had a wonderful time."

She stretched herself and asked, "Maria, who is Debbie, besides been Jacque's girl? She was about to tell me something, but Jacque came and interrupted her. She seemed so sad, lost, and alone. I feel for her."

Before Marie could answer, there was a knock on the door and Carine called to ask if she could come in.

Julie invited her in and Carine climbed on her bed and gave her a kiss on her cheek. She picked up a piece of bacon and chewed slowly, saying, "I tried to reach Louis last night, but he was over at his cousin Nadine's. Did you see him?"

Julie nodded her head to say yes, so Carine asked, "Wasn't he dreamy?"

Before Julie could answer, Carine got up from the bed and twirled with a dreamy expression on her face. She continued, "He's handsome, rich, and smart. I just wish his heart was not as black as midnight."

"Do you know he's coming here for lunch today?" Julie broke in.

Carine stopped turning and exclaimed, "Here! Look at me! I look a mess!"

She ran out the room and down the hallway to her room, shouting for a servant as she ran.

Marie rolled her eyes shook her head in sympathy. "Then it starts. . . . This is the first time Louis–I mean Monsieur Janvier–is coming here for lunch. He always here for business. Never pleasure."

Julie remonstrated, "Really, Marie!"

"Madame," Marie responded, "I'm old, not stupid. Monsieur Janvier wants something. I got a feeling it's here in this room."

Julie looked shocked. "What are you implying?"

Marie looked at her with a smile but didn't reply.

Julie persisted, "Are you saying it's because of me Monsieur Janvier is coming here? He's wasting his time. I'm a married woman."

Marie looked at her thoughtfully. "Yes, madame, you are. You see, I have known Monsieur Janvier for a long time, since he was born. He was a happy boy. Then something happened, and he almost died by his own family's hands. They used black magic to try to kill him. Poison! But his mother loved him so much she could not stand to let that happen. She took him away so they couldn't harm him. I was there. I love that boy."

Julie couldn't understand why Marie was telling her these things. "Why didn't you work for him?"

She shook her head. "I have reasons at the moment. It's better this way. He can take care of himself now."

Julie still needed Marie to give her more information. "But I heard he is really mean, practically evil."

"If you were in his position, you wouldn't be too nice either. He's not evil, madame."

Trying to make some sense of what Marie was telling her, Julie reminded her, "But the other night you said he was bad news. . . ."

"Madame," Marie interrupted, "I know what I said. He's bad news all right, but there is worse news than he. You see, madame, a man does not like a woman to chase him, especially someone as rich and powerful as he is. Some women don't have respect for themselves. They become puppets. They have no life for themselves. Those women are jealous, vicious. They don't know the meaning of love, but I'm sure you know what love means, otherwise monsieur wouldn't be coming here. . . . Monsieur Janvier is coming here because he sees something special about you, or maybe he is in love."

Julie tried to shush her. "Don't talk too loud. They might hear you, and I don't want to hurt Carine. You know she is in love with Fuji."

Breathlessly Marie asked, "Madame, did you say Fuji?"

"Yes, I did," Julie answered. "He gave me this name to call him."

Marie smiled widely. She knew she was right. She remembered only Louis's mother used to call him by that name. No one else would dare call him Fuji without his permission. Marie was still shaking her head as she continued to smile. Puzzled, Julie asked, "Marie, is there something you're not telling me?"

Marie's smile got wider. "You're special, madame. You are special."

Julie still wanted to know, "I want to know why he got involved with Carine and Maxine? Why did he hurt Carine so much?"

Defensively Marie replied, "He never comes near Maxine. She lied to cover up her tracks. Tonight, I will show you who she is sneaking out to meet. As for Carine, she and Louis went on a couple of dates. And that was when they were children, thirteen, fourteen. They stopped seeing each other way before Louis went to America to study medicine. She was dating Brian, his cousin. Her greed got to her—she thought Brian was going to inherit everything. And knowing the way Louis was, they all thought Louis was going to amount to nothing. She did not give a damn about him then. Louis's relatives made a bet with him, his inheritance against their wealth . . . everything they had. Winner took all if he became a doctor. So he did. When he was about to graduate, they tried to kill him with voodoo and poison. When he survived, they all lost everything to him. . . ."

Marie paused and removed the tray of food from Julie and placed it on the table by the window. Looking at Julie, she meditated for a few seconds, then continued, "Brian and Carine dated for years. He thought Carine loved him, and they were about to get married. But when she learned his parents lost everything, she dropped him like a hot potato a day before the ceremony."

Julie remembered her mother had informed her about Carine's engagement. How happy her mother was for her when she heard that Carine was getting married to that fine young man agronomist. She had received a wedding invitation from Carine and her mother while she was away to college. The name just hit her mind—*yes, Brian Bravé*—everything was canceled and because of that she spent her time in Jacmel with her mother. She couldn't believe that Carine broke up with Brian, and she couldn't give her mother a good reason.

Marie continued, "She told Louis she was in love with him. She accused Brian of seducing her. But Louis, monsieur, did not care . . . because he never cared for her that way, and whatever that had happened between them was a long time ago. He let bygones be. He just wants to be friends with her, but she can't accept that. She wants more than what he can offer her, so pay her no mind. She knows, they will never have a relationship. Monsieur Janvier is man of class and good taste. Madame, you may think you are a long way from home. I heard you dream, and in your dream you're torn between two men who love you. For some reason the pictures on your mind are blocked. . . . You may not remember what happened or what took place in your dreams, but believe me when I tell you this. You're not too far from going home. Now, madame, it's time for you to get dressed. Lunch is almost ready. Monsieur Janvier's car just drove through the gates."

Julie got out of bed and went to the bathroom to wash. She allowed Marie to help her dress. She was silent. She wanted to know more but didn't want to pry. She pulled her hair back and put a hair band over it that matched her dress.

Downstairs in the family room, Jacque and his brother Jean were entertaining Louis. Nicole walked in and greeted them.

Louis complimented, "Nicole, you have grown up to be a lovely woman."

Maxine came in behind her. "Hello, Louis, how are you?"

She greeted him with a kiss. Louis returned the greeting and asked, "Fine! Did everything go well the other day?"

She looked at Jacque warily as she answered, "It couldn't be better. I'm so happy you're here."

Nicole walked over to Jacque and kissed him on his cheek. Jacque looked at Maxine, thinking that Louis and she really had something going on. He smiled and said, "Well, Louis, I'm happy to have you for lunch."

Louis replied, "I hope you didn't put me on the menu."

Everyone in the room laughed at his comment. Then Carine walked in, trying to keep a straight face. She smiled as she walked toward Louis, extending her hands. "Hello, Louis. I didn't know you were coming here."

Standing on tiptoes and stretching her neck, she pursed her lips together and placed a kiss on Louis's cheek.

Louis returned the greeting, "*Bonjour*, Carine. It was a last-minute invitation."

Jacque looked around for Julie. "Where is Julie? Isn't she ready?"

"The last time I saw her," Carine replied, "she was still in bed."

Promptly Louis asked, "Is she ill?"

Carine said, "I don't know."

Louis requested, "Can I see her?"

Jacque said, "Yes!"

They both left the room and went up the stairs to Julie's room. Carine, Maxine, and Nicole stood by the door, anxiously waiting.

Halfway up, they met Marie coming down. Jacque stopped her. "Marie."

"*Oui, Monsieur Bassine.*"

He said, "Take us to Julie's room."

"Yes, monsieur," she acquiesced. Turning to go back up to Julie's room, she knocked and called, "*C'est moi, Marie.*"

Julie called, "Come in."

She was standing on the balcony meditating on what Marie had said and at the same time squeezing her hands on her stomach. She could not understand why she was having these feelings.

Marie asked anxiously, "Are you all right, madame?"

"I'm having a strange sensation in my stomach."

Behind Marie, Jacque and Louis had entered the room. Jacque told her, "We were concerned when we did not see you in the family room so we came up to see how you were doing. Are you all right?"

Looking at Louis, she nodded. "Yes, I'm fine. Am I late for lunch?"

Louis was staring at her as he walked closer. This was the first time he'd truly seen how exotic she was. Louis spoke as if words were put into his mouth. "Since I'm here, why don't I give you a check-up?"

Jacque asked, "You need anything?"

"My bag. It's in my car. The doors are open."

Jacque told Marie to fetch Louis's bag. Marie hurried off to get it. Louis asked, "Where can I wash my hands?"

Jacque pointed to the door where the bathroom was. Julie insisted, "I don't need a check-up. I'm fine."

Louis came out of the bathroom wiping his hands on a towel. Ignoring her comment, he pointed to the bed. "Please sit down."

Sitting down on the edge of the bed, she asked him, "What are you going to do?"

Gently he smiled and reassured her, "Nothing much. I want to look at you—I mean your eyes."

Louis took her hand to check her pulse. She wanted to say something but couldn't. Looking at his watch, he whispered, "Be quiet."

She looked from Louis to Jacque and wondered if they had both lost their minds. Marie returned with his medicine bag. She opened it and handed him his stethoscope. Julie stared at Louis as he moved his hands around her neck and asked, "Does this hurt?"

She choked, "Kind of."

She's stressed, he thought. He moved closer to look at her eyes. He whispered, "*Ouvre ta bouche* (Open your mouth)."

He placed the thermometer in her mouth. They realized how close their faces were and how fresh each other's breath was. He kept thinking how much he wanted to kiss her and hold her in his arms. Looking at her marble light brown eyes, he thought, *If she continues looking at me like this, I'll definitely lose control.*

His eyes were mysterious. They seemed to change color, she thought. She jerked her gaze away and looked at Jacque. Jacque waved at her and she made a funny face at him. Louis took both of her arms and lifted them up and down to check her reflexes. He thought, *I want you.*

Shocked, she squealed, "What did you say?"

Startled, Louis wondered if he had spoken out loud. But his mouth did not open to pronounce a word. *Can she read my mind?*

Gripping the sheet, she thought, *His touch is arousing me. Jacque, take this man away from me.*

He was the cause of the feeling she was having. She made an attempt to stand as he removed the thermometer and looked at the temperature. "*Votre température est bien* (Your temperature is fine)."

"I told you, I'm not sick."

He continued talking as if she hadn't said anything, "But your vital signs are kind of low. Are you taking any kind of vitamin?"

"I don't need any vitamin, thank you."

He took out his prescription book and wrote something. Ripping it off, he handed it to Jacque. "I'm prescribing you this vitamin once a day. I think you need it."

Jacque gave the prescription to Marie and said, "Get it for her, please."

"*Oui, monsieur.*" She left to do as he asked.

Maxine knocked and walked in. "Is Julie all right?"

Julie reassured her, "I'm fine, Max."

Julie walked over to her and placed her arm around her shoulder and said, "I'm starving. What's for lunch?"

Louis placed his equipment inside his bag and commented, "I hope you guys have a great lunch prepared because I'm starving." He picked up his bag and handed it to Jacque, saying, "See to this, please."

▭   ▭   ▭

In the middle of the meal, Maxine burst out, "Welcome to our home, Louis."

Carine was still thinking he came because of Maxine. She wanted to get back at Maxine, so she asked spitefully, "How was it with Maxine the other night, Louis?"

Maxine looked at her in shock because she knew she had not been with Louis. Slowly Louis raised his head as he continued chewing. He looked at Carine and Maxine. Maxine's face looked so scared because if Jacque knew who she was really with, he would be furious and he might mess up things for her. Nicole choked on her food. Jean immediately tapped her on her back as he shook his head. Glancing at Julie, Louis noticed she, like the others, was waiting for an answer. He smiled, swallowed, and answered nonchalantly, "I hope the way you truly like it."

Jacque shook his head in puzzlement. He looked at Carine as if she'd lost her mind. Nicole put her napkin over her mouth, and Maxine gave Louis a smile and mouthed silently, "Thank you," to Louis.

With a grating sound, Carine pushed back her chair and walked out of the dining room. With tears in her eyes, she ran to the balcony. Julie pushed back her chair and made to go after her as the men at the table rose up from their seats. Julie said, "Please, be seated."

Louis watched her as she left the room. She went directly to the balcony and found Carine looking straight ahead.

Without turning around to see who had come after her, Carine sniffed. "Please, no matter what you say, nothing will make me feel better."

Julie started to laugh. Carine turned and demanded angrily, "What is so funny, Julie? Why are you laughing at me?"

39

Catching her breath, Julie shook her head. "Oh, no! I'm not laughing at you, but at the situation. What on earth possessed you to ask a question like that at the lunch table? And when you heard the answer you did not like it. He told you the truth, you know, but you did not want to hear it."

Carine was flabbergasted. "You think I want to hear he had sex with my sister, Julie? I don't think so."

"Is that what you really want him to do, Carine, have sex with your baby sister?"

"No, I hate the thought of it," Carine replied sullenly.

"Then he did not have sex with Maxine," Julie assured her.

Carine looked hard at Julie, wondering if she knew more about the situation than she was letting on. "How did you come up with that conclusion? Louis is a hound!"

Julie couldn't believe how Carine could be so blind. "Think of what he said Carine. . . . 'I hope the way you will truly like it'." She took a deep breath to prevent herself from laughing. "He said it in a way that neither you nor Maxine would feel hurt. After all, by asking that question, you did try to put them in a spot. He is not having sex with her. The man is trying to be a gentleman. . . . And because he thinks of you both as ladies, he answered the only way he knew to spare everybody." Taking Carine's hand, she coaxed, "Come, let's go back in there."

Carine hung back. "You don't know him the way I do, Julie." She put her hand over her face. "I'm too embarrassed to go back in there. . . ."

"Well, you've got to apologize, no matter what. That was extremely rude."

She shook her head. "I can't, Julie."

Julie cajoled, "Say, 'I walked out because I should not have asked this foolish question'. Say, 'Louis, I am sorry. Will you accept my apology?'"

Carine was agitated. "What if he does not accept?"

"Don't worry about it, and while you're at it, apologize to Maxine too, and everyone at the table as well. You will feel better."

They both walked back to the dining room. Julie resumed her seat, picked up her knife and fork, and continued to eat. Carine made her apologies as Julie had suggested. Maxine got up from her chair and walked over to her and gave her a kiss.

Louis assured her it was quite all right. Carine looked at Julie with a relieved smiled. Jacque placed his hand over Julie's hand possessively, looked around the table at everyone, and smiled smugly, "I'm glad everyone is feeling much better. Shall we continue with our meal, Roy?"

Roy removed the soup dishes that were in front of them and served the main course.

But Julie's mind was some place else. She missed her son and her mother. She wanted to hold him and feel his baby softness and inhale his baby scent. She wondered where her husband was. She was looking down at her plate as she chewed, forcing herself to make the food go down her throat.

Louis kept glancing at her and wondering what was on her mind. She barely ate. She looked so far away. Returning to the present, Julie glanced at Louis and found him looking at her. She said to no one in particular, "I'm going for a long ride today. It's a nice day."

Concerned, Louis asked, "Are you a good rider, Julie?"

"Not really, but I want to learn."

Looking at his watch, Jacque said regretfully, "I would like to teach you, but I know you would like to spent time in Jacmel, and your return was blunt, and I have to go there to get the place ready for you. When I return, I'll have the time. I'm leaving today. There are a few problems I need to take care of."

Leaning back in his chair, Louis offered, "I'll be very happy to teach you, Julie."

She accepted gracefully, "Thank you, Louis."

"Today," she repeated. "For how long?"

He glanced at her warily. "One day or two. It depends on how big the problem is."

Worried, Julie offered, "Do you need my help?"

Jacque reassured her, "You don't have to worry about anything. I'll take care of everything. I'll call you as soon as I get there. I want the place to look beautiful for our princess."

She wondered what Jacque was up to. Louis offered his help, but Jacque told him he needed to talk in private with him. Jacque and Louis walked away to the library. Louis sat in the armchair with his back toward the door. Julie left the dining room behind them to go for her walk. Passing by the library door, she knocked. She wanted to say goodbye to Louis before he left. Jacque called, "Come in!"

Julie put her head through the door. Louis did not turn around because he was looking at her reflection in the china door where no one could see. She said, "Jacque, I'm going for a walk and if you need me, you'll find me by the river."

"All right, but be careful."

She pulled the door closed behind her and went up to her room to change her clothes. She pulled on a pair of jeans and a cotton sleeveless blouse, climbing boots, her shades, and a baseball cap.

Carine walked into her room as she finished dressing. "Julie, we're going swimming. We'll be by the pool. Where are you going?"

"For a walk by the river. I need to walk and think."

"Okay." Carine shrugged. She didn't notice the tears in Julie's eyes because she was standing on the balcony looking at the view. Julie never turned around to look at her. She could hear the sadness in Julie's voice. She chose to say nothing. Instead she suggested, "Let's have a barbecue tonight. I'll invite a few friends. We're going to have fun."

Julie was about to tell her she was not in the mood for party. She wiped her eyes and turned to give her answer. The door was wide open and Marie walked in. She had returned with her vitamin and a glass of water. She handed her a pill. Julie thanked her and took the pill as instructed. By the time she swallowed her pill, Carine had left. She didn't notice her departure so she looked around the room for Carine, but she was no longer in her room. Walking out, she informed Marie, "I'll be by the river."

She lightly ran down the stairs, bumping into Louis, who was walking out of the library with Jacque. She paused long enough to mutter a word of apology before continuing out the door. "I'm sorry!"

Jacque excused himself and ran after her, calling, "Julie, wait a moment!"

She slowed down as he caught up with her. "I'm sorry, Julie, that I have to leave on such short notice, but I promise when I return, I will make it up to you. I'm leaving in a few minutes. Will you please stay until I leave, before going for your walk?"

"Oh, all right, Jacque. . . . Are you driving down by yourself?"

"Yes."

Purposely she offered, "Would you like me to come with you? This will be a good chance to say hello to some old friends in Jacmel."

Jacque was made nervous by her request, but found an excuse. "No, you came here to rest, Julie. Some other time, but I promise I'll be back as soon as I finish."

Julie looked at him and smiled sadly. "Well all right. I'll see you when you return. Tell my friends I'll see them as soon as possible." Taking a deep breath, she exhaled and offered, "Would you like some assistance in packing?"

He shook his head. "Roy had already prepared my suitcase for me."

She smiled. "Well, you have everything ready."

"Actually, there is one thing you can do for me." He looked at Louis, who was standing at a distance watching them. "I want you to be careful when you go riding tonight. And when I return I will fill you in with what has been happening here, okay."

Louis didn't move as he stood there watching them. He noticed Julie was trying not to look at him while she was talking to Jacque. He smiled when he noticed he was making her nervous and the way Julie nodded her head, trying to pay attention to what Jacque was telling her. The sun was glaringly hot. He removed his handkerchief to wipe his face. Maxine was passing by the door when she noticed Louis was standing on the terrace by himself.

Louis wondered. *What exactly brought her here to Haiti? And why am I puzzled over her so much?*

Realizing what he was thinking, he whispered to himself, "Snap out of it, Louis."

Maxine came over to him and touched his arm. "Louis, I want to thank you."

Still focused on Julie and Jacque and the intense feelings that were raging inside him, he asked absently, "What for?"

Maxine looked at him to see what had caught his interest and saw where his eyes were focused. She tapped him harder on his arm. "For getting me out of trouble with my brother."

Still not looking at her, "Oh, that. . . . When are you going to tell your brother the truth, Max?" he asked.

Maxine replied, aghast, "The truth—are you mad? He'll kill me."

She looked at Louis and then over to where her brother and Julie were talking, folded her arms, and asked, "When are you going to tell me what really brings you here? I know it's not my sister Carine and definitely not Nicole."

Louis swung round as if he had been shot. Smugly, Maxine continued, "You see, Louis. I'm not as naïve as my family thinks."

Louis removed his shades and placed them in his vest pocket, folded his arms, and stood there with an amused look in his eyes. "You tell me, Maxine! You seem to have all the answers."

Stroking her feet on the perfectly manicured lawn, she planted her hands on her hips. "I saw you! I saw the way you were looking at Julie. She's very beautiful, isn't she?"

Louis smiled. "Yes she is."

"She is not your type, Louis." Maxine smiled. "She's too nice and modest."

"What are you implying, Max? I'm not worthy of this modest beauty?"

"You don't know how to love, Louis. You're not ready to settle down, and plus Julie is a married woman. You're a heart breaker. And my friend's heart is already broken. She doesn't need to add to her sorrow."

"Max, be quiet." He removed his left hand out of his pocket and placed the other one around her shoulders. Pointing to where Julie and her brother was, he asked, "Julie comes to Haiti all the time, doesn't she?"

"Yes, she spent most of her time here when she was a little girl."

"How come I never met Julie, and your family never introduced me to her?"

Maxine laughed and said, "Julie doesn't usually go out when she comes here. Last night was the first. She usually kept to herself. She spent more time working on the lands, taking care of her animals, reading, or in the province of Jacmel. That's the place she usually stays. She loves the countryside, especially the mountains of Jacmel. She said the people there are friendly and warm. Not like Thomassin or Port-au-Prince."

Louis purposely asked, "Is there anything going on between her and your brother?"

"Oh no!" Quickly Maxine silenced him. "Don't ever let her hear you say that. She's a married woman. She takes her marriage very seriously. Jacque is like her big brother . . . she's family."

Carine came out then and interrupted, "Who is family?"

Maxine retorted, "Julie!"

"Oh yes," Carine replied. "She's the happy married sister."

Louis, without any expression, ignored the comment and continued to look straight ahead as he was before. Maxine agreed, "You can say that again. She's not like many women. She's very respectful."

"Well anyway, Maxine," Carine cut in, "Julie and I are having a few friends over for a barbecue tonight."

"Tonight!" Maxine exclaimed. "She didn't tell me anything, and plus she is going for a walk."

She stared at Carine then gave her a funny look. She knew Julie didn't have many friends except for them and the province friends. They were not even in town. She looked at Carine and wondered what she was up to.

"Julie's here on vacation, and plus it is a long weekend. I'm sure if you call a few of your friends they'll be very happy to come. We need to show Julie a good time. What do you say, Louis?"

Maxine didn't wait for Louis's answer. She replied, "Louis is a busy man. I'm sure he has other plans."

Ignoring her response, Carine answered, "You're wasting time, Max. Go make your call. And your name is not Louis. Well, Louis, what do you say, making up for the flying trip?"

Smiling, he replied, "It's been a long time since I have had a good time."

Maxine laughed. "Carine, you're crazy!"

Then she ran off toward Julie and Jacque, leaving Louis and Carine standing there.

Carine called, "When are you going to learn to be serious?" Turning to Louis, she shook her head. "When is that girl going to grow up? Louis, will you come tonight?"

Louis took his shades out of his vest pocket and placed them on his nose before answering, "I don't know."

Jacque, Julie, and Maxine were walking back. Suddenly Maxine yanked Julie's cap off her head, allowing her hair to cascade down her back, and took off running. Julie ran after her laughing and trying to grab her cap. "Give it back, Max!"

Maxine ran around Louis, shrieking with laughter. "You can't catch me!"

She jumped and placed the cap on Louis's head and taunted, "Now! Come and get it."

Louis joined in with Maxine's taunting, "Come and get it!" with a smile on his face.

She slowly walked toward them, shook her head, and stretched out her hand. "Can I please have my cap?"

"Sure!" He lifted it off his head and pretended to hand it to her. Then with a flick of his wrist, he sailed it over her head to Maxine. "Maxine!" he yelled. "Catch!"

Julie tilted her chin, looked him up and down, and asked, "Hmm . . . so you want to play as well?"

Jacque walked toward Maxine, took the cap from her, and gave it back to Julie. Maxine stuck her tongue out at him. "You're such a party pooper!"

But deep down Julie was having fun. She needed the little run. Carine looked at Louis. "God! Louis, I'm surprised at you!"

Jacque apologized to Louis, "I'm sorry for leaving you here alone."

"I'm not alone. Maxine is here with me," he said deliberately, which made Carine jealous as usual.

Nicole came out and walked over to Carine. She whispered to her and let her know that she had invited Brian and his brother Patrick to the barbecue tonight. They all said they would come, but she still couldn't get in contact with Sofia. And Debbie was going out of town, so she would not be able to make it.

Jacque asked curiously, "What are you girls up to?"

Maxine chirped, "We are having a barbecue tonight."

Carine was frantically signaling Maxine not to tell him anything, but it was already too late. Jacque rounded on Maxine, "Whose idea was this?"

No one answered, so Julie spoke up, "My idea! Is that a problem, Jacque?"

"Why you didn't you tell me that you were planning this, Julie?"

"Well, it came up unexpectedly. I didn't know you were going away."

Jacque conceded, taking a glance at Louis, "Okay, but no wild things going on here, you hear me?"

"Speak for yourself," Julie retorted. "There are no children here, Jacque, so I find what you just said very offensive. Everyone here is in their twenties and older, and I'm sure we can take care of ourselves. I—we—don't need adult supervision, right, girls?"

They all chorused, "Right!"

They all stood by Julie. Throwing his hands up in the air in a gesture of surrender, Jacque relented. "I didn't mean anything by that. I'm sorry!"

Julie said, "You better be careful where you're heading."

Jacque turned to Louis and pleaded, "Help me here, Louis."

Louis held up his hands in a gesture of surrender. "When a woman talks, a man's best bet is to yield and listen to her commands or her wishes." He stared at Julie, then looked at Jacque and said, "I'll be leaving now."

"So soon," Maxine cried out, holding on to him. She leaned her head against his arm. She turned to Jacque to make an earnest request of him, "Ask Louis to stay here with us tonight."

Louis smiled when he heard what Maxine asked and wondered what her game was. Jacque looked at him and said, "Maxine, I cannot impose on

Louis like this, but if he wants to spend the night," he looked at Carine and Maxine, "it will be fine with me."

Louis responded, "Thank you for the offer, but I have another engagement." Looking at his watch, he shook his head in regret. "See you all at the barbecue. By the way, Julie, later I'll take you riding. Bye, everyone. Jacque, thanks for an interesting lunch."

Louis lightly ran down the steps, got in his car, and drove off.

Roy had already put Jacque's luggage in the trunk of his Jeep. He was ready to go. Julie walked him to his car and waved goodbye to him. He got in and started the engine. "I'll see you soon, as soon as I've gotten everything set for you at Jacmel. I'll return to get you. Take care of yourself, be careful, and don't worry about me. I'll be fine, Julie."

She stepped away from the car and waved to him again as he revved up and sped off down the drive. She turned and waved to the others, calling, "I'm going for my walk now. . . . I'll be by the river if anyone needs me."

Chapter Five

Bittersweet Memories

Julie stopped at the barn to look at the horses. One of the workers was catering to them. She walked in and greeted, "*Bonsoir, Monsieur Pépé.*"

The man was happy to see her. As she entered he greeted her with a smile and stepped aside to give her access to the horse he was feeding. Passing her hands on the back of horse's shining coat she said, "You looked healthy."

Julie petted the horses while she checked on them. The man was telling her how well the horses were cared for. She handed the man an envelope that had money inside it and told him he had done a good job. The man smiled and bowed his head as he took the envelope from her hand to thank her for thinking of him. She didn't stay long. She thanked the man for taking good care of her animals while she was away and told him she had a package for him, so he should drop by to pick it up, then she left the barn.

Julie took her time walking across the field down to the old house where her parents had lived when she was a little girl, before they built the mansion her friends were now living in. Taking a deep breath, she opened the door and went in. She smiled when she saw the family pictures on the wall of the living room and how well the place had been kept. She looked around the three bedrooms. The bathroom was redone, the tub replaced with a two-seater marble jacuzzi, which was olive colored. Even the kitchen was redecorated, too. Everything looked perfect. Julie thought, *I would rather stay here then in the big house. It's cozier here and I could have my privacy. I think I'm going to move here instead.*

Leaning against the wall at the entrance of the house, she looked around and thought Saul must have had Jacque fix that place, because it was fixed just like the one in the Paterson, New Jersey. Was Saul here in Haiti? she thought.

The place was clean and the marble floor was shining. There was no dust inside the place. The chairs had been renewed and the curtains matched the dining room and the living room chairs. Everything complemented each other. Nodding her head, she closed her eyes and saw herself as a child. She remembered the joy she had inside that place. She could see her father tickling her on the sofa, making her laugh, and her mother smiling as she prepared their meal. They would sit around the coffee table sharing their dreams and ideas to improve their lives.

She went to the kitchen to take a bottle of spring water from the refrigerator. Then she walked out of the house and closed the door behind her to go to the back yard and look at her gardens. She passed her hands over the cactus and took a rose from a branch and made her way into the woods. She climbed over the hill, then stopped to look around the field and thought, *I hope the people on the land do not cut these trees down for charcoal.*

The plain was filled with fruit trees, *quênéppe, mangue, corossol* (sour-sop), *chadèque* (grapefruit), lime, sour orange, *grenade* (pomegranates), guyave, *serise* (cherries), *cocotier* (coconuts), and *avocatier* (avocado). There were also a few *banane* (banana) trees in the field. The plain looked healthy and rich with green grass. She looked up at the sunny sky—not one cloud.

"Boy, it's hot!" she shouted out.

She removed her shades from her blouse pocket and perched them on her nose, then took her cap off her head to fan herself some air. She stretched her arms up to feel the wind going through her hair and face.

She breathed, "God is good."

She was glad she had taken a bottle of water with her. She opened the bottle to drink some of the water. She couldn't wait to get by the river to rest her feet in the water. She met a few workers working on the land. She greeted and stopped to talk to them for a few minutes. She called them over to her to give them a few words of gratitude.

They were happy to see her again. There were some faces she didn't recognize. They came forward to introduce themselves to her. She complimented them for the good job they were doing and looked forward to work beside them as well.

They all waved goodbye to her as she made her way further up on the plain. On her way, she thought the Bassine did a good job of taking care of the land.

There were birds on some of the branches of the pines and nests on some of the coconut trees. The sound of the quails made her stop to look around. She smiled when she spotted the nest. Here on the land, she felt it was a safe haven for those birds. She never wanted anyone to hunt those little creatures.

They were the beauties of the land. She remembered when she was seven years old, her father built a nice-sized birdcage for her, and through the years she made sure they were taken good care of. It was not too far from where she was standing. Putting her cap back on her head, she walked toward the direction where the birdcage used to sit.

"Oh my." She smiled when she saw them.

She ran toward the cage. It was rebuilt, and there was a note at the side of it addressed to her. She removed the little note to read. But the words were typed and it said, "I took the liberty to fix up the place while I was here."

The whole area of that section was reconstructed. There were picnic tables and benches and two nice-sized barbecue grills built. She wondered, was Saul in Haiti? Did he build those things?

There were quails inside the birdcage. Then she thought it must have been Jacque. She smiled. "You kept it for me."

There were babies inside the nest that was in the cage. Food and water was well arranged at the side of the cage. Even the tree was well preserved and her initial was still imprinted on the bark. That was one of her favorite trees. She used to climb it. She placed the cap down and fixed her pants on her, making ready to climb the tree, which she did. When she got on top, she yelled, "I made it. Just when I thought I forgot how, I did it."

She laughed like a little girl who just succeeded on her first climbing lesson. *Now*, she thought, *how am I going to come down?* She sat there for a while, swinging her feet, then she went down very carefully. She stretched when her feet were on solid ground. Taking one good look at the quails in the cage, she picked up her baseball cap, placed it on her head, and off she ran toward the river.

She could hear the river. She slowed down to catch her breath. The sound of water running was getting louder. She stopped carefully to look down. She remembered the hill was high like a mountain when she was a little girl. Everything looks huge to anyone who's little and short. Slowly, she descended the little hill going down toward the river.

They kept it clean. She smiled. There was no horse or donkey waste by the river, so one could drink water directly from the river. Carefully she went down toward the river, then she remembered there was an easier way down she had built a while ago.

She walked toward the direction where the steps were. She laughed when she saw the steps had been improved and there were handles on both sides of the steps to hold while going up or down. Her picnic area was well arranged.

Did Jacque build all that also?

There were more trees planted by the river and there was a support wall built to protect the land from eroding so when it rained very heavily the land would not slide.

How thoughtful of him, she thought, making her way down to the river. She walked to the almond tree she had planted when she was five years old with the help of her father. She noticed everyone had trees planted by the river. Her almond tree was the largest one of them all. She smiled as she read the name plates on each tree. Jacque had a mango tree; Carine, apricot; Jean, crab apple; Nicole, peach; and Maxine had planted a breadfruit tree.

Passing her hands over the tree, Julie whispered, "Maxine remembered that was my favorite. One can never go hungry when having a breadfruit tree in your yard."

She looked at the extent of the tree then she hugged it. "She planted you well, my friend, near water. You'll be the most beautiful breadfruit tree in Haiti."

She walked back to her almond tree and sat under it, looking at the river flowing by, remembering the time she and her father planted the almond tree. She loved almond so much that she told him she was going to have an almond factory. She thought her father would have been with her forever. He was her best friend. She recalled the day her father died. He was going to Washington, D.C. That was the first time her father told her she couldn't come with him, but he would meet her mother and her three days after the conference. He would not have the time to go to the museum with her. So she had to stay home with Mommy. Her father was an agriculturist, so he was always traveling, going to different countries for new ideas or how to help the lands. That was the best job to her, because her father was also her teacher. She didn't have to sit in a classroom to learn. His dream was to go back to Haiti to rebuild his lands.

Never in her life did she think her father would have died in plane crash. She was twelve when her father passed away. Her mother continued the work her father was doing. It wasn't easy for the both of them, but she had to learn that her mother had feelings and she needed her to cooperate with her. Her mother couldn't handle the home teaching and taking care of agriculture business. She suggested her mother put her in boarding school, which would be easier for her mother, and she could come home on the weekends. It took courage for her to get on a plane again. She had to, for the sake of her mother.

She had not been back to the land she loved for over five years. Many things had changed and people she knew had moved. Only a few of them were still here in Haiti, and they were all scattered around.

My, she thought, *tonight the girls are having a barbecue. I'm not up to socializing. I need to think how to make my marriage work and find out what's wrong with me. The Bassine think I'm here to party, but I'm not about that. I never was, and I am not about to become one. Do they really understand what I'm going through, and what my position has been as Saul's wife?* It was Saul's dream for them to move back to Haiti to settle here. Now she was here by herself to see if she could make that dream come true.

She inhaled as the tears flowed out of her eyes, wondering why that man Janvier frightened her. She was not accustomed to being puzzled by anyone. And she was going to work on that by facing her fear. Marie made it clear that Louis was there to see her. She was definitely not going to encourage him. She thought maybe if he realized she was a happily married woman, he would lose interest. Why would a man like him wanted to involved with a married woman, unless he was a player. Breathing in and out, she said, "He has to be joking."

She shook her head to remove the thought of Louis out of her mind. She knew her husband loved her and treasured the passion they shared between them. Again she wondered, *Where are you Saul? Are you hurt? Is some one holding you captive? Are you okay?*

She had called everyone she could think of, but no one saw him. She even hired a private detective. So far he had not found a clue yet. She closed her eyes trying to envision Saul before her, to hear his voice and his joyful laughter. Instead she heard the voice of Louis whispering in her ears, *Is that what you're wishing for, Julie?*

Covering her ears, she shook her head to come to her senses and whispered, "No, not you. I don't even know you. You are just the wind whispering in my ears."

She couldn't grasp why was she hearing Louis Janvier's voice in her mind. Why was she being haunted by a man she didn't even know? She leaned her head against the tree as she drifted away, whispering her husband's name, "Saul."

It had been four days since she arrived in Haiti. She wanted to be here with him, at her favorite hideaway, the river. She knew Saul loved that place. She remembered the very first time they were here together. They were married for only nine months. She had to meet him in Haiti, so after the seminar from Paris she went. How they enjoyed the river. They camped by the river and swam naked when everyone left. The water was cold, but their bodies kept each other warm. That night she thought she was definitely pregnant.

Absently Julie picked up a small rock and threw it in the water and watched the ripples it made as it went by. While she was in her deep thoughts, she heard a sound of a motor bike and a voice calling her, "Julie, Julie!"

Wiping her eyes, she turned to look where the voice was coming from. "Over here, Max!"

Maxine sat by her and mused, "You know, this used to be our favorite spot. I usually come here when I need to think."

Julie didn't respond to Maxine's comments. Deep in her own thoughts, she was throwing small pebbles in the water and observing attentively how they glided on the water before sinking. Maxine noticed that Julie was unhappy. She too picked up a rock and threw it in the water. "I'm sorry for everything, Julie."

Julie's head snapped up. "What do you mean? You have nothing to be sorry for."

"Yes I do. You know, the way we all behaved, especially me."

Continuing throwing the pebbles, Julie answered, "I did not notice any bad behavior."

Maxine came and sat closer to her and said, "You haven't been in Haiti since the time you got married. We don't spent time together anymore, Julie, the way we used to when were children. And when I look at you, you look like you were crying. You seem distant. What is wrong?"

"My marriage, Max." She breathed out.

"I thought everything was going well," Maxine responded. "You and Saul were the perfect couple."

"There's no such thing as a perfect couple, Max." She threw a rock in the water. "Maybe perfect intentions, but what he had was good."

"I thought you were going to be a diplomat or a missionary," Maxine commented and asked, "What made you decided to get married? And why did you marry him?"

"I was wondering when you were going to ask me that question." Julie chuckled and said, "It has been over six years. I thought you were no longer interested about knowing my business."

"I was upset." Maxine smiled, "I felt that Saul stole my best friend, but still, I was happy for you. You two did look good together. Now I'm asking, What made you decided to marry that hunk of a man?"

"You know I never dated," Julie replied. "I was always home studying or reading a book or exercising. Most young men who talked to me were airheads and selfish. They couldn't reach my level of thinking. I was hungry for adventure and Mother noticed that. I started to study the Bible, and from what I was learning from it, I was looking for the perfect man. Who would love me, be my equal intellectually, and would kiss the ground I walked on. My mother got worried that I would never get married, because the men I met were not up to the challenge that I was brought up for. . . ."

She glanced at Maxine. "My mother introduced me to him. She met him while she was at Columbia University on a lecture she was giving. He seemed to be very charming to my mother, so she fixed us up on a blind date. Saul was born in Haiti. His father was from Paris and married to a Haitian woman from Jacmel. You've seen Saul. You were always wondering where Saul got his blue eyes and dusty blond hair. I was fascinated by him. He is tall and handsome, full of life and ideas. He is the smartest man I've ever met. . . ."

She breathed joyfully, "The minute Saul saw me he was taken. After a few minutes of talking he said, 'I thought you were just a beautiful face with a gorgeous body', and I felt the same way, too. That was the first time I was having a normal conversation with a man. He had the power to charm."

"Oh yes he does." Maxine smiled. "He charmed your mother and caused a miracle."

"What miracle is that?"

Maxine laughed. "You! Ms. Orderly, he captured your heart."

"He did." She smiled, nodding her head in agreement. "Eight months later we got married."

"I remember," Maxine cut in. "You called me to tell me you met your husband. I thought you were joking, giving me an excuse to leave Haiti. I came to New York the following week. Boy! I remember Jacque was so angry when he heard you got married and he wasn't invited. Carine thought you were being cheap. Nicole thought that Saul was an ugly man, and Jean didn't care."

Shaking her head, she continued, "I didn't want a big wedding, and plus Jacque felt I didn't know Saul well enough to marry him. I didn't want any negative vibes around me. . . . I love Saul. He thought me how to kiss. How to make love. I was like a treasure to him. We made love every day. Sometime five times in one day. I wanted children. . . ."

Maxine replied, "Wow! What were two you running, a marathon? You always wanted a big family."

Smiling at her comment, Julie explained, "For years I've been trying to have a baby for Saul. I traveled all over the world trying to find out why I could not get pregnant. That was one of the reasons you didn't hear from me for awhile. Then one day Saul came to me and told me why I could not get pregnant—he had had vasectomy a while back. And it was irreversible for him."

Maxine cut in, "Vasectomy? He didn't want any children?"

"The strange thing he did was, before he had the operation, he had deposited his sperm in a sperm bank."

"You mean Saul froze his sperm? That is strange."

"Yes." Julie meditated. "But still, I jumped for joy. All that time I was praying, now God finally answered my prayer. Saul said he was sorry, he didn't know how much I wanted babies, so he never told me. Without thinking, I accepted what he told me. The next morning, he took me to see my gynecologist. Saul said we could have a whole lot of babies if we wanted to with what he'd saved.

"The first time we did the procedure, bingo! I got pregnant. Saul seemed to be very happy. He was always taking pictures of me and my stomach, videotaping William's birth. When Bill was born, I was the happiest woman in the world. I thought I had everything. But something phenomenal happened to me. . . ."

Julie paused for a while, looking at the stream running by. "When I got pregnant, I started to have a dream I had a couple of times when I was a teenager, except this time I was no longer a girl, I was a woman. You remember that dream, Max? You were the only one I told about it, about the boy. I couldn't make out his face, but he was dressed in black."

Trying to remember, she nodded her head. "Yes, the one I said might be Jewish or a Druid. I thought that was a funny dream you had, but you thought it was dirty because you two made love. . . ."

"More likely sex. I didn't even know who he was. I never could understand why would I be dreaming of some strange boy. On top of that, we were having sex. We were children, for God's sake! That was definitely nasty."

They laughed. Maxine replied, "And you made me promise never to tell anyone of that dream of the boy in black outfit."

"So you remember it well, Max. The stranger in black in my dream came back. The dream got worse after I gave birth to William. I love my husband and cannot understand why that came back to haunt me. It made no sense at all. Saul didn't give me any reason to think of another man."

Maxine comforted, "Have you seen a doctor?"

"I've visited one." Julie sighed. "But there was not much he could do. He was prescribing me sleeping pills so I could sleep at night, which I couldn't take because I was breast feeding. He wanted to hypnotize me. I would not allow him to put me under hypnotism. I hate for anyone to play with my mind. My problem, doctors cannot solve. Only God could help me with my dreams."

"You're right," Maxine agreed, "but what happened after that?"

"I could not stand for Saul to touch me after giving birth Max."

"Why?" Maxine asked in shock.

"I couldn't understand it. . . . Every time he touched me, I felt like pushing him away. Like I've been punished. Knowing how much he loved and wanted me didn't make it any easier. I wanted to please him but I was unable to. I wanted to love him because he loved me so much. But something held me back. I kept on dreaming about a man I don't even know. Only a glance of the dream I was able to remember, everything else is blank. Then it became a nightmare. Sometimes I woke up crying, 'Where are you, my love? I'm looking for you. I can't find you. . . .' The dream drove Saul crazy."

"Did you ever see the man's face in your dream?"

"No!" Julie paused, sorrow clouding her voice. With tears in her eyes she continued, "Saul started to lose his patience with me. One night he was in his graphic room working on a new project. I was bringing him something to eat. I overheard him talking to himself saying, 'That bastard thinks he could have my woman? I'll kill him. . . .' When I asked who was the bastard he wanted to kill, it turned into an argument. He accused me of eavesdropping on his conversation. I thought he was really going out of his mind. That night he wanted to make love. I tried, even though I didn't want to. I tried.

I was trying so hard, Max, I pretended it was feeling good. When he took me, it felt like I was been raped, like I was being ripped apart. I started to scream. I screamed so loud, because it was painful. Saul was very angry. He jumped off me and stood there, watching me screaming, he thought it was the baby. . . ."

"The baby!" Maxine exclaimed in horror. "Why the baby?"

"I couldn't understand why he said that it was the baby that caused my problems." Julie sighed. "Saul said, 'You know who's the problem . . . it's that unholy child.' It hit me the bastard he wanted to kill was our baby. He ran out of the room to Bill's room. I got up and ran after him. Bill let out a chilling scream when Saul picked him up. I ran inside the room where Saul was holding him as if he was going to throw him on the floor. I screamed for my baby and told him, 'If you hurt one hair on his head, you're going to have to kill me, too. I can't go on living without Bill.' He just handed me Bill and turned and walked away. . . ."

"Oh my word," Maxine said in sympathy.

"The next few days, I slept with Bill. I didn't let him out of my sight. I didn't trust Saul anymore with him. I asked him to give me more time. I was probably going through post-natal trauma. I felt I needed more time. I wasn't ready. He looked at me like a madman and laughed, saying, 'If only you knew'."

"If only you knew what?" Maxine exclaimed. "Didn't he give you any explanation?"

"No. A few days after that, he received a telegram. He just packed his bag, kissed me, and said, 'You have plenty of time to think now and to clean up your act. Hopefully you'll be ready when I return. I love you, Julie, and all I've ever wanted is to make you happy. Everything I do, I do for you and the baby'. He kissed me and kissed Bill on his forehead. He didn't say where he was going. He didn't say when he'd be back. . . .

"His last words were, 'I'll call you'. I spent a month in the house waiting for his call, and my nightmares got worse. I was frightened to go to bed at night. Every little noise scared me. I was jumpy and on edge. So I moved in with my mother. As the days went by, I got more and more depressed. My mother tried to cheer me up. She helped so much with Bill, but nothing worked. Then she encouraged me to come here to Haiti to help establish what Saul and I dreamed of. She said, 'You guys will be good for me'. She personally packed my bags and took me to the airport. Something strange happened the night I arrived in Haiti. . . ."

"Really." Maxine waited with bated breath.

"After everyone went to bed, I was alone in the balcony, looking at the stars. I felt something or someone touch me like a . . . kiss on my neck. And a voice whispered, '*Demande ce que tu veux, mon amour* (Make a wish, my love)'. Oh Max, for the first time in a very long time, I felt good. I wanted more of what touched me. I felt safe. For a few seconds, I forgot about all of my problems."

Maxine was excited. "That was the night Louis was over at the mansion."

Julie nodded in surprise. "Yes."

She stayed silent for a moment when she realized, the very first night here in Haiti, it was his voice she had heard whispering to her. Then she said, "Enough about me. . . . What have you been doing with your life, young lady?"

Maxine stood up with a rock in her hand and threw it in the river. "Max, is everything all right with you?"

She still didn't answer. Slowly she turned to Julie and said, "I'm in love with a man my family will not approve of."

Sensing that Maxine want to share her secret with her, Julie asked gently, "Who are you in love with, Max?"

"I've wanted to tell someone about him so bad and I know you're the only one I can confide in. I met him almost ten months ago. I went to the hospital visiting Louis and there he was, coming toward me. I couldn't stop looking at him, or he at me. Boy! Julie, he is so handsome. He has the most wonderful chocolate skin and the softest hazel eyes I've ever seen. So while he was going by me, I asked him if he knew where Doctor Janvier's office was. He told me that was where he was heading, and that was when we started to talk. As we were walking I took a quick glance at the back of his head. . . .

"His jet-black hair that was well cut made his entire appearance stand out prominently. He gave me his phone number. I told him I would call him. His name is Richard Landers. He is a doctor who studied in Mexico. Do you believe in love at first sight, Julie?"

"Yes, Max, indeed I do."

"This is what happened to me." She moved back to where Julie was. "I love him, and he loves me, too. We plan to get married."

"When will that be?"

"In a year and a half from now. I need time to have the courage to face Jacque and the rest of them. And I don't want Aunt Viviane to be mad at me. . . ."

Julie was confused by her allegation. She didn't understand why Maxine would think her mother would be upset at her. She waited for Maxine to finish her sentence before she cut in. Maxine sighed dreamily. "He's a neurologist, same as Louis. He loves people and he's kind and patient. He treats me with respect."

Perplexed, Julie asked, "Then why are you sneaking around to see him?"

"Because my family will not accept him."

"I don't understand. Why wouldn't they?"

She answered softly. "Because he is Marie's son, our servant."

Julie didn't reply immediately. Maxine got nervous and peeked at Julie. "Are you upset at me, Julie?"

"No, Max," Julie reassured her. "I'm surprise at your family, not upset. One can never tell when or with whom one's going to fall in love. . . . I'm glad to know that you're not a person who judges anyone by their birth right or family title. . . ."

She leaned closer and gave Maxine a hug. Gently, Julie lifted her chin to look at her. " . . . but by their deeds. You can't keep him a secret forever, Max. Invite him to the barbecue tonight. I want to meet him."

Maxine was scared. "What would Carine and Nicole and Jean say if they found out who he is?"

"Don't worry about what they will say, worry about how Maxine feels."

Maxine smiled tremulously. "I feel good, but scared."

Julie said, "It's quite all right. Come on, let's go. You have a mission to work on. . . ."

Maxine's problem had given Julie something else to think about and she forgot about her own problem. Julie got up and stretched out her hand. Maxine hadn't moved. She repeated, " . . . Let's go. I'll race you to the house."

"I have the bike with me."

"Then I'll drive, you'll sit on the back."

Maxine took the outstretched hand and jumped up as they both ran giggling like the schoolgirls they once were to prepare for the night's festivities.

Meanwhile over at Janvier's estate, Louis was in his lounge room by himself playing billiards and wondering what he should really do tonight. Putting the cue stick down across the pool table, he picked up the phone and dialed. "Hello, Patrick, *c'est moi* (it's me) Louis. . . . Did the Bassine's girls invite you to their place tonight? . . . Good! I need you to help me bring something there. . . . My two favorite horses. . . . So Carine didn't waste any time. This woman doesn't know the meaning of love and what love is all about. She is only worried about what I have in my pants. I have no time to waste on her. She asked you to bring three horses to her home tonight?. . . . Bring only two."

He smiled and concluded, "I'll see how lucky that I am tonight. . . . Oh, like Julie said, blessing. And if God finally blesses me. . . . See you there."

Louis sat back on his lazy chair, meditating on his surrounding. Most people thought having lots of money was a blessing, but sometimes he felt it was a curse, because most of them wanted what he had and some wanted him dead. And the responsibility that came along with it was devastating for him. Most of the women loved what they were getting out of him, and they were willing to do anything to be part of his action. To him they were senseless parasites feeding on his flesh. At first, he didn't care about that, because his life didn't have any meaning and he didn't mind the feeding he was giving them. But now there was a reason, and it had been doubled. And for him to put the pieces together–that was where the challenge stood, and he was nervous about it. Never had he allowed anyone to see him sweat, and even that might be the greatest challenge he'd ever face in his life.

He led a rough life, and he usually played hard. And he wasn't the type to settle down. That was not in his agenda. A bachelor he was and a bachelor he was going to stay. One thing he realized was he was attracted to her more than any other women he ever met. And she was a married woman. That wasn't new to him. He had been involved before with many married women, but with her it was different. He actually wanted to get to know her.

Banging his hand on the side of the chair, Louis whispered, "Damn! It is wrong."

He got off and walked to the bar to pour himself a glass of water to calm himself down.

He gulped the water down, then placed the glass back on the table. He couldn't help thinking about Julie and the game they played last night. He felt she was highly intelligent. Never did he meet a woman who was able to express her feelings and thoughts the way she was able to. He laughed when he thought women like her have strong-minded children.

Squeezing his hands against his temples, he wondered what was he thinking. Then roughly he ran his fingers through his hair, backing them away from his face as he walked back and sat on the lazy chair. Stretching himself he whispered, "Julie, the desert plant lady, who are you really? What is hidden in your wilderness?"

He was trying to get her out of his mind, the cactus lady, who claimed she wasn't mysterious. But she was more so to him than he was to her. Several times during the check-up he was giving to her, she was reading his thoughts. And that was something he had never allowed, to let anyone get that close to know what he was thinking, but she was able to do so when they didn't even know each other. How could that be possible? A woman he didn't know was able to sense his feelings and set them on fire.

He inhaled and exhaled to release some of the feelings he was beginning to have. His body felt feverish as he controlled his nerves and his wandering mind.

"Please," he whispered, as if he was talking to someone. He closed his eyes trying to erase her features he thought were present before him. Like a tormented man he was turning, quivering, and thinking. *How did I let this feeling overtake me? What is happening to me? Why are you following me? Please set me free!*

So many questions were running in his mind. He was released from his vision when his butler Francois came to announce that Henry wanted to talk to him.

"Excuse me, Dr. Janvier. Monsieur Henry Claude want to know if he could come in to see you."

58

He nodded his head for yes with his back turned, looking out through the sliding door into his domain. Someone knocked on the door. Louis called, "Come in."

Henry walked in and stood by the door. Louis signaled him to come closer. He sat straight and turned the chair around to face Henry and said, "Are you game? . . . Man, I'm thirsty."

Henry looked at him strangely, "It's been a long time since I've heard you use the term I'm thirsty."

Walking behind the bar, he fixed himself a drink and poured Louis an ice-cold glass of water, he brought it to Louis, handed it to him, and asked, "How was lunch?"

Louis smiled and saluted him with his glass. "I'm still hungry, but not for food."

Henry sat by the bar. He didn't need to ask who his boss was talking about and was hungry for. He knew instinctively that it was Julie.

"I could smell her, taste her. It felt good. I feel alive again, and I know she feels the same way I do, but she is fighting herself. I wasn't planning to go to the Bassine place tonight, but for her I'll go. And plus I have promised her I was going to take her riding later on."

Henry was surprised by Louis's statement and thought, *Did Louis hear what he just revealed to me?*

"You think that's a good idea, Fuji? You yourself told me, she's dangerous goods."

"I don't recall I've asked you for advice, Henry. I'll let you know when I need it."

"You have not been yourself, Fuji, for quite some time. You're not thinking straight. She seemed fascinating and she's very attractive, not only to you, so hands off, Fuji, or she'll crush you. She is not those woman you played with."

"I haven't played for quite some time," Louis said as he got up from his seat to stand by the door looking at the view of his domain. "She's a woman, isn't she? And who said I was going to play with her? She's not a toy."

Picking up the cue ball, Louis threw it onto the sliding door and shattered the glass with such a rage. Intensely he watched how the ball rolled into the garden.

"Fuji, control your temper!" Henry said angrily.

"Who said that I lost my temper?"

Henry reminded him, "That's the fifth time in one month you broke these doors. And I'm running out of excuses for telling people why you keep on breaking on these doors."

Louis said calmly, "Since when did I care of what people think or say?"

"I know you didn't ask for my advice." Looking at the blaze in Louis's eyes, Henry cautioned, "But, brother, you have to admit Julie is a frightening woman. Look at the way you're acting! Doesn't that tell you something–

stay away, danger zone? I never met any woman who was able to get every-one's attention when she's talking. And yours, especially! The power she has in unbelievable. She's very intimidating, Louis, and at the same time she's like a child who's hiding. At Nadine's, I watched the way she tried to avoid eye contact with you. She's scared, Fuji. You know what happens when a rat is cornered."

Looking at Henry he emphasized, "I could tell she's confused and hurt-ing. I hope I'll be able to comfort her and help her to deal with her pain."

Shaking his head, Henry said, "I hope you know what you are getting yourself into. She'll have you as a captive audience and have you applaud-ing for her instead of for yourself."

"This," smirking, Louis said, "I'd love to see. She's on my turf now, and I'm not about to run."

▭ ▭ ▭

Jean and his sisters were preparing for the barbecue while the caterers and the servants were setting up the grills and the tables. While they were setting things up, Maxine asked, "You think it's wise for that hang-out tonight? Julie doesn't like crowds."

"She'll be all right," Carine responded. "It is about time Mrs. Philip start-ed to live life."

Julie was on the phone talking to her mother. "I'll be fine, Mother. I miss you guys. I wish you two were here with me. Haiti is fine, but you know it could always be better. I'm looking forward to going to Jacmel. That province always seemed to bring peace to my soul."

After finishing talking to her mother, she went and stood by the window looking at the view. She wished she could have made all Haiti look like the scenery she was beholding. It's just too bad she was only one person. There was not much one could do, but it was better than nothing. She remem-bered Cité Delmas used to Call First Cité and Second Cité. As a little girl, she used to go there with her parents, visiting some relatives and friends who used to live there. Delmas used to be their first stop. They would make a left driving down the little hill coming from Pétion Ville. As they were going by, across was a little police station, and her father used to wave to the officers as he drove down the hill. Not too far down, the Bassine family used to live. Their parents were like uncle and aunt to her. Her parents were always bringing gifts and toys for the children. Maxine was always the cheerful one to welcome her, and Jacque was always trying to impress her.

She could see the view in front of the entrance where there was an almond tree she used to climb. Also, the front yard was filled with beautiful flowers, and the mint garden and a patio were surrounding by climbing blaze roses and Lord Baltimores. She used to love to sit on the patio to enjoy the smell of the garden. She used to prick off some of the mint leaves and rub them between her fingers and inhale the fragrance. The fences were

60

made with mistletoe cactus and old man cactus. When cut, the fence would look beautifully even. It was always a part when she was in town. Some of the kids in the neighborhood used to stand far away looking at her with admiration. Maxine used to take her around to show her off to her friends around the neighborhood.

There was a boy, she remembered, who used to live across from their house. He used to come and join them while they were playing. After beating him once in a friendly fight, he claimed she was not a girl, she was a boy, because the boy was supposed to win the fight. Since she was not going to let that happen, the boy never played with them whenever she was around. She laughed as she thought of that.

Not too far from the corner of their house there used to be a man who used to sell sugar cane under the lamplight every afternoon and a lady frying pork and green and sweet plantain, sweet potatoes, and dumplings. Her parents didn't want to eat the fritters she was selling, but she used to sneak and asked Jacque to buy her some of what she was frying because it smelled so good. They would climb the almond tree and sit there to eat the fritters. She thought that was fun. And the *chamcham* (roasted corn ground with sugar and roasted peanuts), the cassava, and peanut butter—she had a ball. She wanted to explore the country. And her parents made sure of that.

She remembered her father explaining to her why the people called the passage going up north "Boute Mitan." He said it was because that section was the center of Haiti. And during the time of the chieftain, that was where they would meet for special conferences. In case anyone of them had an idea that could cause a rivalry, they all would be able to get to their province's safe ground. It was an equal distance to where each of them was from. And plus it was a place for ceremony. She thought that was amazing, because they never measured to know the distance was equal to where each one was from. "It was mystical," her father would tell her.

There was a knock on her door that brought her back to the future. She called, "Come in!"

Maxine walked in and said, "The guests will soon arrive. Everyone is ready. Richard will soon be here. And Louis's horses are on their way to the barn. Hope you have a nice ride."

Chapter Six

The Barbecue Night

Everything was set. The clock was showing six, and the guests were starting to arrive one car at a time. The servants had their work cut out for them tonight. Patrick was the first to arrive in a trailer that had two horses. One was jet black and the other one was white, a male and female horse, walking together in rhythm. Jean helped Patrick with them. Brian walked in the yard with Sofia beside him. Nicole and Jean stood by the gate to welcome the guests.

Julie stood at a distance wearing a cowgirl's outfit bearing a blue-and-white striped long-sleeve blouse with matching denim pants with leather fringes running down the side of the pants, watching the comings and goings with a smile. Around her slim waist was a black belt with silver buckle. Her feet were shod with a pair of black cowgirl's boots and she wore a cowgirl's hat that matched her boots. Maxine spotted her and ran over to her exclaiming, "I like what you are wearing. You look good in it. "Stepping back, she spread her hands." Let me rephrase that: you make it look good. And it looks like you're ready to ride!"

She smiled at Maxine indulgently and looked around, amazed. "When did you girls have time to invite all these people?"

"Not me. I only invited one person, Richard. And some of them, once the word got around that Louis was going to be here, jumped at the opportunity to be around him, so they could say 'I know Louis Janvier'. Oh my! There's Richard. Do I look okay Julie?"

Richard was wearing black pants, a white collarless shirt, and black shoes, very simple. Julie looked admiringly at him. He was a handsome enough young man. He didn't look anything like Louis, but he could hold his own with the rest of them. Taking Maxine's arm reassuringly, she complimented, "Max, you're right, he's not bad looking at all. Let's go and greet him and don't be so nervous. You look terrific."

He was about six-two, with black hair. His eyes made him very appealing. He smiled when he saw Maxine. His teeth were white. They walked toward him. Maxine wanted to give a warm hug to welcome him, but instead she withdrew and greeted, "Hello, Richard. Welcome to our home. This is my best friend and sister Julie."

Extending his hand, he said, "Nice to meet you, Julie."

Taking his hand, Julie smiled. "Nice to meet you too, Richard."

Carine looked over and saw who they were talking to. She recognized the maid's son, and with an outraged gasp she said to Nicole, "What is he doing here?"

Swiveling around, Nicole asked, "Who?"

Pointing in the direction where Julie, Richard, and Maxine were standing, she indicated, "Him!"

"He's cute." Nicole grinned.

Carine sneered, "That's the maid's son, Marie."

Nicole's face dropped and the tone of her voice changed. "Oh . . . to think I thought he was cute! Who invited him." She crossed her arms and shook her head in disbelief. "You know what this will do to our reputation? And if Jacque finds out, he will be furious."

She suggested, "Let's go find out who invited him here."

Outraged, Carine and Nicole walked toward the three of them. Ignoring Richard, Carine exclaimed, "Oh, Julie, almost all of our guests are here!"

Richard was standing between Julie and Maxine. Carine looked him up and down with a disdainful expression and snarled, "I don't recall calling to invite you."

"I did, Carine," Julie interrupted, trying to placate her. "I called him and invited him."

Carine looked at him up and down and asked skeptically, "You invited him!"

Calmly she answered, "Yes."

Trying to getaway from Carine's obnoxious behavior, Julie asked, "Where's my table, Carine?"

Carine pointed to the table on the left. Taking Richard's arm, Julie headed off, "Thank you. Richard, come."

Glancing over his shoulder to Maxine, who had been standing silently throughout the whole exchange, Richard whispered nervously, "I don't want any trouble for you or Maxine."

She squeezed his arm reassuringly. "Don't worry, there won't be any trouble."

Maxine was still standing by Carine and Nicole. Carine whispered, "How dare she bring the maid's son among us?"

Maxine shook her head, too scared to say anything, and turned as if to follow Julie and Richard. Carine grabbed her arm and hissed, "I hope you are not going to sit with them."

Pulling her arm away from Carine, she snapped, "That is precisely what I am going to do."

Turning, she walked away. Nicole huffed, "How low can one be . . . ! Oh look, there's Nadine."

She walked to her to say hello. She looked around and asked, "Where's 'Miss Cactus'?"

"Who?" Nicole asked.

"Julie," Nadine replied. She pointed to where Julie was sitting. Nadine said, "Let me go say hello to her."

"If I were you, I wouldn't go by her," Nicole said. "Do you see who she's with?"

Nadine was confused by Nicole's statement. "I don't understand."

Not wanting her to know that they would invite a person who was not of their status, Nicole said, "Never mind."

Nadine smiled as she walked toward Julie's table.

Angrily, Carine replied, "I'm not going to let her or my sister ruin my party. . . ."

As if by cue, Louis walked in the yard. "Oh my! Here comes Louis . . . how do I look?" She smoothed down her hair.

"Nice," Nicole said and held on to Carine's arm. "For the past two years I've heard Louis has been very tempered. And he had become more solitary. He looks at everyone more from a distance. I was surprised to see him sitting at the same table with us having lunch today. And you almost blew it with your question! And he is here tonight. Something is not right, that's not norm for him . . . I don't have to spell it out for you. Be careful."

Pulling her arm away, Carine exclaimed, "Oh, be quiet, Nicole, you're so stupid. You forget Louis promised to take Julie horse back riding tonight. Can't you see the way he is dressed?"

Making sure everything was in place, Carine smiled smugly. She walked away to greet Louis. He was dressed all in black. Around his strong masculine neck gleamed a golden necklace. He removed his left hand out of his pocket and looked at his wrist to see the time. It was 6 P.M. Henry stood beside him dressed in white and carrying a box that was shaped like a bottle in his hand.

"Louis," Carine greeted with a warm smile. "I'm so glad you made it here."

Ignoring his companion, Henry greeted, "Hello, Miss Bassine."

Giving Henry a cursory glance, she replied, "Oh, hi!"

Looking around, Louis asked, "Where is your guest of honor?"

Pointing to the direction where Julie was sitting, she indicated, "She's sitting over there."

Pointing to the bottle in Henry's hand, Louis requested, "Can you put this on ice for us, Carine?"

Taking the package, she looked around for the butler. "Yes! Roy . . . where's this man when you need him?"

The butler hurried toward them. "You called, mademoiselle?"

Handing him the package, she told him sharply, "Put this on ice for me."

While she was talking to Roy, Louis and Henry walked away and headed over to where Julie was sitting. Julie was busy talking and didn't notice Louis' presence till he said, "Hello, Julie!"

She looked up and said, "Hello, Fuji. Henry, *bonsoir.*"

With a grin on her face, Maxine turned and invited, "Hi, guys. Sit with us."

Louis looked at Julie, pulled out the chair that was facing her, and asked, "May I?"

Shrugging her shoulders gracefully, she consented, "Sit down, and you too, Henry."

Noticing the way Louis was looking at her, Julie felt a twinge in her stomach. Trying to ignore the feeling, she continued talking to Richard, Nadine, and Maxine. The feeling was getting stronger as Louis joined in the conversation. Maxine smiled when Louis said, "I want to hear one of your poems tonight, Julie."

"You should give me one," Julie requested.

Staring at her, Louis recited her poem another way:

I am standing on the corner of mind.
I've look at everything that I could see.
But everywhere I've looked,
All I see is you illuminating my way.
At first I thought you were summer,
because I felt so warm.
I thought you were autumn
because I couldn't help falling.
And I thought you were winter,
because I found myself buried alive in your beauty.
Then I realized you were the spring,
because when I saw your face I suddenly arose!

Henry smiled, but everyone else at the table was surprised. Never did they hear Louis talk that long to anyone or recite poetry. Julie couldn't believe Louis could be so bold as he concluded,

"Who am I?"

Maxine said in surprise, "Wishful thinking."

"No," Louis said. "Let Julie figure it out."

"Your word said," Julie answered. "That you're going to be a very lonely man."

Louis smiled at the answer she gave him. Julie was beginning to feel very uncomfortable. She felt her heart pounding faster. She tried to calm herself by taking a deep breath, then she heard him say, "I was hoping that you would have given me a better definition."

"Sorry, that was the best I could do." She looked away.

Carine and Nicole came by to see if Louis was comfortable. Jean came to say hello, then he walked away with Patrick, continuing their conversation. Carine wanted to know if Julie was enjoying herself. Julie told her yes, but she didn't feel right for her to even be there, celebrating with anyone. She whispered to Maxine, "I'm not feeling good. I'm going in."

Maxine looked worried, as Julie whispered, "Don't worry, everything is going to be fine."

Julie called Carine aside and told her to make sure she kept the peace. Looking at Louis, Maxine didn't object to Julie leaving. She understood why she was feeling like that. Julie excused herself. "Nice to meet you again, Richard. Nadine, I have to go in to call my mother to see how my son is doing. . . . And Henry, Louis, good night."

"Good night," Louis repeated softly in disbelief. Julie walked away without giving a second look at the barbecue. She walked toward the mansion.

Coming to his senses, Louis said to Maxine, "I thought she wanted to go riding. What happened?"

Maxine said, "She must have forgotten. Her mind has been worrying too much. She said she wasn't feeling good."

"There are many doctors on the terrace tonight." Removing himself from the table, Louis requested, "And I'm one of them, so take me to her." Looking at Henry and he said, "I'll be back."

He followed Maxine to the mansion. She knocked but there was no answer. Putting her head in her room, Maxine called, "Julie!"

The light was on so she walked in. Julie was not in her room. Looking at Louis she said, "Where can she be?"

Maxine walked to her bathroom. She was not there either. She shook her head and said, "Maybe she's by the pool."

There was no one by the pool. Maxine concluded, "Maybe she's at the old house. . . ." She glancing at Louis. "I hope she is not by the river."

Louis replied, "I'll go look for her. Don't tell anyone where I go, and when I find her, we're going for our ride, just as I promised. That girl is brave. Are you sure she's not meeting someone there?"

"Julie? Only if her husband was here. I'm sure she is not."

They both left the mansion and went their different directions. Louis stopped at the barn to get the horses he asked Patrick to bring earlier that afternoon. He saddled them and mounted one as he held the reins of the other one and off he rode. Carefully he rode across the field. He checked the old house to see if she was there, but the light was off and the doors were closed. He rode down the hill toward the river. Louis noticed the lamplight near the almond tree was on. As he got closer, he dismounted his horse and continued by foot. Quietly he went down. She didn't even notice Louis was kneeling behind her.

He whispered in her ear, "Julie."

She startled. "Louis, you scared me!"

He apologized, "Sorry, I didn't mean to frighten you. What are you doing here alone?"

"I'm enjoying my solitude."

"That's a pretty place to enjoy it. It is peaceful."

"Yes it is." She returned to the position she was sitting in before. She wondered what he was doing here. She asked, "What are you looking for?"

"The word is who. I was looking for you."

She let him know, "I wanted to be alone."

He was the last person she wanted to be here with. She quickly dried out her eyes. She didn't want him to see that she was crying. Louis gazed at her face and thought she was crying.

Louis said, "I was hoping you would stay at the barbecue since it was your idea. And here I come and you left. That wasn't polite, 'Ms. Cactus'."

"I would apologize, Mr. Janvier, if I was the one who invited you." She threw a pebble in the water. "But fortunately I was not the one."

"But you did say I was to take you riding."

"You volunteered." She looked at him and said, "But I did accept. This I will apologize for. I'm sorry, I forgot all about it."

"Your apology is accepted," Louis readily accepted. "It's not too late and I have the horses with me, and they are saddled. All we need to do is to ride them."

She didn't reply. Sitting beside her to look at her and wondering what was on her mind, likewise he picked up a little rock and threw it in the water. "You miss them. . . ."

She looked at him, wondering what was on his mind. He said, " . . . Your family. I usually go further up to sit. I like the quietness of this place. It gives you time to think, but at the same time, it can make you feel so sad. The loneliness of it is unbearable."

Nodding her head, she smiled in agreement. He got her to open up to him. "Yes, it can be. I miss my husband and my son and my mother."

"You have a son?"

"Yes, and he is five months old now." She removed the necklace from her neck to show him the picture of her son and her that was inside the locket.

Looking at the picture, he smiled. "He's handsome."

"Yes, he is."

He handed her the locket and she placed it around her neck. He asked, "Where is your husband, Julie?"

She chuckled. "I wish I knew."

Louis didn't know what to say after his last question, and so he said, "Don't move. I have something that could help make the moment look better."

He ran up the hill and returned with the bottle of Haitian rum and two glasses that was inside his saddlebag. He returned with them and opened the rum and poured her some. She chuckled when she saw what it was as he handed it to her. She took the glass from his hand and thanked him. He poured himself some and toasted, "It's not a martini, but this will do. Here's to loneliness."

She laughed at his toast and agreed with it. She waved the glass to him, then drank. Looking up to the sky she commented, "In New York one can only dream of seeing such wonders, all these stars. . . ."

He looked up and agreed. She softly spoke, " . . . Saul and I used to travel out of New York just to go up in the mountain to look at the stars. They were always fascinating to us. And the sight makes me think of the one who created them, how much power He contains. That's awesome."

He stared at her as she talked. She noticed the way his eyes moved across her face. She said, "It is very rude to stare like that. You're making me feel very uncomfortable."

"I'm sorry, but I can't help to look at you. You're a beautiful woman."

"Do you always flatter the women like that, Louis?"

"Only when I'm lying, but with you there's an exception. It's not flattering; your beauty is very rare."

She smiled and stood up as she handed him his glass. "Thank you, Louis."

As their hands reached, they received a static shock but both pretended they didn't feel anything. Louis responded, "You promised to call me Fuji."

"Fuji," she repeated, "I'm heading back. I'm sure you'll be missed at the barbecue."

"You mean you wouldn't miss me, Julie?"

"No, I have enough trauma. I definitely don't want to add to my wounds."

"Do I look like someone who would add injury to your wounds?"

She looked at him, up and down, then focused on his eyes and said, "Yes."

"Ouch!" He held on to his chest. "You cut me deep."

"You're not bleeding." Taking another look at him she replied, "You'll live."

"You cut me deep inside. It's internal."

She went up the hill, leaving him behind as he called, "Julie, wait. I brought the horses with me."

She stopped as he whistled for the horses. They came galloping toward him. "Maybe a good rough ride will help you relax."

Chuckling at his statement, Julie asked, "What did you say?"

Smiling at his own words he rephrased, "If you go horse riding, it might help you to relax."

The horses cantered to him. She came closer and exclaimed when she saw the two animals. "They're beautiful!"

Introducing her to the horses, he told her their names. "This is Fire and Cliff."

She passed her hand over their beautiful shiny coats, admiring their beauty, while Louis made sure the saddles were secure. When he finished he turned to her and inquired, "May I?"

Helping her to mount the female horse, Fire, he then mounted Cliff and they slowly cantered out across the field. Riding side by side, he engaged her in pleasant conversation to ease her nervousness. They spoke of the kind of riding they liked. She preferred English riding, while Louis preferred bronco rodeo (a type of rough bull ride). Julie laughed at this. She thought Louis was crazy. He reminded her so much of Saul.

Taking the lead, she rode to where she had seen the two men on their horses. She stood at the same spot. Louis wondered what was she looking down for. "What are you trying to see?"

"Three days ago, here," Julie indicated, "two people—I believe they were two men—sitting on their horses looking down at me. I couldn't make out their faces. I was wondering what were they doing on my property, looking at me through binoculars."

"What did you do?"

"If I was riding or had my binoculars I would have known who they were," Julie confessed. "But I got nervous."

"And tonight you were sitting down there all alone."

"I shouldn't be afraid to walk on my land, a place I spent most of my childhood. I know every corner of that land. I was wondering how they entered. And I thought the only way those two people were able to enter my land without any problem was only if you have been giving them access to ride through your land, or the people were you and another man."

Louis said, "So we frightened you away."

"I don't get frightened very easily like that, Fuji."

"A woman," Louis smiled, "and a brave soul."

"I shouldn't be brave, Mr. Janvier?"

"Are you always that confident, Mrs. Philip?"

Julie replied, "I'm a woman who knows what she wants, and I'm careful."

"Can you take a man like me down if he came against you?"

Looking at him she said, "Are you looking for a challenge, Fuji. . . ?" Louis didn't answer, so she added, " . . . Men like you take pleasure going after forbidden treasure."

Louis looked at her firmly. "It's more exciting."

Nodding at his expression, Julie retorted as they made their way back, "I love my husband, Mr. Janvier. . . . He means the world to me. No man on earth can come between us. The love we share is sweeter than milk and honey. I wouldn't change it for the world."

"Now you have me even more curious. Can a woman be sweeter than milk and honey, the drink of the gods? I'm like a bee searching for such nectars."

"I noticed that you have a hearing problem, or maybe you're just trying to be funny," Julie responded. "I think you're the one who really needs to be careful. Do you know what happens to the male bee when it finds honey?"

"No," Louis answered. "But I bet the moment of pleasure would be sweeter than milk and honey."

"That would be the last thing it will enjoy, because as it find the honey its male organ is ripped out its body," she gripped her hand as in a gesture pulling something off, "while it's enjoying the nectar. Like the male mantis who got its head eaten up."

"Ouch," Louis exclaimed as if he felt the pain. "But still I wouldn't mind losing both of my heads for this forbidden treasure."

Looking at him, she wanted to punch him in the mouth for lack of respect and make his head spin like a possessed man for him to come to his senses, but she tried not to show him that she was shocked by his obnoxious attitude. Calmly she continued riding beside him, trying to keep her cool. She rubbed her nose as if she smelt a stench. She couldn't believe that Marie claimed Louis Janvier was a man with class and the Bassine girls thought that he was a smart man, because every time he opened his mouth talking to her, a fly flew out of it. The only thing she felt was going for him was his looks, and if he didn't have any money, without a doubt she knew no decent woman with a brain would have anything to do with him.

Controlling her anger, she thought, *I must swallow this rage that is trying to go forth out of me.* She peeked at him and thought, *You're an impertinent man, Mr. Janvier!*

Then again, she took a good look at him and realized that Louis wanted her to act uncivilized. He was hoping to get that kind of reaction from her. Nodding her head, she couldn't understand why. She thought, *I'm not going to feed, to give you satisfaction, Mr. Janvier.*

She approached him from another angle to put him to shame. "You need to calm down, Fuji. I'm going to give you a word of advice. Only one treasure is worth losing one's life for because hope's laid behind it."

Louis desired to know, "Like what?"

"Searching for the true God."

No! Louis thought. *I want you to get mad and curse at me.*

He was looking for reasons to dislike her because he didn't want to have any kind of affection for a woman with a dirty mouth. He wanted the craving he was having for her to disappear. This time, Louis was the one nodding his head and thought that was not the reaction he was searching from her. He wanted her to jump off her horse and launch at him, slapping him or spitting on him or something. Not this controlling behavior. Why couldn't this woman act like most other women? He wondered how was he going to get out of this conversation and to the solution to dismiss her like he usually did to every women he met. At the moment he felt he should behave himself, like a gentleman.

He was humbled. "That never occurred to my mind, but that would be something I would like to dig into more. I'm one with an open mind and I will like to learn more about hope."

Smiling, Julie agreed. She felt she had gotten through to Louis. She hoped she could help him even more to see that it was unlawful to think or to get involved with a married woman. After that they had a wonderful time riding then she returned to the party with Louis. Carine asked, "Where were you two?"

Smiling, Julie replied as she walked away, "We went riding."

Looking at Louis, Carine smiled as she tenderly passed her hands on Louis's arms. "Are you happy, Louis?"

Without glancing at Carine, who wanted to know if he had a good time, he quickly took her hands and tossed them aside and said to Julie, "We ride again tomorrow afternoon, Julie."

Julie called out over her shoulder, "All right."

She walked to Maxine, where Nadine, Richard, and Henry were still sitting, waiting. She apologized to them for leaving without excusing herself. She sat with them for a while longer then she said she was going in.

"I'm leaving too," Louis answered. "See you tomorrow afternoon, around four."

Julie replied, "See you then."

Julie went up to her room, hoping tomorrow did bring her some kind of hope. As she entered her room, her phone rang. "Hello? Hi, Mother! How's everything? I was outside barbecuing with the girls and some friends they had invited. . . . It's late—ten o'clock. . . . It's late enough for me. . . . Give William a big kiss for me. I love you."

She hung up the phone and got herself ready for bed. She knelt before the bed and said her prayer. She got up off her knees and slid herself under the blanket, then fell asleep. Again the dream returned. Marie was passing by her room when she heard her crying. She opened the door and turn on the nightlight to look in on her. She came closer and passed her hand on her face. Slowly, Julie came out of her sleep, and saw Marie was standing by her bed.

"Marie," she whispered.

She handed her a glass of water to calm her down. She drank a little of it then asked, "Was I talking in my sleep again?"

Marie didn't answer.

"That's the story of my life. I destroyed my marriage with my dreams. . . . Did anyone else hear me, Marie?"

"No. I'm the only one who knew. You'll be okay, madame. I'm sure your husband is fine."

"I wish I could be that confident, but I'm not. It has been over a year since I've been having that same dream. It is just that for the past five months, the dream got worse to a point where it is destroying my marriage. I don't even know the man I'm dreaming about. The scary thing about my dreams is that he stood before my husband and they merged as one, standing before me, loving me. That's all I could remember about the dream. That doesn't make any sense at all."

Her eyes were shimmering with tears. Marie came and sat on the side of her bed next to her and hugged her to comfort her. She hugged Marie back as she cried on her shoulder. "I feel sorry for my mother. She's the one who got us together, now look what I've done. I've destroyed my marriage."

"It's not your fault, child. No one could control their dreams, no one."

Pulling away from her, Marie said, "Listen, I'm sure he is not blaming you for what is happening to you. Everything has a logical explanation. No doctors can give you that answer, only you. Open your eyes and your heart and search for the truth, your true love."

"I thought when I married Saul, I didn't need to search anymore."

Marie helped her get comfortable and fixed the blanket on her and told her to rest. As if Julie was her own child, Marie did not hesitate to give her a kiss on her forehead and tell her goodnight.

In the morning Julie was up early. She did her exercises then she went and took her shower. By the time she came out, Marie had brought her breakfast. She sat by the window as Marie was fixing her a cup of coffee. Julie said to her as she handed her the cup, "I want to thank you, Marie. You are a true treasure."

"Thank you, madame. You're so kind."

Julie smiled at her last statement as she continued to eat her breakfast. Maxine came in her room.

"Julie, get your purse or your bag. I'm taking you for a ride around town today. . . ."

Julie didn't answer.

" . . . No buts or I don't know."

She took the cup from Julie and drank the rest of the coffee. She burped then said as she put the cup on the table, " . . . Now you're finished."

Julie and Marie couldn't help laughing. Marie exclaimed, "She is crazy!"

Julie agreed, "Totally a nutcracker."

Taking Julie by her hands, she turned to Marie and said, "I want lobsters for lunch. I mean a big lunch. When we return, we're going to eat like two pigs that have not eaten for days."

As she was dragging Julie out of the room, Julie waved to Marie, "See you later!"

On their way down, one of the maids handed Julie a small envelope. She took it without looking at the name on it.

Maxine and she ran to the car, got in, and away they drove.

Remembering the envelope, Julie said, " . . . I didn't even look to see who sent me the letter."

She turned the envelope over and read, "It's from Saul. Max, pull over. I want to read it before I leave the yard."

She opened the envelope, and pulled out the letter and read:

Hello, darling,

How are you, my love? I'm sorry for leaving in such a brutal departure, my love. Hurting you was not something I wanted to do. I would have given anything not to see you hurt. I want you to bear this in mind, that I love you. I would do anything to please you and to see you happy.

Believe me when you read these words. I love William with all my heart. He is my best friend as you are my wife, my treasure, my life. Don't be sad, my love. I'll join you in Haiti by the end of the month. At the moment I'm working on my project, and I must see it through. Please don't blame yourself or anyone for my wrong doing. Have a wonderful time in Haiti, enjoy every second and moment for me. With deep regret, I must stop writing and return to my work.

I love you so much.

Saul

Julie had tears in her eyes as she read the letter to Maxine. Turning to Maxine she said, "He'll be here in two days."

Handing her some tissue that was on the dashboard, Maxine replied, "Great, I don't have to worry about you when I'm at work on Tuesday. Now shall we continue on our way."

Smilingly Julie said, "You could take me anywhere around the country. I'm so happy."

She leaned her head back against the seat as Maxine drove down to the city, Julie exclaimed, "Boy, it's hot."

She made ready to bring down the window as Maxine said, "Close your window. Let me put the air conditioning on."

Julie replied as she rolled the window up, "Let's go to Delmas."

It was still early in the morning, when they were making their way down. People were everywhere, rushing to buy food at the Maché Pétion-Ville. They stopped by a bakery to buy bread and cake. They placed the bags and boxes of cake in the trunk. People looked at them like they were tourists. A couple of young ones came and asked them for money. Julie gave each a dollar and Maxine drove off because there were more coming.

Maxine said, "Let me drive off before you go home without any money in your pocket. . . ." Julie laughed as Maxine continued, " . . . That's one of the reason I hate to go any where in Port-au-Prince, someone is always begging you for money. I'm glad they did something at the airport! It was a madhouse. There was a time one couldn't go there without being afraid. I couldn't breathe . . . there were too many beggars."

Julie replied, "There are beggars everywhere you go, Max. I could tolerate the ones on the island, even in United States. There are so many beggars, hungry children, homeless. There's no proper care for the working class. In America, there's no way one could go in the mountains and live off the land."

"Here too, Julie. The farmers don't want to work the land anymore. They would rather come here, in the capital, swallowing dust."

"Someone has to take the lead, Max. I wish I could help. That's one reason I wanted to return and live here in Haiti. . . . To work the lands that Saul and I have. I just hope I find those who are willing to work with me. I love nature. . . . I could live off the land if I had no choice."

"I'm sure you can," Maxine said. "I witnessed how you skinned a rabbit and roasted it. You're unique, Julie. With all the money that you have, you're not spoiled at all. You're so simple."

"Don't be so sure, Max." She smiled. "I'm far from being simple. I'm hardcore, right to the point. That was one of the reasons I never dated. Every man was afraid of me. And I'm spoiled. You guys spoil me with your love and affection. And that caused me not to settle for anything less."

Maxine smiled at her response and thought Julie was right. She asked, "Where would you like me to take you?"

"We're not to far from Delmas. Why don't we go see the old neighborhood?"

"Why do you want to go there?" Maxine said with wonder. "There's nothing to see besides the school yard they built a few years ago."

"I never had a chance to see it," Julie replied, "so there's something new after all."

As Maxine made a right turn on Delmas. She took a quick glance at Julie's face, how she was slowly nodding her head. Her face looked disappointed. "Things sure change around here."

Maxine continued driving through. Julie felt like they were driving through a concrete jungle. The damage the people did to the little Cité she used to know and love. Most of the flowers were gone, hardly a mistletoe cactus plant or a Lord Baltimore. She felt like she had seen more flowers going to a funeral. Maxine pulled the car in front of the house where she used to live with her family when she was a little girl and stopped. They both came out of the car to look around at Delmas. The only thing that was still standing there was the almond tree and the old house. They stood there looking at it sadly. The leaves were ashy and dried out from lack of water. There was a goat tied to it with a rope and a couple of chickens pecking on the ground for corn. The fences of mistletoe cactus were cut down and replaced by bricks and where the mint garden was now sat a lottery stand with people on line buying lottery tickets. The new tenants destroyed the beautiful rose garden. There was nothing left to see. As they were looking, a lady came out of the house. She walked toward them and stood by the gate to ask if they were lost.

Smiling, Maxine answered, "My parents and my sisters and brothers—we used to live here!"

The lady smiled in surprise, she thought they were tourists. Julie smiled back. "We used to play and climbed this almond tree."

The lady answered as she looked at the almond tree, "This tree has no pride. No one takes care of it, but it still stands there giving us shade."

Maxine laughed at the ignorance of the lady. Julie said, "My parents used to spend a lot of their time here when they came on vacation."

Julie removed a picture out of her purse to show the woman how the place used to look. The lady stared at the picture and looked at Julie as she handed back the picture. Julie didn't say much. She excused herself from the woman's place and went back to the car to continue on their tour. The playground where they used to come every Saturday afternoon to eat beef patties, fresco, and roasted peanuts was no longer there. But on the other side they built a nice huge playground that stood in the middle of Delmas by a school they used to call Ducanada; a public school where the ones with a little means didn't want to send their children. That was something Julie could never understand. She leaned against the car looking at the place while Maxine sat inside the car looking at her.

Maxine said, "You like the playground?"

She smiled at Maxine's comment. She placed her shades on her face and sat inside the car. She said "I've seen enough. Please take me home."

"I want to show you Jacque's new place, then stop at the hospital to see Richard before we head back home."

She said, "Fine, let's go."

As fast as Maxine could, she drove away from Deuxième Cité St. Martin, now called Delmas, and headed for Jacque's place. Julie looked around like a tourist. She smiled at the little kids who waved at her as she waved back. Parco was still looking nice, but not as nice as it was before. But one could still see that people with money were still living there. There was tight security since nice big beautiful houses were still standing there. She dozed away, but Maxine let her sleep. Before she knew it, Maxine was parked in the driveway of the hospital. Julie apologized as she began to awaken. "I'm sorry, Max."

"You're tired and I'm glad I was able to put you to sleep, and plus the music was soothing."

She was making ready to leave the car. Julie told her she would wait for her outside. She wanted to check the neighborhood. Maxine said she wasn't going to be long.

Julie walked to the side of the hospital, looking around. She spotted two lizards that were lying on an almond branch. She perched her shades down her nose to watch how the two little lizards were mating. She had not realized that Maxine and Louis had come out of the hospital. Curious of what she was looking at, Louis stood behind her also looking at what had caught her attention.

He whispered in her ear, "It not polite to invade one's privacy."

Holding her stomach, she staggered. Louis held her up as she tried to gather herself. She said, "Fuji, it's not polite to sneak up on people!"

Maxine laughed. "Are you okay!"

"I'm fine," she breathed.

Louis took her hands and commented, "You're cold."

Maxine replied, "Julie must be nervous."

He asked, "What could make you nervous, Julie?"

Looking at him, Julie didn't answer. She felt a bit flustered. Maxine replied, "Maybe you."

He looked at Julie and responded, "Do I make you nervous, Julie?"

Taking Julie's hands out of his, Maxine said, "You have that kind of disease that makes people around you get very nervous."

Knowing she was right, he smiled and replied, "I will see you at four, Julie. I'll bring our favorite horse and a bag full of goodies."

He opened the door of the Jeep for Julie. She sat in and gently he pushed the door behind her. Leaning against the door, he brought his head down to say goodbye. He tapped two times on the side of the car door, then moved back from the car and waved as Maxine drove away.

The road to home wasn't busy. Smoothly, Maxine pushed the gears of the Jeep going up the mountain. The air blew cool and the sun was well set. There were a couple of fruit and vegetable merchants on the road, so Julie bought a couple of sticks of sugar cane from each of them. They bought watermelons and basket full of corn. Everything was placed in the trunk of the Jeep. Julie handed Maxine a cane stick and said, "I remember we used to chew our sugar cane like this."

She took a little bite of it and started to chew. Maxine laughed. "If Aunt Viviane was here she would have say, 'Stop making those noises. Close your mouth when chewing'."

"It was very uncomfortable to chew sugar cane with my mouth closed, like this is fun." They laughed at the slurping sound they were making with the sugar cane. They chewed all the way home.

Chapter Seven

Moment of Truth

It was precisely four when Louis arrived. Carine and Nicole were still at work, and Jean was no where around. Julie wanted someone to go with her on the ride with Louis. Maxine had already had a date with Richard, so she couldn't go riding with Julie.

Maxine apologized. "I'm sorry, Julie. When Jacque is not home, it's a great opportunity for me to do what I wouldn't be able to do when Jacque is home. Have fun and see you later."

Taking her hands to leave, Louis said, "That would give us time to get more acquainted."

"Slow down," Julie said as she pulled her hand out of his. "My legs are not as long as yours. You have me walking behind you like a child."

"Force of habit," he apologized as he took her hand once more and took shorter steps. When they arrived at the barn they brought the horses out and the saddles to put on the horse's backs. Taking her saddle out of his hand, Julie requested to saddle the horse she was going to ride. He moved out of her way to give her access. Louis watched how she was saddling her horse while he was saddling his. He smiled. "Very good."

After finishing saddling their horses, he helped her mount her horse. She stated, "This time we're going up to mountain. I want to watch the sun going down."

They galloped toward the mountain. Louis broke the silence, "I would like to take you riding tomorrow early in the morning, around three-thirty or four, to look at the sun rise."

Julie thought he looked like a man who stayed in bed very late to get his beauty rest, so she wanted to laugh because she thought he was trying to be funny. "You'll get up that early."

"I go to bed late and I get up very early almost all the time. You seem surprised."

"The truth is, you don't look like someone who has done a hard day of work throughout your entire life."

Smiling at her comment, he replied, "You see all that by looking at me? Interesting. Will you join me tomorrow morning?"

"I'm an early bird myself, so the idea sounds nice, but I have to pass. My husband is on his way here to Haiti and I want to look good when he arrives. You know what I mean."

"No!"

"No!" Julie repeated. "How come?"

"I never had a husband. And I'm not about to take a wife."

Smiling at what he said, she asked, "Why wouldn't you?"

He glanced at her. "If I told you, you would not believe me."

"Why wouldn't I?"

"The woman I love is married to my best friend and I can never have her."

"Why didn't you marry her first?" Julie curiously asked.

"He found her before I did. I was not as lucky as he was. Her mother introduced her to him."

Fascinated, she smiled. "My mother introduced me to my husband, too."

"Lucky him," Louis responded. "If only I met her mother first. The craziest thing is, she had my baby."

"My word," Julie sadly exclaimed at Louis's shocking revelation. "Don't tell me you had an affair with her while she was married to your friend." Louis didn't answer. She was frowning. "Louis, that is very immoral. . . . How gross!"

Gloomily he replied, "It was not my intention. She wanted a baby and he talked me into it."

"Are you telling me that your best friend suggested the affair. . . ?"

Louis nodded his head for yes. Julie gasped, " . . . Is your friend impotent?"

"No!" Louis answered. "He's not. He just couldn't conceive and she wanted to have children. And when she got pregnant he made me swear never to see her unless he died."

Julie was really horrified. "So you plan to kill him now?"

"I would never do that," he reassured her. "He is my best friend. I love him dearly. I would have given my life for him, just to see him happy. I would never kill him for his woman, despite that I love her very much."

Julie renamed him. "Does she know how much you love her, Sir Lancelot?"

"I think she does." Louis smiled at the name she called him. "But she doesn't want to admit it. At the moment she would rather live in denial . . . dream."

Wondering, Julie asked, "Did you ever try to see her?"

"No," Louis said.

"Why not?"

He emphasized, "Like I told you before, she's married to my best friend. I think she's seeking for me. Do you think I'll ever have a chance with her?"

Julie replied, "I don't know if she's Guinevere."

"I believe she does love me."

"Then you may have a chance." Nodding her head in disbelief, she said, "I don't believe I'm having this kind of conversation with you, Louis. You fornicated with a married woman, with her husband's approval, so she could conceive a baby. And I believe you weren't thinking when you gave up your child to a crazy couple just like that."

"I didn't give up my son like that," Louis retorted.

"You have a son, too?" Julie was surprised.

"Oh yes," he smiled. "A very handsome son who looks like me, too."

"But you told me you never saw him."

"Not in person," he replied. "I saw his pictures."

Julie moaned, "I know how hard it is for me to be away from my baby. Is it hard to you too, Fuji?"

"Yes," he said, agitating without thinking. "It is very hard. My heart is breaking each day that I don't see him, holding him in my arms, smelling his baby scent. And to tell him how much I love him."

Noticing his reaction, Julie realized he wasn't happy about the whole situation. She suggested, "If I were you I would have fought to have my baby. He could have the woman, but not the baby."

"It is not that simple," Louis repeated and explained. "Like I told you before, he's my best friend. He saved my life. I owe everything I have to him, even my life."

Julie cut him short, "And to thank him he had you sleep with his wife?"

"Something like that." Again he emphasized, "It wasn't my intention to sleep with his wife. He forced me to impregnate her."

Julie could not believe what Louis was telling her. "You and your best friend are both crazy. And that woman is even crazier to get involved with men like you. Did you ever sit back once to think about the trauma your son may face later in life?"

"No." Louis sighed. "It happened so fast I didn't have the time to think it over."

"Unbelievable." She nodded. "She's very sick, too."

Louis laughed. "I'm sure she is. You're the first person I have confided my feelings to about my situation. No one knows what we done, except the three of us and the doctor."

"You mean the five of us."

Louis didn't answer, so she looked at him. "Why are you telling a woman you don't even know your secret, Louis?"

Looking at Julie, wanting her to know his reason for confiding in her, Louis wanted to know her deepest feelings, so he stated, "For some reason I feel like I have known you for a very long time. I could open up to you. And you look like someone who could keep a secret."

She started to feel a bit disturbed by what Louis was telling her. "That is too hard for me to believe. I heard that some women are capable of getting pregnant for another man and telling their husband it's their baby. But I never heard of a man who would let another man sleep with his wife just for the hell of it."

Nodding his head, Louis smiled. "Now you have! But it wasn't for the hell of it."

She shook her head in contempt. "I can't believe that."

"You think it's an easy thing for me to swallow and to talk about it, don't you?"

Wanting to hear a better reason for why he was telling her that, Julie questioned, "Why are you confessing to me?"

"Because you look like someone I could talk to."

Julie didn't want to listen. She felt a little edgy. "You chose the wrong person to talk to. I would really hate to be your best friend, if that's the way you're going to repay me."

Sarcastically Louis replied, "Don't worry, I'm not homosexual. I wouldn't sleep with your husband. He's safe with me."

Angered at his response, Julie lost her temper and spoke sharply to him, "Oh, I see, it's between my legs you wanted to get. . . . You're not man enough to handle a woman like me, Mr. Janvier."

Louis started to laugh. He laughed so hard that he fell off his horse.

"Fuji!" Julie screamed as she watched him going down into the bushy hill. Louis didn't think that she was going to come out so bluntly. He thought she was going to lecture him like last night and advise him to take the right course. Rolling down the hill like a madman he laughed. He thought, *The hell with sympathy*, he was not about to get that from her. Not only he was scum, dirt in her eyes, but also not man enough. He was intrigued by her answer, but at the same time he couldn't help laughing when he saw the look on her face and how she flared her nose and curved her lips to snarl at him.

When she didn't hear him anymore, she quickly got off her horse. Looking down the mount she called out to him, "Fuji, are you all right?"

He didn't answer. He lay there quietly with his face down on the ground. He didn't move, hoping he made her very upset and she would leave him down there. He pretended to be unconscious to see if she would come after him to help him. Worried, Julie thought he was hurt. Rushing to the horses she searched inside their saddlebags for the first aid kit and two blankets. She took them out and held onto the first aid kit and the blankets, then carefully went down to him. She kneeled down at his side to assist him. When he didn't move, she became nervous, murmuring all the while, "Please be okay."

She gently touched his head and shoulders to see if anything was broken or if he was bleeding. Then she folded one of the blankets and placed it under his head. She didn't want him on the bare ground so she opened the other blanket and carefully rolled him on it. Then she turned him on his back toward her. She checked if his face was cut or bruised. She removed the leaves out of his hair. She laid her head over his chest to listen if his heart was still beating, then gently pressed on his rib cage to see if he had any broken ribs. She ran her hands down his legs and checked if his ankles were injured. He made sure he got a good dose of her touch before he opened his eyes and moaned, "Ooh that hurt, my heartache."

After checking all his vital points, she asked, "Are you all right? Can you move?"

Pretending he was hurt, he stretched before he sat up and said, "I'll live. I was hoping that I broke my neck, but unfortunately I'm not that lucky."

She sat by him and wondered and said, "Why would you say something like that, Louis? Do you want to die?"

Looking away, Louis thought she looked a little puzzled, and felt he had her just where he wanted her to be. He said, "I have nothing to live for. . . . Everyone I love, they're all gone. I'm in love with my best friend's wife, my son may never call me father, and I may never see him and hold him in my arms. That's the price I pay for being alive."

Louis didn't realize he had actually revealed his deepest thoughts to her. He thought by telling her he was suicidal, she might say something cruel, like, "Yes, you should have broken your neck for falling in love with a married woman. For wanting your best friend's wife."

Julie started to look at him from a different angle. She felt she was thoughtless, too harsh, and too quick to judge him. Louis's situation was more complex than she presumed it to be. "I'm sure there's another woman out there for you, Louis. You should never give up like that. It's true. One can never tell where their heart is going to lead them. We can only pray that it leads us in a good direction." Gently passing a hand on his shoulder as to comfort him, she said, "Have hope. Don't give up!"

Louis couldn't believe his plan didn't work. He didn't want her to worry, nor did he want her to feel sorry for him. He wanted to dislike her. Instead he found himself drawn to her by every moment they spent together. The marble cold brown eyes he thought she had were warmer than a midsummer day. Unexpectedly he had her revealing her feelings to him. " . . . There was a time I thought I was never going to find a man to love, but I was wrong. I did! And another time I thought I was never going to have a baby, now I found out I could have an army if I want to. So you see, Louis, if I had given up, today I wouldn't know my son William and hope for many more."

"You truly believe that, Julie?"

"Yes, I do."

"Your husband is a blessed man, Julie."

"I think it's the other way around." She picked up the blanket and the first aid kit, then got up and stretched her hands to him so she could pull him up. Looking at her build he said, "No, I'm very heavy."

Julie smiled. "So is my husband. He's as tall as you and physically well built!"

"So my build doesn't intimidate you."

"No, not at all!" She pulled him up and they climbed up the hill together. The horses were waiting on top. Julie laughed. "Look at them—they're laying down."

After placing everything inside the saddlebags, they got on their horses and continued on their way. They went all the way on top almost near his land. Louis took out a blanket from the saddlebag. He lay the blanket on the ground and asked her to sit while he went and fetched the other things he brought with him.

She commented, "You weren't lying when you said you were going to bring a lot of goodies. I'm really going to enjoy the dusk."

He handed her the glasses and poured the wine in them. He laid the bottle beside them as he sat by her. He was about to toast when she handed him the glass and stopped him. "No! This is my turn." Hitting their glasses together she said, "To hope."

He smiled as he repeated, "To hope."

And slowly they drank. Pointing to the sky with excitement she said, "Look! It is coming."

The sun was bright scarlet, blazing, and at the same time it looked so peaceful and happy, Julie thought.

Louis was more interested in looking at the way she was enjoying the sun going down. He smiled as he tasted his drink, then looked at what she was beholding.

Yes, the view was awesome, just like she said. All the birds were giving a last run before the sun fell asleep on that side of the earth. What a dynamic view, he thought. He leaned his head against her head. They were so captured by the sight they didn't realize their heads were leaning against each other.

Julie softly spoke. "Isn't this a beauty?"

"Yes," he breathed out. They sat quietly drinking the rest of the wine as it became dark. A crescent moon was out and one by one the stars appeared like flies that were trapped on flypaper. Without a word they sat back to back looking at the sky. Never in Louis's life did he do something like this, a romantic night without spending a dime. He smiled and he just couldn't help it. Her hair felt soft against his back and the fragrance of her hair was really enchanting.

In harmony with the moment Louis confessed, "I used to fantasize about sitting in a place like this, enjoying a moment like this with the woman I love. We'd be drinking the best wine money could buy, having candlelight dinner. We'll talk about our future and where we were heading. We'd be making love under the moonlight and the stars, just as I'm beholding now."

"That sounds very romantic, Fuji," she agreed, sighed, and asked, "What time is it? I forgot my watch."

Looking at his wrist, he acknowledged that his watch was missing. "I must have dropped my watch when I fell off my horse. I'm sure it's not late."

Louis's situation was pondering on her mind. "I hope you don't give up on your child, Louis, and I'll pray that your friend comes to his senses. What he had you do was madness. Tell me . . . why did you accept to do something like this?"

"Are you planning to write my life story, Julie?"

"Maybe! I want to understand what would possess a man of your status to do something like that?"

"Love, Julie, love."

"Love," she repeated.

"It may sound unpersuasive," Louis closed his eyes to say, "but it was love that possessed us both; it compelled us to do something like that. When he told me his problem, I didn't want to go through with it at first. He pleaded, he begged, he demanded my seed. I refused. I wasn't about to give my seed to any woman I was not married to. Then he showed me his wife's picture."

"You mean when you did that you didn't meet her yet?"

"Never had the chance to." He smiled. "The first glance I took, I was hypnotized by her beauty. He didn't have to ask or beg anymore. So I yielded to his wishes."

"You fell in love with a woman when you only saw her in a picture. Then you slept with her . . . you didn't even know her!"

Louis stared at her while she talked with a recognizing smile in his eyes. "Even though I thought you and your best friend and the woman were mad and very immoral," she emphasized. "But I have to say it was also romantic." Putting her hands over her face, she laughed. "What am I saying? I can't believe I said that, I sound so worldly. . . . So you slept with her and conceived a child for your friend? How many times did you two sleep together?"

"Only once."

Being nosy she questioned, "Did you want to sleep with her again?"

"Yes, but not like that," he motioned with deep feelings. "I wanted to hold her and really make love to her."

Julie chuckled. "Your life is very complicated, Louis. I would hate to be in your shoes."

She got up from the ground and said, "I don't know the time, but I think it's time for us to head back home."

Louis got up on his feet and called the horses. They mounted their horses and off they rode. By the time they reach the house, Jacque had already arrived from Jacmel.

The door opened and Jacque greeted, "Hello, Julie. Where have you been?"

Louis was standing behind Julie, and she answered, "I went riding with Louis."

Jacque looked at Louis, wondering why his shirt had a tear on the left sleeve and why did he have dirt on the back of his shirt? Was Louis lying on his back while Julie was on top of him making out? Jacque walked to her to give her a kiss on her cheek.

She stopped him. "Don't come too close, I smell like a horse."

"It okay," Jacque replied and thought, *I'm sure horses are not the only things you smell like.* "Thank you, Louis, for taking Julie horse back riding."

Louis answered, "The pleasure was all mine." Turning to Julie, he said, "I hope you change your mind. The sun rise will be a beauty."

She smiled. "Why not? I usually get up at that time to go jogging anyway. Three-thirty it shall be."

Kissing her hand he said, "Then I will see you."

"I'll bring breakfast," Julie said as she walked him to the door.

He left without saying good night to Jacque. He stood there looking at Julie, trying to make sense of what took place before him. He said, "Everything is set in Jacmel. The place is sparkling clean."

Julie said, "It was all right, you didn't have to do all that. I would have been happier if I was to go there and help fix the place."

"I'm sorry," he apologized. "I knew you came here to rest, not to work. That's the reason I went up by myself to make sure everything was well taking care of. I didn't want you to go up there and find the place not the way you wanted it to look."

She gave him a kiss on his cheek and said, "You're so thoughtful, but I'm looking forward to settling down here with Saul."

Jacque was stunned when she said that to him. He thought she was just here for a little rest, not for a permanent home. He inquired, "Where do you plan to build a home?"

"Not in the city. I need a place for my animals, big enough for a nice-sized home, nice green grass, and plenty of gardens and trees," she informed as she went up to her room. "I'm hoping Saul finds good land to settle down on."

And up she went. Marie was in the room already preparing a warm bath for her. Julie sat on the chair to remove her shoes. She unlaced them and kicked them off her feet. She stretched back on the chair as she removed her pants and blouse and said, "Marie, today I had a wonderful time. My husband wrote me."

"I'm glad for you, madame," Marie said and informed, "Your mother called this evening too, madame."

As Julie walked to the bathroom she said, "She did? Did she sound worried?"

"No, madam."

Julie laid in the warm water while she was continuing telling Marie about her time. "My husband is arriving on Tuesday, but I don't know the exact time."

She asked Marie to stay with her tonight. For some strange reason she didn't want to be alone. Marie went down to get her something to drink. She laid down thinking that Maxine had not come home yet. Marie returned with a glass of warm milk for her. She carried the armchair next to her bed and sat on it. Julie was telling her what she did during the day, and the joy she had watching the dusk.

"Marie," she said, "the last time we were talking, Louis arrived and we didn't finished our little conversation." Marie smiled while staring at her. She questioned, "Why do you stare at me like that, Marie?"

She replied, "Monsieur Janvier told you his big secret tonight, didn't he? He told you about his son."

"Yes," startlingly Julie answered. "How did you know?"

"Like you," Marie compared, "Monsieur Janvier had nightmares about his situation."

Worried, Julie asked, "I could just imagine. I would have had nightmares too, if I had given my child away."

"He's very tormented."

"I'm sure he is," Julie breathed sadly. "At least he could have joint custody of his son. I don't understand men, Marie."

She replied, "Did he tell you the name of the woman and who was she?"

"No," Julie responded, "but he told me she's the wife of his best friend, a man he would have died for. And yet he slept with the man's wife. He's truly a lonely player."

Marie replied, "Monsieur Janvier revealed a lot about himself to you today. No one has been able to do that. You must be very special, madame."

"Maybe that's because I'm nosier than anyone else," she replied. "He spoke of love. Love compelled him to do that."

"I believe him, madame, because he changed since then. I was surprised to see him talking to you. For that alone, I was happy to see. He hadn't spoken much to anyone since then. If it's not business, he had nothing to say to you. He kept quiet in his suffering. I believe Monsieur Janvier finally fell in love, but he knew he could never have her. His friend wanted children. He couldn't give his wife any. What his friend had Monsieur Janvier do was a cruel thing. He actually destroyed him. Monsieur Janvier's love for his friend is strong. Would your love be that strong to give up your seed for the happiness of your loved one, madame?"

Listening to the sound of Marie's voice, Julie could tell she had a lot of love for Louis. She replied, "I don't know."

"Maybe it's because you never were in that position. What if Miss Maxine Bassine said, 'Madame, I need an egg from you,' would you give it to her?"

"I don't know. I would have to think she wasn't meant to have children, she should leave it as it is or she should adopt."

"Not everyone thinks like you, madame. What if it were you? You can have children and your husband is the one unable to produce children, and the one thing you wanted in this whole wide world was a child, and you were willing to give everything to have this child? Be very careful how you answer, madame."

Julie meditated on what Marie said. She remembered how much she wanted a child. She felt hopeless when she couldn't conceive, but yet she felt she wouldn't have done just anything to have a child. She replied, "I guess they felt Louis was their last hope, but they destroyed him. Louis is suicidal. Does the man know Louis is in love with his wife? He doesn't care about life anymore. He feels life is worthless . . . I pray for him."

Marie warned, "Be careful what you pray for, child. What if it were you in that position? He was in love with you, and your husband died. Would you become his wife?"

"I'm not in that position, so I don't know how to answer your question."

"But what if you were?"

Julie replied, "You're not going to let me out that easy. Well, that would be a different story. I have to think about that. Louis has too many women after him. I wouldn't want to be caught in his web and be one of those women."

"That's not his fault, madame, he's a gorgeous man. . . . I'm sure a lot of men want you because you're a beautiful woman."

"Have you ever seen my husband? He's handsome."

"Yes he is," Marie replied. "What time are you waking up tomorrow, madame?"

"At three in the morning, no later."

Marie tucked her in and turned off the light.

Chapter Eight

Precious Moments

Bright and early, Julie's eyes opened. She stretched for a few minutes then headed for the shower. She was thinking, Would Louis be out there that early waiting for her while she put on her jogging suit? She combed her hair and put her cap on. Marie was in the kitchen fixing her a picnic bag to take along with her. Julie placed her cell phone in her pocket and her locket watch around her neck. She smelled good. She was surprised when she stepped out of the door and Louis was already outside waiting for her. She looked at the time—it was fifteen minutes past three. She thought, *Did he sleep?*

Louis, too, was wearing a jogging suit and sneakers. He took the picnic bag and put it on his shoulder while she stretched before they started to run. Then slowly they ran toward the barn, where they brought their favorite horses out of the barn. Quietly they saddled the horses. Slowly they rode out, in the dark. The lamp light on some part of the field helped them to see where they were heading.

"The horses seem to know where we're heading," Julie commented.

"They have been in these woods so many times they better know the way."

She asked, "Where are we heading this time?"

"To a place I like to get away to when I need to think." Louis was taking her riding on his land. That was Julie's first time. She could tell there were many old trees by the size of them. Trees she thought she would never see in Haiti anymore. She got off her horse to touch some of the trees when she smelled the fragrance. She whispered, "Lilac hedge."

Admiring the way she was enjoying the fragrance Louis asked, "Did you sleep well last night?"

As if she heard him say, "Did you sleep well my love," she asked, "Did you call me 'my love'?"

He replied, "Am I your love, Julie?"

Getting back on her horse she replied, "I want to know, did you call me 'my love'."

Smilingly he looked at her. He understood what she was saying but he was going to play till she didn't want to play anymore. He repeated, "Am I your love, Julie?"

She caught on to his game and exclaimed, "No! I thought you were the one who called me 'my love'."

Again he smiled. "Am I your love, Julie?"

Shaking her head she said, "What are we, Bud Abbot and Lou Costello? Now I see where you got your name. I'm surprised your parents didn't call you after the Three Stooges—Moe, Curly, and what was the third one's name? I can never remember his name."

Louis smiled. "Larry!"

"Yes, that one. You know your pals' name's well."

Louis laughed. "Please, don't make me fall off my horse again. This time you will break my neck. . . ."

"So yesterday it was my fault that you fell off your horse?"

"You always seem to be reading my mind, Julie, or is it me just connecting to you, that you always seem to know what I'm thinking?"

"I didn't know I was reading your mind, Louis. I can't even read my husband's mind."

"Maybe you two are not connected as you and I are."

"What are you? An extension cord?"

"No, an umbilical cord. I'm stuck on you, Julie, can't you see?"

"I hope you don't try to use me as a substitute for the married woman you are in love with. I definitely don't need an extension. I might short circuit and kill you."

Acting silly, he laughed. "What kind of cactus are you?"

"I'm going to make it clear to you once and for all," she said, "saving us both trauma and the humiliation. . . . I'm one who doesn't take pleasure in fornicating and adultery."

Frivolously, he stated, "Don't tell me you were a virgin when you married your husband Saul?"

"Yes I was," Julie answered firmly. "And I would have stayed a virgin if I didn't get married."

"Maybe it's because you never met with a man who could make you lose your mind," he declared. "I wished I had met your first."

Julie thought she was being ridiculed by him. "I wouldn't marry a fornicator like you!"

"So you're going to tell me Saul was a virgin when you two got married?"

"I don't know," Julie replied, "if he was or not."

"And if you believe he was," he laughed, "then you're still a virgin, and your son was conceived undefiled."

She was upset by his response because at that moment, it hit her that her son was conceived by artificial insemination. She galloped very fast, leaving him behind.

"Julie, be careful," he called as he rode after her and pulled on the rope of her horse. "Julie," he repeated, "what's wrong? What did I say to make you so upset? Tell me."

Julie didn't respond. He wanted her to tell him what was troubling her. That was something she didn't want to do, to open up to him, to tell him about the way she had conceived her son. She knew her secret was safe with Maxine. Louis she didn't know him like that. Her own mother didn't even know. Instead, she asked, "How far up are we going?"

He replied, "A little further up."

Something like a bird flew by and caused Julie to startle. "I should have warned you, there are bats in these mountains."

Julie didn't answer, so he questioned, "Can you let me in on your thoughts?"

"I'm thinking about my husband, and how happy I will be when I see him again. I hope I'll be able to satisfy him."

Louis couldn't believe what she said.

"Satisfy," he drearily repeated.

Julie smiled. "Did what I said displease you?"

Again Louis repeated, "Satisfy!"

She was happy because she had let him know how glad she would be to have her husband here with her. "Don't tell me you're jealous of my husband?"

"Seriously, I'd hate to be in your husband's shoes."

"Is that a payback for telling you I would hate to be in your shoes last night?"

"By the way, my shoes are too big for you to wear, and I have to admit I was jealous of your husband, but not anymore after knowing he was just adequate to your needs. I just feel sorry for you."

"Sorry for me!" Julie exclaimed. "Stop being haughty, Louis. I never said my husband didn't satisfy me."

"That's one word I can never deal with, 'satisfy'! . . . If I were to take a wife, I feel I should be able to give her great pleasure, not just satisfaction. I want remarkable! Not good enough. I want her to feel complete, lacking nothing. Satisfaction is not in my agenda. I can't be in between when it comes to my woman. The day before you told me your husband was a man like me. . . . And if he's anything like me, you should wonder how that word must have felt to him. I want to possess her mind, body, and soul, my perfect mate, and she'll be able to do the same to me. Understand?"

"Not that I care what you think, Mr. Janvier." Julie didn't understand why was Louis displaying his anger at her. She retorted, "What does my husband have to do to with you? I didn't think the word 'satisfy' would have insulted anyone, especially a man like you."

From the tone of her voice, he knew she was calling him a player. Perceiving what she said, Louis answered, "More so to a man like me. That is why I never took a wife, Julie. I don't want to feel incomplete, and the same goes for her. Your words told me you're incomplete."

She laughed. "That's nonsense."

"Ms. Cactus," he persisted, "you're missing something. You're hungry and you're still thirsty. . . ."

Julie shook her head to say no, but Louis wouldn't hear of it. He was analyzing her word to the core and make her think about her husband. Where was he to complete her, to help her resolve the mental stress she was undergoing? Louis was right. For the moment she felt empty, lost, and confused. She trembled as he spoke. She felt her world was falling apart. . . . She wanted to cry but she held back her tears. She didn't want to break down before him.

He continued hitting her with words. " . . . It's like I'm hungry, and I would love a nice, tasty, juicy filet mignon and since I couldn't get what I really want, I settle for a T-bone steak. . . ."

Quietly she listened. " . . . No, Julie, the word 'satisfy' means lacking and this is the kind of love I totally avoid because I wouldn't want to feel hungry or thirsty. I definitely don't need that. . . ."

After his statement he didn't say another word till they got there. Louis dismounted from his horse. Julie was still trying to gather herself from Louis's last statement. She was still mediating on her condition while Louis checked the area. To gain her attention, he said, " . . . There's no snakes here."

"Snakes?" she quickly repeated.

"Are you afraid of snakes?" he asked.

"No," she replied, "but I wouldn't want to stop or sit down on one."

Louis reassured her, "There's no snakes here."

Focusing her eyes at Louis she replied, "I'll be the judge of that!"

Louis laughed as he removed the blanket from his saddle and laid it on the ground, then removed the picnic bag off his saddle and placed it on the blanket. He was still laughing while he helped her dismount from her horse. For a moment, he was tempted to kiss her, but he withdrew.

She was trying not to stay upset at him from his last remark. She said, "Thank you."

He replied, "You're welcome."

She went and sat on the blanket, looking at the direction of the moon. It was still dark and she could hear roosters cocking. She looked at him and said, "We are like two critters of the night, out before dawn."

"We are." Louis smiled in agreement, glancing at her. "Most of the time I'm out before dawn. . . . I feel energized at night. I love the night. I used to visualize myself as a star exploring the night."

"You have a great view for yourself," she said sarcastically as Julie rolled her eyes.

"And your ambition is very big?" he ridiculously replied.

"Where and what gave you that idea?" Julie asked.

"The night of Nadine's hang-out. You felt you could reach and take the stars."

"You have good memory, Louis, but that was not the way I meant it."

They frowned at each other. For moment they didn't say anything but stared, then started to laugh at each other's dreams. Then Louis continued to tell her why the night fascinated him. "One of my reasons I love the night is that I fear nothing about what it has to offer. It's quiet and there are less shadows to see."

Struck by his disclosure, Julie discreetly asked, "What are you hiding, Louis?"

Grasping his own words, Louis quickly answered, before she analyzed him, "I'm not hiding, Julie. I'm all you see here before you. You just have to look. I have given you permission to see me for what I am."

"A creature of the night," she said and left it as it was. She didn't want to go further than what he had revealed. They both sat quietly, enjoying the wind on their faces. Across the hill from where they were sitting a group of bats were flying in a circle. The moon made them looked as if they were putting on a show for them. Julie smiled. "I have never seen anything like that."

Louis answered, "They don't usually run every night. Tonight must be a special night to them."

She wondered what was special about tonight. Louis asked her if she knew anything about bats.

She said, "Very little."

Then he told her about the bats he read about and saw in Asia and Africa. He described their wings, how some had spans of nearly six feet and others that could fly in the daytime, not at night. Julie didn't know about that. Anxiously she listened while he was telling her about the two main groups of bats. "They're harmless and gentle creatures of great value to nature."

Louis tried to protect those that were in his land from stereotype people. Julie was fascinated by what he was telling her. She felt there was more to Louis than what people were saying about him.

"The flying foxes have big ears and can see very well."

Julie didn't know that, she revealed. "I thought bats were very ugly with poor vision and carry diseases and so on. The closest I ever came to a bat was behind a glass door in the Bronx Zoo in New York. And when they mate the male bats better to able to fly away before the female bats eat them."

"Like most women," Louis laughed. "I spend so much time in this part of the mountains. I think these bats know me . . . and because I gave donations to help protect those creatures, some who work for me think I'm some kind of a monster."

She was intrigued. Her mind was filled with questions, but she didn't know where to start. She sat there looking at him with great wonder and thought Louis was a rarity.

He took a good glance at her, then closed his eyes as he spoke. His voice was warm. She smiled as she listened to him. "When I cannot sleep, I come up here to look at the moon. I never shared this moment with anyone. Always here alone. This is my favorite spot. I thank you for coming here with me."

She felt the same way too, but she didn't answer. Instead she wondered what was she doing here with Louis and why she was compelled to come out with him at this particular hour. She felt she followed him like a lost child.

She took another glance at him, but he was looking straight ahead.

She thought, *Marie was right. He is very good looking.*

She flashed back on the night on the hang-out at his cousin Nadine's when she first took a good look at his face, how everything was well coordinated and she thought his lip was unavoidable.

For a moment her mind strayed away from reality to fantasy. She spoke without thinking and said, "Saul, what are we doing out here?"

Slowly Louis turned to look at her. With a strange look in his eyes he asked, "Did you call me Saul?"

Julie shook her head to come to reality. She didn't tell him what she was really thinking about. She apologized. "I'm sorry, I was thinking of my husband and what you have told me and for a minute my mind went astray. I thought you were my husband."

Louis replied, "Your husband is that good looking?"

He got her to smile. She replied, "My husband is better looking than you."

Louis said, "You're lying. Take a better look again."

He came closer to her as he turned her face to look at him. He took her hands and framed his face and insisted, "No, don't look away, look at me. Am I better looking or not?"

Her hands were trembling as he held her hands against his face while she was looking into his gothic eyes and his face. *Oh God*, she thought, *I'm about to have a heart attack.*

He pretended he didn't notice she was nervous. He fixed her while he held her hands firmly against his face. Wanting her to take a better look at him, he closed his eyes so she could really see him.

It was easier for her to look at him because his eyes were closed. She examined his features well. She thought his lips were kissable. He was very good looking, but to tell him that he was better looking than her husband, that would never happen.

He was still holding on to her hands, making sure she felt the texture of his face. Like a blind man, he sat letting her paint his features with her eyes. She thought Saul and Louis looked a little bit alike. . . . After a while she pulled her hands away and said, "You're a conceited man, Louis Janvier. But my husband's looks are different from yours."

Louis replied, "For a moment I thought you were going to kiss me, but then again it was just a wishful thinking. Well, I'm not surprised by your answer. . . . Soon you'll tell me that your husband's build is better than mine."

She tittered. "I'm not interested in your body, Louis."

Vainly he replied, "Don't tell me you have not undressed me yet!"

"Like you've been undressing me," she blatted.

"Believe me, when I undress you, you will know. I like my woman aware of every sensation, rapture, and feeling registering in her mind when I'm taking her. I'm direct, not like you, undressing me with your eyes very discreetly."

She launched, "I have no reason to be interested in your body. My husband's body is quite delightful to me. He's very tall, well built, and handsome. I have no reason to need another one, and he's quite a good lover."

Louis replied, "How would you know? You never had another."

"I don't need to have another lover to know that he is. I know how my body feels when he touches me. My body yearns for him."

Mockingly he asked, "Is that really so?"

Julie didn't like the tone of his voice. "You make me feel like I'm lying. Why are you mocking me?"

"Did I?" He laughed. He wanted to agitate her to see how far could he take her, what made her tick, and how she would respond to his mockery.

"Yes! The way you answered me." She mimicked the drag in his voice. "'Is that really so?' You sounded like a prowler, the serpent that was in the Garden of Eden, a deceiver."

Unexpectedly he found himself piqued by her statement. Moving close to her, he pulled her in his arms as if to kiss her and he added, "What if I am that slimy serpent that is prowling around your beautiful garden, and I've deceived you already. What would you do?"

Louis didn't realize Julie had taken her cell phone out of her pocket till he was hit with it.

"Ouch!" Louis exclaimed as he backed away.

She grinned. "Maybe if you have read your Bible you would have known he was bruised on the head. I would bruise you too on the head if you try that again."

Rubbing his head as he looked upon her angered expression on her face, he replied, "You're violent, Julie."

"Only when I'm compelled."

"I see," he said while nodding his head. "I guess I deserved that."

She placed the cell phone back into her pocket, then reached for the picnic bag to take out the food. She handed him a croissant ham and cheese sandwich that was still warm and a bottle of orange juice.

Taking the sandwich out of her hand, Louis thought, *The girl has no fear.* He thanked her and commented, "You're a kinky woman aren't you Julie?"

Sneering at him, she asked, "What makes me freaky?"

"Interesting." He laughed. "I didn't say you were freaky."

"What's the difference? They're both wild."

"There is a big difference. A freak is one who would do anything, tries anything, a very abnormal monstrosity. . . ."

She cut in, "Like you."

Louis wanted to laugh, but he didn't. He continued giving her his explanation: " . . . And on the other hand kinky is a little milder, sexually abnormal, perverse, contrary."

Julie repeated, "Sexually abnormal, perverse, and contrary? I'm not like that, Mr. Janvier."

He insisted, "Yes, you are, you just don't want to admit it. You're not my mother, but yet you beat me then fed me. Some men pay lots of money for that treatment, you know. And here I am getting it for free."

She had to laugh because at that moment she believed Louis was really crazy. "You're sick, Mr. Janvier!"

"I notice every time we don't agree on something you call me Mr. Janvier," he persisted. "Your husband must not have reached that lesson with you yet. Oh, what am I saying! He is the kinky type and a freaky one! My apology, Mrs. Cactus. I forgot that I was the one who wasn't man enough to handle a little woman like you. . . . Well, anyway a man could get turned on in that kind of activity."

"You're the freaky or the kinky type, not him."

"You can tell that I am," he laughed. "Mrs. Cactus is reading my mind. . . . Now you really have me curious about you. I wonder if you have fangs hidden behind those teeth of yours."

Nodding her head she said, "No, I don't have fangs like you."

"So you admit that you do have fangs. . . ."

She ignored him.

" . . . Mine are baby fangs. I don't have much venom, so you see me coming."

Julie teased, "Your baby fangs might be more powerful then the adults. You're pure venom."

"You know about reptiles well, Julie." He smiled into her eyes. She ignored his last statement and told him to eat. Louis thanked her and raised the sandwich to the sky and then removed the wrap to eat. She looked at him and laughed at what he just did. She asked, "What was that?"

He replied, "I was praying."

Julie giggled. "That was praying? Oh my. You mean no one ever taught you how to pray?"

"Would you teach me, Julie?"

She smiled at the way he said her name. The sound of his voice sent a tremor down her spine. She held on to her stomach as she gave him the outline of how to pray. "Yes, Fuji, I would help, but the asking is up to you. You have to bless God's name first. Ask for his kingdom to come. Pray for yourself, the things you would love the most. Ask sincerely, then pray for forgiveness and the forgiveness for your family, for your friends and enemies, and always close your prayer like this: 'I ask you all these things in the name of your son, Jesus Christ. Amen'."

Intently Louis was listening to Julie as she explained to him. Her gentle voice captured his attention. He acknowledged she was a good teacher as he quietly listened to her. She concluded, "Practice makes perfect, so always talk to God, then the words to say will come easily."

"Do I need to be in certain position to pray to God?"

"No," Julie replied. "Just now all you needed to do was to bend your head down and pray."

"Why the head down? You just told me, I didn't need to be in any position."

"Yes," she answered and explained, "but the head down or the bending down of the knees show a sign of humility. Humble yourself before God!"

He was attentively staring at her as he was listening to her. Julie reminded him, "Didn't I tell you not to stare at me? You're making me feel uncomfortable and it's not polite."

He looked down at the mountain to put her at ease as she continued, "Some men claim God is mysterious, but in reality we are. God revealed all his purpose, but men don't know what they will really do tomorrow. We fall in love and out of love in so many different ways, but God's love is forever and perfect. What we think is good may be the things that would hurt someone else. We are mysterious creatures walking upon the surface of this earth. We know so much, but so very little. Our eyes can only see clearly when it's spelled right before us. Today you're a Mrs., tomorrow you're a widow or a widower. What life beholds we don't really know, but one thing we know for sure is death is not mysterious, just as God loves us. Death beholds all living. That is the other thing that is not mysterious to all mankind, as God is. But we as individuals are mysterious in our own ways, whether it is good or bad."

"You said some powerful words, Julie." He wanted to say something else, but instead he bit his sandwich. She did the same. She closed her eyes as she chewed while listening to the sound of the running water. She swayed her head and smiled. "The water makes a peaceful sound. It causes my mind to flow along with it."

Louis couldn't help looking at her and admiring the way she was swinging her head. He whispered in her ear, "Have you ever thought of cheating on your husband?"

Furious at his question, Julie opened her eyes. She couldn't believe what Louis whispered in her ear. Leaning away to look at him, she quickly said, "No! Louis, you're a provoker. Just when I thought you were not going to annoy me, you hit me with this. I cannot put my guard down with you, can I?"

He smiled. "Do you really want me to answer that?"

Going into a trance she looked at him and thought, *Maybe I deserve that. What am I doing here with him?*

She thought about her marital problems. She had not found any solution. Sorrow filled her heart. She couldn't eat anymore. She lifted up the hand that was holding on to her sandwich and threw it down the hill.

Looking at the expression of her face, he knew he insulted her. Louis apologized, "I'm sorry. I was insolent, please forgive me. I didn't mean to make you sad."

"You didn't cause my unhappiness, Fuji. I did. I don't know what is wrong with me. I don't understand why am I here with you. You have had all the reasons to ask that question. I would, if I was in your position. I would want to know if you're faithful to your wife. Look at me, I am sitting on the mountain before dawn waiting for the sunset, sharing my first meal of the day with you. . . ."

She glanced at him as she was continuing to talk, " . . . This is something lovers watch and do together. And here I am, with you, siting on a cliff like two lovers waiting patiently for a new beginning. I didn't even think twice about it. I can't believe that I'm sitting here with the biggest player in Haiti watching the sunset. Either I'm crazy or I'm curious and I wanted to know what made you so sick that you wanted to get in every woman's panties you meet."

Louis could not believe what she just called him and what she accused him of. Vexed by her statement he asked, "Did you just call me the biggest player in Haiti? Where did you get your information, woman?"

"I don't have to inquire of anyone." She wanted to offend him. "I just have to look at you. I'm not blind you know. How your eyes move all over my body."

"Maybe you are blind," Louis replied, "and deaf too, because you cannot see who I really am."

"I know for a fact you're the playboy in town." She continued hitting his pride. "And you want to sample every woman in town."

"For a fact!"

Contemptuously she looked at him, and he felt she meant to insult him. Throwing his sandwich down the hill he vociferously said, "You didn't get that information from me, so therefore it couldn't be a fact!"

Placing his hands on his temples, Louis couldn't believe he had spoken so loud. No one was able to get that type of reaction from him.

"No need to raise your voice at me," Julie responded. "I'm not blind or deaf like you claimed I am."

He was defending himself to her. Never did he have to explain himself to anyone, besides his mother. "With all the diseases going on around the world, a man has to be out of his mind to go around sleeping with every beautiful face he meets. You're wrong!"

"I didn't mean to offend you, Louis." She stood firm. "You can't deny what you are."

He breathed in and out to calm himself down. "Does it ever occur to you that I'm not that way anymore."

"Anymore." She laughed and repeated what he said. "You're not that way 'anymore'. That's what the scorpion told the frog before it stung him."

She was seizing on Louis's own words. He laughed and thought, *She caught on to my words.* She was fast.

"Since you went there," Louis stated, "I'm sure you remember what happened to the scorpion."

"It drowned."

"That's right," Louis agreed, "and I don't want to drown."

"You're suicidal, Louis."

"I may be," he continued, "but I'm not a murderer. I wouldn't take you down with me. Remember, I'm only here to help you with your riding, not to get that close to you. . . . I wouldn't do anything you wouldn't want me to do. Don't you feel safe with me as if you were with your big brother, Julie?"

"Am I, Louis? Am I safe with you?"

She couldn't deny the feeling. She couldn't understand why she felt protected when she was around him, but she never had a big brother so she wasn't really sure. But one thing she knew, she was married and she had her dignity to uphold. She tasted her drink, then stretched, and changed the whole conversation.

"Yesterday, Max and I drove all the way to Delmas to look at the old neighborhood."

He asked, "You used to live down there?"

"In a way." She smiled. "I spent a lot of time down there visiting some good friends. All of them moved. Only strangers live there now, all are indifferent. There was a time one could talk and say good morning to someone, and you would have received a warm welcome. Children used to fill the sidewalk playing, jumping rope, playing tag, and the older ones would keep their eyes on the younger ones to make sure they were playing properly. There was so much laughter, things to do. And they were alive, young and old. Yesterday, I felt like I was walking inside a cemetery and everyone who was living there was a bunch of caretakers. Everything looked dead in my eyes, even the people in it. They destroyed all the beauty and replaced it with bricks. The island is turning to a concrete jungle. How sad. If they only could see the beauty that I envision for Haiti. . . ."

Her voice sounded so sad. Louis could feel her sorrow and how sentimental she was. Likewise, he felt the same way too about Haiti. He was offered a prestigious position in New York as one of the directors in charge of several hospitals, but he felt Haiti would need him much more than New York. He returned to stay to work as a doctor here. He wanted to contribute to the Haitian community. That was one of the reasons he made a home here and had brought a lot of land.

Louis had constructed reasonably size houses for people to live and gave handsome donations for schools, hospitals, fire departments, and recreation places. He helped newcomers establish their ways into the business world. Not just in Haiti but also in America. His ideas had created many jobs for men and women. But still, Louis felt that a woman's place is at home, to help raise the children. He felt that job was already too much for one to handle. Now most women were working because of single parenting. He was now working on establishing a center where single mothers could find financial support to help raise their young ones. He felt the Haitian family values had gone down enormously.

Dreamily Julie smiled. " . . . I'm thinking of putting up a barn for those who enjoy riding horses like me, not too far from the city."

The sun was coming up. Julie stretched her arms wide open and said, "If only I had my guitar, I would sing like the birds in the field, letting my mind fly with them to glorify this magnificent sight."

"Then tomorrow I'll bring a guitar for you to sing with the sunrise."

"Sorry," she said. "I'll be home tomorrow preparing for my husband's arrival. My husband will be here on Tuesday. . . . I would like to introduce you to him. I'm sure he'll be happy to know the man who took the time to take me horse back riding."

"I would like to meet him." He smiled. "What time is dinner?"

"Wednesday at seven. Would that be a problem?"

"No, not at all."

They sat there in silence watching the sun hitting their faces.

Later in the morning Jacque and his family were sitting in the dining room having breakfast.

He asked Marie for Julie. "Where's Mrs. Philip?"

"She went out early this morning, Monsieur Bassine."

"Did she say where she was going?"

"From the way she looked, she look like she was going riding."

"Riding," Jacque breathed under his breath. "With whom?"

"Monsieur Janvier," Marie smiled, "Monsieur Bassine."

Marie left the dining room, leaving an intense atmosphere.

Looking at everyone's expression, Maxine said, "Julie is a big girl. She can take care of herself. No need for anyone to worry about her."

Ignoring Maxine's comment, Carine asked Jacque, "Is the business you're taking care of with Louis on the move?"

"I have a lot of work to do on the matter. We have the money, but it's a matter of putting the plan on paper."

While they were having their breakfast Julie walked in all dressed up as if she was going out to a job interview. "Good morning, everyone."

They all chorused good morning. She sat on the empty seat that was next to Maxine. Maxine gave her a kiss on her cheek then asked, "How was your ride this morning?"

"Beautiful! We went all the way to where you can see the waterfall. The air felt good, and the sight was awesome."

"On Louis's land," Jacque exclaimed.

Julie answered, "Yes!"

Jacque replied, "That's very nice of him. Why don't you eat something, Julie?"

"I already had something to eat, but a cup of coffee will do."

The butler poured her a cup of hot coffee. Carine questioned, "Did Louis behave himself, Julie?"

"Oh yes. Not the perfect gentleman one would take him for, but he seemed decent."

Maxine laughed. "Isn't that the truth? Well said, Julie."

Carine curiously asked, "Are you going riding with him later on, Julie?"

"No, not today. Saul is arriving Tuesday, and I want to look my best."

"You always look your best," Maxine replied. "You can go riding. Like Saul said, enjoy yourself."

Jacque cut in, "Why didn't you tell me Saul is coming here? I have a few errands to run for him."

"No need to worry yourself so much, Jacque. Saul is not in any hurry. I'm sure you'll have plenty of time."

"Saul, your husband." Jacque chuckled as he carelessly said, "The last time he was here, he almost broke my neck."

"When was 'the last time he was here'?" Julie asked.

No one answered. Maxine cut in to defend Saul, "You were being disrespectful to me."

"I was joking with you."

Maxine was upset. "Calling me a female dog wasn't funny."

Jacque was embarrassed. He didn't think Maxine was going to reveal what he had called her. He looked at Julie and said, "I was just playing with her."

Julie looked angry, not only because they wouldn't answer her question, but also because Jacque was very disrespectful to Maxine. She was appalled. She stared at him. He quickly apologized to Maxine.

"That kind of name is unacceptable, Jacque. . . . I don't ever want to hear that you talked to the girls that way. No women should be disrespected, even in a joking way. I'm surprised at you."

"I'm sorry," he said and asked, "Did I ever bully you, Julie?"

"No, Jacque. But you can be rough sometime."

"How true," Maxine said.

Jacque replied, "You ladies have a way of ganging up on me. Look at the way Maxine replied. If I was such a bully, you, of all people, would be the first one to put me in my place."

Julie agreed, "True."

Maxine replied, "Don't be fooled by his angelic look, Julie. You know the saying–the worst liar and killer comes with an angel face."

Carine and Nicole laughed at her comment. Jacque replied, "You see what I mean."

Julie replied, "I see. . . . Well I'm going up. I have had enough for this morning."

"The weather is not so hot," Jacque said. "Why don't you take a stroll with me around the mansion."

Wanting to know what Jacque knew about her husband being in Haiti, she agreed to take the stroll with Jacque. "Let me tell Marie that she could go on and do what ever she wanted to do today."

She left them sitting around the table and went to do what she was going to do. Jacque got up and ran up to his room to refresh himself.

By then Julie was waiting for him outside on the terrace admiring the view. She walked to the cachiman tree and she took one of its fruit. She broke the skin then tasted the fruit. She closed her eyes to enjoy the flavor of it. "Mm!"

Jacque was just getting there. He said, "I planted this tree for you."

"I remember," she replied as she continued enjoying the fruit. "You said every time I tasted the fruit of this tree, I should remember how kind and generous you are. The fruit is sweet."

She handed him half of it to eat while they continued to walk. They stopped before another tree, and she commented, "I never could understand why they call this fruit a cherry. The cherry trees in America are big tall trees and the seeds are hard. They're not that little."

Jacque took a cherry off of its branch and split it open, then showed her the seed. He said, "Ours in the real cherry. Not only the seed splits in half, but it's also soft and juicy." He sucked it.

Shocked by his behavior, Julie gave him a playful push and said, "You're too much, Jacque!"

She took a cherry from the branch then looked at the inside and commented, "You know I never really looked inside it, but you're right," she laughed. "The American cherry seeds are very hard. You could break your teeth on one of the seeds if you are not careful."

Jacque replied, "American cherry is a man, not a woman, or maybe she's just a heartbreaker."

Julie did respond to his comment, so he continued. "You know, I used to think that you and me, one day we would have been husband and wife, but you never looked at me like someone you could love."

"Husband," she exclaimed. She thought that he was joking. She replied, "But, Jacque, I do love you."

"Like a brother, isn't it, Julie? I was never a man to you, but a brother. I hate Saul for having you, but at the same time I admired him, because he was able to capture you. My beloved Julie you will always be."

She didn't answer him. She looked at him as he talked, trying to understand what Jacque was telling her and where he was heading. . . . *Does Jacque want me as his lover? Him and me together like husband and wife?* She thought, *I hope I'm thinking wrong, an I misunderstood what Jacque is revealing to me.*

The thought made her nauseous. She dispelled the idea out of her mind. That was one thing she couldn't picture. When Jacque touched her or gave a hug, she never felt any chemistry between them. Always like a family member. Never did she gave him the impression that one day they would get married, not even when they were children. Why would Jacque think that way?

She silenced him. "Jacque, why must you think or even mention this to me? You now you're my big brother."

Her answer displeased him. Trying to cover up what he said, he gave her a kiss on the cheek. She smiled him off as he apologized. "Well, Julie, I see you enjoy riding. What Louis brought here for you to ride are two very expensive horses. They are Arabian horses. You don't see these kinds in Haiti. He must have bought them from America. I wouldn't want anything to happen to them. He never let anyone ride those two horses. I'm surprised that he did. You better be careful. . . ."

Julie agreed. Then he went on to say, " . . . Louis is a dangerous man. He may appear as a nice man, but he's not. I'm concerned for you, you know that."

She replied, "I know."

"I knew you and Saul were having marital problems."

"How do you know?"

"Since you two got married, you guys are always together. Here you are in Haiti by yourself. You didn't even know that Saul was here in Haiti?"

Julie was puzzled and thought, why didn't Maxine tell her? "No, I didn't know! What was he doing here?"

"He claimed he was taking care of business. He spent almost two months here. And during that time he was going on a rampage with everything you and him have together. He sold half of everything to some unknown buyer."

"Unknown buyer!" Julie thought that didn't sound like her husband.

"He refused to give the name of the buyer. He told me that was none of my business. He never told me who the buyer was. Then a day later, he took a suitcase full of money. The next thing I heard, he went to the Dominican Republic with a couple of friends. I think he went gambling down there because when he returned he had no money. I assumed he was in serious trouble because he told me to give him the rest of the documents he had entrusted me with and to hand them to Henry Claude. . . . Do you remember who Henry is?"

Julie nodded. "Yes, an associate of Louis Janvier."

"They are more than associates, they're partners in crime. . . . Your husband wanted me to give Henry Claude the documents, which you have personally entrusted me with. Everything you have here with him. I thought he was mad. He threatened to kill me, Julie."

She was surprised. "Why?"

"Because I told him I was going to call you to let you know what he was up to. He sounded and acted like madman, Julie! You should have seen the place. I didn't know what was wrong with him."

Julie didn't respond to Jacque's statement. Instead she said, "Maybe he's tired and worried for me."

"I don't think so, Julie," Jacque answered. "He didn't give me the impression he was thinking about you. For some reason he wanted me out of the picture. He offered Jean to take over for him while he was away, but Jean felt he wasn't suitable for that kind of work, so he suggested for Saul to let me continue handling things. That was the first smart thing my little brother ever did that I could remember. I think he wanted Jean to waste everything you and your parents worked hard for."

"Maybe he had his reasons," Julie said distantly, thinking back to the relationship between Saul and her.

"Perhaps, but that didn't give him the right to squander everything you worked hard for. He's involved with the most notorious killer in Haiti, Louis."

"I thought he was dealing with Henry Claude," Julie replied.

"Please, Julie, don't be naïve. He's working for Louis Janvier and they're thieves and killers for all I know. Your husband put the whole family in danger. I believe he's in serious trouble, or he owes someone a large sum of money. I barely saw him after that. He was always on the run. He didn't stay here with us. I thought he was in Jacmel, so I went there after him. He stayed there for only two days, then he disappeared. He was nowhere in town, no one saw him. When I saw him again, he stayed here for a couple of days to fix the barn, then his last night here, he told me he was leaving for some kind a mission, a project he was working on."

"Where do you think he might have disappeared to?"

"Your husband is a clever man. I can't believe you married a man like that."

"Saul is very kind and worked hard for everything he got. I know the type of man he was before I married him. I don't need you defaming his name. Selling what is rightfully his doesn't bother me at all, but what does bother me is you talking about him that way. I won't have it."

"I didn't mean to, Julie. It's that I don't want him to hurt you. . . . If he knew Louis was taking you riding, I don't think he would have approved it."

"My husband doesn't tell me who I should associate with, and I think for your own good you should do the same."

"I wouldn't dare tell you what to do. You're my boss's wife. Like I told you before, Louis's family gave him everything they possessed. He had them all working for him like they were his slaves. On top of that he has women all over town and the city in this little country. And now he's prowling around you. I'm doing business with him because I feel he's the king. One has to go through him to get things done. As you can see, Louis and I are not friends. We're just doing business. . . . Please be careful. He can be very charming, but he is a player, a killer at that. I didn't want to tell you this, but I'm afraid he's sleeping both with Maxine and Carine."

Julie was stunned by Jacque's outburst. She felt bad that she didn't say a word in their behalf, especially Maxine's.

" . . . And keep this in mind—Louis is a liar. He would lie to get his way. He would even create stories and would have you believe in it just to make you feel sympathy for him. He doesn't have a drop of human blood in him."

Julie walked beside Jacque without saying a word. She was thinking, What was really behind all that information Jacque was giving her?. . . . He went on telling her about Louis and her husband. With one breath he told her all that. . . . She wondered if Jacque was in her best interest, and why did Marie tell her those things about Louis, and Maxine, whom she trusted very much, not once mentioned that Saul was in Haiti. Why did Louis tell her such a big secret about himself? At the moment she was giving Jacque the benefit of the doubt. But one thing she had to totally agree with Jacque was that Louis was not one anybody should play with, especially her. Louis was definitely bad news.

Julie thanked him for the information Jacque gave her, but at the same time she was wondering where Saul was and why he was here. Even though the bank accounts were empty, she couldn't bring herself to believe that Saul was here with another woman or gambling. That was not his style, even if she drove him away. Saul wouldn't do her like that. She believed he was here for something else, but what was it?

They continued their tour around the mansion. Jacque was showing her the work he did while she was away. She liked what he did with the swimming pool. Jacque built a bar in the pool so that people could sit and have drinks while they were cooling themselves in the water. The sight was beautiful to look upon. The fall of the water coming down from the roof of the bar, pouring into the pool. The chairs were comfortable to sit on. On the deck was an outdoor custom-designed kitchen. And a romantic corner near the pool where two people could enjoy a quiet moment alone.

When they finished looking around, she said, "You really outdid yourself with the place. I saw your new hotel. It's a beauty."

"Who took you there?"

"Maxine."

"I wanted to show it to you when it was completely finished," he said sadly.

"You could always take me for a second tour," she smiled. "It's beautiful and the name fits perfectly, 'Jacque's Palace'. You're a successful man, my brother. Your place would be a hit. Your engineering skill is a gift from God."

"It's because of you I became an engineer. You like to build things, improving your surroundings. You always said a man should work not just with pens and papers, but also with his hands; touch the soil, the sand, and the water of your field; bring them to life as you go along."

She smiled. "When I said that, I was not only talking just for the male species, but also for the female, Jacque. I like what you did with the place. You even remodeled the servants' quarters. They seem to be very happy. I would like to move in the old place. I like the way it's fixed."

"Saul did the work on it while he was here. I guess he knew you would like that place better than the mansion."

"Don't get me wrong, my brother, I like what you did with the place. You take good care of the land."

"I try to keep the land up. It was your dream. Every chance I had, I had everyone plant a tree, you know, like a school project."

"I see." She smiled. "I saw everyone planted a tree by the river. They're growing nice and beautiful. And the birdcage . . . oh, Jacque, thank you for keeping them alive. I was so wrapped up in my problem I forgot all about them."

"I'm glad that you like everything, and later on, I'm going to show you a property that Saul got. It's in Delmas. He said you'll decide what to do with it. It's quite big with plenty of trees and plants. I planted some of them, you'll love it."

"You think so? Delmas is overcrowded. I was hoping to find a land for horses, donkeys, and mules, a place they could run free. These animals have been neglected, and we have many of those, and here is not a place for them. Jacmel is too far off. I need a good veterinarian just to cater to the animals. When Saul arrives, I hope everything goes well. I believe I'll be the first one to have an animal farm where certain ones could come and play with horses and donkeys and mules. Oh, I almost forgot I invited Louis over for dinner on Wednesday. I hope you don't mind."

"Tell you the truth, I do." He smiled. "But what's one last dinner? Saul may not like his presence. Did you notice the way Louis looked at you? The man wants to swallow you alive. I hope Saul breaks his neck like he almost did to me."

"It's just your imagination." She laughed. "And you're just jealous."

"I hope Saul breaks his neck."

"Saul is not a violent man. He's sweet and kind."

"Tell that to my neck. He almost broke it."

"You're never going to let go of that. You just have weak bones. You need to drink more milk and take your iron."

"Listen to you, defending that mean, arrogant husband of yours."

Julie laughed. "Like you're not arrogant? Please, Jacque."

She dismissed what Jacque was saying about her husband. She felt Jacque should keep his opinion to himself. Her husband was sweet and a gentleman. After their tour around the mansion, she went in for a little rest. Later she called her mother.

Her mother started to tell her that the other night, Saul had dropped by to see her and the baby. He spent the night with them. Then yesterday, he spent the entire day with William up in Spring Valley. Later that evening he brought him back then headed for the airport. He didn't tell her where he was going, but he let her know that sometime this week he was going to meet with Julie in Haiti. She called off the investigation. And she was calling her to inform her about everything, for her not to be worried because her husband looked well. And he was looking forward to seeing her so they could spend some quality time together.

Julie was even happier after she finished talking to her mother. She kissed the phone and said goodbye then got ready to meet with Maxine. Louis called to see how she was doing, but she didn't pick up the phone to talk to him. Marie just gave her the message.

That night Maxine planned a picnic for the following day. She wanted to spend the afternoon with Julie because her weekend was almost over. She invited Carine and Nicole to join the picnic, but both had a previous engagement. Carine had promised Michelle she was coming over to her house to spend the day with her, and Nicole was also going with her.

"Sorry," Carine stated, "I was going to invite you to hang-out with us, but it seems Maxine has already made her plan."

Maxine chirped at Carine while she was talking then yawned. "Okay, we heard enough!"

Taking Julie's hand, Maxine walked out with her and left Carine and Nicole in the family room. As they were leaving Julie took a look at Carine and saw that Carine didn't even care. She turned up the volume and sat back on the sofa with her eyes closed, her head swinging to the music that she was listening to. Then she looked at Nicole and found her looking at her and when their eyes met, Nicole quickly looked at the book that was in her hands and pretended she was reading. Julie didn't say anything. She let Maxine drag her out of the room, wondering what that was all about.

Maxine took her to the kitchen. Opening the cooler she took out a large bag of chicken legs and a ten pounds bag of beef to prepare what they were going to have at the picnic. She said, "I'm glad that I asked Marie to take this meat out of the freezer last night. Now it's ready to be seasoned."

"That's a lot of meat," Julie commented.

While they were getting the things they are going to need for the picnic Julie confronted her. "Why you didn't tell me that Saul was in town?"

Maxine replied, "When Saul arrived here, I was in Florida. I spent two weeks there. . . ."

She took a deep breath and exclaimed, " . . . There was nothing to tell. Saul spent most of his time working and getting the place beautiful for you. For the way the place looks, I assumed you knew that Saul was here. He's the one who did all this constructing and remodeling. He made the place look more beautiful. While he was fixing up the place, he didn't want anyone to disturb him and he made everyone promise not to say a word. I didn't know you were having problems. He seemed to be so happy doing all this work for you. He hired a lot of people around the clock. He was amazing! Saul worked as much as the workers he had hired to get the place fixed. Within two months the whole place was redone. He wanted everything to be perfect for you. He even redid the servants' quarters, bought them new uniforms and furniture. The barn was falling apart and he didn't understand why we didn't have it rebuilt. So he rebuilt it bigger and better. Jacque was upset because he didn't take his suggestion. Jacque only remodeled the pool with the help of Saul. The pool was also Saul's idea. And if Jacque said anything bad about him, it is because he is jealous of him. Saul was upset that Jacque had fired some of the people who have worked for you guys for years and had five children working on the land. He thought that Jacque was being mean."

"Children!"

"Saul took them all to an orphanage. And he made sure they were taken in and they were taken care of. I was there. He gave a very big donation to the place. He reminded me that was your favorite place and I promised him I'd keep an eye on those childrens' progress. . . ."

Julie was happy to hear that her husband did all that and not once did Maxine mention gambling or that he was partying. The work here proved it even so.

Maxine concluded, " . . . Saul worked so hard. He spent most of his time working. He only dropped by the mansion to make sure the room that you were going to sleep in was redecorated for his queen, and everything in the mansion looked beautiful. Everything was well arranged! When he was finished, he gave each of us an envelope full of money, but Jacque wanted all our money for his project. Everyone lied and told him that Saul didn't give us any money. He gave us all gifts. When I told Saul I was preparing myself to get married, he gave me more money as a wedding gift. Then he was gone. Jacque wanted to know what he gave me, so I told him he gave me the key to the Jeep to put away."

Julie laughed at her conclusion and continued their work.

▣   ▣   ▣

The next day it was around ten-thirty when Maxine met Julie by her room. Both were wearing their bathing suits and skirts that matched their suits and sandals. Matching hats and picnic bags held their towels and combs and deodorant. Earlier, Maxine had two of the servants set their picnic items under their favorite spot by the river. The minute they sighted their spot, they ran to the picnic area and put their bags down then ran in the water to cool down. Like two children they played, throwing water on each other's face. Then Maxine went back to their area and opened the cooler and threw a bottle of beer to Julie. "Catch!"

Julie saw the cooler was full of beer and a big bottle of homemade passionfruit liquor.

"That's a lot of beers for two people to drink. We're going to get drunk." Julie laughed, removing her skirt. She hung it on a branch so it could dry then sat by the grill. She took the bag of fresh corn. She opened it and threw corn at Maxine. "Here, clean the corn!"

Throwing it back at Julie she grimaced and said, "They might have worms and I don't want to see it. I would lose my appetite."

Shaking her head Julie expounded, "Girl, you have a lot of nerve!"

She handed Maxine the fork as she removed the leaves of the corn. Julie suggested, "Why don't you lay the meat on the grill, starting with the roasting. . . . I marinated them well. The bonnet peppers smell so good, I could just eat them."

"Yes they do smell good," Maxine agreed, looking at her fingers and staring at the meat in the bowl. Taking a look at her Julie asked, "What's wrong now?"

Again she grimaced. "I don't want my fingers to smell like meat."

Pulling the fork out of her hand, Julie exclaimed, "Why did you bring the grill with you and all this food if you did not plan to roast it yourself?"

"We will be here for a while, so I came prepared, and it's a nice day, and definitely tonight will be nice and warm. And you know I love your cooking. Where did you learn how to cook so well?"

"Something called practice. This is the only way you'll know how to cook."

Maxine laughed. "Domesticated work doesn't cut well with me."

Julie laughed. "And you plan to get married!"

"Don't tell me you cook for Saul."

"Yes I do," she answered, and sighed. "Every chance I get. I like the way he enjoys my cooking. It gives me pleasure and made me want to cook more for him. Maxine, the best thing a woman could give her husband is herself. And I don't mean sex. To know what he likes to eat, wear, and the position he likes you to hold him. The thoughts, the dreams you two share. He trusts you, loves you. And you're the capable woman who can take care of home, making sure your house is well arranged. To have the strength to stand by your man, in helping him make the right decision. You wouldn't fear when another woman tries to enter your home, because you know you have done your job. Your mouth only speaks well about your husband . . . I hope you understand what I'm telling you, Maxine. And I believe Richard loves you. So don't sell yourself short by not becoming a complete woman. . . ."

Maxine nodded to let her know she understood. " . . . And please don't let the corn burn. Just watch them, and make sure to turn them so they are cooked evenly."

"You see," Maxine replied. "I wouldn't know if I have to turn them. Thank you for the lesson."

"It's not a lesson, just common sense."

"To you it's common sense, to me it's a lesson. What's little to you is very big to me. I'm spoiled the wrong way, Julie. I may have to go to colonial school to learn these things." She handed Julie a cup of homemade liquor. "Here, drink that. It will relax you."

Shaking her head Julie handed her a roasted corn as she took the cup from her. While they were enjoying the food and their homemade liquor, they heard motorcycle noises. Slowly Maxine and Julie went up the hill to look. Maxine waved to the people riding the bikes. She smiled. "It is Louis and Richard!"

She noticed Julie was uncomfortable, but she didn't say anything. Julie went back and took her skirt off the branch and put it back on, then sat by the little grill continuing with the roasting. Maxine shouted as she put back on her skirt, "What are you guys doing here?"

"Having fun," Richard replied as he removed his helmet. "We saw your fire, so we came to the rescue."

They both came down together. Louis commented, "I smell something good. What are you two cooking?"

Maxine replied, "We're roasting corn and meat. You want some?"

Julie didn't answer. Louis came closer and said, "You girls can cook. . . ?"

Julie looked up at him and tasted her drink then she continued turning the food on the grill. " . . . Can I join you?"

She looked at Maxine, nodding her head to Julie for yes. Without looking at him, Julie said, "Sure."

Maxine handed Louis and Richard a bottle of beer. Looking at Julie's eyes Louis noticed she was a little high. "How long have you girls been here having fun?"

Maxine answered, "Since ten, ten-thirty."

Louis looked at his watch. It was two in the afternoon. He smiled and thought she must be stone drunk. He wanted to know how strong was the drink she was having and put her vulnerability to the test. Handing Maxine back the beer bottle he said, "I want what Julie's drinking."

Taking the beer from him, Maxine handed him a cup of homemade liquor. He tasted it as he looked at Julie and thought, *Good but strong.* He commented, "Passion liquor, perfect for this moment."

Maxine handed them napkins, forks, and a knife. Julie gave them corn and steak on a plate, saying as she went to sit, "Be careful. It is spicy and hot."

Drawing her beautiful long hair back away from her face she turned her back on them, she took a bite of her corn, nodding her head to a beat of music no one could hear. She closed her eyes and ignored them. Maxine was surprised at Julie's behavior. She looked at Louis and shrugged her shoulders, but Louis smiled at Julie's rudeness.

Placing the plate at his side Louis wanted to call her a chicken for not facing him. He teased, "You don't want us to see if you grew a beak, Julie."

Which caused them to laugh. Still Julie didn't turn. She retorted, "The way you ate yesterday morning made me sick. I don't want to look at you. You'll make me nauseous."

"Touché," Louis replied. He tasted his drink. "Mm! The drink is strong. Maybe the booze is getting to you. You're too young for it, Julie, that's what getting you nauseous."

Maxine couldn't help laughing and so did Richard. Maxine said, "Stop teasing her, Louis."

"Let the fool talk, Max," Julie blurted out as the drink was getting to her. "That's what clowns do best."

Maxine sat there and looked at Louis with her mouth half open. She didn't smile at Julie's description of him. She knew no one talked to Louis that way. She was surprised to see Louis just laughed at Julie's comment and continued to drink. Richard looked at Maxine with a shocked expression in his eyes. Louis got up and stood in front of Julie with the plate in his hand to look at her. She looked up and didn't say anything.

He asked, "You're not going to tell me stop staring. . . ?"

She didn't answer. She handed him her corn.

Taking it from her hand, Louis commented, " . . . Should I do like a rooster, crow for it?"

"I'm sure, you could," Julie replied. "It's your nature."

On hearing Julie's statement Maxine and Richard excused themselves, leaving Louis and Julie on their ranking game.

Louis smiled and sat by her, then asked, "What is my nature, Julie?"

"You like to play with women." She didn't hold back. "Your mind games, making them feel sorry for you and beneath you."

"You seemed to know a lot more about me than I know about myself." He lowered his head to make eye contact with her. "Do I give you that impression about me?"

She didn't answer. She turned her eyes at him then looked away. Feeling peeved he concluded, "You shouldn't talk about what you don't know, woman."

"I know enough that you're a person not to trust."

On hearing her response, Louis removed himself from her side and stood to look down at her. He was not about to argue with a drunken woman, and he felt that was where they were heading. He took her hands and placed the cup and the plate in her hands and said, "Since you know enough about me not to trust me, so let it be."

Louis ran up the hill without a second look, got on his bike, and rode off, leaving Julie and her judgment call of him. He was upset at her last statement. At the moment he didn't care or want to be near her or anyone. He rode past Richard and Maxine, who were embraced in a passionate kiss and now wondered what had taken place between Julie and him. Louis rode faster than usual, going up and down the mountains till he reached the spot where Julie and he sat to watch the dusk! He didn't know what he was doing there but he knew he was not going to watch the dusk with her. He didn't want her there. Rage was going through him. He took his helmet and threw it down the hill and he didn't care where it landed. It rolled in the water.

He sat on the ground not too far from his bike, with his head resting on his knees, folding his arms around his legs. He tried to calm himself down while he thought, *Damn! I can't believe I'm attracted to that woman. She could drive a man out of his mind. Julie is actually getting under my skin. Henry was right, I'm beginning to feel like her captive audience, and I'm not about to let that happen. She's on my turf.*

Bringing his head up and pushing his hair back as if to push her out of his mind, he sighed and thought he had given a lot of people reasons to think he was not to be trusted, but Julie had no reason to claim she knew enough he was not a person to trust. "How dare she!"

Shaking his head Louis tried to regulate the uncontrolled anger he was feeling. He flashed back on his youth. He was bad and he could be senseless. There was one thing he remembered his father saying: "There's nothing in this vain world that you cannot accomplish when you have money.

When someone has so much money he either spends it on worthless things or invests it on something that will make him or her happy. Never love money . . . love a good woman who will know the value of love, someone like your mother!"

He found himself thinking and wondering, was Julie the woman or was that another phase he was going through?

Meanwhile, Julie and Maxine were continuing their conversation while barbecuing.

Maxine commented, "I think Louis is very fond of you, I never saw him talk to or look at anyone the way he does with you."

"That's what players do, Maxine," Julie replied coldly. "They try to use their charm to seduce their victim."

Maxine thought Julie sounded angry. Tasting her wine, Maxine looked at her and smiled. "Does he make you feel like a victim, Julie. . . ?"

She didn't answer. Then Maxine continued, " . . . He had that kind of charm. He is very good looking and rich and very talented. He has many things going for him. Whether he wanted to be a player or not, women would always come up to him. He has it like that."

"He doesn't have to flaunt it," Julie responded.

Maxine laughed. "Believe it or not, Louis is shy."

"He doesn't seem shy to me."

Julie didn't say much after that she leaned her head against the seat with a smile on her face looking at the sky. Maxine asked, "What are you thinking?"

She replied, "I was thinking Saul would be here tomorrow. We're going to the beach and so many other things I want to do with him. I hope my body and my mind don't fail me. I want him so much."

Maxine nodded in understanding. Quietly they sat for while enjoying the taste of the passion liquor, talking about what they would like to see happen in the future. It was getting late so they made ready to go around four o'clock. As they were going up the hill, Maxine yelled, "Look! I see a helmet in the water."

Julie stopped and ran in the water to take the helmet out of the river. She looked at Maxine and said, "Does this belong to Richard?"

"No, it looks like the one Louis was wearing. What is it doing in the water?"

Looking up stream, Julie got scared, afraid Louis might have fallen or jumped off a cliff. She climbed up the hill as fast as she could while she placed the helmet on her head. The thought of what Louis might have done got her very worried. "Max, do you think that Louis okay?"

Breathlessly Maxine replied, "I don't know. . . !"

She tried to keep up with Julie saying, "Julie, slow down. I have too many things in my hands."

"Put them down. We'll send someone to fetch them later. . . ."

Julie tried to get to the barn as fast as she could. Without stopping she said, "Louis could be up there injured or in serious trouble. We have to move."

When they got to the barn, Julie didn't saddle her horse. She just put the guard around the horse's neck, then got on and rode off without thinking. Maxine called, "I'm not good at saddling a horse, Julie!"

Julie called over her shoulder, "Don't worry, I'll meet you at home!"

Without looking back she galloped away. She rode on the path of the river looking for Louis. When she couldn't find him she started to call out, "Fuji!"

She saw something gleaming up on the hill, she assumed that was his bike. Cautiously she rode up.

From afar Louis heard her voice, but he thought his mind was playing tricks on him. Shaking his head he said, "No! That woman is really getting to me, now I'm actually hearing her calling me."

He lay on the ground trying to see if the voice would vanish, but it was getting closer and louder as he felt the pounding of a horse galloping. She spotted him and rode the horse close to him and jumped off it without coming to a complete stop, then ran to his aid.

Passing her hands over his face Julie asked, "Are you all right?"

Holding onto her hands, he flashed, "I was till you came here!"

Surprised by his answer and the tone of his voice, she pulled her hands out of his and said, "I thought you were hurt so I came to your aid and this is the thanks I get for being a good Samaritan."

"Why would you think that I was hurt?"

Removing the helmet off her head, she handed it to him. "Maxine and I found your helmet downstream."

He looked over her shoulders. "How come you came up here by yourself? Where's Maxine?"

"I was in a hurry to come to your rescue," Julie lashed back at him, "thinking you were hurt." She looked at the expression on his face, as if to tell her, *Yeah right! Give me a better reason.* "Why all these questions?"

He cut her short. "So you came running to rescue me, how nice. Now tell me, what really brought you up here?"

"What do you mean?" she sneered at him.

"You know exactly what I mean. You ran up here to beg for my forgiveness."

Stepping away from him she inquired, "Why should I beg you for forgiveness?

"For insulting me, Julie." He got up and stood before her. He said as he slowly moved toward her, "You got all drunk calling me out of my name. . . . For a man you don't trust, why did you come here to his aid?"

"I told you already." She moved back. "I thought you were hurt."

He was so close, to the point where he could just kiss her. She wanted to move but she found herself unable to. She started to shiver as she felt his minty breath close to her mouth.

Grinding his teeth he said, "Don't worry. I wouldn't touch you."

In his heart he knew he was lying. He had to force himself to say that. He pushed his hair away from his face as he slowly moved away from her, trying to calm himself down before he did something stupid. She couldn't believe she was trembling before him, why her body reacted toward him like that. All she could think of was that man was insolent. "As you could see, you make me sick! I wouldn't want to be touched by you either! The reason I'm here was I thought you might have committed suicide."

Looking at her and the horse behind her, knowing the horse she rode didn't like motorcycle noise, Louis got on his motorcycle and jumped started it. Julie was not holding on to the belt so she didn't have the chance to stop the horse and calm it down. She yelled at him. "You big buffoon! Look what you did. You scared it away. It's a long way from home! And Maxine and the others might get worried for me."

He didn't reply. He couldn't believe she called him a clown again. He continued making the noise with his bike. He paused for a moment then said, "Get on."

"Are you commanding me?"

"What do you think? Right now you're at my mercy. So get on and keep quiet."

Julie didn't respond. She looked at him like he was crazy, so he turned off the bike and went and sat where he was before. Julie stretched before she started to jog. He took a quick glance to see if she was still standing there, but Julie had starting to run toward the road that lead down the mountain.

"Damn!"

He motion his head with anger. Louis got on his feet and ran after her. When he caught up to her he apologized. "I'm sorry, my head had not been clear lately. Forgive me. Please let me take you home."

Julie inhaled and exhaled to calm down, she stopped and walked back with him. He took her hand in his to thank her for the concern she showed for him. "You're a brave and loving woman, Julie. Thank you for coming to my rescue."

"You didn't need my rescue."

"More than you think." He kissed her hands to show his appreciation. The feel of his lips quickened her. Louis too felt the stimulation that rose in him. He gazed into her eyes as he held her hands against his lips. She looked away. He wanted to do more. Instead he remained calm. He didn't want to frighten her away. At that moment Louis knew there was something in him burning more than he presumed. He didn't want to say or do anything to jeopardize his friendship with her.

Letting her hands go, he quickly changed the conversation to an airplane that was passing above the air. "That plane must be going to the Dominican Republic. Hopefully one day I'll take you and your husband on a flying trip."

She knew that Louis could fly a plane because the Bassine girls had already told her. She smiled. "You know how to fly a plane, too? Exactly what can't you do?"

"I cannot birth a child by myself, and I cannot stay out of trouble. The list goes on, but right now this is all I could think of."

Julie laughed. "Now you really sound like my husband. . . . Are you sure you two didn't go to the same school?"

Louis stared at her. He didn't seem pleased by her remark. Looking at him she quickly said, "I didn't say that to offend you, Fuji. It's just that I can't help if you make me feel that way. You two have so much in common. Saul designs plane, and you love to fly."

He put her mind to rest. "There is something else on my mind, Julie. . . . When you spoke of your husband, loneliness hit me more then before. The wife of my best friend and my child came up to my mind. How I wanted to hold her and kiss her with passion . . . and I cannot! That made me feel so lonely. I'm torn, and I don't know how long my suffering will continue. I wish the madness I'm having has ended. Instead I found myself loving her more. Wanting someone I know it's impossible to have. And it's hurting me."

Julie tapped him on his shoulder to comfort him and said, "I understand what you mean."

"Do you?"

She sighed. "I want to be touched and held my husband, but I don't even know where he really is. Right now, I want to kiss my baby and hug him, but he's too far away. I think I understand the loneliness you're feeling but all we can do is hope one day you will hold her in your arms and I will hold him in mine."

Louis didn't comment. He helped her get behind him on the motorcycle. Just as they were getting ready to ride off, the sun went down completely.

Embracing the night with his mind Louis said, "Look, the sun has gone."

He turned off the motorcycle so they could listen to the sounds of the night. Julie saw how the moon made the pine trees looked so heavenly. She was hypnotized by the sudden arrival of the night, forgetting herself she laid her chin against his back looking at the sky. Like a miracle the stars appeared. Louis closed his eyes and smiled when he felt her face against his masculine back and her arms wrapped around his narrow waist. He could feel the sound of her heartbeat against his back.

During that time, Maxine was walking back and forth on the patio when she didn't see Julie. I had been over two hours since Julie went up to search for Louis and she had not heard from her yet. She called at Louis's. His butler told her Louis didn't get home yet.

Jacque had just walked in and asked Maxine for Julie. When she told him about the incident, Jacque got upset. He felt that was one of Louis's tricks to get Julie to come to him.

Maxine thought in a way Jacque was right. Why would Louis throw his helmet down the river? Jacque tried to call Julie. Her phone rang. Maxine thought it was Julie who was calling her. So she answered, "Hello!"

Jacque was standing not too far from her when he said, "Julie?"

Jacque looked at Maxine and realized she had Julie's phone and there was no way now he'd have contact with Julie. Jacque got so mad that he snatched the cell phone from Maxine's hand and accused her of plotting against him!

Maxine couldn't make him out. Why would Jacque think such an evil thing about her? She ignored him and went out to the terrace to wait for Julie.

Carine came and asked what was going on. When Jacque told her, she looked at him and remarked, "Mrs. Philip is not as virtuous as you think she is."

Maxine heard the sound of the bike. She yelled, "They are here!"

Louis pulled close to where Maxine was standing. She jumped for joy when she saw Julie. Louis helped Julie off the bike and asked her if she enjoyed the ride. She told him she used to ride with Saul when they first started to date. She had not ridden in years. Tonight Louis brought all those memories back. She felt like an outlaw, but she did enjoy the feel of it. As he was leaving Julie reminded him of the invitation for dinner on Wednesday. Again he kissed her hands and off he rode.

Slowly Jacque and Carine walked to meet them. Jacque wanted to know why she didn't come home with Maxine. She asked him if Maxine explained what happen. He said yes so then Julie felt she didn't have to give him more information. She walked into the mansion to rest for the night.

That really made Jacque unsettled but what could he do? He was only a brother, not her man. And plus she was like his boss, he was working for her. He nodded his head as she walked away from him.

Later the following day Saul called to tell her he couldn't make it to Haiti. It was impossible for him at the moment. The project was almost through, and he wanted to finish with it. Julie didn't want to hear of it, they had been away from each other too long and she wanted to join him. She told him she was afraid to be away from him, she wanted to be near him. But Saul felt she would be in the way and he wouldn't have the time to spend with her at the moment.

"I love you, Julie," Saul said on the other end of the telephone. "Please be patient. As soon as I finish I'll join you."

Saul didn't let Julie finish telling him how she was feeling, how much she missed him. He hung up before she could tell him she loved him back. She was upset. She felt that Saul was doing something she would not approve of. That was why he wouldn't want her to join him. She was afraid he was doing something very dangerous. She tried to trace the call, but the operator was unable to do so. She sat in silence on the balcony looking at the dark sky, her tears running down her cheeks.

It was a clear and bright sky. There were stars in every direction her eyes could reach, but she couldn't see the stars tonight. Everything was black and distressed. The sky was like a lifeless pit of hell as she looked at it. Tears were not able to stop flowing out of her eyes. No one was able to reach her, not even Marie, who was in the same room with her. Tonight the loneliness she felt was unbearable. Now she really understood what Louis meant when he said he was hurting.

Julie thought as she fell asleep, why was she suffering? What graven sin had she committed that her lover left her in the cold?

"God," she cried out, "help me endure! I'm falling and I don't know why. Help me, hold me up!"

She spent the following day in her room. She didn't want to see or talk to anyone. Maxine came anyway to see her before she went to work, but Julie never spoke a word to her. Maxine was worried. She didn't know what to do. She called Louis, wanting to know what she could give her to bring her back to herself. But Louis told her to leave her alone, letting her think Julie would be okay.

On Wednesday evening, Louis was punctual for the dinner invitation. The butler let him in and escorted him to the living room to wait for Julie. When Marie came and told her Louis was there waiting for her she couldn't understand why was he there till Marie reminded her Louis was there for dinner. Dying with embarrassment she quickly put on her clothes, then ran out of the room to meet him.

She apologized. She forgot to call him to cancel; her husband couldn't make it right now to Haiti. Her mind was not there.

Looking at her face and listening to the sorrow in her voice, Louis apologized for not calling her first to let her know he was on his way. He handed her the flowers and the box he brought. Inside was a bottle of an expensive wine. She asked him to stay, not for dinner but for a drink. He accepted the drink. He sat with her for a little while to cheer her before he went home. He spoke of his ranch to her. He would like to take her there and show her the countryside. She accepted his invitation because she was looking for a place for her animals. She was happy that she didn't call him to cancel.

On hearing Louis was on the premises, Jacque quickly came to join in the conversation. Just when Louis got her to smile, Jacque had to come and spoil everything.

As he made his presence known, Louis got up and told Julie he was leaving. Jacque was trying to persuade him to stay, but Louis was not in the mood to converse with Jacque. He said good night to Julie and left.

Julie, too, was not up to socializing either. She explained to Jacque she needed to apologize to Louis, that was the reason he was there talking to him. Now that he was gone, she wanted to go to her room and rest. Jacque wanted to stay with her to keep her company like he did on the night she first arrived in Haiti. On hearing his request Julie thought back on the conversation she had with Jacque on the terrace a few days ago. The protecting loving brother he was, the innocence of the friendship they had shared when they were children was gone, because Jacque wanted to be more than a loving brother to her. She couldn't dismiss the feelings Jacque claimed he had for her. And she wasn't about to pretend she didn't understand what he was saying and encourage it.

"No! Good night, Jacque."

Julie walked up the steps without a backward glance, turning straight to her room. The next morning Julie called Louis and canceled the invitation. She didn't think it was wise to be near him for the way she was feeling. She spent her time helping the workers who were taking care of her animals, planting, cleaning up the yard, and reading, while Jacque and his brother and sisters were at work. She called her mother almost every night to see how she and her son were doing.

Jacque and Maxine joined her on her horse ride almost every day after work. They knew Julie was feeling down, so they tried hard to make her happy. After two weeks of isolation Jacque took Julie to one of the nightclubs in town to enjoy an evening of entertainment.

On sitting down Julie looked straight ahead and saw Louis sitting, with a couple of women and his associate Henry Claude. He was kissing one of the women sitting next to him. As he was kissing one of the women who was entertaining him, Louis's eyes caught Julie's looking at him from across her table.

Turning her head aside, she looked up at Jacque, who was helping her sit, and thanked him. Jacque smiled when he realized Louis was sitting right across from them.

Slowly Louis moved aside from the women and kept their hands off him. Jacque smiled and bowed his head when their eyes met. He knew now Louis had blown every chance he may have had with Julie.

Noticing the way she was looking at him, Louis took out his handkerchief to wipe his lips to remove the lipstick on his mouth.

Looking at his facial reaction, Henry quickly looked in the direction he was focusing at. Getting out of his seat, Louis straightened his tie and walked toward Julie's table to say hello.

"I didn't know you were coming here tonight. Nice to see you again, Julie."

Looking at Jacque, Julie smiled, then at Louis. "My brother here wanted to cheer me up."

"How kind of him," looking at Jacque he replied, and thought, *Touché, you big grump!*

Smilingly, Jacque invited, "Why don't you and your friends join us?"

What a weasel! Louis thought and said, "It's all right, too many of us. See you around, Julie."

Louis went back to his seat. He sat there looking at her. She took his breath away. The way she looked in that red dress didn't make it easy at all for him. At that moment he was starting to feel tempered. He was no longer having fun.

Jacque got up and asked Julie to dance with him. Gracefully she took his hands, then walked with him to the dancing floor to dance. One of the women sitting by Louis wanted his attention, so she touched him. At the way he looked at her, she quickly sat still and looked at the direction his eyes were staring. The woman wondered who that beautiful woman in that red dress was.

Julie was laughing as Jacque turned her on the dancing floor. Then her eyes met with Louis's. She smiled when she noticed the way Louis was staring at her. She didn't understand why was he looking at her that way. Jacque whispered, "I think we made an audience."

Jacque was happy. He felt things were starting to look good, going his way. He felt the night was ruined for those who were with Louis. He knew Louis wasn't enjoying the company he was with. And at the moment all he could see was jealousy that was in Louis's eyes staring at him and Julie dancing before him. And he could tell Louis wanted to hold her to dance with her. And if looks could kill, his arms would have been ripped off from holding Julie.

Henry noticed the flare that was burning in Louis's eyes. He poured Louis some cognac in his glass. He tasted, but it didn't taste good and he was running out patience. He couldn't focus anymore. After a few minutes, without saying good night, Louis got up and headed for the exit. Henry shook his head as Louis was making his way out of the nightclub, then turned to look at Julie in wonderment, who was busy talking to Jacque.

Almost three weeks went by since the last time Julie heard from her husband. And she had been completely avoiding Louis also. She didn't go any place where she might have bumped into Louis. She worked in the yard, cleaning and planting flowers, plants, and fruit trees around the mansion. Several times Louis called to see how she was doing, but she never answered his call or returned his call. That was driving Louis up the wall. Never in his life did he think a woman would avoid him or treat him like he was a plague. Like Julie, he worked hard so as not to think of her.

Then one early evening while the Bassine family was on the patio having cocktail, one of the maids came and interrupted. "There's a delivery from the florist shop."

Carine instructed, "Bring it here."

The servant went and called the delivery men.

Nicole said, "What is that? That's larger than bouquet."

As the men rolled the plant on a trolley car into the patio, Maxine said, "Looks like a tree."

One of the two men asked, "Where should we put it?"

Pointing to a spot next to the table that was nearest to Nicole, Carine said, "Put it there."

They sat it by the table where Julie would be sitting. Carine uncovered it and exclaimed, "A cactus tree! Who is it for?"

Maxine came and took up the envelope that had been pasted to the cover that Carine carelessly threw on the ground. She said, "You should not have uncovered the gift, Carine. You know it wasn't for you. The card says, 'Madame Philip.' It's for Julie."

She smiled and called Marie, "Call madame, Marie."

Marie ran to call Julie, who was already on her way down. She saw Marie running toward her. "Slow down, Marie." She caught her by both shoulders. "Why are you running so fast?"

Breathless and excited, she answered, "Someone sent you a tree, madame."

"A tree!"

She walked toward them, wondering what was going on. Nicole pointed and said, "It's for you, Julie."

Maxine handed her the card and prompted excitedly, "Read the card, Julie."

With trembling hands, she slowly opened the envelope and read, "'Your shining star'."

Carine laughed. "Your shining star! I wonder who that fool is . . . who in their right mind would send a woman a cactus tree?"

Julie said nothing. She just looked up to the sky and wondering as she touched the plant. Inside the golden pot there was a porcelain man doll dressed in black, lying on a crystal sand bed with a generous-sized ruby in the shape of a heart lying on top of it. Beside the sand bed was a golden, empty thermos. Four desert stones–a jasper, an emerald, a diamond, and a ruby– were encrusted in it. There was a hushed gasp as the people standing around all stood in awe at the beauty of the gems. It was a small king's ransom.

Maxine's eyes bugged out of her head. She said in a hushed whisper, "How romantic this is."

The men who delivered the cactus were about to leave. Julie called to them, "Wait! Jean, do you have money on you?"

Jean nodded. "How much do you want?"

"*Cent Gourde* (Twenty U.S. dollars)."

Jean opened his wallet and gave the men the money. They bowed and thanked Julie and Jean. "Thank you, *madame et monsieur.*"

Julie asked one of the men, "Who send it?"

The man smiled and said, "It's from the florist, madame."

Julie, realizing that was all she was going to find out, she did not persist. "*Merci* (Thank you)."

She stood staring fixedly on the tree and the other gifts and automatically she remembered in one of her dreams, she had seen the same doll she was looking at now except the doll had been crying. Slowly she bent down and picked the doll from the crystal sand bed (that was also attached between the shape of the cactus) and gently placed it on her bosom, as if to comfort it. She thought, *My Jewish boy*, because it was dressed up all in black.

A few drops of sand fell on her blouse as she held the doll to her heart.

Meanwhile, back at Janvier's estate, Louis was playing pool with Henry. The phone rang. Louis answered the phone.

"Yes." He smiled. "I'm glad she accepted it."

As he hung up the phone, Louis felt as if he had literally been touched, as if he was being caressed.

He held tight to the stick. . . . He felt like she was close by him, and her heart was in harmony with his. He dropped the stick and held onto his stomach and moaned. He didn't quite understand the feelings he was having. Henry was wondering what was happening to him. He thought Louis was in pain and rushed to his aid.

Louis waved him back. "No! Stand back. I'm not in pain."

Again he moaned. His face was starting to sweat as was his chest. He let out a shivering sound. Henry didn't know what to do and got scared. He had never seen Louis like this.

He called out for the butler, "Francois!"

Louis panted, "No, don't be afraid, Henry. I'll be just fine."

The room was cool, but sweat was all over Louis's face. His shirt was sticking to his body like someone who had been doing a total body work out. Taking some napkins that were on the bar to wipe his face, he smiled at Henry and said jubilantly, "She received my gift and she accepted it. I guess the excitement got to me."

Henry didn't understand what the gift had to do with the way he reacted. "What is wrong with you?"

"I'm not sure," Louis said and paused to think. Henry looked disturbed by his reaction. Glancing at Henry, Louis examined the way he was looking at him and his question. "I'm not sick! I know what I feel. And I told you I felt as if she touched me while I was speaking to you now. I know that sounds strange, but this is how I'm feeling and I feel good."

"That is very crazy," Henry said as he put his hands over his face, trying to reason with Louis. He calmly said, "I think you should keep away from her, Fuji. If she could do that to you without being here with you, the woman is dangerous to your health and your sanity. And everything that you stand for."

"You always call me Fuji when you're getting on my nerves." Louis tried to control his temper. He grabbed the side of pool table and held on to it. He closed his eyes, then he opened them to look at Henry and said, "I will be insane if you keep on contradicting me."

From that point, Henry didn't want to say anything to upset him. He walked to the bar and fixed Louis a drink. Henry felt something phenomenal was taking place with Louis. He wanted to understand. He wanted Louis to level with him. "I've never see you like this, Fuji. What bond do you have between you and this woman?"

Louis sat back and smiled tranquilly. "It's a long story and unbelievable and the answer to all my problems."

Back at the mansion, Julie still held on to the doll. She, too, was shivering at the strong sensations coursing through her. Maxine was looking at her keenly while everyone else was so busy admiring the jewelry that was in and around the pot. Quietly Julie moved away from everyone. She wrapped her arms around herself, trying to catch her breath. Maxine walked over to her and handed her the heart-shaped ruby. She took one of Julie's cold hands in hers and whispered, "You're trembling. Are you all right, Julie?"

"I'm fine," she stammered.

"Do you know who sent these to you?"

Trying to control her body and the feelings coursing through it, she shook her head. "I don't know."

Maxine touched the gift with reverence. "It might be from Saul."

Carine overheard what Maxine said. "Why would Saul send his wife something without signing his name, especially something of value? Unless he is out of his mind to send something so precious without signing his name?"

Trying to keep her silent, Maxine snapped, "Oh! Be quiet, Carine. You know nothing of love."

With a mocking laugh, she sneered, "Who wants love these days? Show me a person who needs love and I'll call this person stupid."

Maxine slammed, "The only stupid person here is you, Carine."

Nodding her head with a look of disdain, she jeered, "Oh really, Maxine? Money, sex, and power—those things are what count these days. If you're looking for love, you'll be in the poor house or worse in the slums of Port-au-Prince. Take Louis for example: He is filthy rich. You think love would have got him this far? I'll tell you what got him this far—power, exploitation, his good looks, and sex. Certainly not love, baby sister."

Seething, Maxine replied, "You know nothing about him, beside him screwing you."

Julie was appalled. "Stop! Stop this arguing between you two. It should be a happy moment, not a senseless debate, I'm sure. . . ."

Before she could finish her sentence Nicole waved and pointed. "Look! Jacque has arrived." She signaled the girls to be quiet.

Carine ran to meet him, laughing and talking, filling him with the details of what was happening as they walked to meet the rest. The butler brought them a tray of fritters. Hugs and kisses were exchanged between them, then Jacque turned to Jean. "I'm surprised to see you here."

Jean smiled. "You're just early."

With enthusiasm Jacque replied, "I finished early today. I wanted to come home and spend time with my family." He turned and said to Julie, "Don't tell me, the cactus is for you. . . . I know it, Julie. I mean Ms. Cactus. I never thought cactus was beautiful."

Jacque was admiring the plant. He ran his right index finger between the ridge of the plant, avoiding the sharp thorns. "It's pretty, but big and green and look, full of sharp thorns. There's also a thermos. . . ."

He bent down to pick it up and looked inside. "It's heavy. Is there a rattlesnake in it?"

Everyone laughed as he read the writing on the bottom of it. "It's gold, made from African desert stones, very expensive, a twenty-four karat gold vase. My! Who sent this, the sheik, the president, or the king? Girl, that's a pretty big snake you're pulling out of its hole. . . . Maybe it's an anaconda, and you may not be able to bring that serpent in."

Maxine shook her head at Jacque. "You are such a rattle brain. I'm sure Julie is a rattlesnake master. She'll be able to bring it in."

Nicole smiled. "Julie, you've got to give me your secret, maybe I should call myself this name, like you."

Maxine looked at her as if she was crazy. Carine snickered. "That strange thing is from an admirer? He did not leave his name."

Jacque automatically knew who sent that strange thing, but he was not about to tell Julie.

Dreamily Maxine sighed, "That's what you call love."

Carine threw her hand up in despair. "Her and her love. If a man really wants me, he better not send me a cactus plant. . . . Twelve or twenty dozen roses is what it will take."

Jacque cut in, "I wouldn't say roses around Ms. Cactus here!"

Carine looked at Julie in surprise. Everyone loves roses. "Why not?"

Jacque replied, "Because Julie believes a rose cannot survive hardships, but cactus can and it grows in wisdom, so here it is!"

Maxine whispered in Julie's ears, "They're just jealous. Don't listen to them."

Julie turned to Marie, "Please, ask the servants to take it up to my room for me."

"*Oui, madame.*"

Marie and some of the workers carried the plant to her room. Jacque went in to freshen up, and Carine went in to place a call, Nicole following her. They were laughing and carrying on. Jean said to Julie and Maxine, "I'll see you girls later," and walked away.

Maxine turned to Julie. "Ms. Cactus! I like that. I got a feeling I think I know who sent it."

Julie answered, "You do?"

"Uh-huh!"

"Well, tell me."

"I think you also know who sent it."

Julie said, "I do?"

She replied, "Uh-huh! Monsieur Janvier."

Julie was shocked. "Fuji?"

She said, "Oh, *oui.* Who else in Haiti besides the president can buy a plant in a vase of gold? Look at the doll's eyes."

Julie looked.

"You see, emeralds surrounded by diamonds. Look at the outfit. Something he would wear. I think you know who your Jewish boy is now, and the cologne—smell the scent of the doll."

Maxine closed her eyes and inhaled deeply. Julie pulled the doll away. "You're crazy, Max!"

She replied, "Maybe I am. Don't you feel there's something strange in the air? I think you need to look at each of us closely, and especially Jacque. Lately he has not been himself. I think he's about to do something devious. He does and says hurtful things. . . ."

Julie couldn't deny what Maxine was saying. She, too, noticed that Jacque's personality was different. She thought that maybe like her, Jacque was having problems in his relationship.

" . . . I know Jacque cares for you very much, Julie. But his ambition is getting overzealous. Jacque tells everyone what to do and when to do it. He's like Doctor Jekyll and Mr. Hyde. No one knows when his mood is going to change. He's becoming a user and a good for nothing man. I felt the money he borrowed from you was uncalled for. You're too generous, Julie. . . ."

"You're my family," Julie pressed.

" . . . I don't want us to take advantage of you. . . . Jacque thinks I'm having sex with Louis. So I let him and all the rest think that way, because he thinks if I'm with Louis, he has a better chance of getting things from him. If he had a chance, I believe he would have prostituted me. He no longer cares about any of us, only about money and making a profit. Louis only helped him because of me. And some other reason, which I don't know. Carine, you know she's living in a dream world since she was a teenager. Her ultimate goal is to marry the richest man in Haiti. She doesn't care who she hurts or how she's going to get it. Believe me when I tell you that at the moment she's plotting on how to get Louis Janvier. And I know Louis wants one person here, and it is you!"

"No, Louis doesn't want me."

"Don't be blind, Julie. . . . Carine is trying to reach for a star, but she doesn't have what it takes to catch one. Lately all she wants to do is to get near Louis. She's going for mission impossible. I think she's mad. She wouldn't mind sharing the same man with you. I know you knew that too, as long as she could get what she wanted. Nicole is a follower. She's like a monkey. Jean is a coward and he's lazy, as we all well know. He never stood up for himself.

"I'm not blind, Julie. I have known you too long not to know when you are attracted to a man. I saw the chemistry between you and Louis. Your hands get cold and your stomach boils whenever he's around you or when his name is mentioned. . . . I admire you very much. You kept silent, you never let anyone see what you're going through. You're so modest, kind."

Looking away, Julie replied, "If you are able to detect all that in me, I'm not so modest, as you can see, Max."

"Yes, you are." Maxine came closer to her and expounded, "You know how to control your feelings. You think of others first before you think of yourself. I want to be this way, too."

"You do think of others too, Max. . . . But please, don't you ever wish to be like me. You'll suffer." She gazed at the moon, then she closed her eyes and said, "My dreams drove my husband away from me. And now I'm receiving gifts from another man I'm trying hard to keep away from, and I wish he would leave me alone, set me free."

Confused by her statement, she asked, "What do you mean by this?"

"I tried to avoid him, but the more I try the harder it gets. And the more I want to know who he really is. I think I'm becoming obsessed with him. I could hear his voice talking to me, Max. I need to keep him out of my mind. I feel like he is ruling me, and I've been abandoned by God."

Taking her hands in hers, Maxine expounded, "You work harder then usual. Your hands are roughened. You work yourself as if you were a slave. . . . Richard told me Louis was overworking himself, too. He saw more patients then he usually does. He spends more time in the orphanage and locked himself in his room more. He speaks to no one and eats less. He even cut his own grass."

Julie replied, "I don't see anything wrong with that, cutting his own grass. That is his back yard."

"Not when you have many workers to do it for you, like you. Why?"

"You should try it sometime, Max. It's fun."

"Fun! Look at your hands." She lifted Julie's hands to her face. "You could chop wood and break bricks with them."

Looking at her hands, Julie laughed. "Has it ever occurred to you that these hands 'can' chop wood and break bricks?"

"I believe you," Maxine informed her. "You're breaking down Louis and chopping him to pieces. I went by the hospital today to see how Richard was doing. When I spoke to Louis, like you, he tried hard not to ask how you were feeling. When I was leaving he said, 'See you later, *Julie*'. I replied, 'See you later, Fuji, but the name is Maxine'. And that was when he realized what he had called me. He looked at me strangely. . . . That look reminded me of the time his mother passed away. His eyes were like one who was also dead. I am afraid for him, Julie."

"Afraid!" Julie exclaimed. "Don't be fooled by that tyrant. Spend sometime with him and see what I'm telling you."

"Louis considered his time very precious to him. He'll give you money faster than to spend his time with you. I must say, I never saw Louis chasing after any woman. They always came to him, but with you it's different. He created time for you and actually showed up and spent the time. One has to be special for him to give her or him the time and day. I believe you're the one."

"No, Max," Julie said. Trying to suppress the discussion, she reminded Maxine, "I'm a married woman. I can't be the one. And I'm willing to do anything to make my marriage work."

Maxine insisted, "Whether you like it or not, you're very special to him. He looked at you as if he could see his unborn child in you."

Julie stood with her mouth wide open at Maxine's outburst. Then she started laughing and Maxine joined her. She wanted that conversation of her and Louis to end. Between gasps of laughter she managed to get out, "Max, let's have a slumber party. I could do your nails and you'll do my nails. Like the old days. Meet me at the old house. Let's ask Carine and Nicole if they want to join us."

Maxine clapped her on the back. "Now you're talking, girl. I'll race you to the house."

They started to run to the mansion, bumping and screaming hilariously into the servants as they raced for the stairs. Maxine shouted, "The last one is a rotten potato!"

Julie shouted back, "So is the first one!"

Up the stairs they ran and down the hallway, but Julie reached Nicole's room first.

"That's not fair," Maxine complained. "Her room is before Carine's."

Julie stuck her tongue out at her. "That's life. But the race is not over."

Waltzing to Carine's room, Maxine threw over her shoulder, "I'll bet Carine and Nicole will say no. See you in one hour, after I finish talking to you know who."

Maxine was right. They felt it was childish and they both had a previous engagement, like the last time. Only when Julie went inside her room did she remember the doll in her hand. She looked at it, kissed it, and laid it on her pillow.

Finishing getting herself ready, she met Maxine in her room. Together they walked to the old house with a basket full of goodies. As they reached the old place there were lights on and soft music playing. Julie wondered, "Who beat us there!"

Quietly they walked to the old house like two sneaky mice. Julie put the basket down on the steps as she and Maxine sneaked into the back door to surprise whoever was in there.

Boy, were they surprised! Jacque was busy in there with a woman and she wasn't Debbie. Maxine almost laughed, but Julie put her hand over her mouth and they sneaked out the same way they had come in. Picking up the basket, they ran back to the mansion, laughing at what they just saw.

Julie said, "I guess I could just kiss my quiet place goodbye."

Maxine replied, "No you won't. Jacque just has to go to a hotel or to his girl's house. He's just being cheap by not taking her or them out."

Julie did not make any other comment as they waltzed back to her room and had their slumber party. That evening she and Maxine had a wonderful time together, just as they planned to do each other's nails and hair. They laughed, sang, and joked about old times. Maxine told her about Debbie, how Jacque lied to her and cheated on her every now and then (which Julie witnessed tonight), how Debbie would defend him and blame herself for Jacque's behavior. She would even help back up Jacque's lies. She didn't understand why Debbie stayed in that crazy relationship and refused to end that madness, but she figured that Debbie was the only woman who would put up with him.

Jean was still running around with the girls in town, nothing serious going on in his life. And as for Carine, she was the only one Jacque allowed to do as she pleased, but every now and then Jacque would stop her, like he did the night Julie arrived to Haiti, because Louis had canceled the flight on her. Louis had a hotter date that night.

"Boy, was Carine frustrated," Maxine exclaimed. "She was sure this time Louis would have taken her offer."

"What was the offer?" Julie asked curiously.

"You know, take her to bed."

"Take her to bed," Julie uttered.

"Louis wouldn't ask Carine to go anywhere with him unless she promised to introduce you to him. That was the only reason she was inviting you to go flying with them, for a 'threesome'!"

"What do you mean?" Julie didn't quite get what Maxine was implying.

Maxine lifted one of her eyebrows to express what she meant. "You know!"

"Oh! Maxine!" Julie shouted. "Louis must have been out of his mind to think I would have participated in something like that. He's a nasty man!"

Maxine laughed so hard at Julie's response that she almost fell out of the bed as she continued telling her about Carine's outrage, how she accused everyone in her death book except for that Canadian woman who was in town. Maxine went on to tell Julie that she was over at Louis's estate when the woman was there.

"She was hot," Maxine uttered, "because he didn't even take her to his room. Louis took her right on top of the pool table. I was sneaking in around the place when I stumbled on the sight. I think he saw me but he didn't give a damn. I tip-toed backward just as we were walking out of the old house. It was around one in the morning. I think it was after Nadine's hang-out."

Julie said, "The nerve of that man! He was upset when I told him he was the running player in town."

Maxine voiced, "You told him that! Julie, you have guts. No one talks to Louis that way. Especially his women."

"I'm not his woman, so I can talk to him how I see fit. He's a player and I will treat him like one."

Teasingly Maxine replied, "You sound like you are angry at your Jewish boy, Julie."

Julie hit her with the pillow. "No I'm not. And he's not my Jewish boy!"

Hitting her back with another pillow, Maxine laughed. "You're jealous of your French Romanian boy then!"

Julie denied, "No, I'm not!"

"Yes, you are so!"

They played pillow fight for a moment as Maxine continued teasing her back and forth.

Curiously Julie asked, "Louis is Romanian?"

"I heard his father's parents were French Romanian. Richard told me Louis knows how to speak the language. I guess that is the reason he is so irresistible, he speaks the romantic language."

The way she said it made Julie laugh. Then Maxine informed Julie about everyone and everything she could remember. They promised never to keep away from each other for that long.

After that, Julie went on to tell Maxine what took place the other morning during her morning ride with Louis. How he was so upset at her for telling him that she was hoping she would be able to satisfy her husband. She felt that Louis was out of place for telling her that her husband was inefficient to her needs.

"My husband is a great lover," Julie stated. "I don't think any other man could be better than my beloved husband."

She felt that Louis had a lot of nerve to tell her that he felt sorry for her and how he would want to love or be loved by his wife if he ever got one. "He wanted remarkable filet mignon, not T-bone."

"Doesn't he make you curious?" Maxine asked jubilantly.

"No!" Julie yelled. "He only made me feel like punching him off his horse that morning and breaking his neck. . . . No man could be better than my Saul. Louis just has a big mouth and he didn't know when to shut it. I'm pretty sure he's just a lot of talk and no action."

Maxine laughed as if to conclude Julie's sentence. "And that's the reason those women keep on coming back for seconds!"

Julie waved her to be quiet, then she moaned, "I cannot believe my body has rejected my husband. I crave him so much. . . ."

Maxine stopped laughing because Julie was serious at the moment. "Do you think Saul is in another woman's arms, doing to her what I should have allowed him to do to me?"

Maxine said, "I very much doubt that."

Julie signed. "I wouldn't blame him. . . . It's me who had pushed him away with my sex dream of another man."

"That's not your fault, Julie," Maxine worded. "I felt something wrong was done to you, and you cannot remember. And that is causing you to have that dream."

"I don't think so, Max. Saul wouldn't do anything to hurt me."

"Maybe not deliberately. Something had to happen to cause you pain when he tried to make love to you. You're a woman who wants to be touched only by your husband, and yet your body refuses to be touched by him. Something he did caused you to change toward him. It just doesn't make any sense, Julie. Saul may know the answer to this mystery dream you are having."

Julie stayed quiet for a moment as she thought that the discussion that they were having was meaningless. She smiled and gasped, "Maybe he has the answer."

Since Julie couldn't come up with better response, she changed the conversation to the gifts she had received tonight. She let Maxine know that she wanted to return these gifts, but because he left no name, it was going to be difficult to do so. "I know he sent them, but he'll deny it just to make me look stupid."

Julie told Maxine about the married woman Louis slept with and the child she conceived by him. And how he loved that woman. When she told Maxine who the woman was, Maxine repeated with laughter, "The wife of his best friend!"

She was shocked, but still she thought with Louis that was not impossible. They sat for a moment in silence staring at each other, drinking their homemade wine, making faces at each other while they sucked on *puenêpe* that had been soaked in hard liquor and brown sugar and laughed about Louis's situation. They knew it was not funny but they couldn't help it.

The following day, it was back to the same old routine. Everyone was busy. Jacque had promised to take Debbie out, but he didn't want Julie to know, so he sneaked out.

Julie went to the orphanage to drop some bags of clothes and shoes she was not going to wear anymore. On her way out she bumped into Louis, who was also visiting. She thought, *Why is he not at the hospital?*

They both were happy to see each other, but they acted calmly as they said hello. Both were heading for the parking lot. Julie didn't say anything and neither did Louis. Then he said, "I want to show you something and I want your honest opinion. It's not too far from here."

Julie looked at the time and agreed. They each took their own car. Julie followed him as he drove his way through the traffic down toward the plain of Port-au-Prince. When they reached there, Julie pulled behind his car and parked. She was surprised to see the project she always had in mind being constructed by the man Jacque called ruthless.

Cautiously they walked through the work field, looking at the work the men were doing. On seeing Louis, the head mason came to greet him and the handed them hats to put on their heads. Julie looked at the place with joy and listened to Louis as he explained the site they were in. She was even more intrigued. She felt that the man could read her heart and put them into action. She said, "Fuji, I would like to invest in the project, to help build more of what I'm looking at."

Louis smiled because she was pleased. Lunch was getting near and he noticed Julie was getting hungry by the way she covered her mouth to yawn. He suggested to talk about it over lunch, then asked her to leave her car. Later he would come for it. They drove a few miles to a nice restaurant. While they were eating, he said, "Definitely the community has to have a restaurant or may be a mall."

Julie smiled in agreement. After lunch he took her back to where her car was parked. She thanked him for a good day and drove off.

▦   ▦   ▦

After that day she didn't hear from Louis. It was over two weeks since she last heard from him. Jacque had told her Louis was out of town but he didn't tell her where he traveled to. While in the family room reading, she overheard Marie telling Maxine that Louis was away to America, in Connecticut. She wondered what was he doing there. She pretended she wasn't paying attention to what Marie said to Maxine.

Maxine came and sat by her and said, "I heard Louis has a very big mansion up there, bigger than what he has here in Haiti."

Julie didn't reply. In a way she was happy to know that Louis was out of town. She didn't hear from her husband either. The following morning Maxine came by her room to tell her she was going to be home late tonight because she was doing inventory at the hotel. Jacque also let her know that he was not coming home tonight because he was going out of town. Everyone had something to do. Even Jean was going to be busy, so tonight she knew she was going to have dinner alone. She stood on her balcony alone, looking at the view of the Bassine mansion. It was beautiful, but there was nothing new for her to look at. Later that afternoon she decided to go by the river to do some clean up. She carried a small basket of fruit to snack on and a big bottle of cold ice water to drink.

After finishing removing the dry leaves and fruit, she sat under her tree looking at the river water running by and dozed off. Deep in her thoughts she heard crunching footsteps. Startled, Julie called, "Who's there?"

Louis spoke from behind her, "Don't be afraid. It's only me."

Looking around, she realized it was dark. She asked, "I thought you were away."

"I returned last night. There was something my best friend wanted me to do for him so my departure was unexpected."

Julie asked, "Did he let you see your son?"

"No," Louis said sadly.

"Have you accomplished what your best friend wanted you to do for him?"

"Tonight I'll know," he replied.

"What are you doing here?"

"I was just riding by," Louis said, "and I was hoping to see you here. I had the feeling that one day you would be brave again to come here by yourself at night, wandering about like this. You might stumble on to a snake."

"I didn't know I was going to stumble on to one tonight," Julie said as she got up to leave the river.

He was standing in her way so she tried to walk by him, but Louis held her back. "Wait. Please don't go. Why are you trying so hard to avoid me. Am I that bad of an influence, Julie?"

"No one can influence me if I don't want to be, Louis."

"Then I shall remember that. Let's go for a good ride for old time's sake. At least you could have given me one last good ride before you disappear on me."

Nodding her head, Julie laughed and said, "You sure know how to put your words together."

Smiling into her eyes he replied, "You know that's what buffoons do best."

Helping pick up the basket and the trash bag, he then crooked his arm for her to hold onto and silently they walked to the barn. When they arrived she questioned, "Why have you not come for your horses?"

"They're yours. I gave them to you. I knew you wouldn't accept them if I had bluntly given them to you like that. I bred them myself. I never let anyone ride them, beside you. Please accept them."

"They're two beauties," she said as she passed her hands over their shiny coats as she helped to saddle them. She was impressed. "Did you say you breed them yourself?"

"Yes," Louis answered while he double-checked if the saddles were secured.

"You're a cowboy at heart." Julie smiled.

"You could say we have a lot in common." When he finished he turned to help her mount the horse and inquired, "May I?"

They rode up in the mountain for a while, then back down to the river. They stopped where she had been sitting before, under the great almond tree. Julie asked, "Did you also send those gifts to me?"

"What were the gifts?" he asked, like he didn't know.

She listed, "The cactus, the thermos, the golden vase, the ruby, and the male doll dressed in black and the card signed 'Your shining star'. Was the doll supposed to represent you?"

"So you finally admit that I look better than your husband."

"I never said that."

"In your eyes I look like a doll. And bright as a shining star."

"In your dream," Julie responded.

He smiled. "For the moment I could live with that."

Admiring the full moon she said, "Look at the moon. Its reflection is so beautiful on the water."

Getting off his horse, he moved toward her and said, "It is beautiful enough to deceive a woman."

Ignoring his comment Julie said, "I want to wet my feet in the water."

She removed her boots and her socks from her feet, rolled up the hems of her pants to her knees, and carefully walked toward the reflection of the moon. Louis did the same. He watched how Julie was enjoying the feel of the cold water on her feet. She spoke through chattering teeth. "It feels good, but it's cold."

She spoke of the time she was a little girl. The memories of her father came to mind, how she used to love coming here by the river with him. She remembered the way he used to carry her around on his shoulders. They used to play in the water like two children.

She glanced at Louis while she was talking. With his hands in his pockets, Louis was regarding her tenderly, but he was listening attentively to what she was telling him. He moved toward her. He couldn't hold onto his feeling any longer. "Can I hold you, Julie?"

She looked at him, stopped talking, and walked out of the water. She went and stood under the almond tree. Tilting her head up, she gazed at the moon's brightness. She held on to the tree, taking deep breaths, trying to fight the feeling she was beginning to have. Louis came over to her, pulled her into his arms, and wrapped them around her.

Julie felt the same sensation she was feeling the night she arrived in Haiti. How she wanted to feel that touch again. She leaned her head back against his chest. He bent his head down to smell the fragrance of her hair. *Acacia*, he thought.

Louis closed his eyes to kiss the top of her head and inhaled the perfume of her hair. He caressed her hair with his cheeks and lips. A soft feeling came over her as he held her within his powerful masculine arms. He gradually turned her around so she could face him, then he lowered his head and tasted her lips. Her rosy lips tasted sweeter than honeysuckle in his mouth. Julie felt the earth moving beneath her feet.

She held on to him tighter as he consumed her with his tender lips. She felt like she was drowning but felt safe in his arms. She was lost in ecstasy. Both were losing control. He felt an electric shock running right through his body. He exhaled a gentle sound as he held her tighter and whispered to her, "I want you."

Sighing, she looked into his eyes and felt his loneliness as he spoke. "I want to make you mine. I need you, Julie."

Shocked at her own behavior, she tried to pull away, exclaiming, "Oh my God!"

Breathing deeply she put her hands on his chest and pushed away from him. Wrapping her arms around herself to stop from shaking, she looked at him with wonder. "I can't believe I did that."

A sad feeling came over her. She shook her head in disbelief at her own action. She held on to herself, wondering what just happened. How could she break her own marriage vows? What possessed her to do something like this? She stared at him with tears in her eyes. She felt pain running through her body and her mind was in turmoil. Her head was spinning. She looked up at the night sky. The feeling of emptiness was stronger than ever.

Cautiously and gently Louis moved toward her while explaining to her, "The loneliness that you are experiencing now is what I've been feeling for a very long time. For almost two years I've dreamt of you, Julie. I think you knew it, too. This is the first time I've felt good holding onto someone. I finally feel complete. You complete me, Julie."

Louis couldn't believe he was pouring out his heart to her. He had to let her know how he felt about her. Louis walked closer to her, pleading to her as once again he wrapped his arms around her, "Don't fight it, Julie. Please don't push me away . . . hold onto me, let me complete you."

Holding her close to him he closed his eyes, kissing her forehead, cheeks, and nose. The emptiness she felt suddenly disappeared. No more pain or loneliness.

He raised her face gently and brought his face down. Parting her lips with a gentle nudge of his, he kissed her tears away. She removed her lips from his and with tears shimmering in her eyes said, "I must go back."

Reluctantly he released her, still pleading, "Come with me tonight."

"What were you expecting, Louis? For me to take off with you?" With a deep sigh she said, "You have got to be joking! What are you going to do with me when I go with you tonight? Have sex with me, add me to your collection, treat me like a whore? What happened tonight would not happen again."

Julie didn't even put on her boots. She ran up the hill to her horse and galloped away, leaving Louis behind as he called out, "Julie!"

She didn't stop, she rode off. Louis was disappointed. He was hoping she would have accepted his request. He stared at the moon, and wondered how he was going to capture her. He walked over to where she had left her stuff. He sat down, picked up her socks and her boots, and placed them beside him. Then he pulled on his socks and boots. He was frustrated. He sat under her almond tree, throwing small pebbles in the water, thinking about his next move.

After a while he got up to remove the saddle on the back of his horse and set it free on the land. He picked up Julie's things then headed for his home. He didn't want to ride home. He walked so he could think.

By the time Julie returned, Maxine was looking for her around the yard of the mansion. She bumped into Julie, who was going to the old house.

Surprised she whispered, "Where were you?"

Julie didn't answer. Looking at Julie, Maxine noticed she didn't have her shoes or her socks on and she looked disturbed and shaky. She followed Julie to the old house, wanting an explanation. "Were you with Louis?"

Like a little girl, she nodded her head to say yes, then whispered, "I let him kiss me. After all the talk you and I had. I kissed that man tonight. I can't believe I cheated on my husband."

"Not yet," Maxine smiled. "You haven't slept with him."

Sadly she confessed, "The way I let him kiss me and how I kissed him, yes that was definitely cheating. My body yielded to his touch, Max! I wanted him. When I'm with him, I seem to forget about everything. I'm losing my mind over that man . . . I already committed adultery. I've been committing adultery for quite some time with him in my mind. It was a matter of the right time."

Julie lay on her bed crying while Maxine tried to comfort her. Nothing she said was going to make Julie feel better. All she wanted to do was to get away. Removing herself from the bed, Julie walked to her closet and took out a suitcase and started to pack.

Maxine said, "Are you going to run away every time a man kisses you? . . . Then again, Louis is not just a man, but still, you know, you should not let him drive you out of town. That's not fair, Julie."

Without stopping from packing, she replied, "Maxine, if I don't get away from that man I could kiss my marriage goodbye. And I'm not about to give up on Saul. He doesn't deserve that."

"Where is Saul?" Maxine asked. "I don't see him picking up the broken pieces of you. Instead he took off on a secret project to get away. He left you to pick up the broken pieces by yourself!"

Maxine was angry because Julie was running away, but there was nothing she could do. Julie was not going to listen to her. She told Maxine, "I'm going to Jacmel to spend some time there. Maybe by then the feeling I have for Louis would be gone."

Maxine knew she was fooling herself. "You did that already and you ended up in his arms, kissing with him. You two are like magnets to each other, don't you see?. . . Louis never rode on our land till you came along."

She stopped talking and let Julie do what she wanted to do. She thought maybe that would make her feel better.

Chapter Nine

Far from Over

Julie went up to Jacmel to her parents' birthplace and spent a couple of days there. While she was there she reestablished her parents' dream, the vineyard passion fruittree plantation. Her mother wanted to help out with the work, but she was unable to at the moment. Everything was still there. All the machines and industrial equipment were still sitting inside the factory. Her mother had put a stop to it because there were too many things for her to handle after the death of her father. Julie felt it was her job to help establish that for her parents. The land was a nice size, and it was under development. She felt the vineyard would be good for the people and she was creating jobs for those who wanted to work. Less then a week later, she got everything together. She was able to hire one hundred people for the agricultural work, and the workers she had before. Like that, things were able to move faster. Together with the help of a few good friends she was able to plant the passionfruit trees on the plantation.

Julie worked hard, and she wasn't expecting less from anyone either. She was so busy she didn't have time to think of her husband or what had happened between Louis and her. She made sure everything was moving smoothly.

Two weeks had gone by when Maxine and Jacque decided to come up to see how she was doing. She seemed to be very happy. Julie showed them the work she was doing. But Jacque felt she shouldn't be working that hard or putting her hands in that dirty soil. She should let the workers do the job by themselves.

Julie didn't agree. One of the important lessons she had learned from her parents when she was a child was, "When you want the job to go according to the way you wanted it to be, you had to do it yourself or be there to help show the person how you would like it to be done."

They only stayed for one day then they went back to the city. She was happy to see them. Maxine had wanted her to return with her, but she felt she needed more time, plus she had a new project she was working on. Things were going well. But at night when she fell asleep the dream came back, it was unavoidable. She prayed that Louis found what he wanted. She knew it wasn't her Louis wanted, he wanted the wife of his best friend. She realized she was more attracted to him then she thought because when the lights turn off, Louis's presence seemed to be with her. She prayed hard to removed the temptation that was befalling her by concentrating on her husband Saul.

She took long walks and rode her donkey and her car around town. She visited friends and relatives. She had brought plenty of dry fishes, a couple of gallons of olive oil and dry milk, and many other things she thought that might help her province friends.

The mountain was beautiful, just as she expected it to be. People there were very friendly. It was always a joy for her to go to Jacmel. She visited the banana plantation where some of her relatives and friends were working and her cattle farm. They, too, were in very good shape. She was happy to see that she was appreciated by the people for the way she took care of things. She helped fixed the barn house for her cattle and some of the projects they were building on the ranch while she was there. She had a good time with the people and it was always a joy for them, watching how she worked hard on helping to fix the place. They had never seen any woman like her. She was beautiful, wealthy, and down to earth. Everyone treated her with respect.

Julie even watched a cock fight. She thought that it was very barbarian, she wasn't happy to see that the people were still doing things like that, but she was glad the roosters didn't kill each other. She was so glad that it was not happening on her land. Before she left town all of them brought plants as gifts and she was happy to accept them. It had been over a month since Julie went to Jacmel when she felt it was time for her to return back home. By then Louis would have run off with one of his women, she thought.

She was brushing her hair while she looked out of the window listening to the sound of the night, thinking how she was way over the incident that took place between Louis and her.

She whispered to herself, "Louis is a man who cannot do without having sex. And by now he's in the arms of some other woman."

She thought, if she ever saw him on the field or out in a nightclub, she would feel safe to face him again.

Back at the capital, Louis was going crazy. He personally wanted to go to Jacmel to bring her back, but Henry talked him out of it. He felt Louis would have damaged any chances he might have with Julie.

"Be patient, Fuji," Henry counseled. "You shocked her. Julie didn't see you coming. She thought she could have overcome the attraction you two have by facing you and being around you. She forgot she was just a 'little cactus' and you are a 'deadly snake' that was crawling up in her desert plant." He smiled. "You have her just where you wanted her to be."

"I wanted her to run into my arms," longingly Louis expressed. "My intention was not to run her off. I wanted her to want me the way I wanted her. I thought she would have understood that when we kissed."

"You have to remember Julie is still married," Henry said as he tasted his drink. "And she wanted to uphold her dignity. Like I said before, she's not like the women we've met in our life. She's going to want more. . . . The woman is like a vampire. I think she's already sucking you dry. You shouldn't give her time to think or breathe when you have the chance. You should have taken her right there and then. And you know you have the upper hand. Right now is the best time to take her. She will do whatever you want her to do. . . ."

Louis stretched back with his hands on the back of his head on his comfy chair to look at Henry while he was talking to him. Henry couldn't make him out. He thought he had Louis's complete attention.

" . . . And at the same time, Julie's no joke." Henry laughed. "She sent you home looking like a puppy. I think you need to go out and have some fun, like old times. There are hundreds of women waiting on line to cater only to you, with no strings attached."

Louis didn't respond, still looking at Henry running his mouth. "Do you hear me, Fuji? I wouldn't be surprised if Julie is having a hell of a good time, just like in the nightclub. You know what she did? I'll tell you since you left all of us at the party very rudely. She danced all night long with that Jacque, laughing and drinking her pretty little head away. And here you are again, right here moping over her. . . . I invited a few of our female friends, and they desperately wanted to come to you, to cheer you up!"

Louis got out of his seat and opened the door. Henry exclaimed, "That's the spirit, brother! Let's go and have some fun. . . ."

Putting the glass on the bar, Henry quickly picked up his vest, nodding his head in a dancing matter, and smiled at Louis, who was holding on to the door for him. He stopped to tap Louis on his shoulder before he walked out of the lounge, then turned to say, "We're going. . . ."

Louis didn't even let him finish his sentence. He slammed the door behind him and locked the door. If Henry didn't take an extra step away from the door, Louis would have hit his face.

Henry stood out of the lounge behind the door calling, "Fuji! Fuji!"

Louis didn't answer. He went right back to the same position he was sitting in before thinking how he wanted Julie and wishing she had accepted his offer.

The following day Louis went to see Maxine. She was dictating to her secretary when he dropped by her office to see her.

He stood by the opened door and said, "I left several messages for Julie and Marie couldn't tell me when would she return."

"You didn't even greet me," Maxine smiled as she walked to give him a kiss on his cheek.

"Good morning, Maxine," he said.

"We'll continue this later." Maxine waved her secretary out of her office so she could talk to Louis in private. With mouth open, her secretary left her office. She was busy looking at Louis with admiration and talking to Maxine, causing her to bump her head on the door while she was leaving the room. As soon as the secretary closed the door behind her, Maxine replied as she walked back behind her desk, "Didn't I tell you to leave her alone? No, you have to put your lips on hers. . . ."

Louis looked at his watch as Maxine spoke, " . . . I see, you don't have the time to hear what I have to say, except what you come here to find out. Well today you will! All my life I've searched for someone nice, and I finally find her–Julie. She is so kind and modest. I heard so many bad things about you, Louis. I have seen what you are capable of doing. But I feel under this metal shield you put around you, there's a heart beating and pumping blood through your body. I don't want to see her hurt, Louis. She is hurting now, please leave her alone. Don't bother her."

Totally ignoring what Maxine was saying, Louis repeated, "When will she return? And please don't make me ask again."

Upset by his response, Maxine pushed her chair back against the wall, got out of her seat, stood up, placed both hands on the desk, and leaned over to look up at him, then said, "And what if I don't!"

Louis put back on his shades and walked out of her office. Maxine sat back on her chair. She didn't like his departure. She got out of her chair and ran after him so she could explain how Julie was feeling when she left town. By the time she caught up to him he was already by his car. It bothered her that Julie left on his account, and that Julie desperately wanted to make her marriage work. Then Maxine told him that Jacque was supposed to pick her up to bring her back to the city tomorrow. She couldn't understand why, with all the women Louis had, he was bothering Julie. She was afraid Louis was preying on Julie because at the moment, she was vulnerable.

"I shouldn't tell you anything," Maxine concluded. "Jacque will kill me."

Louis smiled. "So she's returning tomorrow."

"I didn't tell you that."

"You didn't tell me what?" he responded.

She replied, "Nothing."

Louis drove off and said, "What goes up must come down." Meaning, the city in the mountain where Julie was.

Jacque had returned to take her back home. On her way back to the city, the thought of Louis Janvier popped up on her mind. She shook her head, trying to erase his feature out of her mind. Jacque took a quick glance at her and asked, "Are you all right?"

She told him she was fine and talked about her adventure. The place lifted up her spirits. She felt good and ready to face anything that was before her. She asked him how his relationship with Debbie was going, but Jacque didn't want to talk about it.

He replied, "No better than yours, Julie."

Julie didn't press. She felt Jacque had his say. He mostly wanted to talk about her and what he hoped to happen between them. That was for her to give him complete trust. Julie felt she trusted him enough and she wasn't about to give any man complete trust besides her husband. She changed the conversation on him and talked about the mountains of Haiti and the providence she brought back with her.

She made him stop on Grand-Rue to see an old family friend who was still working in a hardware store. He was very happy to see her, and he promised to drop by to see her soon. Grand-Rue was one of the busiest roads in Port-au-Prince. People were everywhere in and outside of the stores selling their goods. She stopped at Maché Vallière to buy a couple of paintings, some wooden statues, and pottery. Although she loved Haiti, she felt the place needed a lot of improvement. Her heart pained when she looked at the poverty of most people in Port-au-Prince.

Julie spent two months in Jacmel and felt rejuvenated. She felt she would be able to concentrate on all her projects better. She needed a place for her animals, a home for herself, her husband, and son to live. Jacque promised to check on some land, but so far what she was looking for was not on the market. She thought that was strange, because there was plenty of empty land outside of the city. She hoped that Jacque found a property where she could draw well water to irrigate her new place.

Later that night, she asked her mother Viviane to come to Haiti with her son William and she agreed. Her mother felt Julie's son would be good for her while she was in Haiti. She had been away from her son too long. They arrived the following day in Haiti.

Even though Julie looked jolly, her mother knew she was lonely and she was not about to watch her daughter getting depressed on her. She decided to invite a few good friends over the weekend for little cook-out, with the help of Maxine and Marie. Among the guests they invited was Louis Janvier, whom Julie tried hard to stay away from. Jacque wasn't too pleased with the event, but he would not dare tell Aunt Viviane what to do. He could only hope that she left very soon.

Louis seemed to charm Julie's mother. They spent a lot of time talking during the party. Louis smiled when his eyes met Julie's, but she looked away. She thought, *I could just wring Maxine's neck for inviting him.*

She was standing far from Louis, talking to some old friends she had not seen for quite some time. Louis was admiring the way she was holding the baby. Her mother noticed the attraction between them, but chose to say nothing. Louis excused himself and walked over to her to say hello. Her friends noticed that Louis wanted to talk to her. They excused themselves and went to talk with her mother.

The baby started to cry. Putting his hands out for the baby he said, "Can I hold him?"

Julie handed him the baby and the baby became quiet. With tenderness he held on to the baby and kissed him on his little forehead. William took a hold of his nose, which got Julie and Louis to laugh. He went and sat on to the nearest chair with the baby playing with him. That was the first time William gave an outburst laugh. Julie was happy to hear such a pleasant laughter. The baby laughed before, but she had never heard him laugh like that. She sat by him watching and admiring the way he was playing with her son, which compelled her to whisper to him, "I hope you have your son with you and your dream comes true."

Looking at her, Louis smiled and agreed. That was the very first time they spoke since the night they kissed. Maxine came by and commented, "Louis, you look good with the baby."

Maxine watched how Louis held and kept looking at the baby with love and tenderness. He kissed his little feet and hands, causing Julie to blush when he glanced at her. Again she commented, "I never thought you had that side in you, Louis."

Forgetting Maxine was sitting by them, Louis asked, "How about a picnic tomorrow? You know, you, me, and the baby."

Maxine scratched her cheek with a knowing expression, when she heard what he asked Julie. She quickly removed herself from their presence and walked back to Viviane. Julie didn't even notice if Maxine had left their sight. She was nervous when she heard herself accepting Louis's invitation. They sat with each other playing with the baby. Jacque came by and asked if he could hold the baby.

"No," Louis answered without taking his eyes off the baby. "You have plenty of time to play with him and to play uncle. Now if you don't mind, move. You're blocking the light."

Jacque was furious at Louis's rudeness, but more so at Julie because she didn't make Louis hand him her baby. Jacque pulled on one of his earlobes and walked backward, looking at them sitting by each other talking and playing with the baby as if he wasn't there. He backed into Carine, who was also watching how Louis was admiring the baby. Jacque whispered, "That has to stop!"

Jacque walked away and told Carine to follow him. They went and sat in a private corner so he could tell Carine about his plan and her role in it. From a distance, while they were talking, they watched how Julie was smiling while Louis spoke to her. Carine listened carefully to Jacque as he reminded her of their plan.

She said, "Jacque, did he tell you to move away from the baby?"

"Yes!" Jacque said. Carine told him that Louis snapped at her, too, for asking to hold the baby.

Later on that night after the party, Maxine was helping Julie prepare the food for tomorrow's picnic. She said, "Louis seems to be a difficult man. . . . I did not see him eat anything during the party. You think he'll enjoy the beef conch that I'm preparing and the salad?"

"Anything you prepare." Maxine beamed. "I believe he'll eat it. You're a good cook!"

Jacque was passing by when he overheard Julie talking to Maxine in the kitchen. He came in and told her that Saul had called, and he thought she was sleeping so he didn't want to disturb her. Saul wanted her to pick him up at the airport and he would be there at three tomorrow.

She was surprised and happy to hear that Saul was finally coming to Haiti to be with her and he was doing fine. The following day she called Louis and canceled the picnic. She told him about the arrival of her husband. Louis couldn't believe what he was hearing, but he had no choice but to accept her decision.

This time Louis invited her, her mother, and husband over to his place for dinner. She accepted the invitation. That was the least she could do for canceling on him. Viviane didn't go with them to the airport. She waited for them at the mansion instead and had the servant prepare one of Saul's favorite dishes.

Julie and Jacque were at the airport by three waiting for Saul. The plane from New York had just landed. She was all excited waiting for Saul to step outside the plane. Every time someone stepped out of the plane, her heart skipped a beat.

She said to Jacque, "If he doesn't come out here soon, I'll have a heart attack."

Everyone was out of the plane. She watched the workers go out to the plane to clean it out for the next group to board, and still there was no sign of Saul. She asked, "Are you sure it was today or on this flight Saul said he was coming, Jacque?"

"Yes, I'm sure." She went and asked for information about the arrival of her husband. There was no one by that name onboard nor for the following days to come.

Jacque said he couldn't understand that. He exclaimed, "He called last night and told me he was arriving today! Carine witnessed the call. I know I'm not crazy to have you and me come here waiting for him." Jacque went on to say, "How could he treat you like that? I would have never treated you like that."

He acted more upset and was more disturbed then Julie was so that she forgot about herself. He was so unable to calm down she had to drive them home. Viviane was waiting with the baby in her arms on the patio.

"Where's Saul?" she asked.

Julie didn't answer. That was the very first time anyone could actually see the down look on Julie's face. She kissed William on his forehead, then made her way up to her room. She left Jacque to do the explaining. Her mother was horrified by Jacque's explanation. She went up with William to Julie's room. She was lying on her bed when Viviane walked in.

Viviane commanded, "Get up."

She rolled herself to sit at the edge of the bed. "What are you doing? I don't know what Saul is doing but I don't like what he's doing to you. I'm not going to sit here watching you sheltering yourself like that."

"I don't want to go anywhere, Mom, but I'm going for a good swim in the pool."

She got herself ready for a swim in the pool with William. She had a wonderful time playing in the pool with him while Viviane watched them play. Later that evening Louis called to see how she was doing. She told him about Saul, and he still wanted them to come over.

Jacque didn't go to his office that morning. He had lunch with her and William. Every time Jacque tried to take the baby from her, William would cry. He didn't want Jacque near him. He couldn't even play with him. Julie found herself making excuses for her baby. "He's not used to you, that's all."

"Well," Jacque said, "he wasn't used to Louis, but he let Louis hold him. . . ." Talking to the baby, he said, "I'm family, William, not that man, Louis." To Julie he said, "Have you ever considered remarrying?"

"No, Jacque, never."

"I think you should," Jacque stated.

"Do you have someone in mind for me, Jacque?"

"Yes, me."

"You're his uncle," Julie's answer.

Jacque said, "William will need a father to help him balance. I'm afraid Saul doesn't want to take the responsibility of his job. No matter how good the mother is with her baby, a child will always needs its father. I think you'll need my help."

She ignored him with his statement, so he concluded, "I'll be good for you, Julie. Am I so ugly? Is that the reason you don't want me?"

The way he said it made her smile. "No, Jacque, you're very good looking. Your cat eyes are to kill for."

"But I can't kill you with them, is that it?"

"I'm sure Debbie would die for them."

"Like I told you before," Jacque responded, "Debbie is not the woman I'm in love with."

"I'm sorry to hear that," Julie retorted. "I hope you find the one you really love, but it's not me, Jacque. I want you to have a woman who would love you as much as you love her. I would not be good for you and I would never understand."

"I could help you give me a chance. Let me make you love me."

"I love you already."

"Not like a brother," Jacque agitatedly said, "like a man!"

Julie was upset by his request. "You cannot make me love you that way, Jacque. That kind of love you're wanting from me is impossible, it's unnatural! I need you as a brother, not as a lover."

She didn't want to listen to him. She removed herself out of the family room and left for her room with William. She couldn't believe what Jacque was asking her, and why at this time in her life was he pushing her? What was wrong with him?

Jacque sat there looking at her departure. He was furious and wondered was it because he was not rich enough for her, or was it because he borrowed money from her or does she feel more superior than he? He sat there wondering as he watched her heading toward the door with her son. But there was one thing he was not wondering about and that was how to get Louis out of the picture and how he was going to get very rich.

The following day Louis called to let Julie know he would send his car to escort them to his estate. Henry Claude was to pick them up from the Bassine mansion. It was five-thirty when Henry arrived. Roy the butler answered the door and said, "I'm sorry, Monsieur Claude, Madame Philip and her mother are not home. They went out ten minutes ago."

"Did they tell you where they were going?"

"No, Monsieur Claude."

"Oh well, I'll meet them there then." Henry left in distress. He couldn't understand why they left when they knew Louis would send his car to take them to his estate. That just didn't make any sense to him. He drove away as Julie and her mother were walking down to meet him with the baby.

"What happened to Monsieur Claude?" Julie asked.

The butler replied, "Monsieur Claude told me that Monsieur Janvier had a previous engagement to attend, so he sent him personally to cancel dinner and to tell you that he was sorry."

Julie stood there looking at him, then her mother. She was stupefied. "I guess that's a payback for all the times I stood him up. Well, I guess we'll have dinner here tonight."

Viviane couldn't understand why Louis canceled them like that. How disrespectful of him. She didn't let Julie know what she was thinking. She agreed with her and had their dinner at home, but one thing she knew—when she saw Louis again she would give him a piece of her mind.

Jacque was just arriving. He was holding two bouquets of flowers in his hands. He handed Julie and Viviane one bouquet each. They thanked him as he handed them the flowers. Julie didn't ask why he gave them flowers. She put them on the coffee table and ignored him. She continued talking to Maxine and her mother, who was also thinking about what Louis did. By then almost all the members of the family were present, and they were ready to have their dinner.

While they were eating, Louis had arrived at the mansion. Roy had answered the door. The look on Louis's face was not to be lied to. Roy quickly directed him to the dining room. Louis stood by the door with a glare in his eyes and said, "*Bonsoir* (Good evening)!"

Julie was surprised to see him. Placing the napkin on the table, she removed herself from the table and walked toward him and went to greet him. Jacque's eyes flared with anger but were shocked at the same time. He quickly pulled an empty chair said, "Louis, join us for dinner."

Louis was still looking at Julie, pulling his driving gloves off his hands, when he answered Jacque, "No, thank you."

Louis didn't look happy when Julie looked at his eyes. She excused herself from the dining room and walked with Louis to the living room, wondering what was on his mind.

When they reached the living room Louis demanded an explanation. "Why did your butler tell Henry you were coming to my home, and here you are having dinner, while you kept me waiting? At least you could have called and canceled like you always do."

"I thought you sent Henry to tell me that you had a previous engagement and dinner was canceled."

"Did Henry tell you that himself?"

"No, the butler told me." Shaking her head in disbelief, she said, "I smell something very fishy here."

So Julie called Roy. He told her it was Jean's idea to do that. Since Jean wasn't there to defend himself, Julie dismissed him and apologized to Louis. Viviane couldn't believe why Jean would do something like that. Then again, the way he'd been acting lately, who knows, she thought.

Dinner was ruined, but the night was still young. Louis and Julie walked around the mansion, talking. That was the very first time Louis actually visited the place. Julie told him that her father used her idea on how to build the mansion. She was five when the place was under construction. She wanted her room to be high up above all the other rooms in the house, like a princess. She used to make believe that she was Juliet and Romeo would stand right where they were standing, reciting poetry to her.

Louis asked, "Did your fantasy ever come true?"

"No," Julie said.

"Then tonight let me make it come true for you." Turning her face to look at him, he wanted her to go to her room and stand in her balcony. And he would climb and stand on the outer side of her balcony to recite his poetry to her.

"It's quite tempting," she smiled, "but I want to hear you here."

There was a marble bench under her window. Louis helped her sit as he kneeled on one knee before her, holding to one of her hands. He looked at her as he made up one of his own poems to recite to her.

If you look into my eyes,
All you'll see is you and how much I want to love you.
Close your mind for just one moment,
And let my heart touch your heart.
You will feel and see how deep our love really goes.
My darling, please don't push this moment away.
Let me embrace you with my mind, let me kiss you and caress you with my
    words,
Let me love you as you love me, before our time began.
Because on this earth there's no love greater than the love I want to give to
    you. . . .
Of all the great wonders of the world,
None are greater than my love for you.
Eternity is the only enough to show the measure of my love for you. . . .
For you have brought happiness in my life, just when I thought it was once
    upon a time.
Then you came along and changed my life completely.
Never did I dream or thought that I would have found a woman like you.
Your smile, every word you speak, I know you're the one to save me.
And I can't imagine living without you. . . .
With you, I see no darkness,
All I see is my dreams in your eyes brightening my path. . . .
Julie . . . let me be your shelter, your solitude, your comfort,
And all this life would offer you.
You and me together for always,
No more hiding our feelings,
Let us express what has been holding us captive.

Louis pressed her one hand against his chest so she could feel how his heart was pounding inside his chest for her. How his body was reacting to what he was telling her. He declaimed,

Come to me, mon amour *(my love)!*
Let me guide you to the happiness that we're both searching for.
Give yourself freely, willing to me. . . .
Let me love you with my mind, heart, body, and soul.
Let me put your search to rest. . . .

Dream no more, Julie!
The slow dance we're yearning is a fantasy that could come to reality.
Set me free to do your will. . . .

Julie felt that she had heard too much. Her heart, too, was thumping in rhythm with his. She put her hand over his mouth to stop him from continuing. "Please, Fuji. No more."

She got up from where she was sitting and continued showing him around the place. She took him over to the old house where her parents started their lives as a married couple. Julie stood by the door looking around the old place. She breathed, "I've had a lot of good times in this little house."

She offered him a seat in the living room to show him her childhood album. Louis smiled when he saw her naked baby picture. She pulled the album out of his hands and said, "I forgot about these two pictures."

Louis grinned. "You have a beautiful behind."

Nodding her head she replied, "Keep it up, and I will not show you the rest of my album anymore."

He raised his left arm and promised that he'd behave. She offered him a drink while he was looking at her pictures. After giving him the drink and fixing herself one, Julie sat by him as she explain each one of her portraits. Then she showed him the rest of her little place that she loved so much. Louis stood in front of her bedroom where she used to sleep and asked if she had ever made love in that bed. She told him no, because it was a new bed.

They chorused a laugh. She noticed the look on Louis's face. She was afraid he might kiss her again and she didn't want to let her feelings carry her away so she headed back to the mansion with him.

Everyone was on the patio enjoying the fresh air and the clear sky. Viviane handed them a glass of sherry while she spoke to them. Maxine handed Viviane William. She felt that Louis didn't come here to speak to them. Taking Carine and Nicole by the arms, Maxine said good night as she dragged them inside with her. Jacque didn't want to leave. He was still sitting down pretending he was reading his newspapers.

Viviane suggested, "Jacque is reading and we don't want to disturb him, so let's go in."

Jacque replied, "You guys are not disturbing me."

Viviane thought that Jacque was being rude, so she invited Louis to the living room for a comfortable talk. Without a second look at Jacque, the two women walked in from the patio, leaving Jacque with his paper.

Louis spoke of his job and his position at the hospital. He was the chief surgeon of the neurological department, but his main goal was to make time for a family and for his growing business. Viviane told him why they had to settle in America. She was pregnant when her husband left Haiti with her. That was why Julie was born in New York, but she had been raised with

Haitian and Christian values. Her husband did not like the way certain people did things in Haiti, and he did not want to get involved politically. Julie took after both of them. She was outspoken, but with modesty.

Louis smiled at Julie when her mother said that. Every now and then, he looked at the baby in his arms and at Julie while Viviane was talking but he was listening to every word that came out of Viviane's mouth. William was fast asleep in Louis's arms. Viviane looked at the sleeping baby and commented, "I feel the same way too, Bill. I must retire for the night. You two enjoy the rest of the evening for me."

As she was taking the baby, she invited, "I'm having a few good friends tomorrow night for little cook-out. Would you join us, Louis?"

Looking at Julie, then Viviane, he answered, "Yes, I'll love too."

She left the room with Bill, leaving Julie and Louis alone. Julie waved to her mother as she disappeared out of the room. Louis looked at her and complimented, "Your mother is quite a woman."

She agreed, "Yes she is. When my father passed away, if she wasn't the woman she is, I would have been lost."

"She did a beautiful job with you."

Julie smiled as he complimented her and she tried not to blush at the way he was looking at her, soft and different from every other time he set his eyes on her. Louis looked more striking tonight. She wanted to know more about him.

Louis, too, was feeling different. He was ready to be more than being her friend. Both were afraid to get too close, but the urge was stronger than they. Louis observed how she was breathing, the way she removed her hair from her face and gently curved it behind her ears. The way she tilted her head to look at him and smiled. He thought she had the most beautiful ears he had ever seen. He bit the bottom of his lip as he looked at her neck and how well she shaped her dress. She was desirable. He was certain that he was falling for her.

He started to question himself: Would the shadow of the past haunt him, make him cold and unfeeling? Would she be able to remove him from his solitude? She and him forever, would he learn to submit to her? Was she real, the woman who was sitting before him? He wanted her to feel the way he was feeling. To touch her mind, lay her in his arm and let the feeling they both were having lead them to where they wanted to go. Deep in his thoughts he heard her ask, "Who were your parents? Tell me about you, Louis."

Startled by her question, Louis handed her his glass. Never had he opened that chapter of his life to anyone. He looked at her for a while and thought, how would he explain who he really was to her. Would she like the person he really was or see him as the monster everyone portrayed him to be?

Julie got out of her seat to fix him a drink. She didn't say a word while getting him the drink. She waited patiently for him to grasp at his thoughts.

She watched how he sat back to meditate then said, "My parents would have loved you. . . ."

She smiled as she handed him the glass. He took the glass from her hand said, "They were the most loving parents I ever known. They put up with me."

She laughed as she got up to fix herself a drink. "Why did you say that?"

"I was spoiled, never did much physical work. When my father died I had to grow up really fast, but still, I was thoughtless."

Reminiscing about his past, Louis couldn't recall any good times after the death of his parents. The members of his family used every opportunity to try to milk him of every penny after the death of his father. They despised him. They thought he would have amounted to nothing because he was wasteful and a party animal, but to his parents, he was a good boy.

Julie questioned, "Did you act one way when your parents were around and another way when they were not around?"

Louis smiled. "I didn't think so, but everyone was always complaining about me."

Going back to where he was, he remembered how senseless and bad he was. He admitted he'd given his family reasons to think of him that way. He was always in trouble. He had to learn self-defense at an early age. A year after his father's death, the older relatives of his parents came to him and made the deal of a lifetime with him. Everything they had against everything he inherited.

The deal was for him to be a medical doctor, but he chose to be a brain surgeon. Tasting his drink, he smiled. "Boy, I love a good challenge."

Thoughtlessly, Louis accepted without his mother's knowledge. He was eighteen and old enough to make his own decisions. Their lawyer and his lawyer presented all the information before a judge. The agreement was made legal and too late for his mother to do anything.

A week later Louis went to New York to study at Columbia University. That was where he met with his best friend. He helped Louis any way he could to keep him focused on his studies. When Louis explained to him the challenges he faced, he went out of his way to see that Louis would succeed. Louis became the top student in his class. At twenty-two, he was a master in his field.

"My husband went there," Julie interrupted. "Does your best friend, 'King Authur' have a name, 'Lancelot'?"

Louis smiled, "In time you'll know, but at the moment I feel it is best to keep his name out of the story. It's more mysterious and interesting like that. . . ."

She nodded her head in agreement as he continued telling her how his relatives tried to kill him when they heard about his progress. "A sudden death no one would understand or be able to explain. Voodoo!"

"Voodoo!" Julie exclaimed. "Do you believe in that?"

"No, but the poisons are real. They came all the way to New York to work the poison spell on me. I was always invited over at their place. I didn't trust them. I knew they were going to try to kill me, but I didn't know how."

"Why would you think that?"

"My father died of a heart attack, caused by some kind of poison they gave him," Louis stated.

He never thought his relatives would have gone that far till they killed his father. "People who use that kind of treachery are very sneaky. You don't see them coming."

Louis's uncles paid someone to poison him. The first time he was hit, he was at a party with his best friend. It was put in his drink. The person who gave him the drink was living in his home, hanging out with them. He was also a classmate of his. Louis thought he could have helped him by letting him stay in his apartment for free since he was at the university on a school loan. Louis had volunteered to pay for his school loan to help him out because he had a lot of potential. That was the last person Louis would have believed could do something like that. That was another lesson he learned.

"There are those who, no matter how much you do for them, because of jealousy and envy, they wouldn't hesitate to kill you."

The poison was being administered to Louis in small dosages in his meals. He never suspected anything. The poison worked slowly in his body, because he was always on the move and that had slowed the process and helped him to survive.

"How did you find out?" Julie asked.

"My best friend wasn't as naïve as I was," Louis replied. "He could 'sense' when someone is not right. He never liked the way the guy looked at me and smiled. That was something I had to learn, not to be too trusting of anyone who has less than you."

Louis's friend suspected something wasn't right with him ever since he moved in to Louis's apartment. He took over the cleaning lady's job. He did the cooking for Louis, took Louis's clothes to the cleaner, and picked them up. Louis's friend claimed that the guy did his job better than a woman would have. They thought he was amazing, the way he took charge of taking care of Louis's apartment. He even cleaned the windows. Louis thought he was doing all that because he wanted to show his appreciation for helping him.

Then one day out of the blue Louis passed out while he was talking to them. He thought it was because he was over studying and didn't give himself enough time to rest. But the more he rested, the more tired he became. His friend felt something was definitely wrong with Louis, so he set a trap for the guy. He asked the guy to bring Louis a glass of orange juice while he was assisting Louis. The guy thought the coast was clear and took the opportunity to give him another dose. After a few seconds the guy left to get Louis the juice. Louis's friend sneaked in to see what the guy was doing. Just as he suspected, he caught the guy with the potion, mixing it in the glass of orange juice he was bringing for Louis. After he finished confessing, Louis's friend beat him till he was unconscious. Afterward Louis's friend made the guy drink his own potion and sent him on his way. . . . A day later Louis's mother arrived in New York unexpectedly. His friend knew that Louis was in serious trouble.

Louis paused for a moment and closed his eyes, then revealed them to her as he continued telling her how his mother learned of their plans from Marie Landers, who used to work for them. He was already sick to the point of dying. His friend took his mother, Margaret, to a Japanese man named Kinsu, who took care of him. He was able to make him an antidote. Then his friend introduced Louis to Master Toshibi. He became a father to Louis. He taught him discipline and refined his technique in martial arts.

Julie was surprised, "You know martial arts?"

"A little." He smiled. "I practiced while I was still in medical school. One of the most important things I learned was to respect all living things great and small."

When his relatives didn't hear from his mother or from Louis for five years, they all assumed both he and his mother were dead. They didn't search for them, so they celebrated. They started to distribute his inheritance among them when the bet was not yet over to complete the deal. When the day came for the judge to sign over his entire inheritance to them, he walked in the court with his mother beside him and his Ph.D. in neurology. They all thought they were seeing a ghost, but he was real. The court was dismissed; the judge signed everything they had over to him. Three of his uncles died of heart attacks that night.

Louis smiled. "Eight years away can really change a man."

He had a lot of cleaning up to do; he really meant business. His father died at the age of forty-two from a heart attack. His mother was killed while taking a stroll with him in her own backyard. . . .

Louis completely went into a trance as he recalled the day his mother died. All he was able to see at the moment was his mother lying in his arms, her blood pouring all over his shirt, her blood on his face as he tried to revive her. Louis breathed heavily as he relived the tragic moment that had taken place that night.

Julie sat beside him very quiet, waiting patiently for his next words. She noticed Louis was no longer here with her by the way he was breathing and staring at her. She took one of his hands in hers and gently pressed her hands on his then shook them.

Thinking he was at his mother's death site, Louis took a hold on to Julie's hands. For a moment he didn't recognize her. He whispered, "Mother!"

Julie was beginning to feel the strength of Louis's hand against hers. Trying to pull her hands out of his, she whispered back, "Fuji . . . let me go!"

Nodding his head Louis closed his eyes then looked at his hand as he came to his senses and saw he had taken a firm hold of Julie's hands. Quickly he removed his hand from hers and apologized. "I'm sorry!"

He thought he had hurt her. Taking her hands he looked at them and again he apologized.

Julie could see that Louis was traumatized by the death of his parents. She knew she had touched a very fragile part of his life that he had tried to suppress.

Louis put a hand over his eyes and squeezed his fingers over them, suppressing the tears that were shimmering in his eyes. He didn't want Julie to see the pain he was feeling. He exhaled as he put his glass on the coffee table. Louis got up to go, because he was feeling ashamed and weak before her, and he didn't want her to see that.

Julie took ahold of his arm, holding him back, and reassured him that he didn't hurt her. She wanted to know what caused him to blank out like that. She thought about the nightmares Marie said he was having. She felt he was haunted by memories. She felt hurt for him and wanted to help him, "Please, Fuji, don't shut me out. Let me in."

Gently she pulled him back and asked him to sit. He softly looked at her and said, "She was hit with a fatal bullet and I think it was meant for me. She died in my arms, because he felt it was my fault my mother wouldn't date him. . . ."

"Who was he?" Julie tenderly asked.

That was a name Louis had never wanted to mention again since the incident. Between his teeth he said the name as if he was being choked. "Jean Ladin."

"Jean Ladin," she repeated, and thought the name sounded familiar. Then she remembered where she heard the name. She had read about him years ago. And she believed that was the year she was married to Saul and she had to meet her husband in Haiti after her seminar in Paris. She never forgot that because she just got married to Saul. That man Jean Ladin had blown off his own head after he killed his three daughters and those who were in the house with him that night.

Julie wanted to know what brought that man's wrath against Louis.

Louis passed his finger over her cheek and continued, "The truth was, my mother didn't want to get involved with anyone, but not because of me. My mother was happy just being alone. She had dedicated her life to helping children in need. She wanted me to get my life together. She spent a lot of time in the orphanage with the children. My mother used to tell me about a girl she met there, and how she loved to come to the orphanage to play with the children. She never met anyone like her. She wanted me to meet her. But I didn't want to because she might force me to marry her so she could have grandchildren. I believe the girl my mother was talking about was you, Julie."

She meditated on what Louis said and said, "Did she have blond streaks in her brownish hair, slim, and had hazel eyes, around my height?"

Louis nodded to say yes and removed his mother's picture out of his wallet to show it to her. Julie admired the picture. She was sad. "Yes, that's her! She was so lovely and elegant. I used to sit with her talking for hours. She once told me to follow my dream, and I would make an astonishing wife. . . . Yes, Mrs. Janvier. I had called her Maggie. She wanted me to meet her son."

"Yes," Louis said sorrowfully. "Only if I had listen to her, you would have been my wife."

She smiled, "Maybe we wouldn't work out."

"I believe we would have," he said and returned to where he left. "My mother didn't want to remarry, him or anyone else. And plus he was a no-good-for-nothing man. . . ."

Louis closed his eyes and breathed, "He wanted to punish me. To teach me not to be so selfish. . . ."

Julie had tears in her eyes listening to Louis. She sighed. "Did you learn anything from him?"

"Yes," Louis nodded. "I learned that I was the 'Doctor Banner'."

Julie chuckled, because she knew it was a Marvel cartoon and the character appeared gentle till something or someone got him angry; then he would become the Incredible Hulk to destroy anything that stood in his way.

She tasted her drink to cover up her shocked expression. Louis didn't have to give her every detail because she understood what had really taken place in Jean Ladin's house. She could just imagine what that man had unleashed out of Louis and wondered if Louis was alone. Did Henry Claude and his best friend help with the killing?

Many people didn't take Louis seriously because of his youth. He had to show them he was not to be toyed with. He softly said, as he looked into her eyes, "Make no mistake, I would take you for everything you got if you stood in my way. The only mercy I may give is to spare you your life. . . . I became a sign of fear to those who defied me. The thought of coming up against me can mean suicide. I can be fierce. . . . Anything else you would like to know about me, Ms. Cactus?"

Julie couldn't find any other words to describe Louis but to say, "You're a daring man, Fuji."

"Why did you say that?"

"My husband is a man like you," Julie smiled. "One who would take daring chances and he would hurt anyone who stood in his way. And here you are, trying to seduce me."

"For you, I dare anything," he confessed as he once did. "I will lay down my life for you."

Julie didn't respond to his revelation. She tasted her drink then looked at him. They both sat there in silence looking at each other. Julie thought

Louis had told her more then she could chew. The brief summary of his life was astonishing.

He looked at his wrist to check the time. He put the glass down on the coffee table, then got up from the chair and made ready to go. Once more he took her hands to look, to see if he had hurt her. Once more Julie had to reassure him, "You didn't hurt me, Fuji."

He bent his head and raised her hands before his lips, then kissed them. Julie got up to walk him to the door. Louis took her hand and placed it on the crook of his arm and laid his hand on top of hers as they were leaving the room.

Jacque stood in a dark corner of the lobby looking at them from a distance where they wouldn't be able to see him. Watching how Louis was touching her face and caressing her lips with his fingers, and she didn't push his hands away. Jacque closed his eyes and swallowed, hoping when he opened them that it would have been just a bad vision, but it was real. Louis stood so close that he could just kiss her, but he didn't. Louis took her hands, caressing them with his lips before he kissed them. Not once did she back away from him. Then he turned her hands and kissed the palms. Then he walked away, leaving the feel of his lips on her mind. The way she held her hands against her chest and looking at his departure, Jacque knew Julie was feeling something for that man.

Leaning against the wall, Jacque tried to catch his breath. Tears had almost flown out of his eyes. . . . As she was going up the stairs Jacque called out to her, but she didn't hear him. She ran up the stairs as fast as she could to her room. Maxine was waiting for her. As she entered, Maxine said, "I want all the details!"

Like Louis, she sighed. "Are you planning to write my life story, Max?"

Maxine exclaimed, "Look! Don't hold back on me, child. I want to get firsthand news."

Julie smiled, and said, "He went home. I was upset for the way dinner was canceled, even though my mother didn't say anything. She would have looked for Louis to wring his neck. I'm glad he came by, but at same time I wished he didn't drop by."

"Why? You seemed so happy when you saw him."

"Maxine, tonight he revealed that he would dare to seduce me and he would lay down his life for me."

"How romantic!" Maxine sighed, holding on to her chest.

"That's not romantic, Max. Louis is a dangerous man. . . ."

Maxine cut in, "Whom you're in love with."

"I might be lusting for him, you know, and loneliness is overtaking me." She laughed. "Louis is a very attractive man and I haven't seen my husband for over three months."

"You don't do lusting, Julie, because if you were, you would have already been in bed with him. What you're feeling for him is it not a mere attraction. I think you two are in love."

"Louis just wants to conquer me." Holding to her stomach, Julie languished. "And I'm afraid I might just let him."

"He might want to conquer you," Maxine replied, "but at the same time I'm disagreeing with you. Louis wouldn't be as upset as he was tonight for not coming to dinner. He got everyone at the table very nervous when he appeared in the dining room." She laughed. "Nicole thought he had a gun and he was going to shoot everyone because you have refused his dinner invitation. And Jacque was more worried than anyone in there."

"I noticed he was," Julie said. "From what I learned about Louis tonight, I would be too if I was in his shoes. He didn't think Louis would have come in person to demand an explanation."

Maxine said, "I'm glad you didn't believe it was Jean who made that crazy plot?"

"Not a chance. Jean wouldn't do something like that," Julie answered then laughed. "The scarier part was when Louis stood by the door removing his driving gloves and said, 'Good evening'. I didn't understand why he was angry and why did he show up when we were having dinner? I think Louis knew Jacque did it, but he kept his cool!"

"Jacque is playing a dangerous game, Julie. There's no laughing matter about that. he shouldn't do something like that. Especially to a man like Louis, who could pounce on Jacque like a lion. Jacque forgot he is nothing but an antelope to a king lion like Louis. . . . You know Louis was named after the lion."

"How do you know?"

"Richard told me."

"His name suits him well." Julie nodded and said, "Jacque is only concerned about my well being."

"Is he really, Julie? His actions made me worry instead. If Jacque was really concerned, knowing the way Louis is, he would try to get on Louis's good side. He wouldn't toy with him. Louis is mostly famous for war."

"Don't worry, Max. I wouldn't let Louis or anyone hurt you guys."

"I know you wouldn't, Julie, but Jacque is doing things he's not supposed to be doing. He is up to no good and I'm afraid whatever he is planning might hurt all of us. . . . Well anyway, let's talk about something more pleasant."

Julie agreed, "That sounds better."

She change her clothes to her nightgown as she was telling Maxine what took place between Louis and her. Maxine spent the night with her talking about the situation she was in and how she hoped Saul could come and rescue her.

Chapter Ten

You Take My Breath Away

The following morning Maxine didn't go to work. She help Viviane organize what to serve for the little cook-out. Maxine didn't invite Richard. She was embarrassed by the way her family reacted the last time Richard was here. She made sure the outdoor grill was clean and the bar had enough drinks for the cook-out that would take place later on that afternoon.

Viviane was happy to see some old friends she had not seen in years. They sat by the pool while enjoying their deep fried pork, roasted conch, deep fried goat meat, and many other things for them to eat. The servant came by and offered them drinks while Jean started the music.

He announced, "Welcome, everyone! My name is Jean Bassine, and I'll be your DJ for tonight. I hope you'll enjoy the music I'm about to play. And if anyone wants to be part of the entertainment, please feel free to join me and be part of my posse!"

Everyone clapped as the music began to play. It was like a force pulling him to her as the song began to play. Louis stood up, extended his hands, and with a gentle look in his eyes, he said, "They're playing our song, Julie."

In surprise, she exclaimed, "They are!"

Louis invited softly, "Come, dance with me."

Viviane urged, "Go dance, sweetheart."

Shoving back her chair reluctantly, Julie pushed back her hair away from her face and handed her glass to Viviane. She got up, trying not to look at him. Noticing she was trembling and nervous, Louis took her hand gently but firmly in his and walked onto the dance floor. Everyone stood looking at them as they started to dance. Carine stood next to Nicole watching.

Nicole looked at Carine and shook her head in disbelief. "Do you believe that man?"

Jacque's eyes were furious but he pasted a dry smile on his face. Julie and Louis were dancing to an old Haitian song called "Anita." This time it was not avoidable to look at him, because he was looking right at her, capturing her attention. Louis smiled deeply into her eyes as he placed her right hand on his chest, and taking her left hand in his right palm and placing it around his neck. Slowly they danced to the music. Julie was nervous like she had never been before tonight. He held her gently as he turned her around, never once did he remove his eyes off her. He did not care that everyone was looking at them, because tonight his loneliness must end. He dreamt of holding her this way for a very long time, and how he wanted to kiss her again and tell her his deepest secrets.

Viviane jumped up and holding her hand out to Henry, she exclaimed breathlessly, "Let's dance!"

Jumping at the chance to dance with her, he readily agreed. Jacque got up to dance with Carine and joined the other two couples. Maxine and Nadine were at the table eating and talking admiringly about Julie. She really amazed them. Maxine said, "Tonight I would like to hear her sing."

The music was over, but Louis was still holding on to Julie. She reminded him, "Fuji, the music is over."

Stepping back but still holding on to her waist, he apologized. "I'm sorry."

Louis held on to her hand as they walked back to the table. Maxine was sitting with Viviane and Henry. Julie said, "I'm thirsty." She drank some of her soda.

One of the servants passed by Carine with a wine tray. She took two glasses of wine and drank them one after the other. She was trying to get herself drunk. Pasting a fake smile on her face, she walked over to Julie's table. Looking at Julie and Louis, she said, "You two danced well on the floor. If I didn't know better, I'd think you two took dancing lessons together. . . ."

Smilingly Viviane agreed with her. Carine took another drink from a passing waiter. Henry asked, "Whose guitar is this?"

Louis replied, "It's mine. Julie promised she would sing for me tonight."

Shocked, by his statement Julie replied, "I did!"

Viviane, who knew she was the one who told Louis to bring the guitar back him up, said, "You did."

Julie had not played the guitar since she started to have marital problems. She looked at her mother and didn't want to play. Viviane asked, "Can I hear you play, sweetheart, please?"

Everyone applauded. Viviane got up on the stage and announced, "I have a surprise for you tonight. Friends, please put your hands together for my daughter, Julie Philip."

There was loud applause. Julie laughed, a bit surprised and flustered. "Why, Mom!"

"Come on up, Julie," Viviane called. "Please sing for us."

Julie demurred, "I can't sing, Mother. You know that."

Maxine insisted, "Yes, you can!"

She got up from her chair and pleaded with Julie to play for them, "Please, Julie, play for us."

Louis took her hands, handed her the guitar, and urged, "Please, sing for me."

Groaning, she covered her face with her hands in embarrassment. "Do I have to?"

Henry added his pleadings to the others, "Yes!"

They were all clapping and chanting, "Julie! Julie!" as she walked up on the stage.

Jacque shouted, "Sing to me, pretty mama!"

She flexed her arms and legs and made everyone laugh. Carine didn't say anything. She had never heard Julie sing. She thought, *Aunt Viviane is tune deaf, and Maxine just wants a good laugh. The girl is crazy.* Julie would be embarrassed before everyone and especially before Louis.

Carine joined in the clapping and whistling as Julie made her way on the stage. She was the loudest. She got everyone to laugh. Maxine had to tell her, "Enough!"

Julie sat on the chair that Jean had vacated, saying, "Here goes nothing."

It would be nothing for sure, Carine thought, and said sarcastically, "Knock them dead, Julie!"

Placing the guitar on her lap, Julie closed her eyes and started to play. She pulled the microphone close to her mouth and she started humming as slowly she moved her fingers against the cords, trying to catch the tune she wanted. Opening her eyes, she said, "I composed this song a few months ago when my mind was troubled. This song brings me peace and tonight, I hope it will bring peace to many of you here."

Slowly moving her head, she started singing.

> *My world is full of joy, laughter, and happiness,*
> *but these feelings were not part of me and as I'm*
> *isolated in my world, my life meant nothing to me*
> *Or to others,*
> *until one day a stranger entered my world,*

She glanced at Louis and closed her eyes. Louis never took his eyes off her. He was looking at her with naked admiration, which he had made no attempt to hide.

It's like I have had no feeling and someone . . . pinched me,
and suddenly my feeling begins to react,
and I'm beginning to live again.
He is me. I am him, together we are one.
Please, someone, pinch me, tell me this is not a dream,
'cause if it is a dream, I would rather my eyes stay closed forever
because I wouldn't give up this stranger in my world.
When he touches me with his eyes,
I feel I am part of him.
Please, please, tell me this is not a dream.
'cause if it is a dream
I don't ever want to wake up,
because I wouldn't give up this stranger in my world.
When he touches me with his eyes I feel like I'm part of him.
Please, someone, tell me that I'm not dreaming.
What I'm feeling, it's all in reality,
'cause I wouldn't give up this stranger in my world
'cause I love him so.
He loves me so. . . .

As Julie sang, Louis felt the song was for him. He felt he was nothing without Julie. His life was meaningless if she was not part of it. Just touching her hands made him feel alive again. Her shadow fell on him. He sat there listening to the music and thought, *Am I going mad? I can't seem to stop myself from loving her. I feel like I've been spellbound. Please open your heart to me, and end this madness I'm having, Julie. I know you love me.*

She glanced at Louis as if she could read his thoughts and found him looking at her. She stared back at him and continued to sing. Viviane took a quick look to see what she was focusing on and found Louis, too, was lost, looking at her daughter. She whispered, "Is everything all right?"

He didn't even look at Viviane. His eyes were glittering with love. "Perfect. Everything is perfect."

Jacque stood at a distance looking at the way Viviane was smiling at Louis and nodded her head in agreement.

When she finished her song, there was a hush. Everyone was silent and listening in awe. Suddenly there was thunderous applause and shots of "Encore, encore!"

Laughingly, she shook her head. "Uh-huh. One song."

She walked off the stage and headed back to her seat. Carine was burning with rage. She never knew Julie was so talented. Julie walked by her and Carine bared her teeth at her and pretended to be drunk, "You always have to be queen of the manor."

Trying to prevent her from falling with one hand while holding the guitar with other hand, Julie asked with concern, "Are you okay, Carine?"

Pulling away from Julie she snapped, "Like you care!"

Looking at Carine with Julie standing by her, Viviane wondered what was wrong. She glanced at Louis and excused herself as she got up out of her chair. Louis got up and followed her as he walked toward Julie to compliment her. Taking her hand in his, he kissed it and commented, "You sing beautifully."

For a moment they didn't say anything, Maxine came by, breaking up the silence as she asked, "What's next on the schedule, Aunt Viviane?"

Carine replied, "What do you think is next?"

She pushed Julie and Maxine away from her. Carine pretended she was about to faint and fell into Louis's arms. Looking at Julie, Louis said, "I think she's drunk."

Julie called Jacque to help escort Carine to her bed, but Jacque acted like he didn't hear her and continued talking with Nadine, who was standing by Nicole and Debbie.

Seeing that Jacque didn't respond, Jean rushed by to help as Viviane instructed him to help her to bed. Without any hesitation Louis placed her firmly in her brother's arms. He knew that this was just an act. Carine was not drunk at all. In spite of the way Louis dropped her in the arms of her brother, she was still trying to get Louis's attention. "Louis . . . Louis, please help me!"

The look on Louis's face told Jean that Carine was in serious trouble with him. Jean apologized to him as he carried her away. Maxine ran to the stereo to play the music louder so no one would hear Carine's outcry, "Don't leave me, Louis, I need you!"

Walking toward Maxine, Jacque was trying to bring down the volume. With brute force Maxine pushed his hands away. Jacque rigorously said, "What do you think you're doing?"

"Covering up embarrassment," Maxine snapped.

Louis took a glance at Jacque and ignoring Carine, he had already turned his attention back to Julie. "She'll be all right."

Viviane, too, apologized to him and thought, *That girl needs discipline.* Tomorrow she would have a talk with her.

Henry was not sitting too far. He was paying keen attention to the stage that Carine and Jacque had set up for Louis. Knowing what was coming next on the schedule and with a nod of his head, Louis signaled Henry for help by pulling on his left earlobe. Louis saw how Jacque was eyeing Nicole to interrupt his conversation with Julie while she was pretending to talk to Debbie. Leaving his seat Henry walked toward Louis and pretended he had not noticed Nicole all evening. He put ahold on her as she walked by and said, "I thought you weren't here. Where were you?"

Jealously, Nicole replied, "You were busy talking to Aunt Viviane and Julie so you didn't notice me."

"Nicole." Putting an arm around her Henry pulled her away. "I'm sorry. I thought you went some where with Michelle. I didn't recognize you. I saw you but I thought you were a teenage girl. . . . You look more beautiful than ever. Every day you look younger and younger, like a gala rose collection."

He continued complimenting her on her beauty, that it was worthy to be celebrated. As they walked away Nicole waved goodbye to the girls then she looked around to see if anyone was watching her trying to sneak away with Henry. Louis, however, was paying attention to everything that was going on around him. Louis asked Julie, "Let's go for a walk."

Concernedly she looked toward the house. "Just a minute, I want to find out if Carine's okay."

Viviane stopped her. "No, Max and I will check on Carine. Go for your walk."

When Jacque overheard what Viviane had suggested, he quickly came by to ask Julie to dance. Before he could open his mouth to ask, Louis placed his hand on the back of his neck, applying pressure that prevented Jacque from speaking. No one noticed the incident that just took place. Julie looked at her mother as she slowly walked away with Louis, leaving Jacque, who was short of breath.

They walked to the other part of the mansion, enjoying the breeze on their face. They walked toward the old house while Louis was telling her how delightful her voice was and the words in her song. The pleasure of her song rose in his heart. They stopped in the garden to rest for awhile. Louis admired the way she had designed the garden around the house.

"You're a talented woman, Julie."

"Exactly what don't you admire about me, Fuji?"

Lifting her chin to look at him he said, "I don't like your loneliness, your emptiness."

Getting on her feet she replied, "Stop being presumptuous."

Louis followed her in silence, observing her body movement. He noticed Julie was getting nervous around him and she was afraid of being alone with him. Putting her nervousness to rest, Louis told her about his friend. "I spoke with my best friend last night."

"You did!" Julie excitedly said.

"We had a long conversation," he said firmly. "He called to tell me he was going on a dangerous mission. I'm afraid he may not return from it."

Louis seemed worried. The look in his eyes told her so. She stopped walking to listen to him.

"My best friend wants me to help his wife and my son if anything happens to him."

"Wasn't that what you wanted?" Julie hastened to say.

"I don't want him to die, Julie!" Louis replied. He was hurt by the way she eagerly responded to what he said. "You may find it hard to believe, but

160

I love my friend. Death is something I never visualized for him. There isn't any woman worth my best friend's life, understand!"

Julie apologized. Louis went on to say, "I wanted him to go to his wife and son and let me handle the business for him, but he wouldn't let me."

Louis was afraid his best friend wouldn't return from the assignment. Looking up in the skies, he sighed. "If only I could have gone to the past to change a chapter of my life. I would have listened to my mother more and today I wouldn't be in this situation that I'm in."

Looking at him, Julie saw his fear. She comforted, "We all feel that way sometimes, Louis, but we could learn from the past not to repeat history."

Louis lowered his head to look at her. In his heart he prayed for his friend to return alive and in one piece. Louis felt helpless that his friend didn't let him go in his place instead. He felt something bad was going to happen to his friend and he had no control over the situation.

Julie wondered what else was on Louis's mind, the way he was looking at her. For a moment he stared at her with anger then looked away. She smiled because she understood that was one situation Louis couldn't control.

"You're a man, Louis Janvier, not a god, but I think you are very humane for wanting to do the assignment for your friend so he could be with his wife and your son. I believe God is going to repay you for all your good intentions."

They walked in silence for a few minutes. Then she showed Louis the work she did in the yard and her new garden.

He smirked. "Resistance is unavoidable."

Julie questioned, "What are you smiling about, and what is unavoidable?"

"You did all this work in a short time." He was amazed. "You were trying hard to keep away from me, weren't you? Have you not gotten it by now? We cannot avoid each other. You planted all these plants and flowers and you actually helped dig a well and you did the construction work yourself."

Julie had built an old-fashioned type of a water well. Louis tested to see if he could draw water out of it. He turned the handle as he lowered the bucket to fetch some water from the well. Then slowly he turned the handle back and there before his eyes was the water.

Louis took her hands and felt them and said, "You're roughening your hands."

He raised them to look at them. He kissed them and pressed her hands on his face. He closed his eyes and wondered about last night while he stood before her. Julie looked up at him. He wanted to kiss her. She moved back and said, "Please, Fuji, don't."

"Why not?"

Trying to breathe she said, "You're clogging my mind."

He moved closer. "I think it's the other way around, Ms. Cactus."

161

She stepped out of his way. "I'm a married woman, Louis. Being around you is a danger to my marriage. It's unlawful to be around you . . . I don't want to be around you, Louis."

He didn't want to hear it. "You changed me to someone I never thought I could be."

Feeling peeved, she snapped, "I never thought a snake could change its split tongue, except shed skin, just like a tiger that cannot change its stripes. I look at you, like those animals. A beast is what you are. It is your nature, you wouldn't quit, till you got a kill. Isn't it, Louis?"

"I was a beast, but that is all behind me. You helped formed me, beauty."

Julie felt that they had to stop seeing each other. It was madness on both of their parts. It wasn't healthy. She wouldn't leave her husband for Louis. "Please, Louis, don't con me. I'm not a woman you can play with. I'm a married woman. I don't think we should even be friends. I've noticed since you returned from America, you became aggressive toward me. What happened? Did you have a revelation about me, that I'm weakening? I'm lonely, Louis. . . . I don't know what your problems are, but I think your attitude is very disrespectful. All you are concerned about is getting in my panties. Please, leave me alone, with my loneliness. As you can see I'm not complaining about my emptiness. You have plenty of women waiting for you to continue your orgies."

"Orgies," Louis scoffed as he cornered her.

Trying to make him move away, she stressed, "I don't love you! Go away."

Resting one hand against the tree that was behind her, he wrapped the other arm around her waist. Louis pulled her toward him. He raised her face so she could look him in the eyes. He shook his head in disagreement. "Look at me when you say you don't love me, and tell me, why are you trembling?"

"Did it ever occur to you that I might be lusting. . . ?" Wanting to hurt his feelings so he could let her go, she said, "I just feel sorry for you, that is all, what I felt is just an attraction because you reminded me so much of my husband Saul."

Ironically Louis replied, "I thought snakes and tiger were not your type. Don't tell me you were married to one and you managed to come out in one piece."

"Correction." She tried to wriggle herself out of his arms. "I'm still married, and I'm not going to settle for less. As you can see, I'm all torn and confused, because if I did come out in one piece, I wouldn't be here talking to someone as miserable as you."

He felt Julie was running from her true feelings and she was using Saul to keep away from him. He let her know she wanted him as much as he wanted her.

Julie felt he was out of his mind. She wanted to know where he got his information.

"Our bodies told me," Louis whispered in her ear as he sucked on her earlobe. Running his teeth on her earlobe and sucking on it he said, "I dreamt about you, holding you in my arms, making love to you. Like your song 'The Stranger and I'. I want peace, Julie, and you're the only one who can provide me with it."

Holding her tighter, she could feel the strength of his arms holding on to her. She felt safe but afraid at same time. Softly, he rubbed his lips against her forehead, whispering her name and demanded to know, "When I touched you, did you not feel or yearn for me?"

"Please, Fuji, set me free," Julie softly cried out in his arms. "I'm married."

"How could I," he whispered, nibbling on her ears, making her lose her mind. "When you're the one who holds me captive."

He persisted to kiss her and Julie wanted him to let her go. "Then push me away, Julie, because I will not let you go."

She couldn't fight him, because she wanted his touch, the feel of his lips against her cheeks and on her neck and his hand rubbing on her back, holding her tight against his chest, his gentle voice whispering in her ears. She begged him to stop, but Louis didn't want to. She wanted to push him but her body wouldn't let her. She held onto him as he drowned her with his lips. Then he gently moved back as he demanded to know, "Tell me again, Julie, you don't love me, it's just an attraction."

Pulling her back into his arms she begged, "No! Let me go, Louis."

He responded by sealing his mouth on hers, drawing her close to him. Gradually he slid his hands under her blouse, massaging her gently on her back, slowly working his way to the front to caress her bosom.

Julie tried to control the feeling that was overtaking her mind. She took a hold of his hands, pulled them out of her blouse, and pushed them away. She expounded, "You want to hear the truth, I'll tell you. Yes, my body yearned for you. I wanted you to touch me and make love to me till you possess my mind, body, and soul. Is that what you want to hear. . . ?"

Louis didn't answer. "I under estimated you, Louis. I saw the warning and I've been warned. I thought I had the situation under control, and that was my mistake. I should have never gotten that close to you, you are cleverer than I thought. But I'm not going to continue seeing you. The party is over tonight. I'm going back to New York."

Shaking his head in frustration, he made it known, "It's not that simple, Julie. I will not let you go."

She felt Louis wanted to punish her for saying he wasn't man enough for her, and the only way he would be satisfied was to lie down with her. "You won, Louis! You broke me down . . . I'm so sorry for telling you were not man enough to get between my legs! What more do you want from me?"

"I wasn't playing any game with you, Julie. I want you."

"Why do you want to treat me like a whore?" she cried and pleaded. "Please let me go back to my husband with some dignity, Louis."

Ignoring her plea, "I'll follow you," he said.

"My husband will kill you, Louis."

"So let it be," he exclaimed as he boldly pulled her into his arms, covering her with kisses as he was mumbling to her how much he wanted her, and death was not enough to keep him away from her. He molded her mind with his words, sniffing the fragrance of her hair. "I'm not going to let you out of my life. You belong to me."

"No!" Julie protested, as she desperately tried to push him. "I don't belong to you. My husband's name is Saul Philip the Third, not Louis Janvier. Got that!"

"How long have you been waiting for him?" Louis frowned as he pushed her away to look at her. "Over two, three months to be precise. You still haven't seen the picture. Do you see any other man here beside Louis Janvier?"

Julie thought Louis had gone out of his mind. "You're crazy!" she said as she tried to set herself free from Louis's grip.

"Only for you, baby." He held her tighter in his arms to kiss her on her neck.

"No, Louis, you are looking at me as a substitute for the married woman you're in love with. It's not me you want. Or is it something you got for married women? A challenge, is it? Let go of me," she demanded as she desperately tried to get out from under his hands.

"To let you go would be suicide on both of our parts."

"I will scream, Louis, if you don't let go of me."

"You don't really want to do that."

Julie realized that was precisely what he wanted her to do when he created a vacuum with his lips to lock his lips over hers and draw her tongue into his mouth, which she was not letting him have before. Julie became lightheaded as he gently absorbed her mind, drowning her with his sweet lips, capturing the depth of her thoughts.

Yes, Julie let me in, Louis thought. *Let me engrave myself into your mind.*

He continued kissing her for a while then gradually, he loosened his grip. He smiled. "Oh, darling, can't you see we belong together?"

She knew definitely now she had to stop seeing Louis. For some reason she felt like it was natural to be touched by him, but at the same time she knew that couldn't be true because she was married to another, and the feelings she was having must come to an end. She felt it was her fault her marriage was having problems and to leave her husband to be one of Louis Janvier's women would be suicidal on her part. It was impossible! That would be degrading! She couldn't bring herself into that category. She wasn't going to say, "I love you, Louis. Yes I belong to you." She felt that feeling must not escape her heart; that passion was something she must endure.

Louis continued kissing her then kissed her hands as he pressed them against his face. He wanted her to touch him. He opened his shirt and gently took her hands and passed them across his chest, making her caress his masculine back. He drew her closer to him and whispered. "Feel me, Julie."

The sensitiveness of her touch sent pleasure in his soul as she slowly ran her hands over his bare masculine chest and back. She leaned her head on his chest listening to his heartbeat. He ran his fingers through her hair, kissing her as if he wanted to eat her. Julie found herself in deeper trouble than she was before. Louis wanted to make love to her. He was taking charge of her mind and she was yielding to his wishes. Julie was weakening. Louis whispered, "Let me make love to you . . . I want to be one with you. . . ."

He moved two feet away from her, then stretched his arms to her calling her to him.

"Come to me, Julie," Louis softly invited her into her old house. Reaching for the stretching arm Julie walked toward him as if she was hypnotized. His voice, the way he looked at her, and the feel of his hand were so warm, holding, leading her to where he wanted her to be.

"Save me, Julie," he whispered as he opened the door to let her in.

She stepped back to look at him, wondering what exactly did he mean? She thought she was the one who needed rescue, not him. His words got her to think. She assembled herself, remembering the woman she stood for. She jolted. "No. . . . No!" she wrangled, nodded her head to get a grip of herself. "No!" Closing her hands she pushed his hands away and said, "Goodbye, Louis."

Julie started to run. He ran ahead of her and blocked her. "You can't run with those sandals. You can hurt yourself."

Julie was wearing a high heels, a glass-like sandal revealing her beautiful shapely feet and pedicured toes. Louis pulled her up as she tried to remove them off her feet. She pushed his hands because he wasn't letting her take them off. Again she moved back, trying to get away.

"Julie, wait," Louis begged, taking a firm hold of her. He drew her into his arm and entreated, "Please don't go. It's been a long time my heart has being searching. I thought I was never going to wake up. But once I saw you, I didn't have to look or think anymore. I need you, Julie, my love. Let me warm you. When I look at you or touch you, I feel love running through me and every part of me comes to life. I feel love, Julie. I'm lost without you. Please take me. Have me. . . . I'll die if I don't have you. Can't you see, we're both empty without each other."

She wanted to scream as he kissed her on the lips and on her neck, but she softly spoke, "Please don't do this to me. I will not leave my husband for you, Fuji. I can't be one of your women, Louis, I can't."

"My one and only woman," he breathed out as he held her against his chest. "I'm in love with you, Julie."

Julie was stunned. That was the very first time Louis directly said he loved her. She stared at him as she moved back way from him, and that time she ran. She thought Louis was definitely suicidal. She managed to remove the sandals off her feet and took off again, leaving her sandals behind. Louis picked up her sandals and went after her.

She kept on running as if there was a killer after her. When she got near the group, she slowed down to catch her breath and wipe away the tears that were rolling down her face and made sure her blouse was closed and her pants were not unzipped. She ran her fingers through her hair to arrange it neatly and took a couple of deep breaths to settle herself. Louis was not too far from her. He stood beside her and handed her the sandals as he fixed his shirt inside his pants and whispered, "I love you Julie."

She whispered back, "I'll do you just like your best friend and his wife. Keep away for good."

Her words disturbed him. "You can't do that to us."

"There was never an 'us', Louis," she sighed. "Lusted, most likely."

Louis wanted to tell her more. How much he loved her and her son. How he would have loved to make a family with her. He was about to say something, but Julie raised her hand and silenced him. "I don't want to hear it, Louis. Goodbye."

Quietly together they walked to the party. Julie looked flushed. Her mother said as she passed her hand on Julie's face, "You didn't go far at all."

Viviane directed an eye on Louis while petting her daughter's hair. She couldn't understand why she took a liking to him. As Louis sat beside her, she reflected on him. Louis was a very good looking, well built, tall, and successful man. He knew exactly what he wanted and he made no secret of his affection for her daughter and her grandson. She saw Julie, too, was also attracted to Louis as well. Viviane smiled when her eyes met his and how he was looking at Julie. She noticed that Louis was not happy about something. And from the look on Julie's face, Viviane knew her daughter was about to get away from Louis for good. Viviane was happy but sad at the same time because things weren't getting better between Julie and her husband Saul. As they were listening to Maxine's conversation, one of the servants came running to Julie with a telephone in her hand.

She said with urgency, "It's from New York, madame."

Looking at Louis, Julie gave a smile of relief, because she thought it was her husband calling her and he was finally coming to her rescue. Joyfully she looked at her mother as she took the phone from the maid. Louis kept his eyes fixed on her. Smilingly she said, "Hello, Saul."

She moved a few steps away, looking at the watch on her left wrist. It was 9:30 in the evening. She leaned against the pole so she could hear and talk better. Julie looked at Louis while she spoke. Her features changed as she listened. Her mother felt something wasn't right. She came closer as she looked at Julie's facial reaction.

Viviane asked, "What's wrong, sweetheart?"

Looking at the way her eyes were blinking, Viviane and Louis rushed to her side and held her up. The phone fell out of her fingers as she trembled violently and she covered her face with her hands.

"No! You can't do this to me!" She looked up in the skies as if she was being watched.

Viviane picked up the phone with rage and said, "Saul! Slow down, I cannot understand what you are saying."

Taking a deep breath, Viviane looked at Julie and started to cry.

Hurling her cup aside, Maxine hastened toward Viviane with the telephone and took the phone from her because Viviane, too, was shaking. "Hello! I'm her sister. . . ."

Julie was weeping openly. Jacque eagerly kept asking, "What happened? What's going on, Maxine?"

Louis felt despair as he watched the tears flow out of Julie's eyes. He embraced her as she bitterly cried. Sorrowfully Maxine expressed, " . . . Thank you, sir, I got all the information. I'll relay the message to her."

She hung up the telephone, taking a deep breath and turning to the group of people looking at her expectantly. "Saul died early this evening while he was on a mission. The plane he was working on exploded. They found what remained of his body."

Everyone murmured in shock and sympathy. Jean, Nadine, and Debbie walked over to see what the hushed atmosphere was all about. "What is going on?"

Sadly Nicole informed them, "Her husband is dead."

Nadine sat back on the chair next to her, in shock, looking at Julie who was crying and Louis who was sitting next to her.

Looking at Jacque, Debbie thought, *I'm sure he is happy now.* And she gave him a cold look. Jacque looked at Debbie with cynical eyes then walked toward Julie to comfort her.

Regarding Louis, Henry got out of his chair to hand Louis a glass of water. He was shocked as well about the news. He breathed in and out of his mouth to control the feelings going through him. He poured a glass of water and brought it to Louis. Taking the glass from his hand, Louis held it to Julie's lips. She gulped half of the water, then pushed the glass away. He drank the rest.

Julie murmured as she cried, "This was one of the things I kept telling him not to do. He never listens to me. Always going for the rush! Always taking dangerous chances! He knew I wouldn't approve of it, so he kept it a secret from me. He left without saying goodbye."

Julie didn't wait for the rest of the message. She pushed Louis aside and ran from everyone into the darkness away from the mansion. Louis took off after her. Jacque felt now was his chance. Louis wasn't the one Julie wanted near her now. He made ready to follow them. He looked at Henry, who was looking at him, shaking his head at him in the gesture of saying no, telling him not to go after them. Jacque snarled at him, then at Debbie, who held him back. He tried to pull away from her. "No, Jacque, don't! Let Louis go by himself. Right now if you follow him, he will not hesitate to dismember you. And I swear I will help him."

"Don't be stupid," Jacque stated under his breath. "Julie needs me now."

"She needs someone," Debbie whispered back at him, "but it's not you. As you can see he went after her. Don't spoil the moment or otherwise you'll regret it."

Jacque didn't listen. He pushed her away, and ran in the direction he saw Louis go. Debbie stood there watching him take off, then turned to look at everyone who was busy murmuring about the death of Saul. She was angry, but she went and sat by Viviane, who was crying while Maxine explained what the man told her.

With tearing eyes Maxine continued to inform Viviane, "The American ambassador will come for her tomorrow at noon. The Marine Corps wants to meet with her. They want to take care of his memorial service and they want her approval. . . ."

Louis found Julie sitting inside of the old house crying, holding Saul's picture. He walked in without a word. He came and sat by her and pulled her into his arms while she was crying. She was telling him about the last time she spoke with Saul. She felt he was doing something dangerous. He didn't even let her say what she wanted to say to him. But now he was gone. She would never be able to let him know how much she cared for him and loved him. She couldn't believe that he was really gone.

"Maybe I misunderstood what the man said on the phone," Julie said as she straightened herself. She raised her head to look at Louis, who himself seemed lost. She wiped the tears that were running out of her eyes. "He's in the hospital injured and he wanted me at his side to take care of him. You know, that's the wife's duty, to nourish her husband back to health."

He didn't answer, but he sorrowfully nodded in agreement with her. He was worried how she was reasoning. She was telling him how fun Saul was, and if Louis knew him Louis would have liked him a lot.

She got up on her feet then looked at Louis who was still sitting on the sofa, looking up at her, crying. For a few seconds Louis's eyes were shimmering with tears. Quickly he got up on his feet while he came to his senses and inhaled and exhaled out of his mouth to hold the tears back. He passed his arms around Julie's shoulders, walking out of the old house and slowly headed back for the mansion, listening to her talking about Saul.

On their way they heard Jacque calling her, "Julie, where are you?"

She didn't answer. His voice was coming from the direction they were heading. When he saw them, he ran toward them and asked, "Are you all right?"

Julie looked at him, but she didn't say a word. Tears were running out of her eyes as they continued walking. Louis said, "You don't have to go back to excuse yourself to anyone. They would understand if you were to go inside."

"It's okay," Julie replied. "I'll be fine."

When they arrived, everyone was still there waiting for her. Maxine was afraid to talk, because when she looked at Julie and Louis's eyes, she felt that they both looked totally out of it.

While Maxine was informing Julie about the rest of the arrangements, Henry came and stood before her, blocking her view of Julie and Louis. She thought Henry was weird. How rude of him and what was wrong with him. She didn't say anything because she felt it was not the time to tell Henry he was being rude. She continued giving the information to Julie and ignored Henry's expression. "Louis, can you help take her to her rooms?" Louis nodded in consent. "Jacque, help Aunt Viviane. Marie, come help me pack their luggage. Julie and Aunt Viviane are leaving tomorrow."

Feeling helpless Jean asked, "Is there anything that I can do, Julie?"

Sobbing bitterly, Julie replied, "No." She looked at Louis, tears streaming down her cheeks. "He was going mad. . . . I think I drove him away."

Maxine consoled her as she passed her hands over Julie's face. "No, you didn't . . . that was his job. . . ."

Julie was crying so hard that her head started to spin and her stomach hurt. She was in severe pain. She held onto her stomach as she cringed and cried. She sat on the chair with her head bent. She was unable to walk. Maxine cried, "Help her inside for me, Louis."

Jacque was mad at Maxine. He felt that Maxine was taking over. She was ordering him around and asking Louis to help Julie inside. But at the moment he couldn't say anything. Gently taking Julie's arm from Louis, Jacque said, "That's okay, Louis, I'll take care of Julie."

With glaring eyes Louis looked at Jacque and made him move out of his way, then gently lifted Julie into his arms and carried her up to her room. Debbie, who was looking at them, saw the look in Louis's eyes. She shook her head at Jacque, who was trying to act normal. He followed them as if he was the guest and Louis was the host. Louis carried her and headed for the mansion. Jacque opened the door for them. Viviane went in with the baby in her arms and Louis went in with Julie in his arms without saying a word while she cried.

Viviane didn't say much, she was crying as well. Silently they all went up to Julie's room. She knew how it felt to lose a husband. The thought of her daughter becoming a widow at such an early age of life was very sad to her. The way her husband died brought back the day when Julie's father's plane went down. Quietly, she went up the steps as Jacque helped her up.

As they went in the mansion, Nicole put her hand over her mouth in shock. "Do you know what you just did, Maxine?"

She didn't understand Nicole's question, but she answered as she cleared her throat, "Yes, I sent her to rest. That is what she needs at the moment."

Nadine and Debbie went standing beside Nicole. She spoke as if they were not there. Thoughtlessly she replied, "Jacque will kill you tomorrow. You sent Louis in Julie's room, with her! Do you know how that looks, Julie crying on Louis's shoulders when she is supposed to cry in Jacque's arms, not Louis's."

Henry was still sitting not too far from them, listening to Nicole and Maxine dispute. He was thinking, *Why would Nicole say something so provocative and insensitive like that? Her mind is so twisted. Nicole needs help.*

Maxine snapped disgustedly at her, "You're sick, you need help. What do you think is going to happen, Nicole, Julie is going to have sex with Louis, Aunt Viviane, and the baby in the middle for finding out her husband is dead?"

As Maxine lashed at her, Nicole glanced at everyone. Then she noticed Henry was listening to their conversation. She felt embarrassed. She looked at Debbie and Nadine and replied, "That was not what I meant. It is just that Jacque doesn't want Louis near her or her mother."

Maxine thought she was stupid. "You have got to be joking!"

She shook her head at Nicole as she walked away from her. Without a word of good night Jean left the premises, leaving Henry talking with Maxine. Nicole looked at them talking, then she ran inside the house. She could not believe what just happened. By then almost all the guests had gone home. Sadly, Maxine sat back to massage her shoulders. Richard sneaked in the yard looking for her. She excused herself when she noticed him.

Calling Maxine, Marie admonished, "You two are going to get me fired."

"Good," Maxine said carelessly, grasping her hand, then ran toward Richard in the dark.

Louis laid Julie on her bed then removed her sandals. He gave her a pain reliever that was in her bathroom cabinet with a glass of water. Her eyes were filled with sorrow. She looked around the room looking for her mother. Louis stood by her bed looking at her, hoping she would be fine. She asked, "Louis, where's my mother?"

Viviane answered, "I'm here, darling."

"I need to change," Julie said.

Louis kissed Julie and Viviane good night and left the room. Henry was down in the lobby waiting for him with Nadine, who was also crying. Louis didn't look at them. He walked right out of the mansion. Henry and Nadine followed him. Louis went and sat in the car on the passenger side without saying a word. Henry got in the driver's side and drove Louis and Nadine home. Louis didn't open his eyes till Henry drove through the yard. Henry parked the car in front of the door of his estate. Louis looked at the time. It was a little past midnight. He forced himself to walk up the steps. Henry was afraid for Louis as he watched him going up. That was the first time Henry whispered a word of prayer for his friend. "Please God, help him."

Francois was at the door waiting for him. Marie had called and informed him of Louis's situation. Louis removed his tie and handed it to him as he carried himself to his bedroom. He gently laid his body onto the bed. When he opened his eyes, he realized he was lying down and Francois had followed him to his room.

"Francois, get my passport and my briefcase for me. I'm leaving town."

Back at the Bassine mansion, Viviane was making sure Julie had everything she would need for the night with the help of Marie.

"Thank you, Mama." Turning to Marie she said, "Marie, you have been on your feet all day and night. It's time for you to take a rest."

"Thank you, madame, but I'll be okay."

Making ready to go, Viviane took Marie's hand to walk out and said to Julie, "I will not be far."

She looked at her gratefully. "Thank you, Mama."

Viviane too was mourning the loss of her son-in-law. Her heart was suffering as she turned to leave the room. Getting off her bed, Julie undressed and stood under the hot stinging shower, crying for a long time. Finally she cried herself out, and utterly exhausted she turned the water off and stepped out. She put on her nightgown and crawled into bed. She lay down with tears in her eyes and fell asleep. During the night she was dreaming and sobbing out in her sleep.

Viviane was coming to the room to check on Julie when she overheard her cries. Slowly she opened the door to go in and realized Julie was still asleep. There was no one there with her. Julie was tossing and turning, crying out. That was the first time Viviane had ever heard her dream and she listened.

Viviane was flabbergasted by Julie's outcry. She whispered, "My word!"

She thought, *Is that the nightmare Julie has been having and she couldn't remember? My God! Why is she having that kind of a dream?*

Viviane heard enough of Julie's dream. She carefully awoke her. Tears were shimmering in Julie's eyes as she awakened. She asked, "What happened? Was I dreaming again?" Julie felt embarrassed. She apologized for keeping her awake. Viviane didn't tell her what she heard her say in her dream.

She said, "Eventually you'll know what your dream meant. Then you'll find out how to solve it."

She spent the rest of the night with Julie. Early in the morning Marie was coming up with a tray of breakfast for Julie and to assist her. But Julie was all dressed up, going down the stairs. "Madame, you're already awake."

Julie replied, "Marie, finish preparing my bag for me, please. I'm leaving for New York in four hours."

"*Oui*, madame."

Hearing Julie's voice in the hallway, the three women came out. Maxine walked over and hugged her and kissed her. "I thought you were still in bed. You are early, Julie."

Julie's face looked sad but fresh. She reminded them, "I'm going back today. My flight leaves in four hours. The Haitian ambassador will meet us at the airport."

Carine, trying to drum up some false sympathy, asked, "Why don't you let Jacque escort you to New York?"

Glancing at her, Julie replied, "Jacque needs to take care of himself. . . . I already made arrangements for someone to pick up my plant and the rest of my things for me. I want my things to be in the guest house when I return."

She handed Maxine the list of the things she would need when she returned on a sheet of paper. Carine thought she was joking. "In the small house, Julie? Your place is here whenever you come to Haiti."

Nicole gave her a hug and said, "I am going to miss you, Julie."

Maxine kissed her on her cheek regretfully and asked, "When will you be coming back?"

Julie sighed. "Probably in about three weeks or so, I don't really know. . . . I'll call you to let you know the exact time."

While they were talking, Louis had dropped by to see her. Slowly they walked to the living room, leaving everyone behind.

Maxine was silent, lost in thought about Louis. The sorrow she saw when she looked into his eyes was unbearable. Without talking she could see Louis was afraid of letting Julie go, afraid of losing her.

Louis offered to escort them to New York, but Julie refused. He wanted her to promise him she would return to Haiti and when she did, he wanted to be the one to pick her up at the airport. He didn't let her know the thought of not seeing her anymore wasn't easy for him to visualize. That wasn't the time or the place for him to pour out his feeling for her. He knew he had to let her go so she could sort her way and prayed she would keep him on mind.

Julie cried openly before him. She didn't know what she was going to do at the moment and where life was really going to lead her.

Maxine stood from a distance looking at them. She knew inside Louis was crying out his heart. She could see that he couldn't bear to see Julie leaving. As he was leaving Louis took his handkerchief to wipe her eyes and held it tight between his hands then made his way out of the mansion. Maxine put her hands on her chest, trying to suppress the tears that were trying to escape her eyes. She watched how Louis rushed out of the mansion. He didn't look back, afraid he might break down before her. Maxine was sure now that Louis's feeling was deeper than what she had presumed them to be. He truly loved Julie.

Jean was talking to Jacque in the lobby. He was informing him about their departure to New York. Jean wasn't able to find reservations for him and for the rest of the family today. Only in three days, and he hoped they would arrive for the funeral in time.

Walking to the living room, Maxine offered, "Can I drop you off at the airport?"

Gratefully, Julie replied, "Thanks, Max, that would be appreciated."

Carine stood at the entrance of the living room looking at the departure of Louis. Still she had not offered any word of sympathy or looked Julie in the eyes. Marie came in to let her know she got everything ready for her. And she had them placed in the back of the car that was going to take her to the airport.

It was ten-thirty when Jacque had come down, he said, "You're not leaving that early are you, Julie?"

"Very soon. Is my mother ready?"

Viviane was coming down with William. She called as she came down, "Yes, we're ready."

Julie picked up her purse and prepared to leave. "Good, it is time for us to go."

She got up and walked away. Maxine picked up her purse and followed her. And Jacque took the key from Roy since he was the one who was going to drive them to the airport. Carine, Jean, and Nicole walked them to the car. Julie waved goodbye, and said, "Tell everyone else, I'll be back soon," as they drove off.

It was very heart breaking on the way to the airport. Julie handed the doll she had received to her son and held on to him, trying to draw comfort from him. She kissed him and cuddled him tenderly in her arms and found some solace in the fact that he was part of Saul she was holding on to.

<u>Chapter Eleven</u>

The Return

It had been over twelve months since Julie went back to New York. Jacque was returning from Jacmel, heading for the mansion. On the way he kept thinking about how would he get Julie now that she was an official widow. He was even happier, because he had heard that Louis had left town right after Julie's departure and spent almost five months away, and by now he felt Louis would have gotten over Julie for good.

He thought of Saul's will. Why wouldn't his lawyer read the whole testimony to her? How dare he tell her the rest was not for her to hear! Exactly what did Saul leave her? He knew Saul's firm made a lot of money. Why did Saul sell out?

"I thought he was going to put me in charge of the firm," Jacque murmured under his breath. "Instead he did that."

Saul's lawyer didn't read the estimate of the business to Julie. Instead he just handed her the paper. Jacque wanted to know how much was he showing her.

"Right now," he said out loud to himself, "Julie is desperate and vulnerable. She'll accept anything I say. She's already married and had a child, and now definitely she will need a father for her son."

He thought of the hotels and the lands that Saul had left in his care and wanted him to hand all the documents to Henry before he died.

"That stinks!" he shouted, and thought of all the documents he had entrusted to him. *Saul was a bastard and he deserved to die. He took all his properties and put them under his wife's name and emptied the bank accounts. When I was the one taking care of them for him. The money he was paying me was petty,*

*compared to what he really had. Saul had given me an acre for me to built my hotel,
a lousy acre of land, when he had hundreds.*

The thought of Saul angered him. He ground his teeth together. "All
your work was in vain, Saul, because I'm going to possess them all, even
your woman. How dare you sell half of everything you had to that crazy
bastard and leave me out in the cold. Now Julie possesses everything you
had, plus the money."

Then Jacque glanced at the passenger seat next to him as if he was speaking to someone there. "I'm a man, Julie, and I patiently waited for you. I
know you are an understanding person and reasonable as well so, Julie,
please give me a chance, let us work things out together. Let's have the family we always dreamt of."

He was so deep in thought, fabricating out loud what to say to Julie, he
almost missed Louis's car passing by.

"Fuji!" He jerked out of his thoughts. Jacque wondered vindictively, "He
has so many people kissing his butt as it is. Everyone is catering to his rich
ass, doing this job or that job for him, while he's out here having fun. That
bastard almost popped a vein in my brain the night Saul died just for wanting to dance with Julie. Then he seduced my woman right before my eyes.
He slept with her the night that Saul died. She was looking all worked out
then she got the nerve to cry for her husband. She deserved an Oscar for
best performance." He laughed. "What a woman! I don't care if he had her
So Louis," he shouted to the passing car, "if it makes her happy, she can
screw you all she wants."

He looked at himself in the rear view mirror, grinned, and slid his tongue
over his top row of perfect teeth. "Boy, am I good looking or what?"

As he drove through the yard, Roy saw him, greeting him as he walked
into the house. He ran up the stairs and found that no one was home. Carine
was not in her room. Running back down the stairs, he shouted, "Roy,
where's everyone? Where's Carine?"

Roy replied, "They aren't home sir and as for mademoiselle, she is by
the pool."

Jacque yelled, "By the pool? Where's Maxine? Did she say when she is
coming back?"

The butler replied, "No sir."

Turning away, Jacque ordered, "I left a few things behind in my car. Get
them out for me."

Maxine and Louis had been at the airport since 3:00 P.M. They sat in the
dining room anxiously awaiting the arrival of the plane. Maxine jumped up
excitedly and said, "Louis, the plane landed. Look, people are coming out."

Taking a deep breath to calm himself, Louis too stood up. "Max, in all
my entire life this is the second time I can recall that I have gotten nervous."

Maxine touched his hands. "Your hands are so cold, like ice! Julie's hands get like that too, you know, when she's nervous. I thought that was weird. You two are meant for each other."

They walked down toward the landing site as they saw Julie emerge.

Maxine said excitedly, "There she is! Oh, and my Aunt Viviane and the baby! They return also."

Julie and Louis slowly walked toward each other. He bent down and gently kissed her. Maxine kissed Aunt Viviane on both cheeks and took the sleeping toddler from her hands.

Placing the salutary kiss on both of her cheeks, Louis greeted, "Nice to see you again, Mother."

Turning to Maxine with the child in her arms, he eagerly held out his hands to take the child. "Max, can I hold him?"

She smiled as she handed William over to him. "Yes."

Gently he took the toddler from her. William opened his eyes and looked at him. He kissed Bill on the forehead. Holding the toddler close to him and wrapping his other arm around Julie's shoulder, they turned and walked toward the car. Under her breath, Julie said, "How's everything with you?"

"I'm happy you returned," he replied.

With a straight face, she replied, "You are."

Julie's eyes looked sad. Louis didn't say much because he was afraid she had not gotten over the death of her husband. He held her tighter as they made their way to the car.

Back at the Bassine mansion, Carine was walking down out of the lobby. Looking at her one would think she was one of the most beautiful women in the world. She was nicely shaped and all her proportions were well placed, and a beautiful face to go with it. Despite all the beauty she possessed, she was always unhappy, with a down look on her face. She walked across the floor toward the library. Before she reached the door, Jacque flung it open and pulled her in. "Where have you been?"

"By the pool." Enthusiastically, she hugged him. "Brother, you're back!"

"Why didn't you call me?" Jacque snapped.

Carine replied in a fake crying voice, "Your phone was constantly busy. I couldn't get through. How was Jacmel?"

"Everyone is fine," Jacque answered, then informed, "Julie has hands of gold. You should have seen the passion tree vineyard plantation. That woman is a gift from God. I've tasted one of the bottles she had prepared, boy! That was the best passion liquor I've ever tasted. It got me so horny that I had to share my passion with a few of the province women. . . ."

They chorused a laugh!

"She's going to make a lot of money. I was surprised when I got there. Her friends weren't too happy to see me. As soon as I get her signature of those documents, I'm going to fire every last one of them. Saul had sent some machinery down to the plantation to help cultivate the lands better before he took the big dive. They're really great. I was surprised to see that the workers knew how to use those machines. They were pretty good at running them. She hired a security company for her plantation. Isn't she so modernized?"

Looking at Carine closely, he said, "Your silent voice sounds sinister. . . . Is there more information that you haven't told me yet? Well, spit it out! I can take it."

Walking to the other side of the room to gain time, Carine said, "I'm so glad to see that you have enjoyed yourself. Since you left, everything turned out wrong here. Maxine was constantly arguing with me and frustrating our plans. She did just as Julie asked. Got everything sent to the old house just like Julie wanted. . . . Did you know Julie is returning today?"

"Today!" he yelped. He didn't know she was returning today. "Why did no one call to inform me?"

"I didn't know myself she was returning till Nicole told me this morning."

Jacque replied, "I knew there was a reason for me to come home today, but I just couldn't pinpoint it. Why haven't you got the place ready? Get flowers and sympathy cards, so she would think we were thinking of her!"

She stared at Jacque, trying to assimilate his expression with a malicious smile on her face. Jacque closed his eyes, and with a huge grin on his face, exclaimed, "Do you know, how . . . *RICH* . . . she is?"

Carine smiled. "Jacque, I never heard so much glee in your voice before."

Hugging her and turning her with glee, he gloated, "That's how . . . *RICH* . . . she is! She inherited everything that man had, plus what she has. Her husband had a successful architectural firm, and he did business with a lot of different firms all over the world. He designed buildings, planes, boats, and many other things. That's the reason he was always involved in military affairs, especially with the Marine Corps. They even made him a diplomat, that's how important he was! Several times he almost got killed, but this time, he finally did it. But one thing I couldn't believe is that he sold his firm."

Nicole, hearing the commotion, entered the library. She asked, "What's going on? Oh! Jacque, you're back."

Carine roughly said, "Why are you home from work so early?"

"Julie is returning today," Nicole replied, "so I want to be here to welcome her home."

Disdainfully Carine regarded her and asked, "Since when were you interested in her coming to Haiti?"

"I was always happy when she is in town," Nicole defended. "I just never showed it. She's moving to the old house and I was helping Maxine with the fixing of the old place. She called Maxine two days ago to let her know she'll be here today. Maxine went with Louis to pick her up at the airport."

"Louis!" Jacque exclaimed with rage and picked up the crystal vase that was on the coffee table and threw it over Nicole's head, shattering it on the wall of the library. Nicole trembled with fear as she looked upon Jacque's outburst. "That man never quits. Why didn't one of you go with her?"

"Julie had requested for Louis to pick her up at the airport," Nicole replied.

Jacque then said, "Carine, you know what to do."

Carine nodded her head in understanding. Jacque, looking at Nicole who was standing there looking at them in fear, said, "Do you know what this means? Get the move on, get the place ready, call everyone, don't just stand there."

They all started to get the place sparkling clean for Julie. Everyone was moving like they were running a race. Before you knew it, the place was bright and clean.

Jacque came down stairs looking good. He asked, "Maybe I could make it to the airport. What time is her plane landing?"

Looking at her watch, Nicole said, "It's too late, she is on her way home. Her plane landed at three and now it five-forty."

Carine, who was coming in the family room, announced, "She is here! I saw Louis's Jeep just drive down the hill heading toward the old house."

Rubbing his chin, Jacque mused, "So she's here! I've got to find a way to get her complete trust. I have big plans for that lady."

Feeling remorse Nicole asked, "Don't we owe her money, Jacque?"

"Do you have a million dollars to pay her?" Jacque was relentless. "If you do, then pay her."

He sat back on his chair as he continued in a callused tone, "If we have to kiss her ass to get what we want, that is what we have to do. . . . So be it!"

He asked Carine to fix him a drink.

Listening to the way he was talking, Nicole realized that Jacque was becoming more unfeeling and untrustworthy. He was turning into a real monster. How would he ever repent? Carine was the same, cold and selfish. "Maxine is with her."

Maxine was just arriving. She opened the door as Nicole mentioned her name. "I heard my name. What do you want with me?"

After she finished mixing the cocktail, Carine handed Jacque his drink. Taking the drink from Carine's hand he said, glaring at Maxine, "Where's Julie?"

With a gleeful smile, Maxine said, "She's at the old house. Guess who returned with her?"

Moving himself from the chair he said, "So she returned with the little prince. . . . His mother needs a king."

Knowing exactly what he was thinking, Maxine replied, "Oh, most definitely she will need a king and I know just the person for it, too." Turning, she walked away, throwing over her shoulder, "I'm not going to be here for the weekend. I was invited to Louis's ranch. Oh, and by the way," she reached the door, "Aunt Viviane also returned with her too."

Carine turned to her brother as they made ready to go to the little house, wondering how he would react to this new development. "What's your plan now, Jacque?"

"I'm thinking of it," Jacque replied as they left the room.

The following night Louis invited Julie and her mother to dinner. It was six-thirty when they arrived. As soon as they stepped out the car, the rain started to pour as if the gates of heaven opened up on them. Francois rushed to open the door.

"*Bonsoir*, Francois," Julie greeted.

Francois responded, "Come in, come in. It's pouring rain out there. You're all wet. Monsieur Claude, the baby."

He quickly took the toddler from Henry. They were drenched from head to foot. Louis ran down the stairs and called out to Richard Landers, Francois and Marie's son, who was also living with Francois on Louis's estate. "Richard, please help take them upstairs to dry off."

Taking the toddler from Francois, Louis quickly ran back up the stairs. Shouldering open the door of his bedroom, he laid him on his bed, and as fast as he could, he removed the toddler's wet clothing and enfolded him with the soft blanket that was lying on his bed. Henry, too, went up to change. And since Julie had followed Louis, Richard took Viviane to the guest rooms where she could remove her clothes and find the towels and robes set out for her.

Julie was so excited over the events taking place that she failed to realize that she was in Louis's room. Louis had not left the room. He had walked into the back of his closet to find William something to wear. Not paying attention to where Louis had gone to, she removed all her clothes and looked around for something to put on.

Louis walked out, holding up two shirts in his hands, talking to the baby, saying, "Billy, which one do you want to wear?"

He stopped dead in his tracks, still holding the garments in his hands. Julie was totally nude, facing Louis. He stood completely mesmerized by her sight. She was speechless . . . quickly she moved and grabbed the closest thing to her (the blanket covering the baby) and covered her body while he stood swallowing from the sight he had just beheld.

He turned his head away and apologized in a husky voice, "I'm sorry."

She looked around the very masculine majesty of the room and saw she was in his room. She apologized. "I'm sorry, I thought you left the room."

Louis tried to pretend nothing had happened. He crossed to William, covering him, and folded his silk shirt and made a diaper and put it on Bill. Bill was laughing while he was playing with him. Julie walked over and held out her hand for the other shirt. "He has extra clothes and diapers inside his bag. Can I have the other shirt?"

Holding out the expensive silk shirt to her, he offered, "Oh, yes! Anything of mine is yours."

Taking it from his trembling hands, she took it and turning her back, she shrugged into the shirt. "Where do you keep your underwear? I need some."

"In there," he said, pointing a finger toward the closet door. It was a huge walk-in closet with wall-to-wall drawers and cabinets with mirrors. She opened one of the drawers and inside were several pairs of underwear. She pulled a pair out and held them up, asking, "Can I wear these?"

It was a pair of black silk boxer shorts. He smiled and nodded. "Yes, if you promise to return it unwashed."

Ignoring his comment and without any sign of embarrassment, she slowly lifted her legs one at a time to pull them on. Pretending he wasn't looking at her out of the corner of his left eye, he softly said to the toddler, "William, your mother is naughty, but she is extremely beautiful."

As if he understood, Bill gurgled, and Louis said, "I could not agree with you more. I, too, am gaga over her."

Francois brought the baby's bag. He knocked on the door and handed it to Julie. "Oh, thank you, Francois."

She smiled and took the bag and pulled out his bottle and a change of clothes for him. "Are you ready for your last bottle, honey?"

Sitting down on the edge of the bed, she pulled the toddler toward her. "Good, now you can give Monsieur Janvier his shirt back."

She turned the toddler over and prepared to remove the shirt off him. She scolded him softly at the wet spot on the shirt. "Bill, you peed on Fuji's shirt." Apologetically, she handed Louis the soiled shirt. "I'm sorry."

Louis looked at it and shrugged. "For what? It's washable." He tossed it over the chair.

She took out a diaper to put on him and something to wear. After she finished dressing him, she took out his bottle and settled him in her arms to feed him. Louis spoke up, "You're not going to breast-feed him, are you?"

Smiling and tickling the baby, she unthinkingly replied, "No, I breast-fed him for the first four months, then I stopped. Sometimes I feel like I still have a little milk left in my breasts."

Julie wasn't looking at Louis so she didn't see the effect her words had on him. Swallowing hard, Louis softly said, "Julie."

She looked up at him from feeding the toddler. He said, "If I was your baby I would not . . . I mean, I would not want to stop breast-feeding."

Laughing at his comment, she shook her head. "Fuji, you're crazy."

There was a knock at the door. He got up and went to open it and invited Julie's mother in. "Come in, Mother."

Viviane was wearing a robe that belonged to Louis. She headed straight for the toddler. "How is he doing?" her mother inquired, brushing her hand over his soft head.

Julie answered, "He's doing fine."

Turning toward the door, Louis looked down at his clothes and remarked, "I'd better go change."

"Why" You look fine to me." Julie didn't see any need for him to change.

"No, I will not feel comfortable if I don't wear a robe, too." He indicated their attire.

Louis didn't want to feel left out. He also didn't want his guests (especially Julie) to feel uncomfortable. He went into his closet, quickly changed his suit, and donned a silk black robe. Everyone had robes on. Henry was out in the hallway waiting when they walked out of the bedroom. They all trouped downstairs to where Francois was waiting to serve dinner. "Dinner is served, *mesdames et messieurs.*"

"Good," Viviane said in anticipation. "I'm starving."

Francois opened the doors to the dining room. Inside it was tastefully decorated, but not to Viviane's taste. She turned to Louis. "Fuji, you need a woman's touch here."

Nudging her head, Julie protested, "But, Mother, it looks nice just the way it is."

Viviane chuckled. "I didn't say it wasn't nice, dear. It's so 'masculine', that's all."

Louis looked around at the décor as if really seeing it for the first time. "You're quite right, Mother." He looked straight at Julie. "It does need a woman's touch."

Taking Viviane's hand as they walked in, he seated her to his left and Julie to his right while Henry sat in the empty chair beside Viviane. They had a wonderful three-course meal, which was lobsters with steamed artichokes, watercrest salad, and broiled fish stuffed with shrimp. When the meal was over, Viviane got up from her chair, saying, "I'm stuffed."

Louis invited them to his lounge room for after dinner drinks and a comfortable talk.

Henry and Julie excused themselves and went to play pool while Louis and her mother were talking. Louis glanced at Julie as she hit the cue ball and thought she was quite good. Viviane smiled when she saw the way he looked at her daughter and how every now and then, he looked at her so she would know he was listening. She thought, Louis still has affection for my daughter.

The butler came to let Louis know that he couldn't get through on the line of the Bassine mansion then left. Looking through the sliding doors they could see the rain was pouring outside. Julie commented when she heard the thunder, "I could just run in the rain and let it fall all over my body."

Louis and Henry smiled. Viviane replied, "That's the child in you talking. This rain would get you sick."

Julie said, "I wasn't planning to play in the water, but I'm tempted."

Viviane went on to say, "When Julie was a little girl she used to love playing and running with nothing on."

Louis and Henry were laughing. Julie replied, "You guys acted like you've never done that!"

They nodded. "Never!"

"Then you've missed a whole lot."

Looking at Julie, Louis saw she was wondering how they were going to go home. Louis didn't feel it was safe for them to leave tonight. William was fast asleep in Louis's arms. Viviane looked at the sleeping toddler and yawned. "I feel the same way too, Bill. Can someone please show me where Bill and I can sleep? I'm sorry, I'm not young anymore."

Kissing her hands, Louis said, "You'll be young forever, Mother."

Francois was summoned to show them to their rooms. Taking the sleeping baby, Julie walked behind her mother to go put him to bed. Louis touched her arm gently. "I'll be down here when you're finished."

She turned and looked at him. She felt the same attraction he was feeling, but she was fighting herself.

Viviane chattered all the way to the room that Francois showed them. The blanket on the bed was turned down and everything had been made ready. Julie pulled back the blanket for her mother and carefully put Bill down in the middle and prepared to slide in on the other side of the bed. As she was about to climb in on the other side, Viviane stopped and commented, "Aren't you too old to be sleeping with your mother?"

"No!"

"The night is young," Viviane suggested. "Go have fun, let me and William rest. I'm sure Louis is waiting for you. Go shoot some pool."

Julie reluctantly obeyed her mother because she didn't want to be alone with Louis. Louis was at the lounge waiting for her. Henry had left for the night. Julie stood by the lounge door and said, "Rack them up. I'm going to kick your butt in pool."

"Is that a promise?" Louis answered as he formed the triangle shape on the pool table. He was happy to see her here with him. She laughed and thought Louis had not changed at all. He was still crazy because she remembered the last time she hit Louis he claimed a man could get turned on in that kind of activity.

They laughed and joked about each other. She beat Louis in the game of pool.

She said, "Saul couldn't beat me either, no matter how hard he tried. I'm really good at playing pool. Saul just couldn't win. One day he got so upset he told me I have a lot of male hormone."

Louis laughed and agreed with what her late husband had said. She laughed in disagreement. "I don't think so. I'm more feminine then masculine. And he knew that, too."

Louis smiled and didn't argue. She definitely had a woman's body from what he had beheld before him tonight in his room. For a moment he had a flashback of what he had seen. She was definitely a woman, but it felt good to tease her and she teased him back. He knew he was definitely attracted to her, but was he really in love with her, or was it just infatuation. He wanted to kiss her as she laughed at his jokes.

Julie made ready to hit the cue ball. She peeked at Louis, who was busy looking at her. She remembered what Maxine had seen him doing here on top of this pool table with a Canadian woman. While she hit the ball, she buzzed, "If only this pool table could talk, boy, would it tell a thousand tales."

Louis laughed in surprise at her comment. "What would you like it to tell you?"

"A few secrets about its master."

"Secrets," Louis repeated. "I tell you this—today when I held William in my arms, I felt so good, like my dream is about to come true."

He spoke of his son to Julie. William inspired him to seek for his son. As they were talking, they shared a glass of wine for the blessing to come.

Taking a deep breath, she stepped away and said gaily, "When are you going to show me the rest of your place?"

He invited, "Why not now! It's not that late."

Placing the glass on the bar he walked toward her and took her hands. He led her first to the library, then the museum. He was an art collector. She could see he loved gothic art and he was an avid collector of the Middle Ages. Then they went to see his car collection, his music room, his living room tastefully decorated in beige and gold, his exercise room with its complete gym, and the many other rooms; rooms he did not even remember he had in the house. Finally he headed toward a huge, brass-trimmed mahogany door. It was a beautiful door with oriental decorations on it.

"You skipped this door twice, why is that? What's behind this door?"

Louis thought, *Julie is an observer, one who pays attention.* "What lies behind this door is not something I take very lightly."

"Oh, I see."

She stood calmly waiting to see what his next move would be. With a serious expression, Louis turned and looked at her. "You see, behind these doors is something very sacred to me. It's a ritual that my ancestors did, and it was passed down from generation to generation. I can only open these doors to the woman who is willing to be my wife. . . . I will not open these doors to you, unless you are willing to be my wife. And if you say 'yes' and then change your mind, I may quietly go out of mind. I might even flip . . . and might possibly even kill you."

"Oh really, I see." Nodding her head toward the door she ordered softly, "Open the door. I dare you."

"You're a daring one . . . aren't you," he commented admiringly as he opened the door.

Inside the open door was a huge ballroom, so glamorous and grand. She walked inside and said in awe, "Shall we dance?"

She sang and twirled around hugging herself. That was the first time since her husband's death, Julie was dancing and smiling like the way she used to. He stood by the door smiling, watching her dancing and turning around and around to imaginary music. She twirled around so much that her shirt parted, revealing a peek of her breast. She came close to him, taunting and calling him to her. Teasingly she twirled around him, but before she could move away, he turned and with one swift, smooth move, he grabbed her before she could run away from him. He took her arms and slowly placed them both around his neck, moving closer to her, like a tiger that had found its prey. He tilted her chin and tasted her lips, which he had desperately wanted to do as he gently ran his hands through her luxurious hair. He bent her slightly over backward, grazing his lips on her neck and inhaling the fragrance of her body.

He whispered, "I missed you so much."

He felt her body trembling under his touch. He quickly lifted her up in his arms, kissed her, and carried her up to his room. She put her arms around his neck and laid her head against his chest. The door of his bedroom opened to him like some unseen person was expecting them, and he kicked the door closed behind him. He laid her on his blue satin blanket. Swiftly he removed his shirt and his underwear that she was wearing. Without any form of embarrassment, she looked at his masculine body as he removed his pants and robe, then he, too, stood naked. He was six-nine in all his masculine glory. She thought she was seeing a Greek god in the flesh. He moved without haste toward her and knelt before her.

Julie implored, "Please, have mercy on me."

She closed her eyes tight and put her hands up in front of her, as if warding off some invisible force. Louis moved back and looked at her smooth, silky, shivering body. Taking deep breaths, he tried to calm the pounding of his heart, making an effort to understand what she said and why she said it. He sat in an armchair that was against the wall with his head down and his hands hanging loosely between his knees as he tried to make sense of the emotions raging through him.

Julie moved off the bed, pulled up the sheet, and wrapped it toga style over her nakedness. She walked toward him and placed her hands in his hair. It felt as soft and silky as a baby's. He looked up at the tears in her eyes. Patting his knees, he indicated that she should sit. She sat on his lap like a child who needed protection.

Burying her face in his bare chest, she sniffed, "I'm sorry."

Stroking her hair and rocking back and forth, he replied, "It's okay, my love."

She continued in a muffled whisper, "I do want you, I want you so much that I can taste you. . . ."

Pulling back she placed little wet kisses all over his face. " . . . I'm a woman who wants to hold on to her dignity. I believe sex should only be in a marriage. I beg you, don't make me out to be a cheap, unworthy woman. I do love you. If this is what you want, I will let you take me."

He looked at her wonderingly, then bent his head to kiss her. She kissed him back. She started to rub her hands over his chest and hairs, caressing him. He caught her hands and took his lips off her lips, smiled, and said, "I, too, am a man with integrity, and I would not want to take the woman I love and turn her into a cheap, unworthy purpose. Holding you like this, at this moment, is enough for me."

Placing his lips on each of her eyelids, he instructed, "Let's go to sleep."

She closed her eyes and fell asleep with his arms wrapped around her. He gently laid her on his bed, put back his robe, then quietly opened the door to leave. She opened her eyes and she realized that she was lying down on the bed. Although she was still hurt by her husband's death, she could not help seeing the passion that was burning in Louis's eyes. Drowsily she asked, "Louis, where's the restroom?"

Louis took her hand and walked her to the bathroom. "Thank you, Louis. Good night."

Making ready to go, Louis assured her, "I will not be far. Just press this button if you need me."

She looked at it gratefully. "Thank you."

His eyes were filled with joy as he turned to leave the room.

While she was dressing, she accidentally pressed against the button and turned on the intercom. Finishing putting on the shirt she took out the male doll that was inside William's bag, gave it a little kiss, and laid it on the pillow. She crawled into bed. She lay down with tears in her eyes, thinking about the way Saul had died, and was that the right decision, to make a home in Haiti the way Saul wanted? Was she ready for a new relationship? That same old questions she'd been asking herself since her very first night when she returned a year earlier. She realized she had told Louis she was in love with him and noticed there was a lot of changing in him.

Before, she thought, Louis would have dismissed what she pleaded and had his way with her. Tonight she had witnessed something new about him. She questioned, did Louis still have other lovers in his life? His eyes told her many tales, but what were they?

She fell asleep as her mind wandered off. Sometime during the night she had her dream. She was sobbing out in her sleep.

She was running in the yard, enjoying the drops of the rain pouring on her. She opened her arms while she looked up in the heavens. She slowly turned, smiling, passing her hands over her face and on her hair. She couldn't see anything but rain falling down her face. He came after her, standing behind her, enfolding her into her arms.

He whispered, "Julie!"

He turned her to look at her, but she couldn't see his face because the rain was pouring very heavily on her face. She closed her eyes while he kissed her. He held her tight against him, kissing her, letting the rain fall all over their bodies. He started to undress her, removing the shirt she was wearing. She glanced to look where they were at and saw they were in the yard of the Bassine mansion, where Louis was reciting his poem the night before the death of her husband. He carried her and laid her on the marble bench that was under her bedroom window. He continued caressing her while he removed the black suit he was wearing. Likewise, he was completely naked.

"My love," she cried out while he was making love to her.

Saul ran toward her and tried to pull her away, but he was unable to do so. Nothing mattered but them two.

"Don't leave me, release me from this madness I'm having," he moaned. "Julie, my love, release me from my solitude."

The feelings hit her unexpectedly. She told him how she'd been searching for him, and she would not leave him. How she wanted him. . . . Saul stood from a distance watching how she was pleading. His body was numbed and his mouth was sealed. There was nothing he could do or say, but to watch how he was making love to his wife, draining his life force out of him.

"Look at me," he demanded of Julie while he moved and sank deeply in her. "Tell me you love me."

She opened her eyes to look at him, grasping her mental view. He whispered, "Yes, look at me."

She whispered back, "How could that be?"

He sealed his lips on her, kissing her with passion. She moaned out his name, yearning for him. "It's you I really want. . .! Take me!" she pleaded over and over. She grabbed him, holding him closer to her. Responding to him as he made his way into her. "Yes, I love you."

Surfacing from sleep, Louis heard her cries and came running to her room. When he opened the door, he noticed she was asleep. He turned off the intercom. He dimmed the light as he watched her tossing as if someone was touching her, caressing her, and crying out his name.

"Louis," she cried over and over, grabbing the blanket and the pillows under her neck. "My love, Fuji. . . . Mm," she moaned. "Louis, yes speak to me. Never set me apart from you. . . . Louis!"

Standing before the bed, Louis was stunned. Never did he see or hear anything like that. He felt some invisible force had yoked them together. He slowly slid himself on the bed next to her side and held her in his arms. She startled and opened her eyes, and saw Louis next to her looking at her. He hushed her as one would a small child. "I'm here, Julie, I'm here."

Julie realized she was crying out again in her sleep and this time the mysterious man was here to the rescue. Aware what she was dreaming about, she covered her face with her hands. She became a bit flustered knowing Louis was at her side because of her cry. She couldn't make sense of why she was dreaming about Louis. And for quite sometimes she'd been having that dream. My God, she thought, did Saul know who Louis was?

He pulled her up closer to him and kissed her on her forehead, rocking her gently back and forth, softly caressing her face. He helped her back to sleep and told her that he loved her. He spent the rest of the night watching over her while thinking about the dream she had. That must have been the dream that drove her husband out of his mind.

He closed his eyes as he kissed her head and fell asleep. In the light of morning as he was about to leave the room, he noticed the doll lying on the floor. He smiled, picked it up, and placed it back on the pillow beside her. Later in that morning Louis took them home.

Jacque was coming to the old house to meet them with a big smirk on his face. He couldn't believe it rain so hard like that last night. He felt that Louis must have cast a spell to cause that deluge. It hadn't rained in Haiti for some time. Last night was unbelievable, the thunder and the lightning was unbearable. The noise kept him awake all night long and Julie with her mother and baby were with Louis through the storm. What did they do besides having dinner? Was he playing with Julie like he did with every woman he met? Was Julie enjoying the company of that playboy Louis?

Jacque looked at Viviane and thought, *She's a very attractive older woman. Knowing Louis, he probably seduced them both. Look at the way Viviane is smiling, touching his face.*

So many questions and thoughts ran on in Jacque's mind that he lost his senses for a moment.

Julie greeted him, "Jacque, how are you? We tried to call last night but the lines were down."

"I was worried," Jacque said, looking at Louis as he kissed Julie on her cheek, then informed her, "I called the telephone company already. By the end of the afternoon, they'll have the lines fixed."

Julie seemed so happy as she walked in the house holding on to Jacque's arm but she clung to Louis. Viviane noticed when Julie was around Louis, she seemed to forget her sorrow. She saw how her head leaned against Louis's arm.

Louis giggled when he felt William was walking between his legs. His little hands were holding on to each of Louis's legs as he walked in with Julie holding onto his arm. Everyone laughed when they saw where William was.

"I think he's trying to carry me on his shoulders."

Wow! The creature could actually laugh, Jacque thought, trying to take William out from under Louis's legs. William screamed. Louis said, "No, let him be. . . . He's not bothering me."

Viviane suggested that Louis and Julie should go horseback riding and for them to return with a basket of mangoes for her. Julie thought that was a rather long trip, because those mango trees were a long way. Viviane didn't care. She felt the ride would do her good. And the joy she saw on Julie's face brought some happiness in her heart. Jacque had wanted to take Julie for the ride, but Viviane had wanted to talk to him about Julie's gathering.

"Take your time," Viviane suggested and sent them on their way. They rode by the river to see if the rain had raised the water. She was surprised when they got to the river. It was not high at all and there was no garbage or debris in the water. Julie got off her horse and removed her shoes to play in the water.

She called Louis, "Come in the water. It's warm."

"Only if you promise to kiss me."

"Come in," she waved.

"Then I shall!"

Louis jumped off his horse and removed his shoes and socks. He rolled up his pants then ran after her. She screamed and said, "I cannot run in the water, there's too many rocks."

He carried her as she struggled to get herself loose from him. Gradually he let her down as he gave her a passionate kiss. She had to pull away because Louis was going to keep on kissing till her mouth got sore. She reminded him why they went riding, and they would have to hurry up to get those mangoes her mother wanted before it got dark. Louis wanted to make it even easier so they could spend more time making out.

He suggested, "Let's go buy those mangoes."

Julie couldn't believe what Louis suggested. Shaking her head, she laughed. "You really are bad, Louis. You want me to lie to my mother."

"It wouldn't be a lie, Julie. She wouldn't know, we just wouldn't tell her."

She said, "Fuji, put your shoes on and let's go. You're a sex maniac!"

"How do you know?"

She looked at him and didn't answer, just continued playing with her feet in the water.

"Did you see that in your dream, Julie?"

She blushed and threw a handful of water on his face because she remembered every detail of the dream she had last night. He smiled as she threw the water on him and looked away, avoiding eye contact with him. He took her hand and together they walked out of the water to put their shoes on. They stopped to check and feed the birds. They didn't stop for anything after that. Carefully they rode to the mango trees.

Louis seemed lost in thought. Julie wanted to understand what made him look so distant. Last night while they were talking, not once did Louis mention of his best friend. The only person he spoke about was his son. Julie remembered it was on the same night when her husband died Louis told her his best friend was going on a dangerous mission. And while she was in New York, they spoke several times on the phone. Louis even wrote to her. He never told her the outcome of his friend's mission, and she wondered why. And the thought frightened her, knowing how much he said he loved them, especially his friend's wife. *Why is Louis so enraptured with me? He wants the wife of his best friend.* Pondering these things, she galloped ahead to control her feelings.

Louis watched how fast she was going. He yelled, "Yahoo!"

Rapidly, he rode aggressively after her. She laughed when she heard the sound he was making as he rode past her. They started to race. She yelled back, "Yahoo!"

The run did her good. Louis was happy to see how she was enjoying herself. He thought, *The girl is dangerous, look at how she's moving.* She loved the rush she was getting.

He slowed down because he didn't want her to fall off her horse, or worse, to get hurt. He called, "Slow down, my wild cat."

She looked back and saw he was no longer racing with her. She cantered back, "What's wrong?"

Louis pretended something was wrong with his horse. "I'm afraid Cliff wanted me to slow down."

Julie passed her hand over his horse's shining coat and together they harmoniously rode. Louis noticed something was bothering her, but she didn't want to say anything. He got an idea what was troubling her. He wanted her to come out and ask him without him initiating giving out the information she wanted to know.

She took a deep breath to gather up the courage to ask. *Here it comes,* Louis thought.

"Have you heard from your best friend?"

Closing his eyes, Louis sorrowfully sighed. "He didn't make it back from the mission."

Grievously Julie said, "Why you didn't tell me?"

"You have enough on your mind. I didn't want to burden you."

"It would not have been burden at all . . . I'm sorry." Dejectedly she said, "How is his wife and your son?"

"They're fine. As a matter of fact, they're in town."

Again Julie was shocked. Louis glanced at her, watching how she was holding on the buckle of her belt, squeezing on her stomach as if someone had ripped her guts out. Louis pulled closer and quickly took a hold of the rein of her horse to hold on to her. He thought she was going to faint and asked, "Are you all right?"

"Don't mind me." Taking a firm hold of her emotions she made herself smile and look at him. "I'll be just fine." She gently moved away from him to sit straight on her horse. "I don't want you to worry about me, Louis . . . I'm a survivor. God has giving you a chance to make things right. Don't let anyone stand in your way, especially me."

Her voice sounded sad but firm as she declared her thoughts to Louis. He was surprised by the way she openly made him know how she felt. She was clear, right to the point, he thought and said, "Life can be cruel, Julie, if you let it. Don't you want me, my love?"

Julie closed her eyes when she heard his whispering voice say, *Don't you want me, my love*, like a song in her ears, caressing her mind. She thought back to the very first night she arrived in Haiti. Alone she stood on the balcony, the wind sounding like his gentle, soft, and deep masculine voice whispering in her ears. Taking a deep breath she tried not to show any remorse.

"I would hate to stand between you, and your happiness, Fuji." Her heart ached as she grinned, a few words of happiness for him. "At last one of us could be happy. That was your hope, to have your son and the woman you love with you. Now it is your chance to do so."

"I wish it was different, because death was not something I wished for my best friend. I'm going to miss him."

"I know what you mean," Julie replied as she drifted in space. "I, too, will miss my husband, but what can we do? We can't bring them back . . . but one thing I know is that I love you too much to stand in the way of your happiness."

"You love me, Julie?"

"Yes." She glanced at Louis and smiled. "I would like to meet them."

"Who?" Louis was lost. He was thinking that was the second time she had said she loved him.

"You know," Julie smiled. "Your son and the woman who captured this untamed stallion."

Louis smiled and said, "In due time I will introduce you to them. She'll be very surprised to meet you because I told her about you."

She was astonished. "You did! Didn't she get jealous?"

"Yes!" Searching for her smile, he said, "She almost cried when I told her I was hopelessly in love with you."

"You are?" she said softly as she breathed a sigh of relief with a hint of happiness.

"Yes, hopelessly in love with you, Julie! She was hurt," Louis added, "but she held back her tears. I've noticed she is a woman full of pride. She didn't want me to see her grieving over me. I cannot help the way I feel for you. . . . She can't wait to meet you, too."

Knowing Louis was capable of having two women, she curiously asked, "What are you going to do with her? Are you going to marry her as you wanted?"

"Only if you approve of her." He took a good look at her facial reaction, then rode away, leaving her behind to wonder. She galloped after him and caught up. "What if I don't approve?"

"Then you would have to marry me."

"You cannot have the two of us, Louis. I'm not cut out for that kind of drama."

"I'm not planning to have two women, Julie. I only want you, can't you tell?"

She didn't answer nor did she ask any more questions. Silently she galloped after him, trying to keep up as they rode up and down the mountain.

Thinking back on the conversation they just had, she thought, *Now I understand why Louis took mercy on me last night. The mother of his son is in town, too.* In her heart she thanked him for not going through with the feelings they both were having.

Breaking off the silence she asked, "Have you ever had fight with a man, Fuji?"

"No, never!"

"Never?" Julie repeated in disbelief.

"You find it hard to believe that I never had a fight with a man."

Julie thought he was fibbing. "Then why were you always in trouble when you were a child?"

"Even then I never had a fight with a boy. It was always two or three trying to kick my butt."

Julie laughed. "So I see—not with *a* man, but with *several*."

"That's right!"

"You're a tough guy, aren't you?"

He cantered very close to her and said, "Feel and check for yourself."

"That's not what I mean." She laughed and pushed him away. "You told me you know martial arts. So I want to know the degree of your fighting technique."

"You want to teach me, Julie?"

"I want to learn."

Nodding his head, Louis simpered, "Now I really believe that you're very kinky."

Julie laughed. "No, I'm not the freaky one. You are!"

"Freaky one," he repeated and laughed like he once did the night she clubbed him with her cell phone. "Very interesting!"

They rode all the way to the mango trees, back and forth, teasing each other.

The following evening Louis had to work late, so he called Julie to see how they were doing. Henry had come by his estate to drop some documents.

"Tomorrow is a special day for me. You know I've invited Julie, her mother, and Maxine over to the ranch. After Julie's reunion, hopefully everything goes well there. I want you to meet me there the following afternoon."

Taking a good look at him Henry asked, "Are you sure you're in love with her, Fuji?"

Closing his eyes, he sighed raggedly. Louis opened his eyes and looked at the ceiling. "*Je suis sûr* (I am sure). I could smell her, taste her, it feels good. The other night I made a promise to her that I never thought I would hear myself say to any woman."

"What was the promise?" Henry asked with concern.

"I promised I would not make love to her unless we're married."

Henry almost choked on the drink he was having. "No you didn't," he said as he started to laugh. "How are you going to keep that promise, Fuji?"

Removing himself from the chair, Louis went to the bar and fixed himself a drink while he watched how Henry was laughing at him and choking on his drink. Tasting his drink, Louis said, "You're laughing at me like I'm some kind of fiend who has no conviction or pride when it comes to sex."

"No." Catching his breath, Henry replied, "That's not what I mean. Can you actually keep your hands off that beauty, Fuji, and remain faithful to her, only to her, until you two get married? And to continue loving her till death do you part?"

Staring at Henry agitatedly, Louis responded, "I guess 'not dating for over a year' doesn't count."

Ignoring Louis's response, he added, "Would she be able to satisfy all your needs and serve your purpose? The last time we spoke of Julie, I warned you about her. She'll have you as her captive audience and you'll be the one doing the applause."

Replying to Henry's statement, Louis said, "Do you also remember that I told you that you talked too much? . . . The important thing is that I feel alive when I'm around her, and I know she feels the same way I do. Everything about her entices me, even when she insults me. I can never stay upset at her. I enjoy looking at her, talking to her. I love that woman, Henry, do you understand that? I found my perfect mate. I don't need any other woman. I need and want Julie. I am going to have her, her son, everything. Do I make myself clear?"

"I just don't want to see you heartbroken, Fuji."

"Stop contradicting me, Henry. Don't you get on my nerves! I will go out of my mind if I don't have her." He was so lost in his reverie he didn't realize he was holding the glass so tightly it shattered in his hand and blood started dripping on the floor. "Do you understand!"

Henry jumped up and grabbed some napkins from the bar. "Are you okay? You're bleeding! Francois!" He shouted for the butler.

"No, I'll be fine," Louis answered with annoyance. He removed his handkerchief from his pocket and wrapped it around his hand. Francois came running into the room. Henry instructed, "Louis needs a bandage for his hand."

Louis waved him away. "No need to get anything. The only thing that will heal my wound is her touch." He looking at Henry. "I'm sure she is 'the bone of my bone'."

Francois smiled and inquired, "Doctor Janvier, are we to expect them soon?"

Louis answered, "Do you believe in prayer?"

Francois replied, "Oh, *oui*, doctor."

"Then start praying and you too, Henry. Pour three drinks, Francois."

Francois went behind the bar and poured three cognacs. Louis and Henry took one each and Louis instructed, "You too, Monsieur Landers."

Francois picked up his glass and Louis raised his glass. "To my future."

Henry and Francois raised their glasses and repeated, "To your future."

And they all drank.

Chapter Twelve

The Remembrance

Over at the Bassine mansion, Jacque was up early having breakfast, sipping his coffee, and reading the newspaper. Suddenly he stopped reading to speak to the staff. "Today is a special day. I want everything to do well for Julie and her guests. Make sure the ballroom looks very beautiful. I want everything perfect."

Maxine came in and said, "What sinister thing are you planning today, brother?"

She took a cup of coffee and stood by the kitchen cabinets. Jacque said, "What time does your weekend start, Max?"

Looking at him over the rim of her coffee cup she replied, "At three. Why?"

"Good," he replied. "That gives you enough time to do something for me."

Turning, she put the cup down. "What do you want me to do?"

"I want you to pick a document for me from Constant."

Looking at her watch, she sighed. "All right, I have to run. I don't want to miss Julie's talk."

As she walked away, Jean walked in and said, "Good morning."

Behind the paper Jacque replied, "What are you up to? I haven't seen you for days, little brother. We have to make sometime for each other."

Jean couldn't tell whether the statement was genuine or a show, because it had been over ten years since the last time they hung out together. Peeved he replied, "Like the last time?"

"Yeah," Jacque repeated twice. "Yeah, like the last time."

Not once did Jacque look up at his brother while they were talking. He was all wrapped up in the newspaper. Jean looked at him with anger and hate in his light brown eyes and thought, *Jacque has no respect for me at all. He treats me like a nobody. This has to stop. Why am I so afraid of him?*

Then Jean remembered an incident that happened between them ten years ago:

He had just turned twenty. Jacque took him out to celebrate his birthday. They had a drink or two at a café. Louis was at that café that night and he was also celebrating with a couple of his friends. He was on vacation from school in New York. One of Louis's friends invited him and Jacque to join their party over at his house. The night was young and there were plenty of women for all of them.

The alcohol was flowing. Then something bizarre happened. Louis's friend Henry, who was sitting by him, moved from the sofa and left Louis alone sitting with a couple of women who had started to cater to him. Henry and his other three male friends each took a corner with a couple of women doing the same thing.

Jacque and Jean were left alone sitting down with no women. Louis glanced at Jean and told one of the women who was with him to cater to Jean, since it was Jean's birthday. Pulling Jean away from where Jacque was sitting, she went and sat on a single chair with Jean. Jacque was left all alone without a woman.

Jacque was not about to sit back and watch the show. Seeing Louis with more women than he thought necessary, Jacque got out off his seat and pulled one of those women caressing Louis off him. Pulling away, she refused to participate with Jacque. She told him to let her go, because Louis didn't give her the permission to go to Jacque.

"Don't touch me," the woman growled.

Louis was in a good mood. He looked at her and waved okay to her. Jacque felt insulted because the woman had to get Louis's approval. He got angry and pushed her so hard that she fell and hit her head on the coffee table and fell onto the floor. She was hurt.

Louis got up to see if she was okay. She was almost unconscious. After assisting her, Louis punched Jacque in the face for hurting her. Jacque tried to fight back. He threw a punch back at Louis. But Louis received Jacque's fist in his palm and squeezed it and made him kneel before him. Everyone sat back looking.

Realizing no one was going to separate the fight and Jacque was no match for Louis, Jean quickly removed himself from his seat and asked Louis to release Jacque.

"Please, Louis, let him go."

Louis pushed Jacque aside and caused him to be even more frustrated. He threw another punch at Louis.

"Jacque, stop!" Jean shouting, feeling embarrassed. "Jacque, enough!"

Jacque wouldn't listen. Twisting his arms behind his back, Louis held Jacque at the back of his neck. Louis's friends and the women were laughing because they were kind of drunk. Henry, who was also laughing, opened the door for Louis as he threw Jacque out of the house and closed the door behind him.

Jacque was mad. He was cursing at Louis. "Who the hell do you think you are? Carine was right for dumping you, bastard! Brian will always be a better man than you . . . you no-good bastard! A bum you are, a bum you will always be."

Jacque went on, his vocabulary becoming unwise. Jean went out to Jacque to calm him down before Louis got really angry. He told Jacque to wait while he went back in for his shirt and shoes. When Jean went back in, instead he apologized to Louis and everyone for Jacque's behavior.

"Jacque had a quite a few drinks," Jean said, expressing his regret to Louis, but the guys had already forgotten about Jacque and they continued their party. Seeing they were no longer interested about Jacque, Jean resumed his former position with the woman Louis had given him, plus the woman Jacque pushed on the floor, while Jacque sat outside in a corner of the patio looking at them through the window waiting for Jean. They were laughing, drinking, and dancing as the party continued. They were having fun, and it was Jean's birthday.

Jacque realized that Jean forgot all about him. An hour went by, and he was still waiting for Jean to come out. Jean was the loudest in there and Louis and his friends were laughing.

The next day Jean walked out of the house and went to the car and found Jacque sleeping behind the driver's seat. Jean was laughing as he looked at Louis and said, "Thanks for the good time. That was the best party I ever had."

Jean was still drunk when he sat in the passenger side and he continued on to talk as Jacque turned the car on and pushed on the gas pedal. Jacque put his hand over his mouth to prevent him from saying anything. Louis looked at him as they drove away from his friend's house.

While they were in the car going home, Jean thought everything was over. Jacque should have calmed down by now. Jacque stopped at the edge of Bourdon Mountain going toward Pétion-Ville. Jumping out of the car, he told Jean to get out. Thinking something was wrong with the Jeep, Jean hastily got out. Jacque opened the hood and told him to look, so he did. Suddenly, Jacque slammed the hood on his head. Blood was streaming down his head and gushing out of his nose. He was almost unconscious with the pain. Everything was spinning.

Then Jacque grabbed him and dragged him to the edge of the cliff and held him over the rails, threateningly saying, "Don't you ever go against me in front of anyone! I thought we had come to the party together and you left me standing outside all night while you're in there having fun with Louis and his whores! And you never came out till this morning." Sarcastically he said, "It took you that long to get your pants and shoes! I was the one who took you out to party tonight! You forgot all about me, letting your brainless head take over your mind! And to top it all off you apologized to Louis. You made me look bad in front of him and everyone who was in there! You should have stayed quiet! The next time something goes wrong and you're not on my side, it's best for you if you stay quiet. . . . If you want to say something, it had better be to agree with me . . . or I'll break you, little brother!"

Jacque pushed Jean into the car through the driver's side door. Jean was in pain and almost sobbing with fright. Jacque opened the glove compartment and handed him a towel to wipe his face and continued driving as if nothing had happened. Jean couldn't believe what has just happened. He was dazed and in pain. He said nothing, only holding on to his aching head. Jacque put his right arm around Jean's shoulder when he noticed that blood was gushing out of his nose. Jean looked at Jacque as if he was seeing him for the first time. Jacque was six-four as he looked down at him with his green eyes. Nodding his head, Jacque said, "Don't ever turn on me again, little brother."

Suddenly it dawned on Jean that Jacque was mad. He was capable of hurting someone if that person stood in his way. . . .

The rustling of Jacque's paper brought him out of his memory. Jacque looked up from the paper. "Oh! You're still here?"

Jean was holding the coffeepot in his hand. Jacque continued, "Pour me some coffee," indicating his cup.

Jean wanted to throw the coffee in his face, but he poured it in the cup.

"By the way," Jacque continued, "make sure all the security staff are in uniform. Julie's mother wanted that. After all, she is our godmother. I don't want to disappoint her."

Jacque finally looked up to see why Jean did not reply. "You're still here? I thought you were gone to do what you have been told to do. And when you see Nicole, tell her I want to see her now."

Totally ignoring Jean, he went right back to reading his paper. Jean walked away from the kitchen and did what he asked.

Maxine had just reached Constant's place to pick up the documents Jacque demanded she picked up. He was so happy to see her. Constant asked, "To what do I owe this pleasure?"

Maxine smiled and kissed him on the cheek. "Hello, Constant, *comment ca va* (how are you)? It's always a pleasure to see a happy face."

With a gleeful smile he asked, "How can I help you?"

"I want some information about Mrs. Philip III."

Feigning ignorance, he replied, "I don't know what you're talking about."

Maxine said, "She was here with Jacque over a year ago."

"My, you're direct," he answered. "You know I can't give you that kind of information. It's personal and confidential, plus it's illegal to give out information about your clients."

Looking at him, she said, "Since when did you practice that law? This information, I need it desperately. Those documents were supposed to be handed to Henry. I don't want you to get involved in Jacque's scheme. You know what Louis will do to someone who double-crosses him. So far Louis had been patient. And once he loses his temper, he'll come here and ask you himself. I don't want to see you get hurt. If Jacque is paying you to do that, I don't think it worth losing everything you have. Stealing from Mrs. Philip would be a hazard to both your health and finances, because I've learned Louis owns half of those properties."

"How do you know that?"

"It's obvious," Maxine replied. "Why would her late husband tell my crazy brother to hand Henry Claude those documents? I thought you would have more sense than that. Louis is her partner and you're helping Jacque to keep those papers. And this is how Louis is going to see it when he rips your heart out of your chest and your head off your neck."

"Why must you try to scare me? I wasn't trying to steal from her or Louis Janvier."

"Good, I hope not," Maxine replied as she sat on the chair in front of his desk.

With a sigh of resignation, Constant complied. "Okay, not one word of this to anyone, except Louis. Jacque brought her here, letting her think she was here for a divorce matter. But in reality, he tried to get her signature on a marriage certificate and documents that contained one hundred and sixty-two acres of land that her husband had bought next to Louis's ranch. These lands were supposed to be where they would have built their home. It was a surprise gift from her husband for giving him a son. Jacque found out Saul was having marital problems. . . ."

"So?" Maxine said.

Constant continued, "He took advantage of the situation for his own benefit. He wants to put his hands on this land so he can turn them into a resort and make them his own. And if he marries her Jacque would run everything she has, not just here but also in the United States."

Maxine was horrified. Jacque's deception was more than she thought. She didn't know about the ranch house Saul was constructing for Julie, plus a home for her animals just as Julie dreamed of. Now she understood why Jacque wouldn't submit the documents to Henry, when it was Saul who told him to do so. At that moment she understood Jacque's plan. He wanted to possess everything she had. She asked anxiously, "Did Julie sign any papers?"

"No," he replied, "she did not. Julie said she had a lot to think about. It was too soon for her to think of divorcing her husband. She seemed to be upset at Jacque when he told her that was why he had brought her here. I left them alone in the office so they could talk things over. He didn't look too happy when I returned, because Julie told me to get the papers out of her face. Then they left the office. . . ."

He walked away from her and went behind his desk. He removed a set of keys out of his pocket and unlocked his desk. Taking out a brown envelope, he placed it on his desk.

"Are those the papers?" she asked, looking at the envelope on the desk. She demanded, holding out her hand, "Give them to me."

"I have to make copies of them. . . ."

He walked to the copy machine to duplicate them. " . . . Don't let anyone know! Louis is already giving him problems. He said he won't give

Jacque a dime if he does not show him proof that the land belongs to him. Jacque told him he'll soon have all the papers to show him. So he's trying to get her to sign them over to him, and if she does, he's home free, and Louis will have invested millions of dollars on Jacque's projects. I heard her husband passed away. Poor girl."

He made copies of the documents and handed Maxine the original copies. She looked at them and placed them inside the brown envelope and stood. "Oh, I almost forgot. He sent me to pick some papers for him."

Constant replied, "Those are the papers."

"No!" Maxine yelped. "These documents belong to Julie. Get this straight in your mind, Constant. You've been our friend for quite some time. We went through so much in the past. This is one thing I don't want you to get involved in. I don't want Louis finding a trace of these documents in your courtyard, get that! Give me the copy. Do you get my drift?"

Shaking his head he handed her the duplicate of the papers.

She placed the originals inside her purse, then took the copy from his hand. She kissed him on his cheek and said, "Be careful . . . okay?"

Constant requested, "Please make sure Louis knows I gave them to you willingly."

She called over her shoulder, "Don't worry!"

Maxine didn't waste any time. She drove as fast and as carefully as she could, hoping it wasn't too late to calm Louis from going on a rampage with her family. She went directly to Louis's estate to drop those documents. She apologized to him for having those documents too long in their presence. Louis reassured her not to worry about it, then asked, "Did Constant volunteer to give you these documents?"

"Yes he did," she responded, breathing a sigh of relief for Constant.

"Good," Louis replied. "He was supposed to give Henry the documents a year ago. . . . Thank you, Max."

He gave her a kiss on her cheek then he walked her to her car. He said as he reached her car, "I'll see you at the mansion during Julie's talk. Be careful."

Feeling relieved she agreed, "All right Louis. Bye-bye."

After she handed Jacque the documents, Maxine went to her room to get herself ready for the gathering.

Meanwhile over at the Janvier's plantation, it was a scene of activity. Six trucks of fertilizer were being delivered.

There were trucks of carpet grass and huge cactus plants of different sizes and with different kinds of roses: Angel face, Chrysler Imperial, so many different kinds, just to name a few; Lupines, bee balm, Monarda, etc. A truck was carrying mango trees, avocado trees, coconut trees, lime trees, breadfruit, sour-sop, pears, apples, and many other fruit trees, and also another truck of sand and colored gravel.

The workers were wondering what was going on. Brian Bravé was in one of the trucks directing them to where to put all the stuff. They were heading toward the area where Jacque's firm had been hired to construct another ranch.

"We have to hurry up," Brian urged. "Monsieur Janvier is coming and bringing some special guests here for the weekend. He is also bringing a baby with him. Make sure that no dust is found in the house and fresh flowers are everywhere." Everyone began scurrying around like ants. "The king of the ranch will be here soon."

Back at the Bassine mansion, Julie was returning from jogging. She walked in the living room and greeted her mother with a kiss and a cheerful, "Good morning, Mother. . . . lady," referring to the servant.

Returning the greeting, her mother introduced her, "Hello, darling. this is Loziane. She's going with us to the plantation. She will be looking after William."

Walking over to shake the other woman's hand, Julie replied, "Great. Welcome to our household. I look forward to getting to know you better!"

Bill was in his grandmother's arms. Julie took him from her and kissed him and tickled his tummy. Her mother reminded, "It's time for you to get ready. Your guests are about to arrive."

Handing Bill back to her mother, she went to the bedroom to shower and get dressed. As she was leaving her mother complimented, "You look like a flower blossom this morning."

Thanking her mother for the compliment, she smiled and said, "I look that obvious? I better be careful."

Walking to her son, she kissed his forehead and said without thinking, "You look so much. . . ."

She caught herself from what she was about to say, and turning, she left the room. Her mother sat back looking at her grandson and wondered what was on her daughter's mind.

Loziane asked her, "Is everything all right, madame?"

Shaking her head in wonder, she took a deep breath. "Everything is fine."

Loziane wanted to know if she could hold the toddler. Viviane handed the toddler over to her, who had fallen asleep in her arms.

At the ballroom in the mansion, it was a hub of activity. They were arranging the room for Julie and her guests. People were already arriving. Security was tight. Those arriving were shown to their seats by the head of security. Louis, Nadine, and Henry Claude were among the guests she had invited. They were sitting at Julie's table, deep in conversation.

Jacque was walking across the floor with the widow Casimir clutching his arm. His eyes were everywhere. Then he spotted Louis and Nadine, who were talking to Henry, but before he could come over, he showed her to her seat. He pulled out her chair for her to be seated and whispered something in her ear that made her smile. He excused himself and walked over to Louis's table. Looking at Louis, he said, "Hello, Louis, Henry."

Turning to Nadine, he extended his hand in greeting, kissing hers when she held it out. "Nadine, it's nice to see you again."

Louis excused himself, got up, and walked toward Madame Casimir.

He greeted her with a bow, "Madame Casimir."

Kissing him on both cheeks, she returned the greeting. "Oh, Louis, *comment est tu* (how are you doing)? Sit down please?"

Pulling out the chair meant for Jacque, he accepted her invitation and sat down.

"Oh," she complained, "Louis, I've been having such bad luck."

Louis glanced over at his table, but Jacque was still talking to Nadine and Henry. He looked back at her as she continued talking. Knowing Louis was able to help her she told him about her situation. "One of my restaurants in New York was totally destroyed by fire. Three people got killed. Now the family of those people killed is suing me for liability . . . My head is down under water."

Louis tried to be sympathetic. Taking her hands in his, he said, "I'm sorry. I hope everything works out for you. We'll talk later."

Jean announced, "Please, everyone, take your seats."

Louis got up, kissed her on her cheeks, and prepared to walk back to his seat. "See you later."

He passed Jacque on the way but didn't stop to talk. Resuming his seat, he pointed out to Nadine, "Our hostess is about to arrive."

Nadine looked around at the prestigious gathering and commented, *Le président et sa femme* (the president and his wife) are here."

Jean announced, "Ladies and gentlemen, it is an honor to introduce Madame Philip the Third."

Everyone stood up and applauded as she walked across the floor. She was wearing a black two-piece suit that enhanced her shape perfectly. Her hair was combed up to reveal her pearl earrings and necklace. She walked proudly with stature and grace with her son, who was wearing a white suit and holding onto her hand. Her mother walked beside her, dressed in a dark beige outfit. She, too, looked elegant. They complimented each other.

"And Madame Bertrand," Jean continued. She walked up to the stage while her mother went to her seat with William. Their table was placed in front of the two-foot tall stage. Viviane looked up at her daughter with admiration as Julie began to speak.

"Thank you, Jean. *Monsieur et Madame* President, ladies and gentlemen, thank you all for your warm sympathy. Please be seated."

She waited for the audience to be seated before continuing, "God created men with the desire to live forever. So what happened? We can never accept the death of our loved ones. I well know he is at peace now, because death has no conscious of anything at all. There is no function, nor knowledge, nor planning *she'ol*. . . .

She bent her head, closed her eyes, and meditated for a few seconds. Then she gathered her composure, took a deep breath, lifted her head high, and continued, "One writer said, 'Only by becoming aware of the anger and not acting on it, but knowing you feel it, can you be free of its destructive effects'. Yes, I am hurt to know that Saul is really dead. I was angry till I opened my Bible a few nights ago. The Bible assures me that God is near to those who are broken at heart; and those who are crushed in spirit He saves, which is stated at Psalms 34:18. It also urges me to throw my burdens upon the Almighty God and he will sustain me. And I also talked my feelings out of sympathetic friends and that helped, too. . . ."

She paused as if to gather courage, then she continued, " . . . The help that God supplies does make a difference. And that I may be able to comfort those in any sort of tribulation. Talking about the sorrow does not eliminate the pain, but it can make it easier to bear. I will not forget Saul. His gentleness, his love for me, and his son." Looking at William, she smiled. "We will miss his laugh, his ideas, and most of all, his dreams. I hope this experience make me more understanding and sympathetic in helping others to cope with a similar loss. . . ."

Again she paused as she closed her eyes and took a deep breath as she looked at the audience. Feeling her sorrow, Louis wanted to go to her and comfort her. " . . . Your presence here gives me courage. Thank you for your tender affections. I will never forget the kindness I see here today. You showed me that you all care and share a special memory about my husband Saul, and how all of you were touched by him. I am happy to see all of his good friends. I thank you for your presence and your compassion in my time of distress. Thank you."

Julie walked off the stage amidst thundering applause. The president and his wife walked toward her and greeted her. They both kissed her on her cheeks.

The ambassador, the senator, and their wives all came up and greeted her. Everyone came to greet her and extended their condolences.

Louis stood at a distance, taking a keen interest in the activities going on around him. The president and his wife came over to say hello to him. Taking his hand in a warm grasp, the president clapped him on his back and invited, "Let's have lunch."

Smiling, he replied, "I'll let you know."

One by one the guests left. Only a few people remained. Beside Louis, everyone including the president wanted some kind favor from her. When the crowd thinned out, Louis walked across the room to her with Nadine and Henry following him. He kissed her and her mother on the cheeks. Nadine and Henry did the same. Louis took Bill from her and sat down with him in the crook of his arm. Nadine and Henry came forward and peeked at the toddler. She said, "Boy you're growing up. Look at him, he's so handsome."

Sitting opposite Louis and the toddler, Nadine looked with interest at him, then looked at William and remarked with a puzzled frown, "Louis, he resembles you a lot."

Over hearing Nadine's comment, Julie looked at Louis to see if what she had said was true. Nadine held out her hands to take Bill, looking toward Julie for permission. "Can I hold him?"

Seeing the way Louis was looking at the toddler in Nadine's arm, Jacque was jealous and he started to rage inside. He couldn't control the emotions he was having. He felt that Louis was trying to get Julie's attention. Jacque didn't like the way Julie was looking at Louis and thought Louis was becoming more of threat to his plan and the relationship he wanted to have with Julie. Jacque approached Julie as she was talking to his sisters. Jacque kissed her on her cheeks and purposely started to cry. "I'm so sorry about your husband, I am truly sorry. I love you, Julie. I wanted to tell that since the very first time you returned to Haiti. But you were married. Please give me a chance to prove myself to you, how much I love you."

Boy, was Jacque glad Debbie was not present. He was able to act out his part to the fullest. He poured out his heart to Julie before everyone who was still there.

Everyone was still. Louis looked up at Jacque as he was crying out in the open to Julie. Jacque knew at that moment Louis wouldn't dare try anything. He would just have to sit there and listen to what he had to say to Julie and make sure Louis understood that Julie was his woman and he better move on to another like he always did.

Louis could not believe what he was hearing–the audacity of that man! He realized that Jacque was more dangerous than he thought, and Jacque had stepped on his heart and caused it to bleed. He knew that Jacque was not going to get away from him without being humiliated just like he did to Julie today. Just when he thought he was through with Jacque, he handed him a blank page to write a new chapter for him.

Julie handed Jacque a napkin to wipe his eyes, trying to hide her embarrassment. "Julie, my beloved, you're the only woman I truly love."

Wishing the earth would open up and swallow her, Julie tried to shush him. "All right, Jacque, I heard enough."

She wanted him to just shut up. Julie couldn't believe that Jacque went there. She thought, *I was wrong to ever think that I was a sister to Jacque.*

Looking at the way Aunt Viviane was watching him, Jacque apologized to her. "I am sorry, Aunt Viviane, I can't help it. I love her so much. . . . I should have been here to pick you up at the airport. I'm the family here, not Louis." Turning to Louis, he looked down at the baby and said, "Oh, Louis, can I hold my future son?"

Louis looked at Julie. She made a gesture with her shoulders to say *I can't handle another scene.* Louis relinquished the baby reluctantly, but kept a careful watch. He looked at Jacque without emotion. Jacque couldn't tell whether that was good or bad. He didn't care because at the moment he felt like he had the upper hand. As he took Bill from Louis, the toddler began to scream, piercing screams like something stabbed him.

On hearing William's cries, Julie quickly took him out of Jacque's arms. "What did you do to my baby?"

Letting go of the baby, Jacque held out his hand helplessly. "Nothing, I'm sure I didn't do anything. . . ."

"Give me my baby," Julie exclaimed, trying to protect the baby from some unseen force of evil, turning away from Jacque. Bill stopped crying instantly as his mother soothed and crooned to him.

Jacque looked at Louis and said, "You're good with babies. You must teach me your secret."

Viviane was shocked at Jacque's outburst. Never in her life she would have thought that Jacque would have looked at Julie as a woman for him to get involved with. She had helped raise him as a brother to Julie. Viviane thought he was distorted. Furiously, she grinned. "You need serious help!"

Louis walked toward Julie and the toddler and asked anxiously, "Did he upset you?"

She shuddered. "Yes, for scaring Bill. This is the second time I've heard my baby cry like that."

"You see him for what he is, don't you, my son." Louis looked down into the baby's strong emerald green eyes. He asked Julie, "Are you ready to go, darling?"

Handing him the toddler, she said, "Yes, as soon as I straighten out Jacque and change my clothes. . . ."

Julie left the room and went to the library to talk to Jacque. "How dare you do this to me!"

He pretended he didn't understand what Julie meant. "I didn't know I was doing anything wrong by wanting to hold William."

Shaking her head she replied, "No, Jacque, the long speech you gave out there. You deliberately wanted to embarrass me."

"I didn't know expressing my feelings to the woman I love was going to make her feel embarrassed."

Shaking her head she snapped, "Spare me the showmanship, Jacque! What do I have to do to make you understand what you want from me can never happen?"

"We're not brother and sister, Julie."

"True, we're not, but I was brought up to know you as a brother."

"All right!" Jacque blasted back. "Since you went there, I'm not stupid. I know where you are coming from. You think Louis Janvier has a lot to offer, don't you? I tell you this. You see Louis Janvier wants one thing from you, and it is between your legs. And once he has it or uses it enough, out of the door he'll go, just like Saul. . . ."

Julie couldn't believe Jacque went there. She realized that he wanted to crush her spirit. She became numb. She couldn't say anything on Saul's or her defense. Jacque took ahold of her arm and pulled her toward him as he concluded his statement and breathed these words on her face: " . . . I'll be here, Julie. I'll be here like I always am, waiting for you to come to your senses."

Then he stepped aside and made his way out of the room, slamming the door behind him, leaving Julie with tears in her eyes. She stood there shaking, trying to calm down before she went to face Louis, who was waiting for her.

Jacque went to his room to wash himself from head to toes, to calm himself down, talking to himself. " . . . I hope Julie comes to her senses, I hope she. . . . Damn! That baby, that little brat! That child needs discipline. . . ! He needs a good guardian, someone who can teach him respect. Louis has nothing to teach that boy except how to be a player! And she's falling for him, a dirty player."

Maxine knocked on his door. Jacque called, " . . . Wait, I'm coming."

Putting on his robe and drying his hair with a towel around his neck, he walked out of his bathroom to open the door for her. "Are you leaving now?"

"Yes," Maxine said, "but before I leave, I want to let you know that you are out of your mind. I may be wrong. You may be blind! You're trying to get in an elephant's way. What is wrong with you! You've challenging the wrong man, brother."

"Maxine, who are you going out with this weekend?"

Stepping away from him, she replied, "I told you already, with Louis. He's taking me to his ranch."

He came close to her and sneered, "I heard a rumor about my baby sister."

Hesitantly she asked, "What rumor was that . . . brother?"

Jacque said, "Carine told me . . . I told her you wouldn't be that stupid. That's nonsense. She saw you kissing Marie's son, our servant. . . . His name's Richard. I am going to give you a little warning, baby sister. I don't give a damn that Julie approves of him, but I tell you this! It had better be Louis's ranch you're going to this weekend."

She tried to back away. "What if I'm not going to Louis's ranch?"

He grabbed her arms so hard that she started to scream, "Let go of me! Let me go! You're hurting me!"

Jacque yelled, "Don't make me hurt you! It had better be Louis's ranch you're going to and make sure he keeps away from Julie. Carine may be wrong, you may be right. How do you like my little rhyme!"

She screamed again. He pushed her hard and let her go. She ran out of his bedroom sobbing and got out of the house as fast as she could. As

Maxine was leaving the mansion she bumped onto Jean, who was coming in with Nicole. Jean called to her, "Troublemaker!"

Maxine was already frustrated. She walked back to Jean and looked at him with an unrecognizable emotion in her eyes. "Is that all you can think about me, Jean. . . . Well, let me tell you how I really feel about you, so you can put your mind at ease."

Her eyes were filled with tears as she continued talking. "I see you as an ungrateful puppet, a coward, a lazy man who does not stand up for himself or for his rights. You expect everyone to feel sorry for you and take pity on your cowardly ass. A man with no self-esteem."

Looking at Nicole who was standing by Jean, Maxine shook her head at her. Without a backward glanced at Jean, she walked away.

Jacque got dressed and met with Carine in the library. The butler brought them refreshments on a tray and placed it on the coffee table. Fixing them their drinks, he handed them to them. Carine dismissed him with a wave of her hand. "That will be all for now. Thank you, Roy."

Roy left the room, closing the door behind him. She eagerly said, "I like what you did after the service."

Rubbing his chin, he said, "Interesting. Even the president came to pay his respects. Everyone important was here."

In awe she said, "I can't believe I was surrounded by all these important people. I always knew Julie's husband was important, but I never thought he was that important." She looked at him with raised brows. "What's wrong?"

"The child." Jacque meditated for a few seconds. "Something about that boy. For a split second, and if I didn't know any better, I would have to think he was Louis's son."

Staring and drinking in his every word, Carine sat up straight. "What makes you say that?"

"The way the baby loved him, how he played with the child. But I know better. Louis studied Julie well and he knows exactly where to hold her. It is through her child. Show a lot of affection, and mother will follow, and grandmother too."

Carine was laughing. "Aunt Viviane thought you're insane."

"She has not seen my craziness yet." Jacque stretched back. "I'm going to have her daughter eating out of the palms of my hands before the end of this month."

Jacque was looking at her in displeasure. She asked, "What happened?"

"Why didn't you go with them to the ranch?"

Carine explained, "When Maxine told us about her weekend at the ranch, I went up in my room that same day, to call Louis to ask him if I was also invited. But he told me if I showed up unexpectedly, he'd make sure I don't return permanently!"

"What did he mean by that?"

Feeling disturbed and angry she replied, "You forget that Louis could make one disappear like the great Houdini. I felt alarmed by what he revealed to me. Louis didn't want me there. He said he'd kill me if I even thought of tagging along or asking Julie if I could come along."

"So, he had every corner covered," he reflected.

She got very nervous, so Jacque got up to fix her a drink. He shook his head, wondering what was going on while he fixed her a drink to calm her down. He said, "Louis has Maxine, Julie, and her mom and child over at his ranch! I wonder what he is cooking. . . ."

Chapter Thirteen

Deceit, Deceived, Truth, and Honesty

At the Janvier ranch, everything was set. Louis and his guests arrived at the gate of the plantation. The guard at the security house swung open the gate. The place was beautiful. As they were driving through, they could see the waterfall cascading down the side of the mountain. The view was awesome, with the colorful-looking gardens. Louis leaned over Julie, who had dozed off, and kissed her on her forehead. She opened her eyes, blinked up at him sleepily, and asked, "Are we here?"

"Yes we are, my love."

Julie stretched her arms and accidentally hit Louis on his face. She apologized as she caressed his cheeks. "I'm sorry. . . . How's William back there?"

William was sleeping soundly. Loziane spoke up, "He's fine, Madame Janvier."

Julie swung around in surprise. "Who told you that I'm Madame Janvier?"

Loziane answered, "Your mother, madame."

Turning to Louis, Julie made a face. "Uh! My mother? I have to talk to that lady. Fuji, she's at it again."

Julie's eyes looked sad. Louis wondered what was on her mind. He grinned. "She doesn't mean any harm. By the way, it sounds nice."

"What sound nice?"

"Madame Janvier. . . . Oh! We're here!"

Brian and Patrick Bravé came down the steps. The servants came off the porch and walked smartly to open the car doors and get the luggage. All the servants on the plantation were on hand to greet them. The whole group trouped inside. Louis called to his manservant, "George, show everyone to their rooms."

Bowing, he answered, "*Oui*, Doctor Janvier," and started issuing orders to the other servants.

Louis called out, "I want everyone to return here in thirty minutes, so just freshen up then come back down, all right?"

Everyone followed George and the maids up the stairs. Louis held onto Julie. "Not you. I'll show you your room later." He pulled her close to him. "Ever since we left town, there's something that I desperately wanted to do."

"What is it?"

Wrapping his arms around her narrow waist, he fitted his body to hers, tilted her chin, and groaned as he bent his head and plastered his lips on hers.

Julie folded her arms around his neck. She opened her mouth to allow him access to her mouth while he drank sweetly as if he was drowning. After a long while he lifted his head, allowing them both to breathe in deep gasping breaths. Rubbing his forehead across hers he sighed deeply. "Uh, Julie. You don't know what you're doing to me. . . ."

Julie felt like she was floating. Her eyes were still closed. She wrapped her arms tightly around his neck. "I want more."

Holding her tighter, Louis obliged. She kissed him back without hesitation, pouring out all her love in that response. They were so wrapped up in each other, they completely forgot about their guests. Maxine and Richard had stopped on the balcony of the stairs and were staring down at them, at the fire that was consuming them. Viviane came out of her room, wondering what Maxine and Richard were so engrossed in. Noticing the focus of their attention, she walked toward the balcony and looked to see what was going on. A little shocked, she whispered, "Julie." But she did not respond. She said louder, "Louis!"

Louis and Julie remembered they were not alone. Slowly letting each other go, they stepped back and looked up the stairs. Everyone was looking at them.

Like two children they laughed. Maxine ran down the stairs to them. "You look so good together."

She kissed them both. Louis looked at the others and shrugged. "It's no secret. Everyone knows how I feel about Julie, but only she can explain how I really feel about her. So, Julie, welcome to my home and I hope your stay will be as pleasurable, enjoyable, peaceful, adventurous, and romantic as I think it will be. . . . Tonight, we're all going to explore the ranch so we can all be familiar with the place. Then tomorrow we will explore the rest of the estate."

Turning to Julie and placing his hands on hers, he bowed and asked, "My heart . . . where would you like me to start?"

Laughing and playing the lady of the manor to the hilt, Julie curtsied and motioned with an imperative sweep of her hand. "Here, my lord."

Turning to the others, he solemnly said, "My lady has spoken. Let's start here in the lobby. Come, everyone, come down. Oh, and bring Billy. We can't leave him out of the tour."

Viviane protested, "He's in his room with Loziane. He's sleeping."

But Louis insisted, "Please bring him down. There are a few things I want to show him."

George ran up the stairs to tell Loziane to come down with the toddler. Loziane brought Bill down to Louis and handed him over. Bill, who was now awake, pinched Louis's nose.

He said, "Thank you, Bill. Now, everyone is here so I can start."

Kissing Bill on the forehead, he settled the toddler in his arms in a comfortable position and continued, "Like I was saying, to my right," he opened the door, "is where I keep some of my trophies and things that I've collected over the years."

Everyone was admiring the paintings on the wall and the many trophies sitting on the shelves. On his desk there was a picture he didn't want anyone to see. Walking sideways, he thought, *Damn! Patrick forgot this picture.*

Pretending he had dropped something on the desk, Louis quickly removed the picture and placed it inside his desk, hoping no one had noticed his actions. He turned to the group and asked, "Any questions?"

Julie pointed to the sword. "What's the story behind this sword?" She picked it up with both hands and turned it over.

He warned, "Be careful, my love. Remember, I studied the martial arts while I was in America with Master Toshibi."

Julie was examining the sword with keen interest. She knew that it was something that was achieved with great skills. One had to be excellent at the martial arts to receive such an instrument. "You must be good. You have to show me your moves sometimes."

"I'm not that good at all."

Avoiding eye contact with Julie, he continued to answer other questions on the different pieces in the room. Looking at the sword closer, Julie remembered that her husband had a similar sword like that. He had told her the story behind the sword. One had to be master to possess such a sword. She wondered, *What did he place inside the desk?* Her anxiety was rising. She wanted to know what else was in the desk. She looked around surreptitiously, to see if there were any other familiar objects.

To put him at ease, she asked, "Who's the artist of this painting? It's quite expressive and unusual."

He explained to her who the artist was, "Boyé Simon. He's quite talented. This painting was especially made for me."

But Julie already knew that. He took them from one room to another for about one hour. It was a huge lobby. Along the hallway, his servants stood offering drinks. After the tour, they all enjoyed a country-style meal, which was very informal. Louis never put the toddler down. He held him in his arms even when they were eating and fed him from his plate.

Finally, Viviane said, "I need to rest. It's been a long day. . . ." Putting her hand over her mouth to smother a yawn, she got up to go to her room. " . . . I must say good night."

She kissed Julie, Louis, and Bill, waved goodnight to the others, and went off to bed. Loziane came forward for the toddler. "Monsieur Janvier, it's time for Bill's bath."

He kissed William and gently and reluctantly handed him over. She took him to Julie, who kissed him too and said, "I'll be up to tuck him in."

Julie noticed that Maxine and Richard were in a deep conversation. She saw Richard move closer to kiss Maxine and lifted her arms to put them around his shoulders. As he raised her arms, she gave a painful sound. With a look of concern, Richard asked, "Are you all right?"

Grimacing, Maxine said, "My left arm hurts like crazy."

Gently he rolled up the sleeve of her blouse. Her arm was badly bruised black and blue and swollen. Due to her fair complexion, it was easily seen. Richard was shocked. "What happened?"

This was no ordinary bang on the arm. Julie and Louis got up out of their seats to see what was going on. "What's wrong?"

Richard looked trouble. He showed them the arm. "Look!"

Julie asked, "How did this happened, Max?"

Hesitantly, she replied, "I fell. I didn't think it was this bad to leave marks on my arm."

Louis was silent. He didn't buy it. He knew someone had hurt her. Gently he took her other arm and said, "Come, let's go to the medical room."

The medical room was at the end of the hallway and off to the side. Louis asked her to sit on the examination table so he could examine the bruise. Turning to Richard he asked, "Richard, can you please go get my medical bag for me in the trunk of my Jeep?"

Richard left to get the bag. Louis lifted Maxine's face to look at him. He gently but firmly demanded, "Now tell me who did this to you, and no lies, Max."

With tears in her eyes, she whispered, "Jacque did this to me. He grabbed me so hard I thought he was going to break my arm. He said if I disobeyed him and continued to see Richard, he'd really hurt me."

"How dare him," Julie angrily said, as she handed her some napkins to wipe her eyes. Louis was silent with rage as he opened the cabinet and took out an ointment to put on her bruises. He remembered how he once punched Jacque on the face for behaving roughly with a woman and since then their friendship was never the same.

Maxine was crying openly. "I am scared. I'm afraid he'll hurt Richard if he gets an opportunity to."

Julie spoke up. "I thought after the last confrontation he had with Saul he would have stopped bullying you girls around! Man, was I wrong! What is wrong with him?"

Louis stopped dead at her sudden outburst and asked with deceptive calm, "Did he ever hurt you, Julie?"

Hastily she set his mind at ease. "Oh no! He knows who to do this to. He's got his entire family afraid of him and now he's going after Maxine."

Richard returned out of breath saying, "Louis . . . I did not . . . find . . . your bag."

"I'm sorry," Louis replied, "it was here all the time. I gave Max an ointment to put on her bruise."

Richard looked closely at her arm and said, "That doesn't look like a bang or anything. It looks like someone deliberately grabbed you, Max."

Trying to turn his suspicions off, she put her sleeve down, jumped off the table, and said, "Take me for a walk around the place. It will take my mind off the pain, although it does feel better. Louis, is that okay with you?"

He reassured her, "Of course, it's fine. You know you don't have to ask, Max."

They walked out of the clinic. Louis turned to Julie and lifted her up so she could sit on the examination table, then carefully pulled the ribbon out of her hair, watching it fall against her chest as he ran his hands through her hair. He said, "Now it's time for your check-up."

He kissed her lips. Absently she said, "What am I going to do with that man?"

His lips on hers, Louis instructed, "Kiss him back."

"Not you, silly, Jacque."

He pulled back to look at her. "Oh! Then let me rephrase the sentence for you. What am I going to do to Jacque? Why not let me handle Jacque?"

Knowing Louis was capable of hurting Jacque both physically and financially, she kissed his ears as she whispered, "That is why I'm afraid for him."

Louis didn't reply. Instead he said, "Now, please close your eyes and take your medicine."

Holding the back of her head with one hand and holding her steady with the other one, he brought his lips down on hers. She held on to him as she reveled in the sensations rippling through her body.

She needed to get closer to him. Moving her hands to his shirt, she unbuttoned it, and sliding her hands in his shirt, caressed him softly across his chest and back. Pulling him closer to her, she parted her lips as he continued kissing her. She kissed him on his neck and gently gave him a small bite on his shoulder. She continued kissing him as she tried to remove his shirt. She was touching him slowly, sending fire raging through him. She moved her hands down to the buckle of his pants. She opened it and put her hands on his belly button. She pushed his pants halfway down and touched him through his revealing silk boxer shorts.

Liquid heat pooled into his stomach. The feel of her touch caressing his masculine body was very desirable. He wanted her . . . but Julie, on the other hand, wanted to know if Louis would lose all his control and take what she was offering to him or would he remember the promise he had made to her.

"Julie," Louis whispered and pulled her hands out of his boxer shorts, then held them tightly between his. "No, Julie, no."

Easing away from her before he lost total control and took her right there and then, he pulled his pants up and buttoned his shirt, pushing it inside his pants as fast as he could. He made no effort to hide his feelings.

Julie asked, "What are you doing?"

Breathing hard, Louis answered, "What does it look like I'm doing? I want nothing more than to make love to you, but a few nights ago, I learned an important lesson about the defilement of the body. I learned sex should only be in a marriage arrangement and this is when it's clean. So if you want to have sex with me, you'll have to marry me! Please, Julie, say yes. I need you so much."

Julie couldn't believe her ears. In her heart she smiled. *He took my words seriously. Louis does love me.*

She sat there silently as Louis carried on. She looked at him and pushed her hair back from her face. He finished dressing and looked at her, still frantically pleading, "Please, stop torturing me, Julie. I'm only flesh and blood."

Getting down off the table, she held out her hands to him, saying, "You're right. I'm sorry for losing control, let's go."

Opening the door, she held on to the door handle, turned, and kissed him, saying, "Thank you. Now show me my room."

"Before I show you to your room," Louis said, "there's something I want you to hear."

Taking her hand, he led her to his entertainment room. There was a baby grand piano. He walked toward it. He sat down and said, "I want you to hear this."

Julie leaned against the piano, looking at him while he played. She was hypnotized by his voice; Louis had the sweetest masculine voice she ever heard. She listened intensely to his words as he looked at her while he played and sang.

> *When the first time I met you,*
> *I knew you were mine.*
> *And the first glance I gave you,*
> *I knew you belonged to me.*

It's not that easy for me to fall in love,
But there's an exception for you, Julie.
'Cause one look from you,
Makes me feel brand new.
One word from you,
Tells me all about you.
Julie, I love you,
Julie, I need you,
Always and forever,
I will always love you.
It's not that easy for me to fall in love,
But there's an exception for you, Julie.
'Cause one touch from you,
Makes me feel so good.
One kiss from you,
Makes feel near you.
It's not that easy for me to fall in love,
But there's an exception for you, Julie.
Make my dream come true.
Make me feel you're real.
And help me smile once again.
'Cause one look from you,
Makes me feel brand new.
One word from you,
Tells me all about you,
'Cause one touch from you,
Makes me feel so good.
And one kiss from you,
Makes me feel near you.
It's not that easy to fall in love,
But there's an exception for you, Julie.

He finished the song. Julie had tears in eyes as she embraced him and kissed him. She said for the third time out loud, "I love you. That was beautiful."

"Yes, it was," said a female voice behind the door. Louis and Julie turned around to see Maxine and Richard standing by the door. Maxine had tears in her eyes. She wiped her eyes with the back of her hand as she came closer to them.

Julie smiled as she wiped her eyes with her fingers. Louis turned to the other two. "I thought you guys were already in bed."

Richard said, "We were on our way, but couldn't help it when we heard the piano playing. You haven't played the piano or sang since . . . I can't even remember."

Louis pulled Julie closer to him, removing his handkerchief out of his shirt pocket to wipe the tears in her eyes. "You know I don't play the piano just for anyone."

"Can you show me my room now?" Julie asked. Louis stood up and took Julie's hand. "This time it's officially good night. See you guys tomorrow."

Putting his arm around her shoulders, he directed her to her room. They walked up the stairs to the lobby of the second floor. They were pictures of Louis's parents hanging on the wall. Julie asked as they made their way down the lobby, "Who is this man and the woman? You resemble him a whole lot."

"They were my father's grandparents." Louis stopped to reply as he informed her, "They were the ones who built the ranch house. They were French-Romanian."

Julie smiled. "French-Romanian. Can you say something in that language, Romanian?"

"Only I love you," Louis responded and said in Romanian "I love you" to Julie. He went on to explain why he wasn't Romanian. "They are a people of culture. And culture was something my great-grandparents were trying to avoid when they left Europe to settle here in Haiti."

As they continued going down the lobby she stopped to look at every one of the portraits of Louis ancestors, down to his parents' portraits. He had let her know he wasn't Romanian nor was he a French man because he was not born in either of these two countries. So were his grandfather and father. They had never practiced the Romanian culture. The language died with him completely, but French language remained since they were settled in Haiti.

He concluded, "The reason my picture is not hanging on the hallway is because I'm still alive." Flinging open the door with a flourish, he said, "*Voilà* (Here it is)."

He stood aside for her to go in, leaving the door wide open behind him. She looked around the room with her mouth wide open. It was something out of a fairy tale, fit for a princess or a queen to sleep in. She moved toward the huge vase of flowers that sat on the table, hundreds of roses and a mix of all the different kind of flowers he could think of. He looked on indulgently as she moved from one thing to another. She picked a flower from each different kind and made a bouquet.

She walked toward him and handed it to him and kissed him on his lips, mouthing a thank you. "Everything is lovely. Thank you, Louis." She pointed to a closed door. "Now what's laying behind this door?"

He laid the bouquet of flowers on her bed and answered, "Open it and see."

Pulling the door open, she caught her breath. It was the connecting door to her son's room. It was light blue and light yellow, and there were toys piled in every corner. Big ones, small ones, big bears, and small bears. There were balloons, blue and yellow with the writing: WELCOME HOME, MY SON. She tip-toed into the room. Louis followed. Loziane was there with Bill, putting his things away. "I'm almost finished, madame."

Julie picked Bill up and handed him to Louis. Louis cuddled him close so he could smell his clean baby scent.

"You smell so good, Bill," he said and kissed him on his forehead.

Julie stood beside him, watching as he played with Bill and thought, *He's a natural father.*

Loziane said, "I never worked with a baby before like that. He is so well behaved and he's so quiet. Were you quiet like that, madame?"

"Not me," Julie grinned, "and his father said he was a pain in butt. . . . William must have inherited the quietness from someone. . . . I don't know." She looked at Louis and laughed.

"He is handsome," the sitter replied. "He looks like both of you, but he looks like his father more."

Julie wanted to ask the sitter if she had met Saul, but instead she looked at Louis and did not say anything and kissed William's cheeks. "You are handsome, my boy, and one day you'll be a handsome young man."

She took him from Louis and laid him down and tucked the blanket over him. Then she turned and looked at the rocking chair and sat down, resting her head on the back of it. Louis couldn't take his eyes off William lying in the crib.

Julie said, "I need to rest." She got up and said to Loziane, "If you need me, I'll be next door."

Louis followed her as she left the room. He revealed, "I was a quiet baby."

"You were?" Julie replied and kicked off her shoes, then flopped back on the bed with her arms flung wide open, and sighed in relief. "I'm pooped! I need to rest."

Louis walked over and stood looking down at her. He was about to lie down with her, but he stopped. Noticing her exhaustion, he agreed, "Yes, you are."

He pulled her up and kissed her goodnight, then laid her back down and tucked her in like she did with Bill, took the bouquet of flowers she had given him, and walked out the room. Opening the door, he looked back and saw Julie watching him. Throwing her a kiss, he pulled the door closed behind him. Julie got up and prepared herself for bed.

Lying down and looking up at the design on the ceiling, she wondered what the meaning of all this was. *This is the first time I'm not thinking of anyone else, except how I feel. Louis already has a family waiting for him, so why am I destroying what he wanted for so long now that he has his chance? I feel so selfish!*

Then a thought hit her—what would people say if she married Louis? *It's only been a year since my husband died. . . . He wanted to marry me, but he hasn't actually proposed. He was indirect. For the first time in my life, I'm yearning for a man, why now? Why did I come here? What am I looking for? My mother seems to be okay with it. But then she's from Haiti, so she's no stranger to the country. Why does this bother me so much?*

Jacque came to her mind, the words he had spoken to her in the library. She could hear him yelling his vicious words out of his mouth to her: *He'll do you just like Saul did you!*

She put the pillow on top of her head, trying to block Jacque's voice out of her head. Nodding her head she thought that Jacque wanted to get his way with her by using effective mind words. The words did hurt, but one thing she knew was that Jacque would never get what he wanted from her. One important thing Jacque should have remembered was how she was. When they were children, he should have remembered about her that she wasn't the type to submit to abusive language or threats. Just when she thought Jacque understood who she really was, he proved to be more confused than any other man she had ever met. Jacque didn't know half of her problems. He was just assuming and thought he was right. What a fool!

Jacque knew nothing about her husband. Saul was very kind and gentle to her. A loving man he was till she started to have that crazy dream.

Julie cried and thought she would have left, too, if he kept on dreaming about another woman and yearning for her. There was nothing her husband could have done to help her. Maybe that was the reason he was in Haiti without her, searching for the same answer she was looking for. Did he ever find the man? Did he know it was Louis Janvier she had kept on dreaming about? What would Saul have done if he found the answer?

During the time they were married, she knew that Saul was a daredevil, and he would not let anyone stand in his way of being happy. Saul practically ran away to let her be, for her to find her own answer. She was willing to set Louis aside to make her marriage work. And she felt she would have succeeded in doing so, if Saul had given her the chance. Saul and she weren't the first to have marital problems. She was willing to go to therapy so she could help cope with her situation. Why wouldn't Saul talk to her? She was willing to listen and do everything he would have told her to do to help their marriage succeed for the sake of their son William, whom they loved dearly. Now, it was too late to do anything because he was dead. And Jacque dared to speak of him abusively when Saul did nothing but helped him so much? Never did he say thanks to Saul, except to criticize him. All kinds of questions were churning in her mind about Jacque. The only thing that Jacque was able to do was to make her wonder about him. She would not allow Jacque to keep her down, not in this life!

Then she remembered the sword. What took place earlier . . . what was Louis hiding in the desk? Why did Louis have a similar sword as her late husband Saul?

Getting out of her bed, Julie quietly opened the door, not knowing that Maxine was about to knock on it. Julie startled a little since she was not expecting her. "What are you doing here?"

Julie pulled Maxine in before she answered her question. "I couldn't sleep from all that excitement, so I assume you were up, too."

"I was about to step out to check on something."

"On what?" Maxine asked.

"This afternoon, while Louis was showing us his trophies, he hid something that he didn't want me or anyone to see."

"I didn't see that," Maxine replied.

"I know," Julie breathed. "He did it so fast that no one saw him do it, but I did. and he got me very curious about that."

"I don't think we should pry on that, Julie. If Louis wanted you to know he would have shown it to you."

Julie ignored her and opened the door to leave. Cautiously she stuck her head out, looking up and down the hallway. It was dark and quiet. No one was there. She stealthily crept down the stairs as Maxine followed. At the bottom, the huge mahogany clock facing them read 11:15. Looking around cautiously to see if anyone was up, she opened the door and they softly slipped in, closing it behind them.

Maxine was scared because she knew that Louis wasn't someone to snoop on and she felt that Julie was invading Louis's privacy. She held on to Julie's hands and whispered, "No, Julie!"

Removing her hands off her, Julie whispered back, "If I'm going to take Louis seriously, I need to know everything about him, even his dirty secrets. I want him naked before me. No hidden surprises, understand? Now move and keep an eye out for me."

Julie walked directly to the desk and pulled out the chair. The desk was locked. Maxine whispered urgently, "Hurry up."

Julie sorted out her tools, pulled out a hairpin, and started to play with the lock. There was a click. Excitedly, she said, "I got it."

Maxine didn't think Julie was able to open the lock. She was surprised when Julie did. "Where did you learn to do that?"

"Living with a man like Saul, I've learned many things, and this is one of the skills." Julie opened the drawer and found a school picture of Saul and Louis together. She frowned and said in wonder, "My husband never told me he knew Louis . . . and Louis never once mentioned to me about knowing Saul."

Maxine looked at the picture and said, "Remembered they went to the same university."

Rummaging through the drawer, she exclaimed, "Look here–there are two videos in here!"

Julie picked up the tapes from the desk and replaced the picture. She closed the drawer. "Let's go up to watch them."

They quietly ran up to Julie's room. Julie looked around excitedly. There has to be a television and a video here."

They searched around the room.

"Here," Julie said, "this button here says: PRESS FOR TELEVISION."

She pressed the button and the wall slid open. A big screen television appeared, with a stereo and a VCR. She turned on the television with the remote control that was lying beside it, placed the tape that said NO. 1 in the VCR, turned the volume down, and pressed play. As they watched the pictures playing across the screen, Maxine said, "It's a picture of the womb of a woman. She's pregnant."

The picture showed a three-month sonogram through nine months of pregnancy. Julie said with trepidation, "This doesn't make any sense. It's showing a pregnant woman carrying a baby boy in her womb."

Maxine removed the tape and placed in the second one. She said excitedly, "Now she is about to give birth. It doesn't show the woman's face, nor the doctor attending her. This is gross. It's physically repellent. This picture is making me afraid to have a baby."

Julie laughed and gently patted her back and said, "It's unpleasant but after you have finished giving birth to your infant, you just want to see it and hold it. There's nothing to compare to the feeling that you get."

Maxine started to fast forward the tape. Suddenly Julie grabbed her hand. "Stop! Go back! Play it slow. . . . It's my son! It's me giving birth to my son!"

Maxine was shocked. She looked at Julie and said, "Are you sure!"

"Look," Julie exclaimed, "I should know how I look and my husband." Grievously, she looked at how Saul was smiling kissing her, passing his hands over her face, kissing her forehead, and the baby that was lying on her chest, telling her how much he loved her. Tears ran out of her eyes as she watched how happy Saul looked. "There! It's another picture of Bill getting older, up to four months . . . Max, this looks spooky! Why would Louis have videotape of me giving birth to my son? How come he has it?"

Maxine said, "There's got to be an explanation to all this. . . . The way he sang to you tonight," she jumped from one topic to another, putting her hand against her chest as she pressed the remote control to turn off the video. She didn't want Julie crying." I was amazed. I never heard him sing to anyone or play the piano, nor laugh the way he does now. I was moved . . . I didn't even know he knew how to sing. Richard said he'd only heard Louis sing once before, and that was a gift to his mother and father when he was a boy."

Waving her off Julie, roughly replied, "Max, I don't care if he had a great voice or never laughed. All that concerns me at the moment is why Louis Janvier has movies of me having my baby?"

"One thing I definitely know is that Louis loves you. He wouldn't do anything to hurt you or Bill.

Julie was frantic. "I don't know him . . . I don't really know anything about him."

"You love him."

"That is beside the point," Julie growled. "Louis doesn't talk much about himself to me. He only told me what he wants me to know about him. He's more interested in learning more about me. I don't like that, Max."

Maxine answered, "The way his eyes light up when he sees you. I never saw Louis in any long-term conversation with anyone besides you. I thought he had a speech problem . . . it was always 'hi' and 'goodbye' and 'have a good time'. then he'd walk away so fast you wouldn't see the back of his head leaving. I was the second woman besides you he ever had a civilized conversation with, and that was when we came to meet you at the airport. Then I realized that he had a human side." They giggled softly. "I don't think he means you or Bill any harm. Bill looks so much like him. When I looked at Bill, I see Louis. They even have the same gothic, green eyes. He has nothing for Saul. If I didn't know you any better, Julie, I would think you're the wife of his best friend who Louis been telling you about, or you and Louis had an affair and Bill was the result."

Maxine got up to rewind the tapes. Julie sat down on the bed and asked with a puzzled frown, "Oh my God, what if I did?"

Maxine didn't even turn around. "You know I won't buy it. You're not the type."

Julie insisted, "But what if I am the woman and I did get pregnant by him without having sex with him."

Astonished at what she was hearing, Maxine stopped what she was doing. "How's that possible?"

"You mean you didn't believe me when I told you how I got pregnant? It's not impossible, Max, not with science and new technology," Julie exclaimed. "For years, I've told you, I tried to have a baby for Saul, till he told me he had preserved his seeds. The first time we did the procedure, bingo! I got pregnant. Saul seemed to be very happy. He was always taking pictures of me and my stomach, videotaping William's birth. I have many videos of my pregnancy. You remember the woman I told you Louis was in love with? He never give me their names. All he said was the wife of his best friend. What if I am the wife of his best friend he spoke of?"

"But you told me he slept with her to impregnate her."

"As a matter of fact, he never told me he actually made love to her." Julie flashed back. "His words to me when I think back were he wanted to really make love to her, not like that. I just assumed he did, and he let me think that way to throw me off track. He didn't literally sleep with her to impregnate her. He told me he fell in love with her picture."

Maxine didn't know what to say. At the moment Julie looked angry, then Maxine said, "What if he is the one that gave Saul his sperm to get you pregnant, and Saul lied about the whole story to make you think that was his sperm he gave you?"

"What am I thinking?" Julie retorted. "Saul wouldn't do that to me without my consent. No!"

"What if he did?" Maxine pressed. "That would make Louis the real father of your baby."

Not wanting to believe, not wanting to think Saul would do that to her, Julie said skeptically, "I don't know. Why am I getting myself all worked up? It is maybe just a coincidence. They went to the same school, that's why Louis has his picture, and as for the videotapes, Louis is a doctor, and Saul had sent him these tapes to study the trauma of giving birth. Plus, two days ago he told me she wanted to meet me, and he let her know that he is hopelessly in love with me."

Maxine insisted, "Don't dismiss the possibility, Julie. Louis may be the father of your son. For some reason, I'm sure of it. Like I told you before, when he looks at you, it is as if he saw his child in you."

"Or maybe it is because he watched those videos too much," Julie exclaimed.

Declaring firmly, Maxine rejoined, "Julie, can't you see? The answer to your dream. Louis gave you the child you always wanted to make you happy, and Saul sacrificed his life when he realized he had caused you and Louis to bind with each other. So to make you happy, Saul got out of the picture, your life. Two men devoting their lives to serve you. . . ."

Julie removed herself from the bed, pacing back and forth on the floor. She was agitated. Maxine was afraid Julie might do something very bad to Louis if she couldn't get her to calm down. She knew Julie was compassionate woman, very gentle and kind. But at the same time, Julie could become headstrong once she got angry, and it would be very hard to reason with her.

Carefully Maxine stated, " . . . It looks like Louis was preparing to meet you and Bill. Everyone who used to hang around him saw the changes. He gradually put them out of his life since the very first time you returned to Haiti. I've seen a lot of changes in Louis. He used to have female companions all the time around him. They all disappeared. He called you on the telephone all the time. He looked for you. Sending you gifts, and not just anything, things he well thought of. Look at the way he fixed this room, and William's. What did the logo say when you read it?"

Julie replied, "Welcome home, my son."

"So you see," Maxine continued, "Louis has been giving you hints since you met him at his cousin Nadine's for the very first time. And William's room declares it all."

"That just tells me he wanted to have his son home and the woman he is truly in love with here with him. It's not me or my son, I'm just a fantasy to him."

"I believe it's you," Maxine said softly. "He wants to be around you. It's amazing the way he changed and the way you kept his interest. Louis was like a navy man. Never was he in a long-term relationship. He was always on the move, he never got too close to any of those women." She chuckled softly. "Seems to me the man is saving himself for you now, and you have no choice but to take him."

Julie shook her head at Maxine's ridiculous notion. "Max, you always seem to turn a shocking situation into a pleasant moment."

They laughed. Then Julie got serious. "How can I explain this situation I'm in to my mother? I can't even explain it to me."

"Have you looked at your mother?" Maxine replied. "Julie, really look at her. I wouldn't be surprised if she knows that Bill is Louis's baby. She loves Louis and Louis is fond of her, too . . . the way he calls her 'Mother', it's almost as if he already sees her as his mother. I was touched when I saw the way he took her hand and passed it over his face. You don't have to worry about Aunt Viviane. . . . My concern is you."

"I'm scared and thrilled at the same time! The evidence is in front of me. I see the truth, but my heart won't accept it. William is all that I have left of Saul for me to hold on to."

Maxine consoled, passing her hand over her shoulder. "I'm sorry, Julie."

Julie was crying. "Saul is dead and it hurts, and I'm here having fun with his friend, or maybe his killer."

Maxine disagreed, "No, Julie, Louis loves you. And you love him, too. Don't even think that way. Now when I think back on the night Saul died, Louis looked so disturbed, so hurt. I could swear I saw tears in his eyes. But he shields himself against you. He was also grieving for Saul. And he couldn't express his feelings."

"What made you come to this conclusion?"

"When I was giving you the information the man gave me, Henry was standing in front of me. I thought he was rude and weird. He was worried when he looked at Louis's face. He didn't want anyone to see the tears in Louis's eyes. Now I understand why he did that. He blocked my view so I wouldn't see Louis's pain." Maxine sounded more concerned than ever. "My word, Julie! Louis needs you . . . that man has had so many tragedies happening in his life. Losing you would be the final blow to him. He wouldn't kill Saul knowing that this might jeopardized his relationship with you. The way I look at it, for Louis to give Saul his seed to give to you, they were the best of friends, like brothers."

Suddenly there were footsteps coming toward the bedroom. Maxine quickly snapped the light off. The footsteps stopped at Bill's door, quietly opened the door, and walked in. Julie put her fingers to her lips. "Ssh!"

Wiping her eyes, Julie hurried to her son's room. Maxine slowly followed her. She heard Bill crying, then he stopped. Julie silently opened the door, then gasped in shock when she heard him say, "Daddy."

Maxine whispered, "Daddy! Who is he calling daddy?"

Julie made a gesture for her to stay back behind the door and walked into Bill's room and found Louis sitting in the rocking chair with Bill in his arms. Looking around the room for Loziane she asked, "What are you doing here?"

Louis, still rocking the chair, looked up at her. "I heard Bill crying so I came to see what happened."

"Huh," she said. "How did you hear him cry when your room isn't near here?"

He showed her the transceiver that was attached on the baby's bed. She was astonished, because she had not even thought about that. She wondered about what Maxine had just told her.

Without turning to the door he asked, "What are you and Max up to?"

Her jaw dropped open. "Where do you see Max?"

Chuckling, he said, "I don't have to see her, I have a good sense of smell. I smell her perfume."

Acting nonchalant, she said, "Really."

He smiled and called, "Really . . . come here, Max."

Maxine walked in smiling. Louis said, "Good night, Max."

Maxine smiled and stuck her tongue out at Louis. "See you later, Julie."

Shaking her head wonderingly, Julie said, "Good night, Max. See you tomorrow."

She walked to Louis, who had the baby in his arms, and said to Bill, "Why aren't you asleep, young man."

Loziane finally woke up and quickly came in to attend him. "I'm sorry, madame, monsieur. I did not hear the baby cry. That will not happen again."

Julie reassured her, "That's all right, Loziane, you had a long day and you're tired. Bill usually sleeps all night. That's the first time he ever woke up at this time."

Loziane moved closer to take the toddler. "Madame, monsieur, why don't you go back to bed and let me take care of the baby."

She repeated, "It's okay, Loziane. You go back to sleep."

Loziane protested, "Madame. . . ."

Julie said, "I insist. Go."

Loziane reluctantly moved back to her room and went to sleep. Bill had also gone back to sleep in Louis's arms. He stood up carefully with the toddler and moved toward his crib, trying not to wake him. Gently he laid him down. Louis covered him and tucked him in. He put his finger to his lips to signal silence as they both tip-toed out of the room and walked back to her room.

Turning her to look at him, Louis touched her face, running his fingers on her cheeks. He felt that Julie was crying since her eyes were still moist.

He said, "I, too, have a keen sense of hearing, and I'm sensitive to your needs. Good night, my love."

He kissed her hands as he gazed into her eyes and hurried out of her room. She quietly replied, "Good night."

Moving toward her bed she realized the tapes were missing. She thought that Maxine had returned them. She slid herself under the blanket, wondering how would she approach Louis about that mysterious woman whom he claimed had his baby. Before falling asleep she whispered, "God help me."

The next morning everyone slept for an extra hour or two. Beside the servants, Louis was also up bright and early in his secret room, the room he didn't show to anyone. He turned on the camera to record his moves before he started. That was the room he usually meditated in when he was in town, where he did his exercises and practiced his martial art techniques. He wanted to record his sword skill techniques. As he was meditating, he started to remember how close he used to be with his best friend.

Louis picked up the sword, making believe he was practicing with him, fencing and turning as if someone else was there with him. While he was practicing, Julie's voice penetrated his deep concentration on the other side of the wall, calling, "Is anyone back there?"

He stayed quiet, hoping she would leave, but she persisted. She was determined to know what was behind that wall. Unexpectedly, she found the secret panel to open his secret place.

Swiftly and quietly he laid the sword on the floor and put on one of the masks that hung on the wall on his face. He wanted to scare her, so she would lose interest about this room. She pushed the door open and hesitantly walked in, calling, "Is anyone here?"

The door smoothly closed behind her. Silently, he moved as a cat and grabbed her. Before he could get a good grip of her, he found himself flying through the air across the floor. Julie picked up his katana. She gave him no time to think or even talk. She was kicking and punching, chopping and slapping him like a punching bag.

The girl has superb skill, he thought as he defended himself. Trying to strike him, she swung the sword high and low. He realized she would chop him unless he identified himself so he hurriedly called out, "I'm at your mercy, my love."

She slowly stepped back and dropped her arms but with the sword still pointing at him. As he removed the mask from his face, Julie lowered the sword. "Louis, you scared me!"

She put the sword down carefully and knelt over him and touched his face tenderly. "Are you all right?"

She ran her hands over his chin and jaw. Taking her hands to look at them, he kissed them and folded between his. Her manicured fingers looked so small in the palm of his hands. With wonder, Louis laughed and said, "Woman, you scared me! Where did you learn to fight like that?"

"Like you, I was always in trouble," she replied, "so I had to learn self-defense, and later on Saul refined my skills." Looking around the contents of the room, she commented, "So this is your secret place. I'm sorry, I didn't mean to invade your privacy."

Nodding his head, Louis laughed ironically. "Really!"

Then looking at the clock on the wall he said, "I thought you would have stayed in bed to rest. You're up early. It's not even four o'clock."

"I couldn't sleep." Nodding her head, she said, "I was surprised you didn't invited me to see the sun set and you know I'm an early bird. I have to run. . . . I was on my way out when I heard someone shout behind the wall. I thought it was a secret room in the house you didn't show me or you did not know about. I was afraid someone or you might been in trouble. I searched and bingo! The wall opened. I must say this is a smart hiding place. No one would have thought about it."

"But you did." He got to his feet and pulled her up close to him. "Then again, you're not just any woman, you're a cactus, the desert plant."

She laughed because she felt Louis was calling her nosy. . . . She snuggled in his arms. "Now it's our secret place."

He wrapped her in his powerful arms and kissed her . . . thoroughly.

Chapter Fourteen

Ties of Love

As the eyes of dawn were opening, the roosters were crowing, and the dogs were barking, one by one the natives came down onto the streets of Haiti. Some were walking, some were riding on their donkeys, and more were driving. Haiti had barely changed. It didn't look much different. It was still full of poverty, making you wonder if there were any rich people or millionaires in Haiti. But at the same time it had much beautiful scenery outside of Port-au-Prince, the capital city. Still, in this hot and dusty place, there's always an exceptional group. Those good people, those who will do anything for you in the name of "love." One such group was on Louis's ranch. They were preparing and planting all the trees that had arrived the day before.

Louis and his workers were cleaning up a part of the ranch along the boundary where the river ran. Louis was wearing a farmer's pants without any shirt, and on his feet he had working boots. He had a shovel in his hands, digging the ground, removing the rocks from the surface. Some of the workers were piling the rocks to the side. It was still early in the morning, about 6:30, but already he and his workers were out in the fields. The area where they were working was almost cleaned for his project. After removing the rocks, he had the steamrollers roll on the ground to even it out. The workers brought the trucks of soil and dumped them on the ground evenly. Then they spread the soil and laid the grass on top of it. He excavated out three joined circles and planed the three cactuses in them. Carefully he put sand around them. It was unusual but beautiful when it was finished.

Julie stood at a distance watching the men work. She could not believe her eyes when she saw how Louis participated in the work they were doing. He wasn't there just for managing. He was working as well. The sun was rising and soon it was going to get hotter. Julie drove back to the house on a motor bike she had taken from Louis's garage to prepare food and lemonade for Louis and the men. Maxine and Loziane were enlisted to help.

One of the servants in the house was telling Loziane not to touch the glass. "These crystal glasses are not for workers to drink from."

Frowning Julie said, "*Mesye te di w sa* (Did monsieur tell you that)?"

The maid answered, "Non, madame. *Kòm sèvant nou sipoze konnen plas nou* (But as workers we know our place). Just because monsieur is kind, that does not mean we are at his level or rank."

Julie said, "It's okay. Ninot, I'm sure monsieur will not mind. So stop talking and give us a hand. The men will be hungry when they return."

Appalled, Ninot thought, this woman could not be Haitian to think she could drink from the same glass with the servant. She replied, "We're not suppose to cook for the men, madame. It's not our job. Our job is to care for monsieur and his guests."

Annoyed, Julie said, "Enough, Ninot! Are there any napkins in the house?"

Another servant quickly answered. She didn't understand what was wrong with Ninot. "*Oui, madame*, I'll go get them."

As the servant left to do what she had requested, Ninot followed her. When they reach the storage room, the young maid rebuked her, "*Sa k ap pran w la, Ninot, ou avèg? Ou pa-wè ki meum ki tap pale a* (What's wrong with you, Ninot, are you blind? Did you see who was talking to you? . . . ")

Ninot ignored her. She did not reply as she helped to bring the napkins out. " . . . *Li pa janm trò ta pou moun aprann. Madame nan gen anpil amou. Mesye a ap fache, si l konnen jan w pale avèk madam li* (It's never too late for anyone to learn. Madame has a lot of love. Monsieur would be very mad if he knew the way you talk to his woman)."

Everyone was busy. Viviane was on the patio preparing the plates on the table. Julie brought out several thermoses and set them on the table.

Feeling her arms Maxine said, "Girl, you're strong. I like the way you take charge of things."

Smiling, Julie replied, "Put ice in them, Max. Come, Loziane, help me bring the rest of the things out."

Following Julie readily, Loziane replied, "*Oui, madame.*"

As they were working, Maxine continued talking. "Aunt Viviane, Julie is always encouraging. I never thought I could enjoy cooking and serving people. Julie helped me to see that to give is to be happy. I'm happy doing it, especially knowing that Richard is going to taste something I helped prepare."

Julie and Loziane brought the rest of the things and two servant women brought the food and set it on the table—salad, potatoes au gratin, onion steaks, and hot biscuits and a big pot of rice and kidney beans.

Looking at the table Julie asked, "Do we have everything?"

Everyone assured her, "Yes."

She looked over to where the men were working. "Good. The men are returning, so we're just on time. Where's the hose for them to wash their hands?"

Walking to the other side of house and picking up a hose attached to a pipe, Ninot said, "Here it is, madame."

"Good, give it to me." She took the hose from Ninot.

As they got closer to the house, the men noticed the table with the feast prepared for them. Patrick was walking beside Louis, and Brian and Richard were a few steps behind them, with the rest of the workers following. As usual, Louis stood out in the crowd. He looked good in his farmer pants, with broad shoulders that made him look even more appealing and masculine. His cut off t-shirt revealed his biceps, triceps, deltoids, and a chest that made him more attractive than the other men; Louis's boots were covered with fertilizing soil, as were his overalls and some parts of his face and body.

Julie stood there wondering to herself, *I've never seen a man that's as dirty as a pig and looking so good. Fuji is the dirtiest of them all. I wonder if he has dirt in his underwear.* Louis removed his goggles as he got closer to Julie. She looked at them and burst out laughing, pointing an index finger at him.

He stopped, looked around, and asked, "What's so funny, Julie. . . ?"

Tears were running down her cheeks, she could not stop laughing. " . . . *Chat pran lang ou* (Cat stole your tongue), Julie?"

She got everyone laughing and wondering what was so funny.

She finally calmed herself down to say, "I always picture you as a bureaucrat, Fuji, but never, I mean never, as a groundhog."

Twirling his goggles around on his fingers with a naughty smile on his face, he replied, "Really. . . ?"

With a sudden lunge, Louis grabbed her and kissed her with complete satisfaction and with everyone looking on. Raising his head, he said, " . . . There, the groundhog kissed you."

Wrinkling her nose, she pushed him away. "Louis, let me go. You smell like manure."

Realizing the men were waiting, Louis spoke up. "I'm starving."

Everyone washed their hands and faces, then Julie invited, "The girls and I prepared some food for you men, and we hope you'll all enjoy it."

Julie looked at Louis. "You look hot."

"That's you, baby." He smiled. "I always wanted to look hot for you."

Ninot handed them a glass of lemonade as they walked and sat on the patio steps. Julie took out her handkerchief to wipe Louis's face. He looked at her with a straight face as she wiped the dirt off and wondered how he was going to explain the situation he had with her. Ninot brought them two plates of food and a pitcher of lemonade. They thanked her. Some of the workers were sitting on the benches and some were sitting on the floor.

Maxine and Richard came and sat three steps down from them. She looked up at Julie. "Julie, this is good."

Chewing on his food, Richard agreed, "Did you prepare the meal, Julie?"

She nodded. "Yes, but I had a lot of help from Maxine and the servants, of course."

Maxine smiled as Richard gave her kiss on the nose. Louis took a bite of his food, closed his eyes, inhaled, and speared a big piece of potato and meat, then shoved it in his mouth and chewed. Julie, Maxine, and Richard looked on in amazement at the way Louis was attacking the food.

Maxine said, "Louis, Louis!"

He pointed his finger down toward his plate and continued to chew as he answered and swallowed. "That's the best steak and onions I've ever tasted."

He put down the plate, leaned over, and kissed Julie and said, "What else can these hands do?"

The girls looked at each other and laughed as he picked up his plate and continued eating. When he finished, he said, "Well, men, break is almost over, so Patrick. . . ."

Promptly, Patrick answered, "Yes, sir."

He said, "Finish instructing the men about the job."

Patrick got up. "Okay, Louis. Hey, guys!"

He called to the rest of them, "As soon as we finish with lunch, we're heading back. And make sure you have large hats!"

"All right," the men chorused and prepared to go back to work.

Louis turned and asked Julie, "Are you game?"

She looked him up and down. "It depends on the game."

He jumped up, brushing his hand across the seat of his pants. "Horse back riding."

She jumped to her feet with excitement. "I'm game."

He waved to Bill and Viviane. Viviane was making Bill wave back. Louis turned to Julie. "Why don't you and Max go change into something more comfortable. . . . Hey, Richard, where are you going?"

He called, "Back to the fields with the men."

Louis said, "Come on, go change. We're going riding instead . . . I need to soak."

Putting his arm around Julie's shoulders, he kissed her on her forehead, and touched her nose with his fingertip. "See you in an hour and, please, don't keep me waiting."

Louis and Julie walked inside the house, and Richard and Maxine walked in right behind them, hand in hand, to change for their ride.

An hour later, Louis was wearing a white ivory silk shirt with black jeans, at his narrow waist a silver belt with the buckle of a horse head, and on his feet he wore a pair of black cowboy boots. Two buttons of his long-sleeved shirt were open to reveal a little of his masculine chest, making him look very sexy. Richard looked nice dressed in blue jeans and white shirt. They were sitting around the swimming pool, having cocktails with Viviane and William while waiting for Julie and Maxine.

Coming down the stairs, Maxine knew that Julie wanted to talk with Louis in private. She said, "I wanted to stay and talk to Aunt Viviane. I want her to know to get to know Richard, so we want to stay and have a little chat with her."

As Julie and Maxine walked in, Louis was looking at his watch while he was talking to Viviane and Richard. Julie was dressed similarly to Louis, except she was wearing a pink blouse. Maxine said, "Hello guys. . . ."

Looking at the expression on Louis's face, which said, *I don't like to be kept waiting,* Julie looked at her watch. " . . . Your watch is fast. You're early."

Picking up his cowboy hat, Louis took Julie's arm and said, "Let's go, darling."

They went through the back door and left the house. He opened the door of the passenger side of his Jeep and helped her in. They drove to the barn. When they got there the horses were already saddled waiting for them. One of the workers brought them the horses. Louis double-checked the saddles while Julie touched their noses, tenderly talking softly to them.

Standing between the horses, Louis helped her to mount her horse, then he mounted his. They rode for a distance away from the barn. Louis pulled ahead and stopped under a great lush tree, dismounted, and waited for her.

Surprised, Julie stopped. "Why did you stop here? I thought you were going further."

He helped her to dismount off her horse, gently patted the horses, and commanded them, "Go!"

They cantered off but not too far. She wondered and said, "The horses, they're leaving."

He pulled her close, kissed her, and said, "Don't worry, they won't run too far away. It's cool and shady here."

Knowing she had watched the videotapes, Louis said with urgency, "Julie, do you know how much I love you?"

"Yes, Fuji, I do."

"Then you know I would not deliberately try to hurt you. I'm sure you wondering why I have a school picture of Saul and what am I doing with your pregnancy videotapes?"

"That had crossed my mind," Julie replied.

She looked at him as he talked. "There are many things I want to tell you and share with you."

Under the tree there was a big rock, maybe four feet high. It was kind of flat on top. Louis lifted her and sat her on it, then leaned on the side of the rock and started to explain to her. Louis looked worried as he mentally replayed the reasons behind the tapes she found and watched last night.

"Thirty-two months ago," Louis sighed, "I was in New York on business. As usual after dealing with business, I would meet your husband Saul in our secret hang-out in Brooklyn, a place called Coney Island Aquarium. Saul was already there, waiting for me. He didn't look happy. After ordering us both drinks, he explained his situation to me. How much he loved you. . . ."

Louis closed his eyes for a few seconds then opened them to look at her as he spoke. "I never had a chance to meet you, but Saul told me you were beautiful. . . ."

Gently, with the back of his hand, he passed his hand over her face, trying not to stare at her too much, and said, " . . . We left the aquarium and walked down the boardwalk. Saul explained how he wanted to give you children, but was unable to. He wanted my help. I was reluctant, but Saul started reproaching me. . . ."

Louis has a flashback to what happened thirty-two months ago.

"For all those times you needed me," Saul flared, "I was there for you. I even saved your life. So therefore you owe me!"

Saul took her picture out of his wallet, looked at it with tears in his eyes, crying and saying, "You owe me your life, Louis."

He showed Louis her picture. The moment he laid eyes on the picture, he was hopelessly in love with her. Now, he understood what Saul was going through. He sat on the bench facing the ocean and looking at the face in the picture. Then Saul dropped his bombshell. "I'm demanding your seed."

Louis tried to reason with him. "Why me, Saul?"

Saul was desperate. "I don't want anyone else's seed. I want yours . . . " he pleaded, "because you're my friend, and I love you, man. We look alike, and we're like brothers. No one will suspect that the baby is not mine."

He was crying like a baby on Louis's shoulders. People were passing by looking at them funny, thinking that they were lovers. Two homeless old ladies pushing their shopping carts called them names. "Disgusting! Don't you people have a home?"

Saul kept pleading, "I want her to have your baby. I will love him or her like my own. I will keep you informed of everything that's going on in his or her life, and if anything happens to me, I want you to take care of my wife and our child for me. . . ."

Saul sounded sick, like a madman. He was beginning to sound scary. " . . . You see, I want her to be happy. She wants children and I can't give her any. I don't have the heart to tell her I cannot produce any baby."

Louis took out his handkerchief and gave it to Saul to wipe away the tears on his face. He tried to calm him down. He'd never seen him like this. Saul was always in good cheer. Saul was always there when he needed him. Louis thought, Even though Saul sounded like a sick madman, this is the first time in our friendship, Saul wanted something from me. For the first time, I would truly be helping a friend. Not just any friend, but someone like a brother. That's what he was to me. If this is what will help Saul to be happy, I will do it for him.

He handed the picture back to Saul and consented to do what he wanted. Saul took him to a clinic to see his long-time friend who was a doctor, and made the "necessary" arrangements. After everything was over, Saul took him out to celebrate their new future. "Friends . . . forever!"

On his way back to Haiti, he wondered about her. How much he wanted her and how much he had fallen in love with a woman he'd never met. Then he realized he didn't do it for Saul, he did it for her, his Julie. His life had changed ever since then. He became a completely different person.

He began to feel more unfulfilled. Nothing, wine nor women, could satisfy his hunger. He grew more distant. He lived on those tapes Saul was sending him. His relatives and friends couldn't understand what he was going through. They thought the death of his mother had finally gotten to him. He developed a temper. Everyone steered clear of him. He was in love with a woman who could never be his, that was driving him insane! The wife of his best friend! He needed her. He wanted her so badly, he ached day and night, plus she was having his baby. The sad part of it was she didn't even know he existed. He may never see her and his son . . . that was driving him crazy.

Then twenty months ago, Saul came to Haiti and spent two months with him. Upon leaving, he handed Louis most of his property documents, even his will.

"And Jacque will give you the rest of the documents," Saul stated. He told Louis his wife and his son belonged to him. Louis didn't understand his words. So he ignored Saul's statement.

"Julie is very innocent. No other man except me had ever touched her. I felt that I have ruined her. Louis, what have I done?"

Louis was trying to make an effort to say a word of comfort. "You love her, Saul. That is your crime, and you will do anything to please her."

Listening to the sound of Louis's voice as he tasted his drink, Saul wondered what was on Louis's mind. Jacque wasn't joking, he thought, when he said he heard Louis was going mad. He tried to make eye contact with Louis "Why are you wearing a pair of dark shades indoors, Louis, talking to me? What are you hiding?"

Removing his shades, Louis answered calmly, "Myself, Saul, just myself."

Suddenly it dawned on Saul what was bothering Louis. Angered at Louis's dead look and answer, Saul snapped, "You're something else! What happened? The woman last night didn't fill your appetite? What do you want now, Louis. . . ."

Louis looked away and didn't reply. Saul blurted, "All the women you're running around with are not enough to satisfy your hunger . . . damn! You have to fall in love with my wife. You don't even know her, Louis. You're crazy." He put his glass down. "You're in love with my wife!" he shouted. "You're the cause of her nightmares, Louis. . . . You think you can hide this from me or take me on, Louis! Look at me, you destroyed my life!"

Louis couldn't believe Saul accused him of doing that. He calmly said, "I destroyed your life? . . . . I wasn't the one who came to you and begged to impregnate your wife. Now when things went wrong, you got the nerve to come here to blame me for what happened. What's next, Saul? I'm the cause now for your unhappiness."

"Tell me you're not in love with my wife." He stood in Louis's way with a maniacal look in his eyes. Saul wanted to fight him. He made a lunge for Louis, but Louis stepped back out of reach and turned away from Saul. He could not deny the truth of Saul's statement, but he was not about to pick a fight with his best friend. Saul shouted, "You're insane! You want my wife, don't you, Louis?"

Louis tried to reason with him. "I never asked for that, Saul. She's your wife. I may be out of my mind, but this is where I'm going to stay."

Louis walked behind the bar to fix himself a drink. Saul watched how Louis drank down his cognac like it was water. Louis troubled him. Never had he seen Louis drink that much in one round, plus it was only six in the morning.

Taking ahold of Louis's hand, Saul exclaimed, "What is wrong with you? Let me tell you something, if you do anything to hurt Julie, I swear, I'll return and haunt you like the dog you are. And I'll chew you without mercy. I didn't believe you were that crazy. I was out of my mind to think I could get away with what you did?"

"Excuse me! You mean, what you did?"

"Oh I see," Saul ground between his teeth. "You're not going to share the blame. Let me put it to you this way—when my wife finds out, you think she's going to look at you as if you were some kind of victim? My wife would want both of our heads. And the truth is, I don't want to be near either one of you when this goes down. It's your problem, because William is your son, not mine. And don't think she's going to hand him to you. . . . She's not going to make it easy for you. She is not like those women you've been encountering. She's out of your league."

"You know I'm out of my league, why are you worried so much?"

"Are you challenging me, Louis?"

"I would never challenge you, Saul. Everything I have is yours."

"But you're in love with my wife. . . . I want my wife back, Louis!"

Saul grabbed him and punched him on the face. Louis didn't retaliate. He stood there and accepted the punch from Saul. He didn't believe that Saul wanted to hurt him. Calmly he reminded Saul, "She never left you, Saul, you did. All you have to do is go back to her and consort with her."

"How could I," Saul shouted, "she's not dreaming about me!"

Louis was beginning to understand what Saul was telling him and why was he so enraged toward him. He didn't want to ask what was his wife dreaming about. Quietly he stood behind the bar looking at Saul explaining his situation to him. . . .

Why Julie, who Louis never met, dreamt about him, calling his name in her dreams, which she did not remember when she woke up. Louis was astonished as he carefully listened to Saul. Saul was furious and confused about his situation with his wife, as he explained to Louis.

"I never thought anyone would have come between me and my wife, my one and only true love. I'm hurting. She was my most beautiful dream. I never would have thought I would have been the one to hurt her. I cannot explain the feeling that is

232

*burning inside me for her. I wanted so much to take good care of her, giving her every-
thing she ever dreamed to have. She's my life and I destroyed her. . . ."*

He cut in, *"Dreams don't count, Saul. Eventually her dream would fade away
just like every other dream. Go to your wife, be more gentle, talk to her, revive your
marriage vow to her, love her not with your body at the moment, but with your
words."*

*In the meanwhile, Louis was dying inside as he was advising Saul. Telling Saul
what to do to gain his wife back. But Saul wouldn't hear of it. He felt he was becoming Louis by listening to how Louis was telling him how to love his wife.*

*"Louis, shut up," Saul exclaimed. "I tried that already, but you kept on coming
between my wife and me."*

*Louis looked away. He didn't want to look at Saul. ". . . Look at me, Louis. . . .
You want her, don't you. . . ?*

*Louis felt helpless. "She doesn't know who I am, Saul, and she never has to know
that I even exist."*

*"How noble of Louis." He laughed. "I always knew deep down you have royalty
in your blood. And today you prove it even so. . . . You want me to kill you, Louis?"*

*Louis started to feel peeved. He felt that no matter what he told Saul, he wasn't
going listen to him. All Saul could see was his wife dreaming about Louis and that
they were having sex, something that didn't even happen in reality. He thought Saul
was as mad as he was. Louis handed him a knife that was under the counter behind
the bar and said, "You should have let me die when my relatives turned against me.
Take me out of my misery. Kill me so you could have your happiness back, you have
the power. I'm already dead. I have nothing worth living for beside these tapes you
were sending me."*

*Louis took out a couple tapes behind the counter and banged them on the bar and
continued, ". . . This is my life living on these videotapes that you are sending me."*

*Louis poured another drink and gulped. Saul looked at him. "I love her, Louis.
She's my wife. She is my dream. Everything I hope to find in a woman. She's all
mine!"*

*Louis provoked him, wanting Saul to stab him with the knife. He grinned. "Not
anymore—past tense, she was!"*

*Angered by Louis's statement, Saul concluded as he threw the knife at the pole
above Louis's head, missing him by a mere inch. "You are a suicidal maniac!"*

*Then Saul started to laugh like a madman. ". . . You will be fine, brother. Your
madness is about to end." He smiled at Louis as he patted him on his back. "I'm not
going to let you two go out of your minds. She too is feeling the same way, Louis,
without knowing who you are. She is as lost and empty just as you and I. . . ."*

*Saul continued, ". . . Ever since you gave her your seed, I've seen that your mind
has been troubled, Louis. And the truth was, I didn't give a damn! I was willing to
sacrifice your ass to please her. . . . But I'm glad that you know how to keep your feelings for my wife hidden."*

*Louis tried to cut in. Saul lifted his hand in a gesture to prevent Louis from talk-
ing. "Don't say a word, Louis. . . . I saw the way you two looked at each other last*

night. The way you two trembled when you looked at each other, how you wanted to touch her and rudely invited yourself to lunch and forgot if I was there in the next room looking at you. She's already wondering about you. Why she felt a knot in her stomach when she was around you. . . . She wants to know who you are already. It's too late for me. . . ."

"No, Saul, it's not . . . I don't want to know her. Cancel your flight for another day. Give her a big surprise by arriving for lunch today. I bet she'll be real thrilled."

Looking at the excitement on Louis's face, Saul said, "She intrigues you, doesn't she? And she revived all your being."

Louis gestured. "Forget about me. All I want is to see her happy, that's all."

"Her," Saul retold, "a slip of the tongue. You were never a good liar, Louis. I want you to go to lunch."

"I will not go," he replied.

Saul insisted for him to go to lunch, and for him to make her happy. But Louis wouldn't hear of that. He didn't want to hurt Saul. Saul felt it was too late. There was nothing Louis could do or say to change what had already happened.

"I will hurt her," Louis sighed.

"You could try," Saul laughed. "But it's too late, Louis. She has already captured your heart. You could fight it, but you will not win. I want you to promise me that you'll protect her for me."

Saul listened to how Louis was blaming himself for everything that had taken place. He closed his eyes and took a deep breath, trying to hold back the tears. . . . "I don't blame you for having good taste. . . . Nor do I blame myself for making that mistake . . . Prend bien soin d'elle (Take good care of her) for me."

Louis reflected on the last time he saw Saul. He spent two weeks down in Connecticut, and during that time Saul seemed to be happy, living in a different world. He invited a couple of his associates to celebrate his new project, at the same time testing if Louis would have slept with the female friends that Louis once used to date and claimed he still had them in his system. Louis was surprised to see them there at the party Saul was giving.

The party was on the move, and Louis was trying to have a good time. He wanted to prove to Saul that he wasn't in love with his wife. Saul stood at a distance talking to a few good friends, pretending he wasn't paying attention to Louis. He watched how Louis kissed one of the female friends and smiled as he kissed her and gulped down his wine. Then wiped his lips in displeasure.

Louis didn't want to be around those women, but he fought himself to do so. So Saul could go back to his wife, and have the family he always wanted to have. Louis tried so hard to erase Julie's vision out of his mind that night, but he couldn't. He wanted only Julie. He realized he was truly in love with her. He pretended to go out for some fresh air with one of the women. When he was out of Saul's sight, he removed his checkbook out of his jacket pocket and signed the woman a couple of thousands of dollars for her to go home and not to return to the party. She was offended. She tore the check and threw the torn paper on his face and walked away.

Louis took a long walk before he headed home. When he arrived, Saul was sitting in his living room waiting for him with a glass of cognac in his hand. Saul handed it to him.

"Congratulations, Louis," Saul smiled. "Now I can go in peace."

Louis was happy to hear that Saul was finally going home to his wife. He didn't understand what he meant by that "he could go in peace." So he took the glass out of Saul's hand and drank. They sat facing each other without saying a word for a while enjoying their cognac. He was happy because he thought he had finally proved to Saul that he wasn't in love with his wife.

As they were talking, about the future, Saul got off his seat to remove the gold necklace around his neck and placed it around Louis's neck. Julie's and William's pictures were inside the locket. Louis was wondering what he was doing. He thought that was a gift from Saul.

As he was placing the necklace around his neck, Saul stated, "The only man I ever kissed was my father. And now you're the second."

He gave Louis a kiss on both of his cheeks, then shook his hand. Then he poured them another glass of cognac and gave toast as he sat back on his sit, "May God help you, Louis."

Louis wanted to know what he meant by that. Then he explained to Louis his plan, and what he was about to do. Saul was very stubborn. He wouldn't listen to reason. He felt there was no forgiveness for what he did. He made Louis swear he was going to do everything in his power to see Julie happy.

Louis reflected back on the night Saul's jet went down. He wanted to run and scream so loud. To let out the frustration he'd kept hidden for so long. But he couldn't. He didn't know what to do. It was so hard for him to hold back his feelings. His best friend died. And the only two people who knew that were Henry and Nadine.

Louis followed Saul's funeral from a distance. He couldn't go to the memorial with Julie. . . . He watched how Julie wept over her husband's coffin, and how he wanted to hold her in his arms to comfort her. Maxine and her mother stood by her side crying while the rest of the family stood behind her looking at the way the coffin was going down into the grave. No one noticed that he was there or the silent farewell he gave.

"Farewell, my brother, my best friend, Saul."

He was the last one to leave the cemetery. He stood by Saul's burial place in silent solitude looking at his grave and wondering about the lives Saul had left behind. Wondering how would he be able to fix the situation he was in. Alone, Louis was crying for his friend, the way he died, the joy they shared, and the adventures they took. He could hear Saul's laughter and his ideas. He could still see Saul was filled with love and life.

"Saul," Louis cried out loud, falling on his knees. "I would have done anything for you."

He grabbed a hand full of dirt. Louis squeezed it between his hands, weeping over the grave. He spent the whole day and night on his knees crying. He didn't realize the time had gone by. The next morning the caretaker of the cemetery had to let him know that it was the following day. He had to get a grip on himself so he could accomplish what he had promised to Saul. Louis spent a few months in New York taking care of the things Saul had entrusted him to do for Julie. He made sure everything was done before he headed back home to wait on Julie's arrival.

Louis looked down at his boots and removed his wallet from his back pocket. He flipped it open to the pictures, looked at it, then he handed it to Julie.

She looked at the picture. "This is Saul and you."

Sighing, he replied, "We went to the same university. He was my best friend; he saved my life. I owed him everything I have."

Julie almost fell off the rock from the shocking explanation Louis gave her. He quickly took a hold of her.

Louis explained to her the type of life he used to lead. The things he used to do till he met with Saul, her late husband. How his life changed. What completely changed his life was when Saul came to him and told him he was going away on a dangerous mission. Louis tried to talk him out of it, but Saul had already made up his mind. Saul knew what he was about to do might cause his death. But this was a chance of a lifetime. He had just created a new prototype design of a jet. And he didn't want anyone to test it except himself. Louis had flown with Saul before, so he knew Saul was a good pilot and navigator. So he didn't have to worry too much.

Louis was in love with Julie. Knowing if anything happened to Saul, Julie would be hurt, he didn't want to see her cry. Louis was also an experienced flier and a good pilot. He was willing to test the plane for Saul, but he wouldn't hear of it. Saul told him that was nonsense. Everything Louis did was to please her. He never thought there would be a relationship between them, because she was the wife of his best friend. When Saul told him Julie was mental, she needed him, even when she didn't know who he was; their minds were connected. How she constantly dreamt of Louis, and if Saul didn't know Louis any better, he would have came down here to Haiti and buried him alive.

"Somehow you knew me. You sensed my presence with you." He removed the necklace around his neck. "It was not my intention to ruin your marriage. I wanted him to be happy. I thought by doing this, it would have brought you both happiness. I'm sorry that I've helped deceive you. . . . This is what he gave me before he left."

He opened the locket to her picture with the baby.

Julie looked at the picture in the locket. She closed her eyes, shaking her head to get her senses. Julie was in shock. She jumped off the rock and started to run. Her mind was whirling at the thoughts that Saul didn't trust her to tell her he couldn't have any children.

Louis ran after her. "I'm sorry, Julie. I never thought of hurting you."

Louis tried to hold her, but she wouldn't let him. She wouldn't listen to anything he had to say anymore.

Louis took her hand in his and squeezed them. "Please forgive me. Allow me to make you happy. Give me a chance to prove myself to you and to our son Bill. I loved Saul, I would have done anything for him, and he knew that. I never wanted anything bad to happen to him."

Tears were running down Julie's face. She removed a handkerchief to wipe her eyes. "All those stories about your best friend and his wife was to prepare me for 'that crap'!"

Gazing into her eyes, Louis swallowed and tried to hold back his tears. Still holding on to her hand, he kneeled before her, begging for forgiveness. "I love you, Julie, and I love Bill. . . . I don't want to lose you. I would have given anything not to make you cry. I cannot live without you, Julie. But I couldn't live without telling you the truth."

Fighting herself not to touch him, Julie pulled her hands away and headed back to the barn. Louis got up on his feet and followed her. She shouted, "The truth! Get away from me! You are a deceiver! You are liar! Saul wouldn't do that to me."

"You've seen the evidence. How could I have the tape of you giving birth to my son, if what I told wasn't true."

She yelled, "I heard about you, Louis. You would lie, cheat, or even kill to get your way, but not this time. You want me to believe you impregnated me without my permission. . . . You mean you raped me? You violated my body without my consent?"

"You know that's not true." Louis exhaled in shock, remembering Saul's last toast: *May God help you.* "I wouldn't rape you or do you harm."

"Excuse me! And what do you call what you did to me if it's the truth?"

Louis couldn't answer. The impact of Julie's word hit him like a violent blow. He felt she was right. He helped to violate her. They didn't give her the choice. He could not hold back his tears. "All I know is that I love you, I need you."

"Get away from me, you sick, debased man!" she yelled. "And don't you ever put your perverted hands on me again!"

Julie took off. She didn't wait for the horse. She tried to run all the way to the ranch house in the heat. Louis was afraid for her, that she might get dehydrated. He begged her to get on her horse, but she wouldn't. He jumped off his horse and carefully took ahold of her, knowing she knew how to fight and she might flip him. Julie started to struggle with him. She punched him and kicked without mercy. She even kicked him in his testicles. Louis rolled for a few seconds on the ground then launched at her. They were rolling on the ground. Louis realized if he would not use his strength, she would beat him to the ground and she would leave him unconscious.

She yelled, "I'll kill you. . . !"

Holding on to her hands, Louis managed to tie her hand and her feet with a rope that was on the saddle so he could control her. She yelled, "Don't you dare tie me like a cattle. . . !"

He lifted her up and laid her on his shoulder then got on his horse and off he rode.

She screamed, " . . . Let me go! Get your dirty hands off me!"

The farmers stood at a distance looking at them, wondering what was going on. Never had they seen or witness a woman treating Louis Janvier like that. They were all submissive and only spoke when Louis demanded an answer from them. They turned their heads, pretending they were working. Some looked down, continuing planting, looking at them under their large hats as Louis galloped away by them. They wouldn't dare come near to see or ask what was going on between them. But they thought Julie was a tough woman. Louis would not chew her easily.

She yelled, "Put me down!"

Julie was aggressive. She bit him so hard that blood was dripping down his chest, but still he wouldn't let her go. When they reached near the house, he untied her and let her go. Julie punched him in the face as he was letting her go. She threatened, "If you ever come near me, I'll cut off your head!"

She stormed inside the ranch house crying as she ran up the stairs to pack her things. Louis ran after her. He was right behind her. Everyone was wondering what was going on. Viviane and Maxine rushed to see what was going on between them. They saw Louis pleading before her doors, tears running down his face, his shirt was torn was if a wild animal tore it.

Hurriedly they walked down the hallway toward Louis.

Looking at Louis's shirt, Viviane said in horror, "You're bleeding!"

She opened his shirt to see where the blood was coming from. There were rows of teeth marks on his left shoulder. Maxine was shocked when she looked at Louis's face and saw he was also punched several times on the face. Stunned, Maxine handed Viviane her handkerchief to put on top of his wounds. She asked, "What happened?"

Julie opened the door, holding on to her bags. She shoved Louis out of her way and said to her mother and Maxine, "I'm leaving. My welcome here is overwhelmed."

Louis rushed behind her, still pleading as she made her way down. She gnashed, "You make me feel worthless!"

"No," Louis moaned pulling on his shirt as if he was being stabbed. "Please forgive me. I was a thoughtless man."

She went and put her bags out on the porch. When she walked back in the house, Louis was holding on to William, kissing him on his forehead. Furiously she walked toward him and pulled the toddler out of his arms and walked back out. Louis followed them, begging her not to go.

Viviane wanted to know what was going on. She stopped to talk to Louis because Julie refused to answer her. Julie was so mad, she told Viviane, "If you want to stay you can, but my son and I are leaving."

Never did Julie speak to her mother with that tone of voice. Looking at Louis, Viviane didn't say another word. She followed her daughter without saying a word. Maxine was trying to calm her down, she already knew what happened, but she responded to Maxine's question, "You're a romantic, Max, but if you ever mention that man's name again to me, you could kiss our friendship goodbye."

She was about to send Loziane to fetch a local bus to take them home when Henry arrived. Julie rushed out of the house with the toddler in her arms.

"Good! Henry, I need your car," she said, and held out her hand for the key. Looking at Louis, Henry reluctantly handed her the car key. She yelled at Henry, "Hurry up, I don't have all day!"

The tone of Julie's voice made Henry quickly hand her the key. Then she asked him for his address. Henry quickly wrote his address on a card he pulled out of his vest pocket and handed it to her. She snatched the card out of his hand and headed straight for the car. She told Loziane to sit in the back seat behind her and handed her the toddler, who was asleep. She placed her things in the trunk then went to the driver's side and made ready to drive off.

Maxine started to cry when she looked at Louis's bruised face and his bloody shoulder. She felt the effect was a great mental disturbance on Louis's mind. She was distressed. She didn't stay either. Richard stood at a distance looking at the event, watching Maxine following Julie. As she was leaving she gently took a hold of Louis's arms, pulling him back. She whispered, "No, Louis! Let her go. She needs to calm down and think, and you too."

On their way home everyone stayed silent. Viviane didn't question her about what took place. She was waiting till they got home so they could really talk and maybe she could make some sense to what had happened between Louis and her.

▭   ▭   ▭

Jacque and Carine were sitting in the library going over the documents Maxine went to pick from Constant.

As they were talking the butler came to announce to them that Julie and the others had returned. Jacque put away the documents and went to check on Julie to see what she was doing home when she was supposed to be at Louis's ranch for the weekend. Marie was already in the old house wiping the furniture when they arrived. She noticed Julie was not herself, because she didn't greet her and walked right to her room. She entered the room and asked, "Madame, I thought you were going to stay out for the weekend. You are home early."

Julie didn't answer. She placed Bill on her bed to change his underwear.

"Can I get you anything, madame?" Marie asked.

"No," she firmly replied. "I want to be alone with my baby."

Marie didn't say another word. She had a feeling that Julie found out she was the wife of Louis's best friend, and at the moment Julie couldn't cope

239

with it. Quietly she walked out of her room and closed the door behind her. She hoped everything worked out fine for them. She paused by her door to pray for them but especially for Louis. Then she continued on her way to assist Viviane, who was at the mansion.

Jacque had come to see Julie. He was knocking on her bedroom door. He asked, "Can I come in?"

Irritated she answered, "Not now, Jacque. Please go. At the moment I don't need to see you or talk to anyone!"

Jacque smiled when he heard the tone in Julie's voice. He was happy because he felt Louis had blown the last chance he might have had with Julie. He didn't say another word. Quietly he went back to the mansion and to the library to call Louis to know what went wrong between Julie and him. Louis was appalled that Jacque dared to question him. He advised Jacque next time he thought Julie and he had a disagreement, it would be best for him to keep his mouth shut and look the other way.

Viviane waited the following day to talk to Julie, hoping by then she would be able to explain what happen between Louis and her. Julie looked cold and confused. She looked at the tray of food on the table. Julie didn't even taste anything on the tray. Viviane came and stood by her while she was looking out of the window and asked, "Please, talk to me. We've been through so much together, don't lock me out. I'm here to help."

Looking at her mother, she chuckled. "Yes, we have been, but you haven't faced anything like mine."

Pulling a chair, Viviane said, "Help me face it with you."

Putting her hand over her mouth, Julie tried to hold back her tears. Viviane stood up to hug her daughter and asked, "What did Louis do to you that made you so upset?"

"To think I let that pig kiss me and I touched him," Julie exclaimed. "He claimed what he did was an act of love. That man has no idea what the meaning of love is. He's an animal, a savage beast."

Viviane didn't understand why she was talking like that. "What did he do to you?"

"There's no better way to say, Mom," Julie blunted. "He claimed William is his son, that Saul is not the father of William."

Viviane didn't answer. She looked at Julie and sat back on her chair. She took a good look at William, who was playing with his toys, as if she had never seen him before, and saw that William looked like a spitting image of Louis. The child even smiled like Louis. That was definitely a giveaway, not to mention the color of his eyes and hair. Looking back at Julie, Viviane was wondering about that, but she kept silent and just listened to what Julie had to say. Looking at the expression on her mother's face, Julie said, "Don't tell me you believe him."

Her mother's refusal to answer was starting to agitate Julie, so she responded, "For God's sake, Mother, you of all people should have known me better. I never slept with Louis."

"Then why did he claim William is his baby?"

Julie sighed and gasped, "Artificial insemination."

Viviane thought Julie was out of her mind. She knew Julie wanted a family, but she never thought she would have gone that far. Stupefied by Julie's revelation, she asked, "You did what?"

Pushing her hair away from her face Julie repeated, "Artificial insemination. I thought the seed was from my husband. I didn't know Saul would have done something like that to me."

"Are you sure you didn't know Louis?"

Shaking her head at her mother's interrogation, Julie couldn't believe what Viviane said. Fretfully she replied, "No! Saul knew him. They went to the same school and they were best friends. I never knew that. I know it's hard to swallow, but just imagine how hard it is for me."

"I didn't want to bring that up, sweetheart, but you're constantly dreaming of making love with Louis."

Julie closed her eyes, as her mother reminded her of her dream. It all hit her. That was the dream that had driven her husband away. She closed her eyes and let the tears flow. Viviane tried to calm her. She passed her hands over Julie's face and said, "Everything is going to be okay, but what are you planning to do?"

"At the moment, I'm mad," she let Viviane know. "I cannot think straight."

"You love him very much, don't you, Julie?"

"Right now, I'm too upset to love that man."

One thing Viviane knew was that she had to get to the bottom of this. Later in the evening, Julie finally came to the mansion. She apologized to Jacque for the way she had answered him. They went for a little walk, but she never told Jacque what really went down between Louis and her, and Maxine was not the one to tell him anything. The secret remained among them.

Julie had asked Jacque to put a fence around the land. She didn't want anyone, especially Louis, to walk in or ride on the land anymore. Jacque thought it was a good idea. He wanted to do that a long time ago, but he didn't do it because he knew she didn't like the idea of being closed in.

Jacque tried hard to gain Julie's trust and William's love. Every day he would come home with a little gift for William till one day William finally let him carry him. Julie felt that Jacque was very patient and he could be a loving man if he wanted to. She smiled when Jacque was able to hold William in his arms and gave him a kiss on his forehead.

Jacque would take William for strolls around the mansion and even helped Julie build a playground for William. They would play like two children who needed discipline. Julie would laugh when they play fought. And how hard William tried to hit him. She thought that Jacque was right, William would need a father, but still she didn't have that kind of feeling for him. The love she had was the love one would have for his or her own brother.

She was feeling depressed, which she hid well from everyone. Julie felt her pride and dignity had been stripped from her by two men she loved the most. It was almost two weeks since she had found out that she was the married woman Louis was telling her about. She remembered how she laughed at Louis's situation with Maxine, and all that time the laugh was on her. And every time she thought about it, it tore her apart. She looked at William with a smile. He smiled back at her. For a moment she thought she saw Louis looking back at her with his smile. Viviane was also very depressed for her daughter. She saw how Julie tried hard not to mention Louis's name and how she kept working hard till she couldn't move. That was the routine Julie had every day.

At the end of the third week, Viviane decided to go over to the Janvier estate to talk to Louis. He told her the whole story, how it happened, and why he did it.

Louis didn't look too good in Viviane's eyes. What they did was monstrous, but one thing she knew was Julie was in love with Louis, and she was hurt and angry to know that Louis had helped to deceive her and Saul didn't trust enough in her to level with her.

Viviane wanted to know what Louis would do next to straighten out the situation he was in with her daughter. He told Viviane he was working on it, but at the moment he wanted to see William. He didn't want to argue with her and make matters worse. So Viviane arranged to meet him by the river tomorrow at ten, while Julie was busy with her project. She would bring William to him. Louis was happy that Viviane would do that for him so he kissed Viviane on both of her cheeks to thank her. He saw her to the door and went to wait for tomorrow.

For over a month Viviane was taking William for a walk by the river to Louis. Sometimes it was in the morning and sometimes in the afternoon. She had a good excuse. She wanted to spend some quality time with her grandson while Julie was working on the yard and helping around the mansion. Never did Julie suspect that William was seeing his father every day. Then one day while Julie, Viviane, and the Bassine family were having an afternoon cook-out, Jacque was playing with William. He wanted William to call him daddy, not Jacque. William responded in his babbling words, "No, Jacque!"

Jacque was insisting to be called daddy, but William again repeated, "Jacque . . . Louis my daddy!"

Jacque wanted to know who told him such a lie. William shouted, "No, Louis, Daddy, by river!"

He thought the child was making this up. Since Julie returned from Louis's ranch, they had not seen each other. And if Louis had come to the house, his butler would have told him.

Julie didn't say anything. She pretended she didn't understand what William was babbling. Smilingly she handed him a mango.

The following day Julie went to her same routine, helping the maid around the house, working on the yard while her mother took William for a walk. She waved them goodbye and went about her way. After a few minutes, Julie was curious to know where her mother was taking her son every day. She went and changed her clothes and followed her mother to the river to see what her son was talking about. As she was getting closer she heard William's little laugh and him calling "Daddy." Carefully she walked toward them.

Viviane startled. "Julie, what are you doing here?"

Her eyes were filled with dismay. She told her mother, "I thought you were taking him for a walk. I can't even trust you either. So this is what you have been doing."

"Julie, I think you two need to talk."

"I have nothing to say to him, and we already said it all."

Louis protested, "No, we haven't."

"Yes, we did," she replied and lifted William up into her arms.

Viviane protested, "Stop that bickering. You two need to talk. You cannot do this in front of William. It is not healthy. You of all people should know that."

Julie didn't argue. She felt her mother was right. Taking William from Julie's arms, she walked way and said, "You two talk, please, for William's sake. Don't go home till you guys get the situation straightened out."

Julie couldn't believe what her mother just said. She thought the heat from the sun in Haiti was getting to Viviane's head. As they were leaving, William waved and called, "Bye, Mommy; bye, Daddy!"

Louis waved back at him with a smile. For a moment they didn't say a word. Bending his head down to look at Julie, Louis found her staring at him. She didn't look away as their eyes met. She looked angry. His heart boiled, knowing that he had displeased her. He thought, *She is as beautiful as ever.*

He whispered, "I'm sorry."

Julie didn't answer. She went and sat under her almond tree, meditating on what he said. Then she put her hand over her forehead to avoid the rays of the sun so she could see him better. She flashed back on the night she first arrived in Haiti. She heard his voice whispering in her ears, asking her to make a wish. When she wanted to know who he was, Marie told her he was bad news.

She said, "Are you? Or is it just a phrase you just learned to say?"

Putting a hand in his pants pocket he responded, "You're quite right. It's a phrase I just learned to say. I'm not accustomed to apologizing for anything.

Nor am I accustomed to explaining myself to anyone. Your husband had approached me, reproached me, begged me, and cried on my shoulders for my help. My shoulders I don't give just to anyone to cry on, Julie. I'm not sentimental either. He pleaded for my precious gift to hand to you. You felt raped, I felt robbed and despaired. I almost went out of my mind. The truth is, I'm not sorry at all. But it was not my intention to hurt you. For this I apologize. I'm sure you already know the truth, but you don't want to accept it. You wanted to believe that Saul Philip the Third wouldn't do something like that, when for years you tried to conceive his child. He was your husband as he was my best friend. You knew what kind of a man he was, and what he was capable of doing for your happiness."

Scornfully she replied, "Did you ever think about how would I feel?"

"I didn't know you, so how you would feel wasn't something I was thinking about. All that concerned me was to see Saul happy."

"You loved him dearly," Julie retorted. "You would have done anything to please him!"

"You could say that," Louis replied as he looked at her looking at him in disdain. "Like David loved Jonathan. David said he loved Jonathan more than a woman. I'm sure you're familiar with that story in the Bible."

"So I should just swallow it and be thankful for your precious gift," Julie answered. "That might have been a very nice speech should you have been talking to one of your bimbos."

"Wasn't that what you wanted out of life for a very long time, Julie, to have a baby?"

Julie couldn't believe what he said. She hissed, "You have no discernment between what is right or wrong do you? You're like an animal, living one day at a time."

"You're wrong!" Louis shouted. "I do know more than you could imagine! I'm not an animal, as you perceive to see me. Look at me for what I really am for a change. I love you! That's my crime! Not because I'm an animal, I was a man who wasn't thinking straight. Maybe you were not meant to be with Saul, I don't know, but one thing I do know is we're here. And my son is in the middle of this catastrophe. . . . For years you wanted a child, now you have him. . . !"

Julie placed her hands on her temple to control the rage that was about to run out of her as she wondered how he knew that. Louis paused to examine her reaction, then calmly said, " . . . You seem surprised that I know that. I was informed about you. There were times life didn't have any meaning to you, too. You took dangerous chances because you felt there was nothing to look forward to."

"I never felt like that!"

"But, my love, you did, by your actions. You lived your life as if you were a missionary, going to where the need is great. That was one of the reasons we never had a chance to meet in person. Saul watched how you worked with these needy children and how you dragged him along with you, constantly telling him how you would love to have a child of your own."

She sniveled. "Don't try to make me feel guilty for the act of sacrilege you've done to me!"

Julie was feeling hurt. She blamed him for everything. At that moment Louis realized that Julie loved him more than she thought. "I'm not trying to make you feel guilty. I just want you to remember how your attitude was. I think you should be grateful and thankful."

"How would you know what my attitude would have been?" she lashed. "Did you ever talk to me to know how I really feel? If those dreams didn't happen to me, you would have kept it a secret for him. Did you also have permission to pursue me from Saul?"

"I thought I told you that already," Louis replied looking away.

"You arrogant men," Julie exclaimed. She closed her fists, holding them tight against her chest because at the moment she felt like beating Louis's head in. She flared with anger. "Who do you guys think you are? Playing with my life the way you did, and thought nothing of it . . . you degraded me and make your plans. I have nothing to say. You raped me!"

"Rape," Louis repeated. "Now you're acting like William wasn't a gift at all, more like a rape. You didn't think twice, Julie my dear, when William was being given to you. You jumped right to it. Deep down, you didn't give a damn where Saul got it! You just wanted a baby that came from your womb. You knew there were no problems with you, so therefore it had to be Saul. You're not mad at me, but at yourself, because deep down you knew my son didn't belong to Saul. You knew! Now you're acting like you were victimized. I'm the real victim here! I have had a lot of headaches and pain in my life. Never have I faced anything like that. I want you to know I spent over two years with this nightmare. And this is one nightmare I will not live again. Do I make myself clear . . . do you understand that!"

Feeling contempt, she warned, "Are you threatening me, Louis, because if you are, you're trifling with the wrong woman."

Trying to make her understand, he calmly said, "I wouldn't dare threaten you, Julie, or play with you, and you know that. I just want to make it clear to you to keep that secret from you wasn't easy for me, and that I'm not about to give up on my son. . . !"

Looking at him Julie picked up a rock and threw it in the water to calm her anger. Noticing she really wanted to throw the rock at him Louis replied, " . . . That's the spirit, Julie. Don't just sit there and let me do all the talking. I have you to thank. You have encouraged me to seek for my gift and the hell with the woman."

"I thought the woman you've spoken of had accepted to sleep with you. That's the difference between me and the story you were telling me. I didn't know you were referring to me. You have a lot of nerve, Mr. Janvier, to think that I would have accepted to do something so profane. First, I wouldn't

245

accept to be impregnated by you or any other man while I was married to Saul. And second, you know I wouldn't give my son to you."

"What do you want me to do?" he said agitated. "Give me an option! Tell me–give up on you or our son?"

She didn't answer, so he came closer and sat by her feet to talk to her. "I'm not asking you to give him to me, but for us to be a family. We can share him like you said."

"How do you know he's your son?"

"Our son, I'm quite sure."

"No," she snarled. "I'm not convinced by your words. Saul isn't alive to tell me himself that he isn't the father of my baby. You think I'm going to accept your words and a couple of videotapes and a stupid school picture of you and Saul, his necklace with the locket of a picture of me and his baby, which you could have found on the streets of Haiti? If you believe I'm going to accept that I'm the woman you have been telling me about just like that, then you really are out of your stupid mind. You're not trustworthy. You're a liar, a deceiver. . . ."

Sardonically Louis replied, "Is that's all you can come up with? Please don't try to be kind, Julie my dear. Don't forget that I'm a killer! And when I want something I take it!"

Sneering at him Julie replied, "I don't get scared that easily, Mr. Janvier. You need to take a DNA test, you dumb S.O.B." (Senseless, Outrageous, Boy.)

Louis's left eye started to twitch from all the blows he was receiving from her. He got on his feet to look down at her and breathed, "I have no problem taking one. . . . If I didn't love you, Julie, I would wring your pretty little neck. . . . I didn't deceive you, your husband did. When the test is over and I prove that I am the father, I don't want any arguments from you, concerning our son. You get that, woman!"

Louis didn't wait for her response, again he found himself walking away, leaving her sitting by the river under her almond tree. He felt taunted by her.

He went home and got in shower to cool down because he was going crazy. He called his doctor for the test. Later in the evening, he let her know he had made an appointment for them. A day later they went to take the DNA test, then went home to wait for the results to come in two days.

Jacque was just getting home from work when Julie walked in. He smiled. "How are you doing?"

She yawned as she walked by with the sleeping toddler in her arms. "Tired!" then she asked, "Where's my mom?"

Jacque answered, "She is by the pool with Max and Nicole."

She made her way to the pool to say hello. Loziane came and took Bill from her. Carine was just getting home herself. She saw the back of Julie leaving. She greeted Jacque and asked, "How's the princess doing?"

Jacque replied, "Tired!"

Later that evening, Louis called Julie to see how she was doing. He wanted to see her, but there were too many people around, so she asked him to meet her out in the field by the river. By the time she got there, Louis was already there, waiting. He tried to help her off her horse, but she pushed his hands away. "Don't touch me!"

Louis moved back and watched how she jumped off her horse. Then they continued walking on foot in silence for little while. Losing her patience she asked, "What did you want to tell me that you couldn't tell me over the phone. . . ?"

Louis didn't answer. He stopped to look at her. " . . . Why did you come here?"

"The same reason you accepted to come." Louis smirked as he took a long inhaled and exhaled through his nostril.

Frowning she asked, "And what reason is that?"

"I wanted to see you as much as you wanted to see me. Don't tell me you came here just to hear what I have to say."

Shaking her head, she replied, "I thought you have the results of the DNA test."

"The results have not come yet."

"You have so many tricks under your sleeves," Julie said. "I didn't think that would have been any problem for a man like you to get the results."

"I see," Louis replied. "But my reason for coming here is because you wanted to see me as much as I wanted to see you."

"You're wrong." Nodding her head she informed, "I don't want to see you, Louis. I thought you did have something to tell me, some more degenerating news to tell or deject me some more."

Julie got back on her horse and made ready to ride back. She pulled on the rein. Louis held on to the guide of her horse. She tried to take control. "Let go of the guide before I kick your head in."

Louis closed his eyes for a moment to think when she kicked him on the face. Blood was coming out of his busted mouth, but he still wouldn't let the bridle of the horse go. He opened his eyes, to look up at her and said, "I wish there was another way, words that I could say or do, to change what happened between us. Except stop! Enough. I cannot change what happened, it's already done, and Saul got the worst end of it, he's dead. And we don't have that kind of power of bring him back. I don't want to waste anymore of our precious time arguing about our baby that we both want, stop torturing yourself and me. . . !"

She tried to pull the rope out of his hands. Moving closer to her, he whispered, " . . . I want to know . . . are you happy, Julie? Because I'm not! Is everything going well for you? Don't you miss me at all? I miss you so much!"

Again she repeated, "Let go of the rein, Louis."

He still wouldn't let it go. He took a firmer grip of the horse's throat latch while he spit out the excess blood that was inside his mouth. Wiping his mouth with his long-sleeved ivory shirt, he then pushed the same hand into his pocket. He fished out some chewing gum. Peeling off the papers with his front teeth, he removed the gum, then shoved it inside his mouth, and chewed.

Julie stared at him as he did all that and thought that man was really mad. She tried to back away with her horse. She yelled, "Move back, you crazy man!"

He didn't answer. With one spectacular move, Louis pulled her down off her horse and took her into his arms and kissed her. She pushed him away and slapped him. Louis stood there letting her unload the brief spell of raving fury she kept bottled up inside. He knew the slaps were well deserved. He allowed her to slap him four times, but on the fifth, he held her hand and pulled her back in his arms, holding her tighter, and kissed her again.

A tender feeling, which she was trying hard to conceal, starting to stir up in her. She tried to pull away from his embrace. Slowly, he was calming her down as he consumed her rage with his lips and his words. Taking the hands that were hitting him he kissed them as he was telling her how much he wanted her and needed her. He wanted so much for her to love the way he did. "Please, Julie, forgive me. . . ."

She closed her eyes as he continued caressing her with his words. "I'm lost without you, Julie."

She felt like a butterfly as he gently passed his hands on her face. She was yielding to his touch. Gently, he took her arms and put them around his neck, kissing her, and drew her closer to him.

She responded by touching his bruised face and lips. The feel of her fingers touching and running through his hair, caressing his face, were arousing joy in his heart. After a few minutes of passionately kissing, he nibbled on her ears as he continued kissing under her neck and her lips. Calmly, he spoke to her.

"I love you . . . I'm crazy about you." Quietly he cried, hoping that he had captured her heart once more. He whispered, "Please, Julie, don't make me suffer anymore. I belong to you. You're in my heart. I love you, Julie. Keep that in mind."

Louis kissed her once more, then he moved back away from her. He didn't want to cry anymore before her. He got on his horse and rode away, leaving Julie standing there breathlessly with her mouth wide opened. Julie couldn't help but cry. She, too, was feeling crazy. She knew in her heart, like he said, they belonged together. Taking some deep breaths, she leaned her head on her horse, crying about her situation. She knew she didn't just want him as a friend, but much more than a lover. She got on her horse and she, too, cantered away.

Jacque was coming across the field when they almost had a head-on collision with their horses. She laughed at the way they bumped into each other. Looking at her eyes, he thought, *Was she crying?*

He looked further up in the mountain and saw Louis sitting on his horse, standing on top of the hill looking at them. Jacque thought, *Definitely the fence must get put up.*

Jacque didn't say anything. He asked her to ride with him. She didn't refuse him. Looking at Jacque as they rode on the field, she remembered that Jacque, too, was a cruel man. They rode beside each other without saying a word, letting the moon and the stars and the sound of the crickets and the frogs do the talking for them.

Without looking at him, she said, "I need a vacation. Since my mother and I returned to Haiti, we have not gone to Jacmel or Grand-Goâve to see anyone."

When Julie mention Jacmel, it hit Jacque. Julie needed to sign the papers he got from Constant. He thought, with Louis in the picture, it was going to be very difficult for him to convince Julie that everything he did or said was in her best interest.

He reminded Julie about the property on Delmas, telling her that land was wasted land, she couldn't do anything with it. But she let him know that land was to build a family center and the area was perfect for that because there was a lot of people living there. Jacque wasn't pleased when she informed him that she had asked Richard Landers to take charge of that project and he was glad to accept her offer.

"Richard Landers," Jacque clamored, "but that's Marie's son, your servant!"

Julie smiled. "And he's a good doctor, perfect for the job."

Jacque didn't say anything for a while, and neither did Julie. He thought Julie was being spiteful. He was hoping she would have given him the land to build another hotel or a couple of houses for him to rent. He wondered, how much fluid cash did Julie have?

He exclaimed, "What part do I play in that project that you have offered to Richard Landers?"

Julie replied, "It's all up to Richard. He's the one in charge. If you want to be the engineer for the job you have to ask him."

He looked at Julie as if she was out of her mind. Julie ignored the look and pretended she was enjoying the ride. She thought about the land she had asked him to search for her, and it had been over a year since Jacque told her that he was looking for the land. And still he had not told her anything. She asked, "Have you found the land that I wanted for my animals?"

"I did," Jacque answered, "but because you're not a citizen, the government wouldn't allow you to purchase all that land. You're not a Haitian born. You need to marry a Haitian born. That would be the only way you would be able to possess all that land you wanted."

She was surprised. She never heard of that. Her parents were Haitians and she was married to a Haitian, but she didn't want to dispute that with Jacque. She let him know maybe the president would be able to help her. Jacque felt that was not wise of her. If anything were to happen, she might lose her land. It was best to leave him out of it. She didn't protest.

She concluded, "Do what you think is best for me. I'm sure you'll find something for me. I'm getting restless. I'm not accustomed to depending on anyone."

Jacque replied, "I'm not just anyone, Julie. I'm the man who loves you and wants the best for you and your son. So don't worry, everything will be taken care of, but I need your signature on the documents before we could do anything. And if you married me, you will not have any problem of buying land in Haiti. Please think about it. It doesn't have to be a real marriage, just for business."

"Marriage is a serious thing, Jacque. One should never play with that arrangement, and I take marriage very seriously."

Jacque quickly replied, "I want it to be serious, but you don't love me like that, and you need the land. I'm willing to sacrifice my life for your happiness."

Nodding to his noble gesture, Julie smiled. "I heard that before, and it caused me a broken heart and a husband."

"Think about it, Julie," Jacque suggested. "That's the only way, the best way. Don't dismiss my proposal."

Julie didn't reply. She looked up in the mountain and saw Louis was still on the land looking down at them from where she had once seen the two men looking down at her. Nodding her head, she realized the two men were Louis and Saul, who were looking at her that late afternoon.

Jacque also looked at the direction she was focusing on and voiced, "Louis is trespassing. It will be good when I have the fence put on. That would keep him out of our land."

"I was being irrational when I told you that," Julie replied. "I like riding on his land, too. He has the best view of these lands. I've changed my mind. I don't want the fence put on anymore."

Jacque didn't know what to make of her. "I thought that's what you wanted before. Why the sudden change?"

She didn't reply. Angered by her silence he snarled, "Julie, don't let Louis play with your mind. If Saul were alive he wouldn't want you to associate with a man like Louis. You know he wouldn't approve of him being your friend."

His hypocritical assent sickened her. "You always seem to know what Saul would have approved of when it serves your purpose."

She rode off, leaving him behind, and headed for the barn.

The day after, Julie and Louis met over at his estate for the results of the DNA test. Viviane was present with William. Louis was in good cheer; he knew he was the father of William. He had no doubt in his mind. He glanced at Julie as the doctor read the results. Louis got out of his chair and asked to hold William, who was being youthfully zealous, wanting to play.

Finishing listening to the result, he asked them to stay for a while, but Julie didn't want to. She looked disappointed and unhappy. She watched them as he played with William. He watched how her mouth trembled as if she wanted to say something, but she was holding back. . . .

Her appearance displeased him. Louis thought, *She thinks I'm swindling her, I'm a liar, a deceiver, not trustworthy, that is what I am to her.* He felt offended by the way she looked at him. A feeling of indignation grew inside of him as he lifted William in his arms to kiss him. Sharply speaking, Louis suggested, "If you still have doubts, we could always go to America for a second opinion."

Looking at her mother, Julie replied, "Maybe we should."

Without hesitation, Louis picked up the phone and dialed, then asked the person who answered the other end if there were four seats in first class section going to New York leaving today. The man told him there were. So he booked them for that night. The plane would leave at six-thirty. Then he called his butler in the United States to pick them up at the Kennedy airport. Julie, too, phoned the Bassine mansion and asked Marie to prepare a bag for traveling for her son.

Viviane felt that was foolish on both of their parts, but what could she say. She was just a grandmother. She felt she was being dragged, but her daughter wanted to make sure Louis was not lying to her.

By the time Maxine and Jacque came home, they were already heading for New York. She left a note for Maxine with Marie to inform her. Two weeks later Julie got the same result from her own two doctors. She could no longer deny Louis, who wanted to be part of his child's life. They had to work for the best of William's interest, but still she couldn't believe what had really happened to her.

After the DNA test fiasco, Julie went up to Spring Valley, New York, to her home, where Saul and she had been living. She walked all through the house with William, looking around the house as she had not been there for a while. She removed all the white sheets she had covered the furniture with and placed them in a plastic bag so she could wash them. She did the wiping and the vacuuming all around the house. William got her to give a little smile as he held the dustpan for her. After she finished cleaning, she lifted him up into her arms to hug him, then she kissed him and thanked him for his help. She looked around once more to see if she had missed anything, but everything was sparkling clean. After she finished giving William his bath and got him ready for bed, Julie then put him to sleep. She stared at him in her arms for awhile, looking at his little face, which was a portrait of Louis. While holding onto her son, she started crying because she was hoping he was Saul's baby.

Julie gave him a kiss as she placed him on his bed, then she went to her room to take a shower, getting herself ready for bed. While lying down, she was turning and tossing, unable to sleep. So she got out of bed to do some summer cleaning around the room she had shared with Saul. She decided to empty Saul's closets to give his clothes to charity. While she was cleaning the closet in her bedroom, she came across one of Saul's personal small square metal box. She opened it and found pictures of Louis and Saul at a new year party and letters that Louis wrote him and inside, a brown package that was addressed to her. Inside the package was a videotape with the title, "Play Me."

"Saul," she whispered, nodding her head, and placed the tape on the floor by her. Then she took the letter that had the earlier mailing date on it. She opened it and read the last adventure Saul and Louis shared.

Hello, brother,

Congratulations! You finally meet your perfect match. I'm so happy to hear she's the perfect woman you've been waiting for. I must say I was glad we had that moment together, because your banquet days are over!

Mother was wondering where we had disappeared to. You're going to laugh when you read the answer, so get yourself ready:

Disney World!

She said she wanted to go, but she never had a chance to. Don't laugh because I promised her I would personally take her in the spring. And we'll drop by to see your wife-to-be. When I told Mother you're getting married, she jumped for joy and hopes I'll do the same, too.

Me!

I haven't taken Rome out of my systems, and those Brazilian women. . . . I wouldn't dare to ask you to go with me on that adventure because you're no longer searching. So the banquet is all mine now. And the truth is, I'm starving. I need a good woman who could fill my hunger and thirst. I need to slow down.

Mother wants grandchildren to play with. But you and I both know, none of the women I met, and you've seen most of them, have the credentials to have my children or even to be my wife. So I'm counting on you to fill our home with children and maybe like that Mother would get off my back.

Nadine was a little disappointed. She was hoping you would propose to her. I told her she's the little sister you never had.

Oh, guess what?

Brian and Patrick want to work for me. They want to help me run things here in Haiti. I told them I demand their complete trust and loyalty, otherwise working together wouldn't work out. They swore their lives to me. So far they prove to be sincere. Mother was happy that I took them in. I was happy to see her smile. I know you would've been happy to see that smile on her face.

She misses you, too. I told her at the moment you're on a very important mission and hopefully Julie Bertrand accepts your hand in marriage.

When I read the name to Mother, she told me that was the girl she wanted me to meet. I shouted, "Whoopee! I'm glad I never met her, because look at my brother. He is head over heels about her. Better him than me!"

So, my dear brother Saul, may this woman Julie bring you all the joy, happiness, and above them all love!

Agape,
Louis Janvier

She opened another letter to read.

Hello, Saul,

Congratulations with your newborn son. I hope this child brings both you and wife Julie great joy and happiness. You will not see me this year. At the moment I need to work out something with myself, and I don't know how long it will take for me to solve. It's nothing for you to concern yourself about, brother, it's just that I need to get myself together on searching for a wife, too, so we could really enjoy each other's company. I don't want to feel left out. So far I haven't had the luck of finding a capable woman. And you know I can be crazy and I'm too much of a skeptic and I don't really have the time, so definitely this is something I need to work on.

Like you, I need a family, a loving wife, and a very, I mean VERY, understanding woman.

I thank you for the tapes you're sending me. I wish I could have been there when William was born. What a miracle he is.

I'm glad to know that you decided to settle here in Haiti. It will be good for your son William.

I'm looking forward to seeing you, neighbor.

Agape,
Louis Janvier

She read the last letter from Louis.

Hello, Saul,

It's been over two months since the last time we heard from each other. I'm working on your projects. I have a lot of men working on the lands, getting the place ready for you. I hope I could be more at your service.

I'm looking forward to seeing you again, brother. And I'm hoping the difficulty you're facing in your marriage at the moment will be solved by then. You must keep in mind that it's part of life. I'm sure it's just a phase she's going through, like we all go through sometimes. Julie loves you, even though I never had a chance to meet her. She will definitely overcome the trauma.

253

Remember she just had a baby. It's women's tendency to become overprotective of their babies. Her body just went through a great trauma.

I'm a doctor, I should know about things like that. Your lives will return the way they were before. Now that you two have your son, I'm sure things are going to turn out for the better. Have hope, brother, don't give up like some of us do. Your life has meaning now, and a future that is shining ahead, waiting for you. Please go forward for me. I need to know that you're going to try everything in your power to make things work out for you. And be happy!

I love you, brother. You know I'll do anything to see you happy. You're the reason why I'm still alive. And if I have done anything to displease you, it wasn't my intention to do so. I humbly ask you for your forgiveness. Please forgive me.

Your friend always,
Louis Janvier

After finishing reading the letter, Julie picked up the small metal box and went to her study to continue reading the letters. She fixed herself a tall alcoholic beverage. She placed the tape inside the VCR, then sat back to watch the videotape. She smiled when she saw Saul's face and her son. She thought, *That must have been the day he spent the time with William when he returned from Haiti.*

She paused the tape to admire his features. Saul was tall, very good looking, and well built, with a royal attitude. Sadly she pressed the remote control, watching how he smiled as he held William in the crook of his arms to kiss. Gently he held his little hand up, making William waved to Mommy, then took Julie's picture from the dresser table and kissed it too. He looked at it for a few minutes with tears running down his face. He pulled out a tissue from its box to wipe his eyes. He placed the picture back on the dresser, then sat back with the baby in the crook of his arms and looked as if he was talking to her.

Saul said, "Hello, my love. You're crying . . . I'm sorry, you have all the reasons to. I wasn't thinking when I committed such a deceptive act toward you. You may wonder what did you do for my crime against you? Please don't think too hard, you didn't do anything wrong. You are the purest person I've met. When I met with you, I knew one of your dreams was to have a nice-sized family. It was also mine, too. But when I found out that it was my fault that you were unable to conceive, I couldn't bear to tell you the truth, feeling that I would have taken that dream away from you. Thoughtlessly, I thought I could have gotten away with this without you knowing.

"I hurt the two most important people in my life and robbed our son of his real father. I'm a traitor to all three of you, and I'm a coward! I was afraid to face the truth and ended up making matters worse. Louis may never forgive me. He maybe wishing he was dead. You may hate me, wishing you never met me. I don't blame you at all. Believe me when I tell you this. With every fiber in me I love you more than life. I didn't mean to hurt you. Please forgive me. . . ."

As she was watching the videotape, Louis was standing by the door looking at her crying. Slowly she raised her head to look at him, wondering how he came in.

"I'm sorry," he said. "I didn't mean to startle you, but when you didn't answer your doorbell I got worried so I picked your lock to come in."

Julie laughed with tears in her eyes. "I knew there was something that I forget to do."

"What was that?"

"Turn on the alarm," she said sadly. He walked toward her and knelt before her and pulled her into his arms. Feeling that what she watching was making her sad, he turned off the video.

Julie said, "No, I want to hear what he had to say."

Louis, too, fixed himself a drink, then sat by her watching the tape. He was surprised that Saul had left a testimony of what they did. They both sat quietly listing to Saul's last words. There was no better proof than what Julie was watching and listening to. Tears ran down her face as she listened to Saul.

Saul continued explaining the wrong he did and the only way he could make it right was by stepping aside and giving her the true happiness she deserved. "I gave away all my rights to him when I did that. Without knowing, you knew something was not right. Subconsciously, you dreamt of him. You loved him and you didn't even know him, but in reality you did. I've put him in the most sacred place in you, your womb. Somehow you know him and he knows you. You belong to that man now. You're no longer mine. I have destroyed my right of being your husband.

"When you see this tape you'll realize I will never return in your life to cause you two trouble. . . . Louis loves you more than life. I know he does because he couldn't deny the love he had for you when he knew I would have killed him for you. He was willing to die. I hated him for that, but it wasn't his fault. Louis felt obligated to me. I think I'm mad. No, I am mad! And my excuse is lame. Tell Louis that I'm sorry, and I don't hate him for falling in love with you and for wanting you. Tell him I love him, he's still my brother. He was my only true friend and I used him to deceive you. I love you Julie, and do kiss William for me. And tell your mother that I love her, too. I know this is not a proper goodbye, but it's better this way. Goodbye, my love."

The tape was over.

"I made my husband afraid of telling me the truth."

"No," Louis comforted, "he chose to seal the truth from you. And I helped him. I, too, was a coward. I didn't help him face the truth. I was afraid to hurt his feelings."

Nodding her head while she regarded Louis, she said, "I never want that to happen again."

That night Louis spent the night over in the guest room, meditating what he was to do here next for Julie. The next day he helped her around the house. He even helped wash the dishes, wiped, and put them away. Then he gave William a bath. Julie watched him as he did so. There were a few things that needed to fix around the house. Louis wanted to show Julie he wasn't just a pretty face so he told her, "No need to get a carpenter to fix the back door, I'll do it myself."

Julie wondered if Louis would be able to remove the door and replace it with the new one. It was not like putting a couple of dishes on a dishwasher, and yet he broke a couple of plates and glasses. She didn't say anything, but she thought, *If he makes a mess, all I have to do is to call my carpenter to do it right.*

She was surprised to see that Louis was great with his tools. He even knew the name of each piece he used. She was impressed to see that he was able to replace the door without any problem. "When did you learn to do that kind a work?"

"I always liked to do different things when I was a child," Louis confessed. "I just couldn't make up my mind. And no one took me seriously when I told them I was a handy man."

Julie laughed while he put up the door. She was happy to help because she, too, liked that kind of work. Louis told her about the work he did around his ranch and the remodeling of his bedroom. Together they worked and fixed the things that were needed to do around the house. That had helped Julie with her depression.

Louis was a great help to her. He was able to get a real smile out of her and teased her like he used to. He practiced with her and took Bill for his morning walk. Some of her neighbors had mistaken Louis for Saul when they saw Louis with the toddler. They thought they were seeing a ghost. Some watched him reconstruct her back fence from afar, wondering who he was.

Julie stood at a distance and watched him at work. It was hot a day, so Louis removed his shirt to wipe his face, then placed it on the toolboxes next to him. He was concentrating in his work, so he didn't realize he was causing that kind of affect on her. She was enjoying the sight, admiring Louis's well-cut body. How he raised his long leg on top of the board he was cutting. She inhaled and exhaled when she felt under her belly button jump. She held on to her stomach and thought, *Marie was right, Louis is gorgeous.*

She started to think about the sex dreams she kept on having about Louis, and the thoughts aroused her. But Louis had also caused an audience with her neighbors. One of Julie's next-door neighbors boldly crossed her fence to bring Louis a cold glass of soda. She was watching how the sweat was running down his back, the movement of his upper body, and how the sun was glimmering on his hair. To get his attention she cleared her throat. She handed the tall icy drink that was sitting on a silver tray to Louis.

Louis smiled and thanked her as he took the glass from her tray. He didn't taste it. He placed the glass on his toolbox while wondering what was she here for. The woman made no effort to hide her lustiness. He put back on his shirt while she spoke to him. She made an attempt to help him button up his shirt. He took a step back away from her. Biting her thumb, she looked upon his masculine chest, shoulders, and arms. She invited him for an evening snack at her place. He smiled as he turned her down and told her he was engaged to Julie.

Julie was upset when she saw how the woman was flirting with him. Feeling he was being watched, Louis looked at the direction of the house and saw Julie standing by the door, looking at them. He took a long fixation on her as the woman spoke to him. He answered as if he was talking to an unseen person, wondering what was on Julie's mind.

Julie wasn't smiling. She stared back at him, then she went inside to make him lemonade and a sandwich to eat. She brought the tray of food out to him then fixed a blanket for them to sit on. They sat together to eat and to enjoy the ice cold lemonade she made. William was inside taking a nap. Julie didn't ask him what the woman wanted from him. He sat by her feet while he ate and drank what she brought him. She took a look at the woman's glass and saw that Louis never took a drink from it. Julie smiled as she took the glass away from the toolbox. She went in with it to pour the drink in the sink and washed it then she brought it back to her next door neighbor. She also thanked her neighbor for her thoughtfulness and handed her the glass. But Julie knew what she was really out there in her yard for. Julie saw what Maxine was telling her, the women came to him. More than twenty females driving by stopped to flirt with him, young and old. Even a couple of men made passes at him. Julie thought, *I might have to get a shotgun.*

In less then two days, Louis was done with the reconstruction of her fence. Julie commented, "You would have finished faster if you didn't have all those flies bothering you."

He smiled because he knew what she was referring to. They were able to accomplish a great deal of work. She was realizing that they made a pretty good team, and the time was well spent. One night during that week, Julie had her dream again. Louis was still spending the night at her place. He was a light sleeper. He became awakened by her calling out his name. Thinking she was in trouble, he hurried to go to her aid.

Slowing opening her door, he quietly walked in and stood before her bed, watching her moving and calling out his name. The sound of her voice raised the urge in him as he was listening to her. Calming himself, he bit on his hand to gain control of his nerves. He made an attempt to shake her to wake her up, but he didn't. He let her go through her fantasy while he was wishing he was in her mind to see what exactly he was doing to her. He sat on a chair that was by her bed, listening to every moan and groan she was taking from him in her dream. He was getting more aroused. How he wished it was reality. At that moment he wanted her so bad. He wished he had not heard her cry. His need for her was driving him crazy.

Again Louis made an attempt to wake her, to give her what she was craving, but he was afraid she might get embarrassed. Softly he breathed to let out some of the tension he was having. He was rescued by William's cry, calling out for his mommy.

Louis moved so fast out of her room. One of the reasons was that she had not invited him in yet. And in less than six seconds Julie was awake when she heard William's cry. She hurried up out of the bed and rushed to him and didn't put on her robe. She found Louis in William's room, holding him in the crook of his arms. He smiled when he saw her entering the room. He tried hard not to look at her body through the revealing nightgown.

Concerned about her son, Julie forgot that her gown had revealed her body and walked toward Louis, who was holding on to William. He swallowed hard as he controlled his hunger for her. William was sound asleep. She thanked Louis for putting him back to sleep. He corrected her statement, "That is my duty, too."

Gently he laid William back in his bed. She looked at him for a little while, then turned with Louis and walked out of the room. In the hallway she asked, "How come you're not in bed sleeping?"

Putting his hands on top of his head, he ran his fingers through his hair and exhaled, then whispered, "You kept me awake."

She apologized. "I'm sorry. I thought I was free from that dream."

He pressed his hand against her cheek. "How could you be free from it when we haven't brought it to reality?"

She thought about her dream, when Louis pulled her into his arms and kissed her. The feel of his touch holding her in his strong arms, but that was not the way she wanted to make love with Louis. How happy she was when she woke up, opened her eyes, and saw she was just dreaming. The reality was yet to come.

Gently she pulled away and headed back for her room, leaving Louis standing in the hallway looking at her going into her room. She didn't look back. She was happy to see that Louis didn't make a fuss of wanting to hold her, because she felt she would have let him. She closed her door and leaned against it to catch her breath. When she looked at herself in the dressing mirror, she realized her body was showing through the nightgown she was wearing, and she wasn't wearing any underwear. Her breasts, nipples, navel, and vagina, which she shaved—everything was exposed to Louis. She covered her face, feeling embarrassed. She breathed, "My word, what is wrong with me?"

She lay back on her bed. She prayed to be free of the dream she was having about Louis.

The succeeding day, Viviane came to get William. She kept him with her for the next three weeks. She felt they needed the time together, to date and learn about each other. They really needed to know about the things they were not going to put up with from each other.

Louis had already known one of the bad habits Julie wasn't going to put up with. But to get her on her nerves, he acted like he didn't know. That night after dinner Julie asked him if she was the only woman in his life. He felt Julie should know that she was the only woman in his life. She didn't need to ask him that question.

Louis laughed. "I didn't know I have to give up any of my women to be with you. I thought you were going to accept me just the way I am."

That made Julie very upset. She knew Louis didn't have any other women, only her. But she still wanted to hear she was the only one. Instead he dished that answer to her. Wrong answer, she thought. Without any further words, she pointed her finger to the door and said, "Get out!"

Stretching himself to get more comfortable on the sofa, with an intimidating look on his face, Louis frowned. "I have my shoes and extra changing clothes in here . . . I'm not going anywhere!"

Julie replied, "Then I'll make you."

Without any hesitation Julie punched him right on the jaw and told him if he didn't leave she would burn him with the blowtorch that she used to flambé the dessert they just ate and which she was holding in her hand.

Holding on to his jaw, Louis exclaimed, "You almost broke my jaw."

"That wouldn't be the only thing that would break if you don't leave."

He started to laugh. He couldn't believe Julie had taken him so seriously. Julie didn't see anything funny. He said, "Julie, can't you tell when I'm joking?"

"When it comes to things like that," Julie stood firm, "I don't joke. I'll kill you!"

"I see," Louis said taking the blowtorch out of her hands by surprise and kissing her. "You're a short woman with very short temper. . . ."

He pulled her down on the sofa. He held her down as he tickled her, because he didn't think it was proper for a man to hit a woman back on the jaw.

Rubbing his jaw on her face he said as she screamed out his name, " . . . I'm learning about you the hard way."

Two days later they went back to the city. While they were in New York, Louis handed Julie all the documents Saul had entrusted him with. Again she was surprised to see that Louis did just as Saul had asked him to. Julie told him he could have kept them, she wouldn't know. He let her know his conscious wouldn't permit him to do something like that, especially to the woman he loved. He had his own money. He didn't need hers. Later that day Julie cooked for him. During dinner Louis told her he couldn't stand lateness with anyone. He felt if he had an appointment with someone, this person shouldn't keep him waiting, and Julie needed to know and understand that. He wanted to know if Julie had understood what the value of being on time meant to him, so he invited her to one of the conferences he was giving and emphasized to her to be on time.

Of course Julie was late, not deliberately, but due to traffic. So when she arrived the meeting had already started. Louis had given his secretary a direct order not to let anyone in, and when Julie arrived for her to inform him. She did precisely what her boss told her to do . . . she called him to let him know Julie was waiting for him.

"Ms. Bertrand is in the reception room waiting for you, sir."

Louis replied, "Tell her to wait, and don't call back to disturb me again."

Julie heard him in the receiver. She looked at her watch and she was ten minutes late. She told the lady she was leaving, but she insisted on Julie to stay and to wait for Louis, because her boss wouldn't be pleased if she didn't wait for him. Julie thought that woman and her boss were both insane if they thought she would have stayed after what she heard him say. Julie perched her shades on her nose and walked out of the reception office, ignoring the lady's plea to her.

Julie took a taxi to midtown to have a good lunch at one of her favorite restaurants her friend owned. She dropped by to see how he was doing. He was happy to see her again, because he hadn't seen her since the death of her husband.

While she was at the restaurant her phone rang. Louis was on the line. He wanted to know where she was. She told him. Fifteen minutes later, Louis was at the place she mentioned. His eyes looked furious when he walked in and saw it was a man making her laugh and that he kissed her hand as he left her at the bar. Louis didn't wait for the waiter to direct him to where she was sitting. He walked right in and stood before her, looking down at her while she tasted her drink.

Looking up she said, "Louis, you got here real fast."

"Not fast enough," he replied with an attitude, as he looked at the tall, dark, and handsome man who had just kissed her hands and made her laugh. A few minutes later, her friend returned with a menu under his arm and a bowl of seafood salad for Julie. He placed the plate on the counter then handed Julie the menu and said, "Here, darling, I hope you'll enjoy it. I prepared this especially for you, my dear."

Taking the menu from his hand Julie introduced him to Louis. After the introduction, Louis requested to speak to her in private. Julie didn't feel like talking at the moment because she was hungry and plus, she had come by to see an old friend.

"Relax, Louis, " she said and tasted the dish before her. She closed her eyes as she chewed with great pleasure and said, "Mm! This is delicious."

She took another and stretched her arm before Louis's mouth and asked him to taste. He said, "No!"

Julie didn't insist. She pretended she didn't see he had an attitude. Making herself more comfortable, she ordered another drink. She told Louis to sit on the empty high chair that was next to him to wait till she finished enjoying her meal and talking to her friend, or he could leave and she would see him later. Turning to her friend she said, "I like what you did with the place. And you definitely have to give me the recipe to this seafood platter, it is excellent!"

Boy, was Louis mad. Julie could tell by the way his nose flared when she hastily looked at him in the mirror that was on the wall behind the bar. She pretended she didn't notice his behavior. She continued enjoying her meal, and each bite she took, she held on her chest like the food was making love to her.

Louis thought, *How did I get myself into this situation. She got the better end of me again. She was the one who was supposed to be sitting waiting for me in the lobby of my office, not the other way around.*

He realized he had to get adjusted to her attitude. He sat back as he ordered a drink while he waited for her. He thanked the bartender who served him the drink. Julie continued to talk like he wasn't there. Carefully she peeped at him in the mirror again. She noticed he was impatient, but he was trying to make the best of the situation he was in by playing with the peanuts that the bartender placed before him.

A woman who was sitting alone at the other end of the bar who had noticed him since he had walked in the restaurant came closer to offer him a drink. "Hello. You seem lonely here. Can I buy you a drink?"

Julie turned with a smirk while petting Louis to let the woman know she was moving in on her territory. She answered for Louis, "He'll accept only if you're buying his woman a drink, too."

Her friend laughed at her response and nodded at the woman's boldness.

Still the woman wouldn't move. She responded, "I'm sure he could talk for himself!"

Looking at Julie with a straight face, Louis didn't even shake his head to say no to the woman.

"You're a big wimp," the woman said looking at the back of Louis's head and did not bother to look to her. She didn't say another word. She felt embarrassed. She picked up her purse and left the restaurant. Julie resumed her former position, continuing talking to her friend.

Louis thought, *Julie is something else.* He hoped she didn't put a dog leash around his neck with a tag that read, PRIVATE PROPERTY, NO TRESPASSERS.

He pretended he was having a good time by himself. She felt she made him wait enough. Then she told her friend she would drop by another time when it was more convenient. He kissed Julie on her cheeks and shook

Louis's hand, as they said goodbye. Louis didn't say a word, nor did he say a word when he got inside the limousine.

Louis told his driver take him to his condominium in Manhattan on Park Avenue. That was the first time Julie was going there. After entering his luxurious condo, he asked her to make herself comfortable. When she sat down, he pointed his finger at her and flared, "Don't you ever walk out on me again! When I tell you to wait you better wait, because next time I would have you walk back by yourself to me! And that 'darling' and 'dear' that man was calling you, I don't like it! I'm the one who is supposed to call you darling and dear, not him, got that!"

Listening to the tone of his voice, Julie crossed her legs and gently replied, "You're an insolent man, Louis Janvier. I'm a woman . . . no man keeps me waiting without a good reason and that goes for you especially."

Louis disputed, "When I told you to wait I meant it! Don't you ever have me running after you like that again!"

"You need a dog," Julie yawned and stretched, "not a woman, and I'm not about to play sit and fetch with you. You got that? . . . Do you care to know what had happened to me and why I was late?" He didn't answer. "I was stuck in traffic, that's the reason I was late. I don't like to wait for anyone, so I wouldn't deliberately keep you waiting without having a good reason. Understand, Mr. Janvier, because next time you pull a stunt like that on me again, running around town would not be all you'll be doing."

Louis couldn't believe her response and how calm she was when replying to him. Not once did she raise her voice or make any faces while correcting him. She had put him to shame for his bad attitude. True, he should have shown concern about why she was late. Something bad could have happened to her. By being upset, he showed a lack of love and respect on his part. He apologized, but he pretended he was not okay with her going to the restaurant and that man kissing her hands. He fussed as he dropped himself on the seat that was facing her to stare at her as he loosened his tie.

She didn't blink away. She said, "Is it okay with you if I stretch my legs?"

He got out of his seat to lift her legs and laid them on his lap. He was continuously regarding her as he removed her shoes then massaged her feet. She reminded him he was a rude man for staring at her like that. He should make himself more useful by getting up and fixing her a martini. He did just that as she instructed him how she wanted it to be. After mixing the drink he poured it in the martini glass and handed it to her on a tray.

"Anything else, your majesty."

"Kiss me," she requested. Holding him by his tie, she pulled him down and kissed him to her satisfaction, then she pushed him away and said, "That would be all at the moment."

She tasted her drink while she fixed her eyes on him and ran her tongue around her lips. Then she stretched herself on the sofa to relax. Louis was spellbound by her ways, but he was trying not to show it. He sat on the other chair, fixing her with his gaze to see how long it would take her before she blinked away. She fell asleep while they were staring at each other.

Later that evening he took her up to Connecticut to his mansion where he stayed when he was in town. By the time they arrived Julie was asleep. He carried her to where she was going to sleep and laid her on the bed. Julie didn't wake up till the following morning bright and early. She realized she was still dressed and Louis didn't remove her clothes. She smiled as she took off her clothes. After taking her shower, she noticed the boots and the socks she had left by the river were standing before an armchair and a set of riding clothes was laid out on the chair for her to wear. There was a note on the seat of the chair. She read, "I'm waiting for you in the hallway."

She hurried up and got dressed to meet with Louis, who was already waiting for her in the hallway. He smiled when she stepped out of the bedroom. She smiled back and said, "Good morning."

He replied the same as he took her hands and walked down with her. They had a very light breakfast. After that he took her to the barn. After a good tour around the place he stopped with her by the pond to look at the swans and the ducks in the water. They saw a couple of deer on his land. She got off her horse to look at them, as they were running away from them. The area was nice to look at and to enjoy a good picnic she thought.

While they were walking, Julie removed her boots and socks to walk on the grass. She stepped on a thorn. She lifted up her foot from the ground and moaned, "Uh!"

Louis asked, "What's wrong?"

"My foot."

Louis bent down to look. There was a small thorn in the middle of her foot. He lifted her up into his arms and carried her to the nearest comfortable spot he could find, then gently laid her down. Going down to her feet, Louis lifted her right foot to look, and placed his mouth under her foot with his tongue to guide him to where the thorn was. Gently he sucked it and with his teeth he pulled it out without giving what he did a second thought.

Julie gasped. She breathed in and out of her nostrils when he did that. She was afraid because what he did aroused her. Louis kissed her feet and said as he looked up at her, "There! Do you feel better?"

Feeling excited by what he did, Julie got up real fast and it caused her to stumble. Louis thought she was still hurting. He quickly caught her and lifted her up again in his arms. She thanked him and said, "I'm sure I could walk now."

He apologized as he gently put her down.

She jumped and twirled and said, "I feel good. Thank you, Fuji." She jumped to kiss him on the lips.

Louis had not heard her call him like that since she had found out he was the father of William. He smiled as he held her in his arms. "You're welcome."

She pulled back her socks and boots on. Taking her hand, together they walked back to their horses to continue the tour around the mansion. The following day he took her to his yacht. The captain of his yacht was happy to see him again with the crew. They were excited when Louis's secretary called to let them know he was going to use the yacht over the weekend because Louis was barely there to enjoy his yacht and the workers were going to give their best to please him. He spent every moment with her, making their own memories that they would never forget. Every moment he spent with her was precious to him.

She was surprised when she saw the name of his yacht, JULY.

He smiled in surprise when he realized that was the name he had given his yacht. He showed her how to steer the wheel of his yacht. The weather was nice, the sky was bright, so they decided to spend the night in the yacht. They spent the night talking and looking at the stars and the moon drinking and eating caviar.

Louis sang to her as she laid her head on his chest. She closed her eyes to consume every love word that came out of his mouth. Her body was starting to crave him more than before. She prayed in her heart to uphold her virtue.

Julie laughed as she was getting drunk. She stood up to dance the Haitian congo for him. Louis was banging on the side of the boat, making a drum sound so she could dance. He was smiling as she was dancing and twirling, moving her hips to the beat he was making. When the dance was over she sat back on the comfy. He poured her more wine.

"Louis, the wine is getting to my head!"

"How deep?" Louis asked.

"Very deep," she laughed, and dropped herself on him.

He put the wine bottle down and smiled when he looked at her eyes and thought, *She is officially drunk.*

"Tell me," Louis asked, "when you look at me what do you think?"

"Besides being goofy for getting me high?" Julie giggled. "Tomorrow I'm going to wake up with a hangover . . . No, I will not tell you."

She pointed her finger on his nose and said, "You're a very tall man, Mr. Janvier, and big and strong," she squeezed his arms as she ran her hands on them, "lots of muscles. I wonder how big is it?"

"My arms?"

Shaking her arms in the gesture of saying no, she agreed, "Yes, your arms. How big is your urine injection?"

Louis burst out in laughter. "My urine injection!"

"Yes." She nodded.

Louis wasn't expecting her to ask a question like that. That was a first. No woman had ever asked him that question. "It never came to mind for me to measure it. . . . Why do you want to know?"

Looking at the skies then she tilted her head aside to look at him said, "It's obvious, but looks can be deceiving. I want to know if you will be able to satisfy me to the full like you once mentioned." She motioned her hand and ran her index finger on her mouth, trying to get her words out well. " . . . I'm still trying to understand why a good-looking man like you didn't have a wife yet?" She pointed to her temple with the same finger. "Then I thought maybe you may have a measuring problem, because the last time I touched you, you didn't let me get the full measure of it . . . I don't want to send you back home to your mother for cutting you short."

That had really hit the spot for Louis. He laughed so hard that he made everyone in the yacht wonder what that was all about. He knew she was definitely drunk, because Julie would have never said or asked him a question like that. Kissing her head he concluded, "Ask me that question when you're not out of the world."

Julie spent the rest of the night on the deck in Louis's arms. They named the stars, creating their own heaven.

Chapter Fifteen

No More Tears

By then, Julie was getting over her situation. She had no doubt about Louis being the father of her son. Louis grew to love her more. He wanted to marry her while they were in New York, but Julie didn't want to hear of that. She wasn't ready for that step yet. She thought they should wait a little longer before they jumped the broom and her mind wasn't completely at peace. She needed more time.

Julie told her mother she was warned by Marie Landers to be careful of what she prayed for. She started to laugh as she thought back, because she had spent many nights praying for Louis's dreams to come true, now they were all a reality for him. She prayed for herself to go on with her life.

The six weeks were over and they were flying back to Haiti. Jacque was upset about Julie and Viviane's brutal departure. He was wondering why she went to New York, and Maxine was never a good help on telling him what went down. She irritated him. No one was able to tell him what Julie was doing in New York. He was unable to get in contact with her, because Aunt Viviane didn't want him to bother Julie while she was in New York taking care of her personal business.

Jacque thought, what could be more important than him wanting to know how her daughter was doing?

Jacque was even more inflamed when Julie returned because she didn't call to ask him to pick her up at the airport. His mind was shimmering with thoughts when he saw it was Louis who dropped them off at the Bassine mansion again. He kissed Julie, then tenderly kissed William, who was in her arms, and then Viviane on the cheeks as he was leaving.

Julie smiled as she said hello to Jacque. She looked at his face and noticed he was upset. Jacque felt they owed him an apology, because they left without giving anyone knowledge of their whereabouts. She didn't feel she needed to give him any explanation. Like her mother told him, she had to take care of herself and it was personal. Jacque didn't say much; he felt at the moment he wasn't getting through to her. And since he wasn't going to get an answer from her, he wanted her to sign some of the documents he had mentioned to her before she took off again. He felt she should get it out of the way, but Julie was not in the mood at the moment. It was only a day since she returned to Haiti and she wanted to rest and take some time off so she could think.

She tossed the papers aside. "I'm not in any hurry, Jacque."

In the meantime, at the Janvier estate, Louis was in his office with Henry Claude, going over the documents that Maxine had given him. Louis felt he had wasted a lot of time on taking care of things here for Julie. Henry sat in front of Louis's desk listening to him as he handed him each document he read. He was surprised to hear Louis was sharing his thoughts with him. Louis never mention the tragic death of his father nor did he let anyone know how he felt when his mother was killed. He kept them all bottled up. That was the first time Henry heard him citing a glance of his past and he actually could hear the fear in Louis's voice.

"I cannot understand why Jacque of all people is trusted by Julie. Here I am labeled as a liar, a cheater, and a deceiver, untrustworthy, a manipulator. You name it, I've been called it, and yet Jacque is about to initiate the biggest con on Julie. . . . I don't want my future wife to be hurt by this man. Julie cares for him so much!" Louis put his hands on his temples to massage his head. "I don't want that feeling escaping me again, Henry."

Henry remembered Louis's rage, and that wasn't pleasant. He never wanted to witness that again . . . letting that burning anger out was fatal to those who stood in Louis's way. Louis never expressed to anyone his thoughts. Julie was the very first. Henry nodded his head as he thought about Louis and the woman who came into his life. She was able to bring Louis back to the living. That was the first time Henry heard Louis express his anger in words or any kind of emotion. Only Julie was able to bring that feeling out of him.

For a minute Henry felt jealous. All the years he'd known Louis, no one was able to reach him like Julie. He smiled and sighed as he listened to Louis talking to him. That was the very first time he was doing the listening and Louis was doing the talking, explaining the way he felt.

"How are you going to stop him without Julie's knowledge?"

"I wanted to take her back to the ranch and finish where we left off."

"You think that's wise?" Henry commented.

"It's a must," Louis put his hand on the back of his head. "Most of the things I wanted to share with her are down there. I must be brave."

Henry laughed. "She scares you, doesn't she?"

Louis laughed back. "I'm terrified."

Henry answered, "Jacque is not wasting any time. He had a couple of lawyers and a judge working with him."

"Jacque is trying to intervene. I'm not going to let him mess up my plans. I made a lot of changes in my life. I will not go back to where I was before. I can't go over there to see Julie without Carine trying to get her hands all over me. And I know her big brother is influencing her. I don't want to hurt her, but if she messes things up for me, I don't know what I would do. When I told her she should listen to her big brother, I didn't mean she should listen to his crazy ideas. It was for her to keep away from me. Julie's mother invited me to dinner tonight, and I've asked her if I could bring you along. She said fine, but the question is, are you game to do what needs to be done to keep Carine away from me."

Smiling, Henry replied, "Just point your finger and I will follow."

Henry was happy to see that Louis trusted him more than he thought. That caused him to drift away to the past when he first met Louis.

Henry thought Louis was a racist, impertinent boy. He never said much to him or anyone. His father was working for Louis's parents as an accountant and they used to give clothes that were too small for Louis to him. He used to look sharp in the clothing they had given his father for him. His neighborhood friends used to wish they had a father like him who could provide such good quality of clothes for his family and a nice home. He was enrolled in one of the best schools in Haiti, and he was one of the top students. His father's boss had even given Henry's father a car.

When his father drove that black Cadillac into the neighborhood, people in town thought he had sold his soul to the devil. That day his father came home with three bags full of clothes. One for him, one for his mother, and the other one belonged to his father. He also had the car trunk filled with food.

Henry spent the whole night trying on his outfits and wondering why that boy had his parents buy him clothes and he wasn't going to wear them. Some of the shoes looked like he only wore them once, then he put them away. But he was grateful for the clothes he was sending him.

Henry's neighbors thought his parents were rich, but they were not. His father's boss was a fair man. They didn't live in a mansion, but their little four-room house was well arranged, their little patio had outdoor furniture, and their little backyard was big enough for him. He was able to sit outdoors to chat with his neighborhood friends, and he able to share a plate of food and a glass of soda. They even had a maid to cook and wash their clothes. He thought he had it made. He was a prince in his neighborhood. Like Louis, he was the only child his parents had.

Henry's whole world changed in one night. His parents were coming home from a trip after a long weekend when a truck ran them off the road, down off the mountain of Jacmel. They didn't survive. His father had told him about his boss and his wayward son. Henry was surprised to see Louis and his family at his parents' funeral. That was the very first time he stood that close with mulattos. Louis handed him his handkerchief without saying a word to him, watching him cry with his wolf eyes. Then he walked away and went and sat in the car that had brought them there.

He handed Louis's mother the handkerchief after he finished wiping his eyes and face. Everyone was staring at them as they stood quietly by him, consoling him. After the service, they told him the following day they were coming to take him to their home because they had promised his parents if anything happened to them they would take him in.

He thought that was the most horrifying thing his parents had ever done to him. When Louis's parents broke the news, at that moment he wished he was dead alongside his parents. He cried bitterly. Why did they do that to him?

He was even more hurt when he heard his relatives didn't want him. The neighborhood friends he thought he had were laughing at him behind his back when they saw it was a couple of blanc *that was taking him in. They thought he was going to be a yard boy. He wanted to run off when the mother of one of his friends told him that, but he didn't. He respected his parents' choice for him. Quietly he walked outside of his little house with his head down, not looking at anyone who was standing outside, watching him leave. He got into the back seat of the Jeep and sat down. Louis's father tried to take his bag for him, but he didn't let him. He thought,* You're going to have me carry heavier load than that, so there is no need to take that for me to cover up faces.

He thought he was going to be a yard boy like they claimed he was to be, carrying a water bucket on top of his head to fill their water drums every morning, watching their car and shining their shoes and washing their dogs. From sun down to sun up he felt he was going to work.

He cried as they drove away, leaving all his friends, all he ever knew behind. He hoped one day he would return to visit his friends. He felt like he was going to be a slave to those people. And their wayward son was going to have his way with him. Slapping him, kicking his butt if he didn't call him monsieur. Liquid flew out of his eyes more than ever as those thoughts hit his mind.

As the car was going up the mountain, fear ran through his very soul. He remembered the horror stories that the people were saying about those who lived up in the mountains. They were werewolves and witches and people who practiced voodoo.

Henry became more afraid, because he heard Louis's attitude was worse than anyone else in the whole world. He was like Satan's child, the devil, the anti-Christ. Henry thought he was going to hell alive.

He never saw a mansion before except for the White House and the military base. The yard was huge and beautifully decorated with well-arranged flowers and trees. He thought he was never going to know every corner of that place. They could eat him and bury his bones in their yard and no one would ever suspect anything, because of the way it looked.

Henry was surprised when a man (Francois) dressed up like penguin called him sir and took his bag from him and carried it up to his room. He looked at Louis's parent and thought, Are they perverts? Are they going to make me feel comfortable for sexual pleasure?

He was thinking so badly about them, he was ashamed. Things they were going to do to him. Never had he seen such grandeur. The lobby was big enough to have a festival. The high ceiling was making him feel like he was entering a cathedral. He was afraid to look up because he felt dizzy when he brought his head down. He wondered who were those people? Were they vampires or were they from the Frankenstein family? Only in those two movies he had seen a palace like this.

He put his hand on his neck, following Louis's parents into the mansion and up to the room that was going to be his. The room was breathtaking when he walked in. Everything he ever dreamt of was before him, a walk-in closet full of clothes for him to wear. Everything fit him perfectly, nothing extra so he could grow into them. He didn't bother to take anything he had brought with him, because there was nothing worth taking out of the bag except his parents' picture and his. He even had a beautiful full-size private bathroom.

Later that evening he got all dressed up for dinner and met with the family in the living room. They introduced him to all the servants. All addressed him as Monsieur Claude and bowed their heads in greeting. Louis wasn't present. He had gone riding on the mountain. By the time he had returned, it was dinnertime. They were heading for the dining room. They stopped when they saw Louis going up the stairs, and Francois the butler was talking to him as he was making his way up. His father called him. Louis looked at him and continued walking away without saying a word.

Henry thought that was very rude of him. His heart skipped a beat when he thought he had to face that boy very soon.

Henry couldn't make him out except he was the devil. By the time Louis returned they were already sitting in the formal dining room waiting for him. He thought Louis had done that on purpose, because he was very late. He sat across the table from him without saying a word. His mother said, "How was you ride?"

Louis just nodded his head to verify he had a good ride. He didn't say why he was late when his father asked him. He looked at him, then at his mother. He stared at his father as if they should understand. He removed the napkin from the table and laid it on his lap, picked up his fork and knife, and started to eat. His mother and father smiled when he did that.

Henry thought Louis's parents needed to perform an exorcism on him. If it was him, his father would have held him down and his mother would be the one doing the slapping to remove the demon that had possessed his body. What he witnessed here tonight was new to him. Down where he came from, children answered when an adult questioned them. Otherwise, they would get a beating.

Louis's parents did all the talking. They asked Henry all kind of questions, his likes and dislikes. He was afraid to speak up, so he was shocked when Louis said something to him: "Don't let them intimidate you."

He didn't look at Louis. He was afraid to say anything. Louis sounded too calm for a boy. He thought, He is the devil all right. *Nervously he answered, "I like business law."*

Louis laughed. "We definitely need more of that."

When Louis said that, he took courage to look at him and asked, "What about you?"

Louis made him feel so bad by the way he peered at him and said nothing. He continued to eat, then raised his left hand and snapped his fingers for the butler to pour him his drink, then gently nodded his head at him and waved the butler away. After his drink he excused himself from the table and walked out of the dining room.

A week went by and Louis never addressed him again. They could sit in the same room and he would just look at him . . . He thought Louis didn't like him, because of his dark skin. That was the reason he was giving the silent treatment. Henry talked more with Marie's son Richard.

As time went by, he noticed Louis was a short-spoken type of person. He never spent hours studying or reading. He would just take a quick glance at his work and he was done. He would always have A's when he took a test. Henry thought Louis was cheating on his exams.

Louis had his own two personal tutors from America to instruct him. A year later he joined Louis. He thought he was going to show off to Louis and teach him the things he knew because he thought Louis had a speech and a learning problem.

Boy, was Henry surprised! That wasn't the case at all. He had a lot of catching up to do. Louis was a genius. Louis was never a talkative person. Louis loved to listen, and when one made no sense, he could laugh his head off, and that could be very annoying. And when he talked, it was because he had something worth saying. Louis was more action than words. Henry felt bad for the way he was thinking about them, because if Louis didn't want him there, his parents wouldn't take him in.

There was not one thing Louis said he could do that he wasn't able to do. His personality was to fear. One either loved or hated him. Louis wasn't in between. Henry grew to love him very much. He noticed Louis was always in trouble, even when he was not the one who caused the problem. Louis would never dispute when someone accused of something, never defended himself from anyone. He thought that was something very special about Louis. Not once did Louis act like a snob toward him or anyone else, but a person would have the wrong view of him for his lack of words. And the way he kept on looking at you when talking to him—he barely blinked.

Henry felt if Louis wanted to be a snob he would have understood. With all that money, who wouldn't.

Henry was the one who had become a snob. Louis's parents gave him the best of care, better than his own parents would have ever done. He went to the best schools and wore the best clothing money could buy. He was even more surprised when he received money at the end of each week when all he did was going to school and enjoying life, and he was getting paid. Never did his parents hand him so much money to spend anyway he felt like. He was wondering why were they giving him money when he should be the one paying them for taking him in. He was grateful just to be in their home. That was the first time Louis said more than just five words to him. Louis explained the money was his allowance.

He had seen parents give children money to go to the movie or have a little to eat after, but all that money they handed to him in an envelope for him to spent just for *the hell of it. At seventeen they gave him his own car. He had a nice Jeep to drive around. Louis was happy for him and asked him to take him for a spin around town. That was the very first time he had returned to his old neighborhood. Some acted like they didn't recognize him, and some thought he had returned here just to show off, which was precisely why Henry had visited them. To show those people he didn't become a yard boy as they thought he would. Louis and his parents were very kind, and he had never met anyone like them.*

Some stared at Louis, who was sitting inside the car looking, and some of the children teased him, calling names. "Blankit, blankit kodonié tèt plat, blanc mangé rapadou sou ban. (Whitey whitey shoemaker flat head, white eat candy on the table)."

Another word, feel no pity for the fair skins because they had it made. Henry never understood the teasing song till that day. He stood there feeling hurt for Louis, but Louis was laughing at the boys and girls singing the teasing song to him. And every time they stopped Louis shouted, "Chanté-l ancore! *(Sing it again)!"*

Henry wondered what was he thinking when he returned here to his old neighborhood. He didn't come here to have Louis teased by those senseless and jealous people. He just wanted them to see how good he was doing.

The girls were looking at them, smiling, especially the ones who thought they were handsome. Some came by to say hello. And that got the guys very mad, along with their parents.

Henry gave one of the girls talking to him his phone number and noted to her, to "bring your girlfriend along with you," noticing the one Louis was focusing on, "by the theater tomorrow afternoon," the movie theater that was on Delmas. As she was leaving he slipped some money into her hand. And when she reached a distance she nodded her head in agreement.

One of the parents who was talking to him noticed what took place before him. "You come here to show off, don't you, Henry?"

Henry was surprised when the man said that, but playing it cool, Henry smiled conceitedly. "Oh no, I drop by here to see how you guys were coming along."

Which made some of them angry and want to test Henry's strength. Louis burst into laughter because here Henry had come to visit his old friends and they wanted to kick his butt.

Louis was wondering what they were trying to do, when he saw one of the guys moving around Henry like he knew how to kick box. Louis started to laugh even more, so much, that he was banging his hand on the dashboard. . . . One of them got very angry and wanted to test Louis. He didn't want to participate. He just wanted to watch so he could laugh. One of them started to speak French to him, showing Louis that he could speak French better than him. Louis couldn't help but laugh. He thought that the guy was being foolish. He didn't come here with Henry to debate the French language. He didn't respond to the guy, he just continued smiling like he was an idiot. Then one of them insisted to try out Louis's fighting technique, but still Louis refused.

Then the guy got real angry and hit Henry on the nose and knocked him down. Henry couldn't fight him, (not because he couldn't fight. In Louis's eye they all didn't know how to fight). Henry was not looking when he hit him on the nose and caused him to lose his balance. That was when Louis came out of the car and pulled Henry out of the other guy's reach. Still the guy wasn't satisfied. He tried to hit Louis. Henry didn't know Louis was good in martial arts. He beat up every last one of them trying to jump them. Then Henry and Louis got in the car and quickly drove out of Henry's old neighborhood because more of them were coming with their brooms and sticks, throwing rocks at them and shouting, "Kim-be blanc-an (Hold the white boy)!"

Henry drove off as fast as he could before his brand new car was completely damaged. There were a few dents on the body, and the back window was cracked. Louis was laughing at them while he stuck his head out of the Jeep window, mocking and yelling as they made their way out of the old place, "you guys need to run faster with your skinny legs."

Henry was afraid when he looked in his rearview mirror and saw the entire neighborhood was running after his Jeep. Some were running as fast as he was driving. He was afraid Louis was going to get his head busted with one of the rocks the people were throwing. His mind was at rest only when he was finally out of his old neighborhood and saw none of them were still running after them. He swore never to return to that place, but Louis said, "Why? That was fun. Let's do it again!"

They became even closer than they were before. Louis showed him kick boxing. They started to hang out together more. They were inseparable. They partied together, girls left and right all over town. And with the money that they had, it was very easy for them. By the time Louis reached sixteen, Henry couldn't tell Louis what to do and where not to go. They became so corrupted. They were having sex with two or more women at the same time. They were bad, but Louis was worse! Louis was capable of disappearing for days, and no one would know where he went and no one would dare question him.

Louis showed Henry how to invest his allowance. He never dreamed to have so much money. He was not saying he was worth as much as Louis, but he had enough money to not worry about financial problems in life.

Now he had more family than he thought he had. When his parents died, if it wasn't for Louis's parents he would have nowhere to go. He was almost fifteen. No one would take him in and give him an education. He would have truly ended up cleaning someone's back yard for a plate of food and to have a place to sleep.

Life is even harder for a child who had no parents or family support.

Never did Louis raise his voice at him, even when he was angry. To complain about Louis, Henry felt that would have been a sin. He knew since day one Louis wasn't looking for a big brother. He was four years older than Louis, but one would think Louis was older because he was a very tall boy. Many women wanted to know Louis. That was one part of his life Henry had enjoyed the most. Henry quoted an old comedian's phrase as he thought back. "The world, champagne, beautiful women!"

Henry smiled, returning to the present. Louis was wondering why was he smiling. He nodded. "Tonight everything you hope for is going to take place."

That night Jacque had other plans. He didn't know Louis, along with Henry, was invited to dinner. He told Julie he was going to his hotel to check on a couple of things. Since she didn't sign any of the documents he gave her to sign, she made it hard for him to do anything for her, but still he was working on finding out how he could get all the land she wanted. Julie told him if he found anything he had to contact her at the mansion because that was where she was going to sleep tonight. Then Jacque went his way.

Julie looked astonishing in her low-cut back, black gown that brought out her shape well. She looked glamorous with her hair up and diamonds in her ears and around her neck. Maxine commented, "I think if I was a man I would love to have you, too."

Julie smiled. "You have a nice shape, too, you know."

"Not like yours. You're exotic," she exclaimed. They turned and danced with each other. Maxine said, "I wish Aunt Viviane had invited Richard for dinner too. I want Richard to feel me in this gown I'm wearing."

Julie touched her face when she said that and smiled. "Dreams do come true if you want it so bad."

Letting Maxine go, she turned, all excited and said, "I will dance tonight. I want to be held by Louis."

They both checked themselves once more in the mirror then headed for the door, laughing like they were two schoolgirls. By the time they came down, everyone was downstairs waiting in the family room. Maxine was surprised when her eyes were set on Richard as she walked in. She looked at Julie and smiled then at Aunt Viviane for inviting him to dinner, which had shocked Nicole and Carine greatly, and Jean acted like he didn't care, but he didn't bother to talk to Richard. Marie was so happy to see her son among the Bassines and that Viviane didn't look down at her son. She questioned him like she would do to all the young men who was interested with her daughters.

After dinner they all went on the patio for fresh air. The butler was serving them drinks. There was a soft love song playing very low in the background, but Louis heard it. He asked Julie to dance with him, and Richard did the same with Maxine. They smiled as they took their men's hands to dance. They all were having a good time except for Carine.

Noticing the way Carine touched Louis and the look on Louis's face, Jean thought, *Carine wants to pull the same stunt she did the last time during the night of the barbecue.*

Unnoticed to everyone else, Jean gently pulled her aside and whispered to her, "I don't think you should have any alcoholic beverages, Carine. It makes you act foolish. And Louis is not here to be bothered with you. Did you notice the look he gave you? His eyes spelled terror, keep away!"

She brushed Jean off. As she walked away she whispered over her shoulder, "Mind your own business, little brother."

She didn't care what Viviane had said to her or her sister Maxine, but that time Henry trying to make sure she kept out of Louis's way, preventing her from getting hurt by him. Pulling away from Henry, Carine snapped, "Get your hands off me!"

Nicole laughed and excused herself from the patio to get the family albums to show Louis and the others when she heard Carine. Maxine knew exactly what Carine was up to, she was going to try to ruin things for Julie and Louis, and Nicole was helping her. She quickly excused herself from Richard, who was dancing with her. She came over and took Carine's arm. Giving her a shake, she ground under her breath, "Carine, get a grip on yourself. Your dramatic role would not work tonight. You will be humiliated."

Maxine signaled Jean for help, thinking that he was coming to help, but Jean didn't want to witness what was about to happen to Carine. He felt she was out of her mind and she would get what she deserved tonight. So he excused himself. "Have a good time, guys!"

Jean didn't even bother to tell Aunt Viviane he was leaving and went out for a drive in town.

Viviane was checking in the kitchen to see if everything was going well with the servants. Julie was still dancing with Louis. She was beginning to feel a little bit flustered when she noticed the way Carine was acting. She whispered to Louis, "I guess we better stop seeing each other. I'm afraid my sister is about to have a nervous breakdown if I don't stop seeing you. It's true you did sleep with her. And now you and I."

Julie gently pulled away from Louis, but he took a hold of her and waltzed with her out of the patio into the terrace. He kissed her and said, "I was a bad boy . . . and what had happened between Carine and I was a long time ago. . . . The truth is, I don't even remember dating her, there were so many of them at that time. Remember, she was engaged to my cousin Brian, they were about to get married. . . . Please, Julie, don't let her ruin things for us, and our baby William. She's playing you, knowing the way you are. The gifts that God has given you?'" He kissed her all over her face as he named them. "You're full of love, joy, kindness, goodness, faith, you have self-control, and you are a long-suffering person. You just have to work on your temper. . . ."

He got her to smile so he continued, " . . . You're willing to step down for another person's happiness. She is hoping you do just that. Please, my love! Don't let her loose conduct get to you, her craziness get between our relationship."

Julie laid her head against his chest while he spoke to her, but her eyes were on the patio observing what was going on. Louis was beginning to feel a little bit frenzied. Slowly they walked back inside and Carine was still acting up. Louis stared at Carine, watching how she was carrying on. Her behavior was unacceptable to Louis.

Henry looked at them, they didn't look happy. Louis pulled on his earlobe to let Henry know that Julie was feeling disturbed. Henry took a firmer hold on Carine and held her tighter against him, pretending he was playing with her so Julie wouldn't think much of what was happening and what was about to happen to Carine.

Looking at Louis and Julie's face, Maxine felt embarrassed by Carine's lustful display of desire and jealousy. Roy had walked in just in time with a tray of cocktails. Maxine took the tray from him and served the cocktails herself to them because she was feeling embarrassed.

Henry was pretending dancing with Carine. He waltzed in with her laughing. He tried to cover her mischievous behavior from everyone. On their way in, she was fussing with him.

He whispered in her ear, "Please, Carine, control yourself. Louis promised to bury you alive if you don't behave properly tonight."

Grasping at what Henry said, she quickly glanced at Louis and found Louis and Julie looking at her. Louis shook his head at her hold on his neck and squeezed to show her he was going to choke the life out of her, but Julie was standing in front of him and didn't see Louis's gesture to Carine. She saw Carine clinched in Henry's arms. She laid her head on Henry's chest, laughing as they both waltzed in, away from everyone's sight, to continue to talk in private.

Nicole only witnessed the beginning of Carine's play. She knew Carine was going to act crazy, messing up things for Louis so their brother could succeed at having Julie. She wasn't there to see what had totally taken place, because she had left the family room to get the photo albums in the library to show Louis some family portraits. By the time she returned, the finale of Carine's acting drama had already taking place.

Viviane, too, didn't see what went down, because she had gone in the kitchen to check on things. Nicole returned with the album. They went to the living room to see the family pictures and to continue their conversation. She was so busy running her mouth to Louis she didn't notice that Carine and Henry were not in the living room with them.

Julie was concerned when Henry and Carine didn't return. She whispered in Louis's ear, "I'm going to check on Carine."

Louis kissed her hand and nodded to say okay. She excused herself and quickly made her way to the family room. They weren't there nor were they at the library or the dining room. So she went up the stairs, heading to Carine's room to see if she was okay. She was about to knock on the door when she heard fainted laughter and moaning.

The door was not locked. Slowly Julie slightly opened the door to peek inside the room to see what was going on. Both Carine and Henry were totally nude. Carine was lying on her back on the bed with Henry on top of her, with her legs wrapped around his waist, was moaning and passing her hands over Henry while he was caressing her. Julie was shocked at the sight! She quickly and silently backed out of the room and closed the door behind her. Leaning against the wall, she tried to comprehend Carine's mental state of mind. Shaking her head she walked back down the stairs. Maxine was also coming up to see how Carine was doing, but Julie stopped her. "She is fine, Max."

Looking at Julie's reaction, Maxine advised, "You seem shocked . . . don't be! But I wish you didn't see that!"

On the way back to the living room, Maxine stopped. "I'm going to show you another crazy drama, but promise me you'll not get angry or upset."

"Maxine, after what I saw tonight, there's nothing in the world that could get me upset or angry at this moment. Okay, let's go."

They sneaked by as they were going by the living room. Louis saw them. Julie waved to him to wait as they made their way out of the house. They ran in the direction of the barn toward the guest house where Julie and her son were staying now. Carefully they made their way through the woods. Reaching a hidden spot Maxine, pulled behind one of the trees and hid.

Julie softly said, "The light in my living room is on. Who would be there without my permission?" In surprise she saw who that was. She stated, "It's Jacque! What's he doing in my place?"

Maxine replied, "Watch and see."

They were looking at Debbie, who was walking across the room with a towel folded around her, toward Jacque, who was also half-naked. He grabbed her and kissed her, lifting her up as if he wanted to take her right there and then. He nailed her to the wall, kissing her as he removed the rest of his clothes. Julie turned her head not to look at them and quietly asked, "Why didn't he use the guest house instead of my place?"

"It's too close to the mansion."

She looked at Maxine and asked, "Why are they sneaking about?"

Maxine replied, "Earlier you told him you were going to sleep at the mansion tonight, and Jacque doesn't want you to know that he is still involved with Debbie. So he thought since you were not going to be at your place, he felt it was a better place to entertain Debbie. He was thinking you were not going to find out about that. Jacque has become a liar. As you could see he lied about taking care of business for you. I don't want to hurt you, Julie, but I think you have the right to know, before he goes too far. I heard him speak with Carine about how he wanted to marry you, and he was going to have you whether you want him or not. I feel you trust him too much with your things."

"I will never marry Jacque. Louis had proposed to me, but I turned him down."

"You did what," Maxine exclaimed in shock. "You guys are in love."

"I'm not ready, Maxine. I don't feel it right at the moment, my body wants him, and in my soul I yearn for him, but my mind is debating."

"Over what?"

"Jacque told me. . . ."

Maxine cut her short, "He loves you and you believed him!"

"No, nothing like that," she reassured her. "I love Jacque as a brother, but never as a lover. You guys are like sisters and brothers to me. Whatever I did or do for you and your sisters and brothers, it's because you're my family." Julie patted Maxine on her back. "I came to Haiti to find myself! To understand why was I having that dream, to solve my marital problem knowing that Saul wanted to live here. Instead it took this course and changed everything. . . .

" . . . Something phenomenal had happened to me since the first time I dreamt about my Jewish boy. The flame turned on when I arrived a year ago. It kept on burning and I don't want it to turn off. I want to go through it burning with only one man, Louis Janvier. And we were drawn to each other. And my first night here confirmed it. Since then we have been intrigued by each other, you of all people should know that. And you alone know more about me than any other person. . . ."

While she was listening to Julie, Maxine was happy when she remembered she had given Louis all the documents that Saul wanted him to have. She felt she didn't need to tell Julie about Jacque's other scheme since Louis had all the documents that were rightfully his, and she knew Louis was going to take care of everything.

" . . . Jacque," Julie said and meditated on what she was going to say. "Since I returned to make a home here in Haiti . . . Jacque's mind is running like it had been hit with local motive. . . . And he is becoming more of a stranger to me . . . I don't understand him. I thought he would have been happy for me, that we would be a family once again. Instead he's acting like a jealous lunatic. . . . Like you said, lately he has been acting really crazy. No one knows when his mood is going to strike him. Believe me, I'm not worrying too much about him. I think he has his own demons to fight with, like we all do. I just hope he doesn't step on Louis's toes too many times."

Maxine smiled. "Louis is trying not to kick him off the planet."

They laughed at Maxine's remark and made their way back toward the mansion.

"I'm hoping that Jacque and Debbie work things out and they don't have sex on my bed or William's."

"I understand." Maxine laughed. She listened to Julie quietly as they made their way back to the mansion while Julie explained what Jacque had told her about Louis and it was still on her mind. And she wanted to make it clear to herself that Louis didn't just want her only for her body but he truly loved her, before she accepted his hand in marriage. As they were reaching the mansion, they saw Nicole and Henry kissing and they headed for the parking lot.

"That's one busy man," Maxine commented and caused Julie to laugh in shock. "My word! Is Nicole blind, too?"

Later that evening Louis called her to tell her he had a wonderful time, but going home was heart breaking for him, knowing he was leaving without her. He was thinking of her and he desperately wanted to see her. During her conversation on the phone, Viviane was paying keen attention to what Julie was saying and to her body language.

Julie twirled her finger in her hair, passing her hand over her face, giggling as she was talking, smiling, and whispering Louis's nickname to him on the phone. Viviane couldn't understand why things were procrastinating between Louis and her. She sat with William in her arms, wondering how she could put a stop to all that.

Julie hung up the phone, singing like she was in la-la land, going to her bathroom to get herself ready for bed. She didn't even notice if her mother was still in her room. Julie was still singing when she came out of the bathroom. That was when she realized that her mother was still in her room. She had laid an evening gown on her bed for her to wear and she was wiping her shoes.

Julie stated, "That gown was too sexy. That is the reason I didn't wear it tonight."

Viviane replied, "But you are going to wear it tonight."

"Mother, you need to wear your glasses." She smiled as she pushed the gown aside to slide herself under the sheet. "I'm getting myself ready for bed, not going out."

Viviane sat down on the bed and patting the spot beside her, ordered softly but sternly, "Come around here . . . come right here."

Julie slid out of the bed and moved toward her mother apprehensively. "Mother, what is it?"

Tenderly framing her daughter's face in her hands, Viviane remonstrated sadly, "You have been suffering for a very long time. It's about time you put an end to it."

Julie shook her head to say, "I'm not suffering, Mother."

Viviane insisted, "Yes, you are. Darling, all I ever wanted was for you to be happy."

Julie clasped her mother's hand. "I know, Mother."

Viviane scolded, "I'm not a fool, and I did not raise one. I saw the way Louis looked at you. He showed it, and he does not hide it. And you, my dear, felt his loneliness, his pain, and sorrow. He's empty and you feel the same way, too. He loves you. And your mind is troubled. I know you have great respect for me, and you don't want to do anything to dishonor me. I already see you and him as husband and wife, and baby makes three. I called him while you were in the shower." Smiling she quoted "My daughter, ought I not to look for a resting place for you, that it may go well with you? He's waiting for you, go to him."

Trembling, Julie said, "Not tonight, Mother. Please, do not play Naomi in the Bible. Don't encourage me to go to Louis tonight. I'm not Ruth. I might do something I'll regret later on. I'm afraid to get too close to him."

Viviane hugged her tightly. "I know, baby, I know, but don't be afraid. Express what your heart is feeling. Tonight don't think, just feel. Go to him and make him yours, with my blessings. Stop the madness between you two. You have the power to do so."

"Louis is not Boaz, Mom."

"True," Viviane answered, "but I believe he will do the right thing. He loves you." She smiled. "He'll repurchase us."

Kissing her on both cheeks, Viviane helped her to get dressed and sent her on her way.

Chapter Sixteen

Love and the Pact

The next morning, at 8:30, Julie and Louis were still in bed. They were having so much fun dancing in the ballroom that they didn't go to bed till four. Julie was lying on his bed beside him. She inhaled deeply as she threw her arms over on him and exhaled. He awoke from the layers of sleep with a hit of her arm against his face.

Louis carefully removed her arm off his face then gently lifted her leg off him and laid it on the bed. Mildly, he pulled himself up and sat on the bed to admire her physical appearance. Julie had yellowish cinnamon-gold complexion, her eyes were like a doll's, her lashes were long and curved, her lips looked liked they had lipstick because of their rosy texture, her relaxing hair was reddish-brown with honey-blond highlight. She had nice-sized succulent breasts that every woman would love to have, and a shape one would kill for. From head to toes, she matched. She was perfect in his eyes. He lay on his side watching her softly breathing.

Louis thought, *Julie is the only woman that I let sleep in the same bed where I slept, and this is the first time a beautiful, sensuous woman lay sleeping beside me and we did nothing but kiss.*

He noticed that Julie slept like baby. She had pushed the cover aside while she was sleeping. Her pillows were on the floor and her legs were not closed—one was on top of him and the other leg was at the other side. Julie practically threw him off the bed. He was lying at the edge of the bed.

He smiled when remembering how her vagina looked through the revealing sleeping gown she had on while they were in New York.

He smelled her hair and gently kissed her. Slowly he started sniffing her hands and her arms, under her neck. Getting up on his hands and knees,

Louis moved quietly on the bed as his eyes traveled to the v-neck t-shirt she was wearing, looking at her belly and her fancy beige panty.

Julie slowly came awake to rippling sensations flowing through her body. She opened her eyes partially. She continued to pretend she was still asleep, lying there wondering what in the world Louis was up to.

Feeling naughty, she opened her legs wider to see what he would do. He looked up and saw Julie was still asleep. He continued sniffing her down to her feet, then kissed them. He silently went back to look at her, how beautiful she looked. *She truly is different,* he thought.

Louis stared at her so much that he almost drooled and lost his self-control.

Bad move! He thought closing his eyes. He was wrong to think he could actually sleep in the same bed with her without having any sexual thoughts. He ground his teeth together and breathed in and out of his mouth as he took ahold of his hands, pressing them against his chest so he would not touch her.

"This would not happen again," he mumbled as he remembered the promise he made to her the last time she was here. Louis chuckled, "I am a man with integrity."

His head was spinning with the heady sensations he was experiencing. He looked up, swallowed hard, and groaned, "God help me."

He realized what she was doing. He whispered, "I'm such a chucklehead. . . . Boy! Am I slow."

Louis quickly jumped off the bed and put his robe on and sat on the cold floor. She opened her eyes and saw him sitting in front of the bed with his long legs stretched out in front of him like a good little boy who had been punished enough and was ready to say, "I am sorry, Mommy."

Softly she called, "Louis, Louis."

He looked up at her, but didn't answer. She asked, "What are you doing sitting there?"

She sat up, pulled the sheets up over her, rested her back against the bedhead, and holding out her hand, she invited, "Come here."

Crawling like a baby on all fours, he went to lie beside her. Julie thought to herself, *My tiger feels trapped and he wants to go hunting.*

She touched his face and stretched up to kiss him. Lying back down and resting her cheek on his chest, Louis declared, "The last time I told you reminded me of a rose, you thought it was rather offensive. I don't blame you. You're more than that, a goddess, this is what you really are."

"Oh, no!" Julie laughed. "Now I'm a demon!"

Louis laughed because that was precisely what he was thinking, because she was quite a temptation. He dragged out a laugh. "No!"

"What's next, Louis?" She laughed back. "Soon I'll be your worst nightmare. This is what happens when you take upon your weakly mind to scope me while I was asleep."

"So you were just being naughty." Louis nodded. "You were not asleep."

"I was," Julie said. "You were breathing so hard over my body, I would have to be dead not to feel that."

He pulled her up and kissed her. He was starting to get drunk from her kisses. Then suddenly he pulled away, sat up, and said, "Julie, what time are you planning to get up?"

That wasn't what he wanted to ask her, but that was what came out.

Frowning, she asked, "Are you throwing me out, Louis?"

He jumped in, quick to assure her, "No! I want to take you for an early morning fly."

What he really wanted to shout was, "Will you marry me?" but he felt it was too soon to ask again.

"Flying?" she repeated. "In your jet? Me and you?"

"Yes," Louis smiled. But that was not what she wanted to hear. She was hoping he would propose to her again.

"I want to take a shower first." She got out of the bed and walked to the spacious bathroom to take her shower.

Back at the Bassine mansion, Maxine and the others were already awake. Maxine seemed to be a little happy. She was humming as she was going down the stairs. Passing by Marie on her way to breakfast, she gave her a kiss on the cheek, and said, "Good morning. What's for lunch, Marie? I'm starving."

Marie replied, "It's breakfast time. Lunch is a long way from now."

"Well," she said, "whatever is available. I could eat a horse. . . ."

Carine and Nicole were already down in the family room. Walking in, Maxine cheerily called out, "Good morning, sisters."

Carine gave her a sour look and replied, "Don't 'good morning' me, Maxine."

Blinking innocently, Maxine opened her eyes wide. "I thought by now you would have gotten off your high horse from the rough ride you had last night." She looked at Nicole, then turned back to Carine. "Well don't be upset at me if he didn't give you enough. Blame the other party he had to meet last night. He had a double to do."

Carine looked about ready to hit her. "I heard Julie spent the night at Louis's. Julie slept with him!"

Maxine responded, "Unbelievable."

Indignantly, she said, "You helped her steal Louis from me. I'm your sister, Maxine, not Julie. You should have helped me capture Louis."

Putting her hand over her mouth, she then scratched her hair and said, "Julie is my sister, too. You two may not look at her like that, but I do. I want to make one thing clear to you, Carine . . . Julie didn't steal Louis from you. He never wanted you."

"Julie acted like she's a virtuous woman," Carine stated, "but in reality she's a big tramp. . . . She slept with Louis last night."

Maxine was on a roll, "Wow! Julie had a ball last night. Louis was giving it to her up and down, all night long, no rest at all! You know how Louis is; he can run a marathon. Carine . . . you make me sick! Last night you showed your true colors. Didn't Henry do a good job last night? Didn't you humiliate yourself enough last night?"

Nicole, who was having tea, almost choked. The cup of tea fell out of her hand and shattered on the marble floor. She looked at Carine in disbelief as Maxine continued to talk, "I'm sure he did 'cause you fell right to sleep. You have no scruples. You think a man like Louis Janvier will want a woman like you or even give you a thought? I don't know what game you're playing, but I'm letting you know you are walking on dangerous ground. Can't you see the man doesn't want you? How long have you been trying to get him? Maybe you forget you were engaged to his cousin Brian, whom you dumped at the altar eight years ago because he didn't have the credentials you were looking for. I bet now you regret it, don't you, sister! That's the reason you're making everyone around you miserable. As you can see, Louis is no longer having orgies with you and your so-called girl friends. Your service is no longer needed. Your plots always fail! Last night Henry, his employee and you, he doesn't even want you. . . . The thought. . . ."

Putting her thumbs on her temples Maxine shook her head in disgust to dismiss the vision. "The way you behaved in front of Aunt Viviane and Julie was uncalled for. They had to witness that. You're nasty!"

Carine yelled, "Shut up!"

Maxine went on relentlessly, "Unless you're crazy to think Louis wanted you, sister. Louis is a man of class, a real man. Therefore, he needs a real woman, and you're not it. And you, Nicole, if you aren't careful, you'll end up on the same road she's heading."

Picking up the broken cup on the floor and placing it on the coffee table, Nicole was angry because Henry was secretly her man and now this. She replied, "Leave me out of it!"

Maxine and Julie saw her sneaking out with Henry last night. She looked her up and down and said, "It's too late to leave you out of it. You're already in it. Julie has been kind to us. She helped us get out of trouble so many times. We owe her everything we have. You have never seen her try to put us down. She treats everyone with respect. We're all a bunch of ungrateful users. . . ."

She looked at Carine with pity and anger. "You better wake up, my sister, because when reality hits you, it's going to hit you hard. You're not happy, and you don't want anyone else to be happy. . . ."

With tears streaming down her face, Maxine said, " . . . What you did last night was not only humiliating to you, but to all of us." She yelled at Carine, "You make all of us look cheap! I'll be damned if I'll let you hurt her again!"

Trying to calm them both, Nicole answered, "You have to remember, Julie belong to Jacque."

Maxine could not believe what she was hearing from Nicole. "You're unbelievable. . . . You must be in the twilight zone. Julie was married to Saul, lest you forget. She is not Jacque's woman, Debbie is. Get this in your stupid mind! She does not belong to that lying cheater! She looks at us like family, for God's sake! She grew up with us. We are her sisters and brothers. . . ."

Maxine felt like shaking her. " . . . What world are you living in?"

Looking at Carine, Nicole deliberately revealed, "You know Debbie's pregnant?"

Rounding on her, Carine yelled, "Shut up, Nicole!"

Maxine turned to Nicole. "So, you're holding back secrets from me. Jacque planned to have two women and you think it's okay? You need help! Do you think Julie deserves that?"

Nicole shook her head to say, "No."

Maxine said, "I had enough of you two this morning. I have to get myself ready for work."

She walked away, leaving Carine and Nicole in their own world to deal with.

It was a month later when Louis finally got everything set for Julie. Some of the documents were difficult to get, because Jacque has refused to submit them to him. He had to find another way to get those documents without Jacque's knowledge.

With the help of Marie, who was working there, Louis was able to do so. She had found out where Jacque was hiding those papers and replaced them without arousing any suspicion. Louis did it like that, because he didn't want to hurt Maxine and the rest of Jacque's family, who didn't have anything to do with Jacque's scheme. He didn't want to repeat history.

Louis laid on his bed meditating on the situation he was in again and the pain he could have caused Jacque. His mind wandered off and took him to his past. . . .

Eight Years Ago: Louis had just turned twenty-eight. He was in his flourish of his life. He thought he had solved all of his family problems. One evening, however, after dinner, his mother and he was strolling around the estate when out of nowhere a bullet hit his mother in the chest, a shot he thought was meant for him.

Although the bullet was silent, Louis heard the vibration of it coming when it hit his mother. He was four feet away from her when she was looking at a meteor dashing across the sky. By the time he reached out to pull her away, the bullet had already hit her. Blood was all over him as he held her in his arms, looking around and at the direction the bullet flew from. He saw the back of the man running away through the woods. Without a word he lifted up his mother and carried her inside the house. Marie was coming in with a tray of cocktails in her hands for them to share.

The tray fell out of her hands as she screamed his mother's name, "Mrs. Janvier!"

The sound of Marie's voice brought everyone to the living room where all her blood was pouring out of her lifeless body. Louis held her close to his chest, slowing rocking his body as if to comfort his mother. "Mother, wake up."

Everyone stood there looking at him with tears in their eyes, crying as he kissed his mother's cheeks to wake her up. Tears couldn't flow out of his eyes, he couldn't cry. He was drifting into space, wondering what he should do with his mother tomorrow. That night he was supposed to pick up Saul at the airport, who just got married six months ago. Julie wasn't with him because she had to be in Paris for an agricultural seminar. So Saul decided to come and spent the time with him. Julie was supposed to meet him in Haiti after her seminar. When Saul didn't see him at the airport, he took a cab over, wondering what was going on with Louis and why was he not at the airport to pick him up just as he promised. When Saul's taxi pulled into the driveway he noticed there was an ambulance at the front door of the estate. Hurrying inside, he saw everyone moaning in distress.

He asked, "Francois, what is going on here? Where's Louis?"

Francois was crying out loud, he could barely speak. He pointed his finger to the direction of the living room. Everyone stood outside of the living room crying. Saul rushed to see what was going on. Henry was standing at the entrance of the door crying. Louis was holding his mother against his chest. No one was able to come near him to take her away from him.

Louis thought Saul was moving in slow motion toward him and that his voice sounded the same. Tilting his head at one side to look at Saul, he whispered, "Welcome home, brother. Don't make too much noise. My mother fell asleep in my arms and I don't think she wants to be disturbed."

Shocked by Louis's logic and the sight before his eyes, he held back his tears and whispered, "Let me put her to bed so she can feel more comfortable."

Gently he took Margaret away from Louis's arms and carried her out of the room to her bedroom.

"Francois," Saul whispered, "call the paramedics!"

"Yes sir," Francois responded, with tears streaming down his face. "Dr. Janvier refused to let anyone near him or his mother. They're out in the lobby waiting. I'll go call them."

Richard had let the paramedics in and directed them to Margaret's bedroom. There was nothing they could do. She was dead with the first bullet she had received. Police and detectives were all over the estate grounds searching for clues and questioning everyone who was present on the estate. No one was able to give them a clue as to what took place, and Louis was not about to talk to anyone. They took pictures of her body and then took her out of the house to the morgue.

Many felt it was Louis's fault that his mother was killed. He was too arrogant. They thought by his mother being out of the picture, Louis would lose his strength and they would have the upper hand. Little did they know they had revived "The Lucifer Monster."

Louis never said a word except to Saul, who knew how to get a word out of him. Under his dark shades he watched how everyone acted during his mother's funeral.

Nadine was clinging to him as she cried her pretty head off. Like her, Louis now was totally an orphan. Maxine was there, standing by Jacque with the rest of her family. Saul stood at a distance shedding a few tears for him in silence under his shades, wondering what was on Louis's mind. Looking at his demeanor, he could guess Louis's plan.

Saul's eyes said excellent to Louis.

Henry was standing beside Saul looking at Louis and wondered if he would be okay.

People from different towns came and gave him their condolences, and there were those among them who came to see him wither. Louis had a hunch as to who the person was behind the death of his mother and thought he was safe because he was one of the big guys.

After the funeral, they all clung to his domain like it was their own. They even made plans before him how they would like to buy his place, and the money they were offering was a generous offer. He said nothing. He watched how they debated among themselves as if he was not alive. They had forgotten, at the age of eighteen he was the king of his castle.

Louis felt alone as he cried in silence. Never had he prayed before as he was doing now. In his heart he cried out God's name, asking him for help, because at that moment he was beginning to lose all his senses. His life had come in touch with death and she'ol itself just gave a new birth to him. He began to feel like a monster, and he was now to sit with the dead. . . . With all his physique he was out of strength, like he was being reborn, coming out of his mother's belly. Free from thinking and a man without a conscience he had become; he couldn't remember the joy of being alive. Rage was what filled his very soul, and he felt he was being afflicted, and the only way he was to be free was to let out the raging anger that had filled him. Out of the pit he was coming. His eyes were filled with anguish because of his affliction. No one was able to detect his distress, the terror that was within him, because is acquaintances were in dark places.

He was detestable even to his very own soul, and to everyone who came not to know him, except to judge him without trying to know who he really was.

Among the guests was Jean Ladin, an Assyrian mobster who was born in Haiti. He wanted to take Louis's mother as his wife. But Louis felt he wasn't suitable enough for his mother. Jean Ladin became enraged and wanted him dead for being an insolent child. He had forgotten he had three beautiful daughters. Louis seduced them all. They were able to tell Louis what was going on in their homes. Louis became a good friend of the family, and Jean Ladin thought he had Louis under his wing, finally.

Meanwhile, little did he know that Louis was screwing with his daughters' minds, having all kinds of illicit sex with them and having his friends join him occasionally!

Saul didn't want to bring his wife in the picture because Louis wasn't himself. Although he was in Haiti, because of all the traumas Louis was going through, he never had a chance to meet her. Nor did Saul let her know that he knew Louis or even men-

tion Louis's name, not even around the Bassine family, who knew he was Louis Janvier's best friend. Julie never suspected anything. Saul had her thinking he was in Haiti to buy some land and he wasn't going to leave until he found some nice-sized land not too far from the city for a ranch house and for a coffee plantation. But the real reason was, Saul wasn't going to leave Haiti until he helped Louis solve his problems.

Jean Ladin thought he could force Louis to join his organization. Louis either sold out or had to leave town. Another word—exile. Louis, of course, didn't want to disappoint him, because that was what he wanted at that time.

He declared, "You're the better man, Jean Ladin, and what better man to deal with now if it's not you?"

Boy, was he taken by Louis's charm. Louis was very obedient to all his wishes. It was do what you were told to do, and don't you dare ask any questions.

He gained Jean Ladin's trust and he was telling Louis he looked at him as if he was the son he never had. Louis was happy to hear that. He had a family again, which he told Jean Ladin. He opened up to Louis in less than three months.

Louis studied hard and learned everything he needed to know about the business. Before Jean Ladin knew it, he was signing his wealth away to Louis. Louis talked one of his daughters into asking her father to marry her with him. She was very happy to know that Louis wanted to marry her among her two sisters.

Jean Ladin held a party on that account. He invited some of his relatives and most of his friends to his daughter's engagement party. Some of his friends traveled far to witness the engagement.

The party was going well and the time had come for Jean Ladin to announce his daughter's engagement to Louis.

"Everyone," Jean Ladin stated. "You know today is a special day for me. One of my daughters is preparing to get married to a very respectful young and talented man. I'm sure some of you already know him well. I grew to love him as my own son."

Louis thought that man had to be joking. The murderer of my mother thinks of me as his son. Today I'm going to do something to provoke him more than ever. Death will also come in his household, as he brought to mine!

Louis didn't let Saul in on that plan. As Jean Ladin was talking, Louis whispered to Saul, "I want you to take Henry out of here. It's going to get nasty in here."

Saul asked, "What are you going to do?"

Louis didn't answer. Saul and Henry were surprised when Jean Ladin announced Louis as his future son-in-law, then asked Louis to make a speech.

Again Louis whispered to Saul, "You and Henry get out, now."

Looking at Henry, Saul whispered over his shoulder to him, "Fuji wants you to leave."

"I'm not leaving," Henry whispered back. "I'm going all the way with him, even if I have to die."

Louis stood up with his glass in his hand and said, "I never thought I was going to have a future." He smiled, looking at his daughters. "I love having sex with all you three together . . . I don't know how I'm going to sleep with just one of you. I don't think it's fair to the other two to let you out in the cold. The only way I'll marry you is if your two sisters promise they'll continue to be in my bed whenever I want them to be."

"What is the meaning of this, Louis?" Jean Ladin exclaimed with a killing look in his eyes.

"What don't you understand?" Louis said, tasting his drink. "I'm screwing all three of your daughters. Why give me one, when I could have all three of them?"

Jean Ladin stared at his daughters. He didn't know which one of them he wanted to kill first. But he knew Louis's butt was going to be barbecued. And he was not going to show him any mercy for the humiliation.

Louis toasted to the daughters and the guests. "Here's to foursomes!"

Saul told Henry, "Get ready, it's going to get nastier in here."

Everyone stood in shock. Saul laughed and thought, I hope Henry remembers what we taught him well. There is going to be bloodshed tonight.

One of the man's relatives said, "Insolent child! How dare you insult the family elder!"

"Don't you people know I'm grown now," Louis replied. "I have no parents to answer to, thanks to that bastard Jean Ladin. That makes me qualified to be grown, as old as you old hags here." He pointed his finger to all the older women who were present.

One by one Jean Ladin's friends and relatives left the house, murmuring about what was happening. Before he knew it, the place was left with Louis, his two friends, and the thugs who belonged to Jean Ladin. Jean Ladin's daughters were looking at each other, wanting to die. Their father walked to them and slapped them.

Grabbing his hand, Louis slapped him right back. The girls ran off, leaving the premises. Some of the men pulled out their guns on him and wanted to shoot him, along with his friends.

Louis felt he was responsible for them and he wasn't about to let that happen. He had metal darts in his pockets, which he threw at the men's hands to disarm them. Some brought out their machetes to chop him.

The man who had shot his mother said, "I'm going to kill you just like I did your mother!"

Henry said, "Why does the villain always confess his crime before he meets his maker?"

Before the man responded Louis had already ripped his heart out. The man's body stood in shock and so did Henry. Never had he seen Louis fight like that. He knew Louis knew how to fight, but to be able to rip a man's heart out of his chest was something he never dreamt to see. He had to go into a corner to throw up. His stomach couldn't take what he just witnessed.

Louis was like the devil when Henry looked at him; his eyes looked like they were on fire. Jean Ladin was trying to reason with Louis. He offered Louis everything he had to spare his life. He even promised to leave town just as he wanted Louis to do. Louis was not about to show mercy at the moment.

"Why would you give to me things that are already mine in the first place? You have nothing to offer but your miserable self. Sacrifice it to me, for your daughters' lives."

Louis handed him a gun. He watched as Jean Ladin put the gun to his own temple and squeezed the trigger, blowing his own head off.

Henry went up to check what had happened to the girls. By the time he went up the stairs the girls had killed themselves. They left a note signed, "I love you, Louis."

Afterward, before Saul went home to his lovely wife, he burned his clothes, took a shower, and wore another suit. The following day he took his wife back to New York. He spent three months without hearing from Saul.

The Jean Ladin incident made headlines in every newspaper in town, even overseas. No one was able to pin him for all that killing that took place, even those who had left the party the minute he declared his statement. They wouldn't dare accuse him of such a crime. One had to be a superman to do such an act. And he was no such one. And those who were at the party who went against him didn't live to speak the truth, because to him, they all were a bunch of two-faced murderers. Yes, Louis thought, he bathed in the blood of his many enemies. That was the most violent thing Louis could remember he did. He tried not to repeat history.

He thanked God for the woman Julie was, the loving woman he wanted all his life. She would stand by him and not put up with his nonsense. He had seen the miracle of God. From the pit of hell, God had taken him to instruct him once more about the meaning of life. After all these years in darkness, he was happy to see that God didn't abandon him. He removed him out of the belly of *she'ol* and brought him back to life. Now here came Jacque, trying to revive the monster in him, like an instigator from hell debating for his soul.

Removing himself from his bed, Louis knelt before it with his head down, praying to God for salvation to set his path straight, asking God to unify his heart to fear his name. Like King David he begged God to instruct him, praying God to turn his face on him, to help him to do the right thing. He was feeling distress and he knew God was the only one who could bring him happiness. He recalled the instructions Julie had listed to him of how he was to pray. And he'd been following the guide, calling upon the name of the Lord for guidance and to give him strength not to lose his sanity.

The first weekend of the following month was approaching. Louis wanted to make up for the lost time. He invited Julie and her mother back to the ranch, and also Maxine and Richard.

That next morning, Jacque and Carine were in the library going over the documents that belonged to Julie.

"Cat," Jacque jubilantly said to Carine, "I have all the papers. Fix me a drink."

Walking to the bar to fix the drink, she asked, "Now that you have all the papers, what's holding you back from signing the contract with Louis?"

She handed him the drink. He raised the glass to his lips, smiling like a predator. "Waiting for Mrs. Philip to sign these documents. When she thinks she is going to turn me down, she will be surprised and too embarrassed to do or say anything when she learns I'm her husband and she's my wife. And by the time she realized that, it will be too late for her to annul the marriage. Then we'll move with her to America. That's where the real deal is."

"Julie seems to enjoy Louis's company. She has spent a lot of time with him. Louis doesn't even want her out of his sight. How are you going to get her to sign them and get her to marry you?"

"I thought I told you already," Jacque agitatedly repeated. "So far I let her know how much I love her and how I want to help her. Eventually she'll take it to heart. . . . And for all I care, she could enjoy Louis's company as much as she wants and he's also looking at Viviane, too. Louis is a dog. He is not going to marry her anyway. To me, extramarital sex would be a good advantage on my part. I don't have to give up anything or anyone . . . got that?"

Carine smiled and said, "You have invested a lot of time and effort into this."

She lifted up the papers and examined them. "So many big words in French, it is hard for me to understand. She's going to have a hard time to understanding the documents. Even I have a hard time understanding them, brother."

Carine looked at him admiringly. She kissed him on his cheeks happily. "She will never know that she has signed everything over to you and she herself has become Mrs. Bassine."

There was a knock on the door. Jacque quickly hid everything. Then she moved toward the door. Jacque made a gesture with his hand for her to open the door, saying, "Open the door."

Carine opened the door to see Jean on the other side. "Jean, what are you doing here?"

Looking at her strangely, Jean walked past her into the room. "I live here, you know, and I want to talk to you two."

"About what?" Jacque asked, putting his arm around Jean's shoulders. "It's been a long time since we talked, little brother."

Jean shook his arm off. "I'm as tall as you, maybe even taller, so I'm not little and I would appreciate it if you call me by my name."

Stepping back at the tone of his voice, Jacque said, "Jean, what's brings you here?"

Looking from one to the other, Jean said, "I learned that you never gave the documents to Henry. It's been over a year now."

"What documents?" Jacque asked.

"Don't play that game with me, Jacque," Jean blasted. "I was there when Saul told you to hand Henry the documents for the ranch he was building for his wife and the rest of his property papers! Now, it has been almost two years since you promised you were going to do so, and you're telling me you never did! I thought you were smart. Louis is going to come after us with everything he has! Nicole, Maxine, and I don't want to be part of your trickery! The games you're playing, you two better stop. Eventually Julie and Aunt Viviane will catch on! And Louis will eat our heads alive if you challenge him! Julie and Aunt Viviane don't deserve that. Please, Jacque, don't let your moronic ambition get to you."

"And what game is that, crazy Jean," Carine said as she laughed.

Jean answered, "You two have no decency," pointing his finger at them. "If you don't stop, I'm going to tell Julie what you two are up to."

Jacque sat slightly on the edge of the table, looking at his brother who was calm and looking at him straight in the eye. "You're serious. . . ?"

Jean replied, "You know I am. . . ."

"You're one stupid fool." Jacque gave a deriding laugh as he placed his drink on the table and walked toward his brother Jean. "I should have gotten rid of you a long time ago. You did nothing but run around town having fun, never taking any real responsibilities as a man. If you stand in my way, like I told you before—I'm sure you remember the accident that took place awhile back. Because I never did, I swear, brother, I will really hurt you. You are either on my side or no side at all. You dare to come here to accuse me and to tell me what to do."

Jean laughed. "You watched the *Godfather* too much, the movie got to you. You better come to reality. Michael Corleone, whatever his name was, was a movie character, and the writer sets the plot like that. But the reality is you'll get hurt, maybe worse, killed. Brother, be kind to yourself, be a man of honor. You'll succeed. You already have something big going on for you. Don't blow it!"

"You know why Louis likes you, Jean? Because you are a low-life ass-kisser, lazy, having nothing to offer, and one who cannot stand on his own."

Jacque continued insulting Jean. Jean lifted his hands and punched him in his face. Jacque didn't hesitate. He jumped on him and they started to roll on the floor fighting like two bulls in a pen. Carine screamed, "Stop it! Stop it, you two! This is insane!"

She tried to separate them, she was knocked on the floor. "Please you two, stop!"

"I was out of my mind for too long," Jean said as he punched Jacque on the face, "but I'm awake now, and I say no more!"

When Carine realized Jean was doing a number on Jacque and they were oblivious to her screams, she ran out of the library screaming, "Roy, anyone, help! They're killing each other!"

Jean was punching and kicking Jacque. All the rage Jean had been hiding inside for his big brother was displayed without mercy. Roy and Marie rushed in and found Jacque and Jean at each other. Jean was hurting Jacque badly. Roy and Marie were trying to separate them with the help of the whole staff. Jacque yelled at him, "You're good for nothing! If you think I'm going to let you use the family's wealth to do whatever you want, I'd rather see you dead! You'll not live to see a cent!"

Jean yelled back, "You're the low-life, Jacque, but this time my back was not turned, brother. Max was right. I was a coward not to kick your ass a long time ago and straighten Carine with her bad ways. If you ever put your hands on the girls and hurt them, I will dismember you. Let me go, Roy. . . ." Roy released him. "If it's a challenge you're looking for, you've got one. I will kick your butt if you ever mess with me again or the girls! You're going to wake up one day and find yourself in a poor house. Just remember not to call me, because you are going to stay there."

Carine turned to Jean and screamed like a maniac, "Get out of my house, get out!"

Sneering Jean replied, "Your house? I hope you didn't let Jacque's stupidity, jealousy, and greed get your head, big sister. If you did, you need psychiatric help. The only person who can put me out of this house is Julie or Aunt Viviane, because it's their home. Don't let the Bassine title go to your head. They named the habitation 'Bassine Mansion' because it was Julie's choice. She wanted to make all the Bassine children feel at home. Please remember that you have nothing but helping Jacque with his dirty schemes. You better wake up, Carine. Louis is moving in, whether you or Jacque want it or not. You better get your act together. Louis is going to make you work for every dime you fish out of Julie's pocket. Carine, I feel very sorry for you, because you don't know what lies ahead of you. You better change your ways. When Jacque goes down, believe me, you'll go down with him."

Marie was still holding on to Jean. Turning to her he said, "I'm all right, Marie. I'm not going to waste anymore of my strength and time on those two again. Now I understand what Louis meant when he said, his time is precious and he's not about to waste time on those who have no worth or value."

Marie released him. He walked toward the door to go out of the room. Then Jacque turned on Marie and said, "Tell your son to keep away from my sister, Maxine."

Jean paused and waited to hear her response. She answered with dignity, "My son is a grown man and I don't presume to tell him whom he should talk to or get involved with. I don't tell you how to do your business, so therefore, however my son chooses to run his life is none of your business."

Jacque screamed, "So you think because Louis begged me to hire you, that means I can't fire you? You're fired!"

Marie screamed right back, "No, Jack-ass, I quit!"

She walked out behind Jean, him apologizing for being the cause of her losing her job, "I'm sorry, Marie."

She waved his apology away. "It's time I took care of myself and use my time on quality people. I was only here to serve Julie. I am not about to waste my time on this wastebasket, Jacque."

Without a backward glance at him, Marie and Jean walked out. Jacque stood by the door screaming, "Get out before I kill one of you! Get out!"

Marie went to pack her things. Roy didn't say anything. Slowly he walked out of the door as Jacque ordered him, "Roy, close the door behind you."

Jacque turned back inside the room, fixing his shirt inside his pants. He turned to Carine and said, "Fix me a drink, and this time make it a double."

Carine went to do as he asked. "What was that all about?"

Wiping the blood off his mouth with his handkerchief, he shook his head disgustedly. "Can you believe this? Maxine with the maid's son, and Jean the useless one. What's next? I could just grind their heads in a coffee machine."

Carine handed him his drink, then looked at his face and said, "Your handsome face is not messed up. "It's not so bad. You'll live."

He gulped his drink and took out the documents that they were looking at before. "Where was I . . . oh yes! I'll deal with Jean and Max another time. . . ."

Pointing at the documents, Jacque continued explaining to Carine how happy he was that no one was here for the weekend. He could plan better and have everything straightened out for Julie by the time she returned.

Meanwhile, Brian Bravé was over at the Janvier estate. He was in Louis's office putting some envelopes into his briefcase when he learned that Jacque Bassine had fired Marie Landers. He was getting ready to go to the plantation to meet with Louis. After taking care of some business for Louis Janvier, he asked Francois, her husband, to come to his office.

"You know," Brian said, "you and your family are always welcome at Louis's and he will do anything for you and your wife. Soon I'll be leaving. Louis is waiting for me at the plantation. We have many things to take care of and go over. Do you have the list of things that Louis needs you to do?"

Francois fished it out of his pocket and handed it to Brian. "Yes. It's on me."

The phone rang as Brian was about to leave. He answered, "Hello? Oh, Jacque, what's up? . . . Oh, you do? . . . What kind? . . . What's in it for me?" Brian was surprised when Jacque offered him that much money. "Forty thousand." He sat back, listening to Jacque's proposal. He let Jacque know the partnership sounded great. Jacque wanted him to keep Louis busy till he was finished doing some personal business with Julie. And if everything worked out on Tuesday, Brian would profit a great deal!

Brian assured him, "That's sounds pretty easy, but what's your gain?"

He already knew what Jacque would gain, but wanted to hear his explanation. "You'd better not double-cross me, Jacque. And when will I get my share? . . . All right, I have to go. Louis does not like lateness."

294

He hung up the phone, removed the recording tape from the receiver, picked up his briefcase, and headed out for the plantation. While he was on his way to the ranch, he passed Jean and Nicole. They were also going to the ranch. He waved hello to them and continued driving as fast as he could, listening to what Jacque and he had said. He arrived two hours earlier than Jean at the ranch.

It was 12:30 in the afternoon, and all those who were going away for the weekend had already left. The roads were easy to travel through. Most of the people had already gone away for the weekend. Brian Bravé had all the documents Louis had asked him to bring with him to the ranch.

Louis was sitting with Henry and Richard in his office talking when Brian arrived. He walked in and greeted them. The way Brian looked at Louis told him something was up.

Louis stood up to looked out of the window. He stood there for a few minutes to meditate, listening to Henry and Richard talking. He turned with his eyes closed and leaned against the wall by the window enjoying the feel of the sun on his face. Then he opened them to look at Richard.

Richard got up to leave. Louis asked, "Do you want to be part of our conversation, Richard?"

Richard knew what he was getting involved in, but he looked at him straight in the eye and answered, "Yes, I do, Louis."

Nodding his head in understanding, Louis looked at him and said to Brian, "Talk."

Brian began to tell him what he had learned and all the plots that were being planned. Richard listened carefully while Brian was talking. He didn't say a word. He was listening and learning. He'd always wanted to be part of Louis's regime. It was like a dream come true. He was looking into Louis's eyes and trying to figure out what color they were. He knew his eyes were hazel, but he was never able to make out the real color of Louis's. Were they blue or were they green? When the sun shone in them, they glowed like fire. His eyes were glaring at the moment. Richard thought fire was about to shoot out of them.

He blinked for a couple of seconds to come to his senses. Richard and Louis were not far apart in age. Louis was only five months older than him. When Brian was finished, Louis asked Richard, "What do you think?"

Richard didn't think for a moment. Without hesitation he answered, "I think this guy is dangerously greedy."

Louis was still standing by the window. He crossed his arms and did not say a word for a good ten minutes, looking out of the window through the yard. They, too, didn't say anything. They sat quietly waiting for Louis to snap back to the present. Then he turned to Brian and said, "Did you bring what I asked you?"

Lifting up his briefcase, he took out the envelope and handed Louis the documents. Louis read them, examining each page carefully. He smiled and said, "Well, today, she must know everything."

Richard said, "What would you like me to do for you, Louis?"

"Keep everyone entertained," Louis said and looked at his watch. "Use the music room if you must. I want to be alone with Julie."

Julie and Maxine were by the pool having cocktails when Patrick came in and told Maxine that Jean and Nicole were here to see her. This was even better for Louis, a better opportunity to be totally alone with Julie on their ride. Maxine seemed nervous. "Jean and Nicole are here to see me? It must be very important."

Julie asked her, "You want me here, Maxine?"

She said, "No, I'll fill you in later. Go have fun with your future husband. I'm going to do the same here."

Louis took Julie to the same spot they were before. He wanted to know if Julie had gotten over the situation they had between them. He sat her on the same position she was before she had jumped off the rock. Feeling weird, Julie said, "Is it me? Or did this scene already take place?"

He replied, "When I brought you here the last time, it was to tell you how much I love you."

Julie closed her eyes and sighed as he remembered. Smiling Julie looked at him from her perch of the rock, as if she heard Louis's voice whispering, "*I'm lost without you.*"

She pulled him by the collar to come closer to her. Then she lifted his face to look at her and softly kissed him. "I know."

She hugged him. Louis only knew that he was happy she had gotten over the condition they were in. He moved between her legs and put his arms around her waist. He gently tasted her lips as he framed her face with his hands and kissed her on her forehead and repeated, "I love you, Julie. I love you so much I ache."

He closed his eyes as she opened her lips and allowed him access to her mouth. After a while she lifted her lips from his, and holding his face between her hands, she said, "What's next? Where do we go from here?"

"I want you to marry me," he said as he put his hand in his pocket and took out a solitaire diamond ring. Julie had never seen such a nice-sized rock. "But before you answer, promise me you'll say yes."

She put her hand on her mouth and with tears pouring down her face, joyfully said, "Oh, Louis! Yes!"

Pretending that he hadn't heard her, he said, "What? I don't understand." Julie covered her mouth with her hand and laughed joyously as he tickled her. "What are you saying?"

Taking her hands from her mouth, she screamed with laughter. She had never been so happy. Julie yelled, "Yes, yes, I'll marry you! I love you!"

Louis had yearned to hear her say she loved him again. He grew serious as he took her left hand and placed the ring on her finger. Kissing her fingers one by one he said, "Marvelous."

He tilted her chin and said, "I'll spend the rest of my life to make sure you never regret your decision. This I vow to you."

Possessively he claimed her mouth once more in a kiss while helping her off the rock. He said, "Oh, there's something else I want to show you, come!"

He whistled to call the horses. They cantered up to him. She said, "My, this is interesting!"

They rode back to the barn where he handed the horses over to the barn man. This time they were using the Jeep. As they drove off, she said, "What surprise lies on this road for me?"

Without taking his eyes off the road, he answered, "Over two years ago Saul brought a few acres of land next to my land. This was where he was planning to build his home, where you and Bill were suppose to live."

"We were going to be neighbors," Julie interrupted. "You guys thought of everything."

Louis continued, "Since he passed away, the project took another course. I learned that the engineer he hired planned to steal the land and to turn it into a resort place."

"Can the person do that?"

Louis said, "Only if you sign the papers over. . . . Oh we're here!"

He drove slowly over the land so she could see the extent of it.

"How big is this land?" she asked in awe.

"One hundred and sixty-two acres that stretch to the sea belong to you."

Julie looked at him to see if he was serious. "Why didn't Saul tell me?"

"Because it was supposed to be a surprise."

"These lands would be good for my animals. Who's trying to steal the lands?"

Somehow she knew the answer before he spoke. Sitting back and resting her head on the seat, Julie closed her eyes and sighed. "Jacque! He showed me two acres of land in the city. He said this was what Saul left for me while he was in Haiti. The land was in Delmas. And you know Richard is taking care of that project, the family center. He gave me the papers and every other documents to that land but he never said anything about these lands. Are you sure these are my lands, Louis?"

"I have the deed for these lands," Louis replied. "And many other documents that belong to you. Saul sold me half of everything. I was his partner in the hotels and the shipping company and also the community I'd show you."

"Partner!" Surprised Julie replied, "Jacque told me Saul sold out everything to this unknown buyer, that's the reason he decided to build 'Jacque's Palace' on his own. He told me that Saul told him to give Henry Claude the deed to some lands which he never showed me, and that Saul had gambled away all the money while he was in the Dominican Republic."

"Saul wasn't a gambler," he said defensively, "and he didn't go to the Dominican Republic. Jacque must have been referring to himself."

"I knew Saul wasn't a gambler, but where was he then?"

"When you had arrived in Haiti the very first time," Louis said, "Saul was still here. He was staying with me. I thought I told you that already when I was explaining our situation."

"So much information at once, my mind must have skipped that part." Knowing the type of a man Louis was, Julie sneered, "So Saul was with you!"

Louis smiled. "Saul was a faithful man, Julie. He wouldn't do anything to dishonor you. . . . And yes, he was with me. The night you were at Nadine's, Saul was there, too."

"He was?" Julie said. "Where was he? How come I didn't see him?"

"Saul and I were playing chess in the room when Nadine brought you in to meet me. He wanted us to meet that night. He was hiding. He didn't want you to see him. He felt revealing that he was here wouldn't be good for you or for him. He didn't want to complicate things too much. So the following morning he went back to New York. I dropped him off at the airport before I came for lunch. He made me promise to handle things here for him."

"Is that the reason there's no money in the bank?"

"I have the accounts," Louis said.

"Why?"

He explained, "Saul had transferred the account to your name. All you need to do is just put your signature on them. And plus Saul wanted you to slow down on giving Jacque money. Jacque wasn't satisfied with the amount you had given him. He was sneakily withdrawing money out of the account. You would have to pay close attention to notice that. And by the time you would have realized it, you would have had no money in any of the accounts."

"I knew there were logical explanations to all the mystery going on," Julie said. "There was barely any money in any of our accounts here in Haiti. And Saul was right, I spoiled Jacque. I gave him a lot of money to help him with his hotel. Now I understand why Jacque was furious. He no longer had access to any of the accounts."

"Jacque was going to use your money to invest with you." They both chorused a laughed, then Louis continued, "When Jacque couldn't invest with Saul, he noticed Jacque went mad. And he was going to take over. If he gave Jacque the chance. Jacque would have left you with nothing. He wants to control your means of life. And Jean wasn't up to the part. So Saul entrusted me with them. I have many other documents that Saul gave me to take care of you here. He suspected that Jacque was not leveling with him. Jacque wants to take these lands. Everything! He wasn't satisfied with what Saul gave him to build his hotel."

She was stupefied. "Saul gave him the lands!"

"Jacque didn't tell you about it?" Louis boiled with rage. "Then again, how could he? He's so busy putting Saul down. I guess what Saul gave him was valueless. . . . I have to take over this project without his knowledge. I made sure he wasn't able to come down here to see what was going on. I told him I'll be his partner and I'm willing to put up all the money if he could come up with all the documents of your lands to show me the lands belong to him. Right now, he's occupied on getting those documents together."

They stayed silent for a moment looking at the view, walking around the house that was completely built. There were people wiping the windows and the floor all inside the place. Watching the workers at work, some were planting trees. Julie was admiring the lands and the construction that had been done on the land.

They walked back and sat inside the car. Julie stretched as she admired the richness of the land. "It's so beautiful, so green and peaceful. You did all these works. Are you sure these are mine?"

Clasping both her hands in his, he said, "*Tous c'est pour toi. Je suis sûre* (It's all for you. I'm quite sure). I have all the documents to prove it."

She tried to make sense of the situation she was now facing with Jacque. "I used to think it would have been Carine who would have tried to pull a stunt like that. She always wanted everything I have, ever since we were children. Not Jacque, I tried so hard to help him."

"Maybe that's the reason. Some men can become resentful for that. You help too much."

For a moment, Julie looked remote. Louis watched her as she spoke. "As a child, I used to come to Haiti every chance I got. I love the country, the people in it. It's amazing I never had a chance to meet you."

Louis smirked. "You wouldn't have liked me then."

"You wouldn't have liked me either," she replied. "I was a nerd, I wore braces, I was a tomboy. I used to play with lizards and snakes!"

"So did I. We have a lot in common."

She went on to say, "I was the only girl in private school who could climb a coconut tree. . . ."

Louis burst into laughter and repeated, "Coconut tree? This I would love to see!"

"But then, if you would have come near me," Julie replied, "I would have kicked your butt."

"Believe me," biting and licking his lips Louis replied, "mm! I would have enjoyed it."

Cheerfully Julie laughed at what he said. She exclaimed, "Louis, you can be really funny when the mood strikes you. . . ."

He was staring at her with a gleeful smile. Looking back at him she said, " . . . And stop visualizing me climbing a coconut tree. . . . Well, anyway, Max was always the closest one to me. Jean was always indifferent. I was hoping he had grown out of it, and Nicole was hard to reach. . . . My parents are their godparents so they're like brothers and sisters to me. I never had any siblings, cousins, aunts, or uncles. . . . My parents were also the only children of their parents so my family line is limited. I thought I would be the one to extend the family line by filling the house with children. . . . The Bassines became my extended family."

Louis understood where she was coming from. Likewise, he was the only child. He wanted brothers and sisters. He never got any. He used to feel it was because he was such a spoiled child and that made his parents afraid to have other children. They didn't want to have any more like him. Later in life he learned that was not the situation. His parents wanted only him.

Louis proceeded to say, "Jacque's plan was to have you sign a marriage certificate and other documents on Tuesday. He thinks he is going to trick you into signing everything over to him. He wanted to take charge of everything you have here and have you marry him without your knowledge."

"Marry him!" Julie was adamant. "I will not put my signature on anything he gives me."

Louis said, "Yes, you will sign."

She thought he had lost his mind. "You want me to marry Jacque!"

"No," Louis reassured her. "You're not going to give him your lands or anything. You're going to sign his documents, but we already have the real ones so what he has are just the copies. I already took care of the judge who was working with him."

Julie was apprehensive. "What do you mean?"

Noticing the worried look on her face Louis chuckled. "I didn't kill him, I just had a talk with him. He was surprised. He didn't know he was dealing with me. Do you follow?"

Nodding her head, she whispered, "Louis, you're naughty! I love it . . . it sounds sneaky. . . ." She laughed. "That will be a good lesson for him. All his sick loving words to me, trying to play me look like a fool. Poor Debbie, she's crazy about him. Maxine thought she might be pregnant by him."

"She is!"

"When were you going to tell me this."

"I just did?" Louis replied.

"I thought he was working on paying me back, not trying to trick me."

Nodding, Louis said, "Why did he borrow all that money from you?"

"He told me he found an investor for his hotel, but he was short of cash. He needed money to back him up. And you know Jacque likes to live large."

Louis laughed. "Now you know who the investor is, it's even more interesting. Exactly what does Jacque have besides the new hotel, which I own half of? I saw the work you did on the plantation in Jacmel, and the people there are happy with what you did. That's a very nice job you did down there."

"He knows where I put those documents of those lands," she sighed. "I left them in the library behind the bookcase that stands behind the desk where he usually sits."

"Not anymore," Louis replied. "I had them removed already, and all other documents that belong to you were taken away and replaced. The only document we couldn't find was the deed to Bassine Mansion, and I'm not worrying about that. So whatever is inside the safe are just copies. Jacque thinks he is sneaky, but we're sneakier."

He smiled and pulled her closer to him to reassure her that everything would be okay.

"You are a very generous woman, my love. That is a rare gift you possess. I love that about you . . . but I despise anyone who took your kindness for a weakness." Gently he tilted her chin with his index finger to look down into her eyes with all the love he could feel. He said, "I vow before God, I'm going to do everything in my power to make you the happiest woman in the world . . . kiss me."

He bent his head to kiss her as he whispered, "Now I have reasons to live for."

She kissed him and then dodged away from him and slid out of the Jeep. "Try to catch me."

She took off on a run. He let her run a few feet from him, and then he jumped out and ran after her. Julie was very playful, and he watched her as she ran. Her laughter brought joy to his soul. Louis hadn't played like that since he was a little boy. At the age of eighteen he was already a man, making lifelong decisions for himself. Julie was truly innocent; she brought out the child in him. His smile was real when he was around her. Life had meaning from every angle to him.

He knew that with her at his side, he couldn't fail. He could wake up in the morning for a reason now, because Julie would be there to greet him with her perfect innocent smile and a hunger for adventure.

Julie shrieked when he tagged her. She ran after him but couldn't catch him. He allowed her to catch him. He grabbed her and they both fell and rolled over in the grass. He turned over so she was lying beneath him and said, "I never had a chance to thank you for the wonderful meal you had prepared for my workers and myself the last time you were here. You're not only beautiful, but also a talented cook too, and a skillful swordwoman. The workers will never forget your hospitality. You're truly worthy to be loved by all, and especially by me. I'm your slave, Julie. Your wish is my command."

Julie lay looking up at him with love shining out of her eyes. She was mesmerized by his mellow voice. Tilting her head up she thought, *If he doesn't stop talking and kiss me I'm going to die.* "Come and kiss me now."

Laughing at the command in her voice, Louis obliged. "At your service, my love."

They kissed for a good amount of time. Then he rolled her on top of him. She asked, "What are we going to do with these lands?"

"Anything you like."

"I notice you really put your heart on constructing this land. Not only the animals are going to enjoy it, but I'm going to enjoy running around with William. You did a beautiful job, darling." She pecked him on the lips. "I want to hire an animal specialist, a veterinarian. I feel this place would be perfect. The doctor could live in the house with his or her family. I can't live in two places when I'm married to you. . . ." Louis was staring at her as she spoke. "What's wrong?"

"I was wondering, am I dreaming you? Are you really here with me?"

"Let me bring you to reality," she replied. "Maybe with a kiss you'll wake up and find me here with you."

She kissed him like she had never done before. It was formidable. Louis felt her love was in that kiss she gave him as they drank from the fountain of each other mouths. He thought that kiss was different from all the kisses she had ever gave him. She took his breath away. He ran his hands in her hair, pushing it away from her face to admire her beautiful features. She seemed so feminine and fragile on top of him. He saw her beauty like a nymph vision. Never had he seen a woman as perfect as she was in his eyes. He confessed, "I don't believe in reincarnation, but I do believe each person has a soulmate. You see, the moment I saw your face I knew. From that moment, I knew I loved you. I had to have you, so I could be complete. Like Adam and Eve, Abraham and Sarah, Isaac and Rebecca, Jacob and Rachel."

"Excuse me," Julie broke in. She didn't look too happy. "But Jacob had two wives, Leah was his first, then Rachel."

"True," Louis carefully stated, because he remembered she didn't play when it came to relationships, "but for whom did he work hard?"

"Rachel!"

"He was tricked into taking Leah as his wife, but all his hard work was for Rachel. He served her father fourteen years for her. He worked hard to have her. His true soulmate was Rachel. All the others were thrown at him, they were just extras."

She laughed. He tried not to laugh along with her. He breathed in relief, because he knew better. She might take his head for mentioning the extras.

Kissing her, she smiled. "You're reading the Bible."

"Yes, I took your advice." He smiled. "I found it quite delightful. It's a refreshment to my soul."

Wrapping his arms around her he brought their faces together and parted her lips with his as he drank deeply of the kiss she was offering.

Back at the ranch, Jean, Maxine, Nicole, and Richard were in the lounge talking. Richard got up to leave Maxine with her family to talk, but Jean stopped him. "No, Richard, don't leave. . . ."

He was surprised. He turned to look at Maxine, wondering what was on Jean's mind. " . . . I need to apologize to you. I would like to properly introduce myself to you. . . ." Jean extended his hand to him. "I'm Maxine's second older brother, Jean Bassine."

"Nice to meet you, Jean Bassine," he smiled.

"I look forward to knowing you better," Jean said. "My sister is quite a catch. I hope you continue making her happy. What I'm going to say today is among the family and you are part of the family. You're Maxine's fiancée."

Taking Maxine's hands Jean said, "Maxine, you knew what was going on all along, and I was so blind with anger I failed to help you girls. You were right—I was a coward to let Jacque run our lives like this, almost to the point of destroying us. I let you all down. But I am not going to let that happen anymore. I am so sorry. Please forgive me. . . ."

Maxine hugged him and he hugged her back as he talked. " . . . And I'm going to work hard to set things straight, especially for Julie and Aunt Viviane, who have been supporting us for so many years. Not once did I say thank you to them and show gratitude. I feel so ashamed."

Nodding her head in agreement to what Jean said, Nicole said, "Thank you for the wake-up call, Max. I was heading down to the road of destruction. I was trying to please the wrong people. I was afraid to talk, because I knew Jacque would turn on me and hurt me if I went against him. Carine told me that I better do as they say . . . Carine and Jacque get along well."

Maxine let go of Jean. "Because they're the same, the evil twins."

Nicole said, "I'm sorry, Max. We all knew you were dating Richard, and it was no longer a secret for over a year. I knew you two were dating since the first week. I felt it was your business, not ours. You were grown enough to make your own decision, like Julie said. I couldn't believe Carine would have stooped that low. When I confronted her, she got so offended because I questioned her behavior. She didn't care I was dating Henry as long as he had what she wanted. I feel so dirty and dumb! She thought she got Henry to side up with her. And now when I think back, Henry had stopped taking me seriously because of the way I was behaving toward Louis and Julie, when I knew it was wrong. He warned me but I didn't listen. And I hurt myself by my own deviousness. . . . Yesterday, Carine pretended she didn't know you were dating Richard. She told Jacque. I knew all along and I didn't tell them. Jacque slapped me for not telling him about it."

She removed her shades and revealed the bruise by her eye. Richard then realized the bruises on Maxine's arm were no accident.

Maxine touched Nicole's face tenderly with tears in her eyes and said, "He did this to you? I'm sorry."

Richard quickly got up from his seat to check on Nicole's eye. He was upset. He put his arms around Maxine's shoulder to comfort her while she cried. Watching the tears in her eyes made Richard so unhappy.

Looking at Maxine, Jean spoke up, "That was one of the reason I went to confront them. It's been over ten years since I had kept quiet, but you've given me the strength to stand up for myself and face him, and I did. I fought him early this morning. And I swear if he ever puts his hands on you girls like that again, I'll dismember him." He turned to Richard. "He fired your mother too, Richard."

Richard replied, "I'm glad. Now I can deal with him better."

Aunt Viviane walked in with Bill running behind her. Jean and Nicole went to kiss her.

"Nicole, what's going on with you? . . . Oh, my!" She was aghast as she noticed the bruise on Nicole's face. "How did you get this on your face, child?"

"Jacque did this to me and Carine approved it."

Shaking her head sadly as she held tight on William's hand, Viviane said, "I knew he was a troublesome boy when he was young, but I never thought he was violent. . . ."

She sat with them to talk. " . . . I'm going to give you all a word of advice."

They all went and sat down while she spoke to them. She let them know she had suspected many things were going wrong with them because they used to call and write to her very often while she was in New York. She noticed many changes had taken place. And Maxine was trying to cover up for them. She was happy to see them here today talking about the situation they were in. She wasn't blind to any of it. She was just waiting to see how long they would let this game go on before they did anything. She didn't raise them to dominate each other the way she saw Jacque and Carine running their lives. And she had also seen that Maxine tried not to take their crap, but at the same time she felt alone because she thought she didn't have the support.

"Maxine, you're not alone," Viviane stated. "You'll never be. And Richard is a fine man. . . ."

Richard got off his seat and gave Viviane a kiss on her cheek for the compliment.

During that time while Viviane was talking to them, Julie was going over some documents with Louis and Henry in his office. Louis showed her everything and Jacque's plans. Brian had walked in to join them after he had gone to his car to fetch the tape he used to record the conversation between himself and Jacque. He handed it to Louis so they could listen to what had been said between Jacque and himself. They all listened to it. Julie sat in silence listening to every word that had been spoken between Jacque and Brian. She felt bad because she understood why Jacque chose Brian to help him with his scheme and she was happy to see that Brian was a man with honor, and Carine was a fool for not taking Brian as her husband.

All the while, Viviane continued talking to them, advising them about life. After a while later Louis and Julie walked in.

Julie greeted everyone cheerfully. "Hello, everyone. . . ." Then she stopped dead in her tracks when she noticed Nicole's face, putting her hands against her chest as if she felt her pain. " . . . Nicole, what happened?"

She walked to Nicole to look closer at her bruised face. Gently she touched her face and then looked at Maxine, who slowly nodded her head to Julie. She immediately understood what happened and turned to look at Louis.

Louis said to Nicole, "Have you seen a doctor, Nicole?"

She nodded her head. "Yes, Jean took me to the doctor."

She put her shades back on her face, and said, "Julie, I'm sorry about everything. I hope I can make it all up to you. You too, Louis." She turned and put her hands out for the toddler. "Can I hold the baby, Aunt Viviane?"

Viviane handed Bill over with caution, because she looked so frail. "He's kind of heavy. Will you be all right?"

Reassuring her, Nicole sat on the chair to hold Bill while she played with him. She said, "Boy, you're handsome."

She kissed his tiny hand. Louis walked over to Nicole and held out his hands for Bill. "Can I?"

Bill was almost jumping out of her hands to go to Louis. Handing him over, she smiled and said, "Sure. Look at him, he's so happy to see you."

Louis took William in his arms and gently kissed him and sat down on a single chair. Julie paid close attention to them while she sat talking to Jean.

After a couple of drinks and some good conversation, Jean turned to Louis with a smile and said, "Thank you for your hospitality. And Aunt Viviane, Julie, I'll see you back home. I'm glad that I dropped by. But it's getting late and we must start heading back home."

Louis spoke up, "Nonsense, you two are staying here. I will not take no for an answer. . . ." Loziane had just walked in with Bill's toy truck. "Please call Ninot for me."

She gave Julie the toy and went out to call Ninot as Louis requested. Julie gave him a kiss on his cheek for his thoughtfulness, then kissed Bill gently on the forehead. Julie reached out to take him, but William pushed her hands away and said, "Daddy!"

Maxine, who was standing close to Julie, heard, smiled, and whispered, "Did you hear that?"

Bill was grabbing and pinching his nose. Louis smiled and said, "There's something about my nose that my son just loves—ouch!"

"I think he's crazy about your nose," Julie replied as she removed his little hand off Louis's nose.

Loziane returned to the room with Ninot following behind her. She said, "*Oui*, Monsieur Janvier?"

Louis answered, "Please, prepare two more rooms for my guests, Jean and his sister Nicole, and tell George I want to see him."

Bowing, Ninot replied, "*Oui*, Monsieur Janvier."

She hurried to do his bidding. In less than a minute George entered the room, bowing. "Doctor Janvier."

Louis turned to George while playing with his son in his arms. "What event did you prepare for us, George?"

"Nothing big, sir," he answered. "A little dance and a little feast. It will start in about thirty minutes."

Looking at Julie, Louis said, "We'd better change."

He gave Bill to Loziane, took Julie's hand, and left the room. On the way up, Julie stopped and turned as she said to him, "Louis, is it wrong for me to want you as much as I want you now?"

"Only if you stop wanting me," he replied as he kissed her hands, "and that is when it will be wrong."

Passing her hands over his face, Julie circled his lips with her finger as she said, "Once, you had told me I never met a man who could make me lose my mind. And you told me you wanted the woman to be as much in love with you as you are with her. I want you to know you were right. You are that man and I'm losing my mind over you. And I'm so in love with you, I ache."

Louis smiled. "I'm glad to hear that."

Softly she nibbled his ears, making him lose his mind. She whispered in his ear, "I want you now. Make love to me. I want to make love to you."

Enjoying what she was doing, Louis whispered back, "Would you be able to live with yourself after the love making, Julie?"

"I'll get over it, I'm sure," she whispered as she continued nibbling on his earlobe. "And maybe sometime in the future we'll get married."

He breathed and gently moved away from her. "I wouldn't take that chance with you."

"Are you refusing me, Louis?"

"Yes! I mean no." Louis was all confused. He knew she would hate herself and maybe him for taking her offer. He wanted her much more than she thought. . . .

" . . . I need you, baby," he said, pulling her into his arms. He enfolded her and kissed her deeply. As if he was being tormented he moaned, "Uh, it's not right! That's a test isn't it? How much do I have to do to prove myself to you? Do you want to rip my heart out to check if I'm telling you the truth?"

"Forgive me," Julie answered. "That wasn't my intention."

Her eyes looked with despair as Louis scolded her. He looked at her firmly as she passed her hands over his face and he said, "I have taken your advice very seriously. I take fifteen minutes every morning and fifteen minutes every night reading the good book before I sleep. I prayed. Do you want to know why?"

Julie nodded her head for yes, as he continued, "The truth is, it is harder to keep away from you than for me to read the Bible. . . . Deadening my member isn't easy, and right now, you brought every part of me to life. I'm about to go crazy. . . ."

Louis again pulled her back in his arms and kissed her like a hungry man, then pulled away because that time Julie was not pulling away. She was drowning him with her passionate kiss. " . . . Please, Julie, stop torturing me. . . . I love you so much. What will it take, Julie, to prove my love to you?"

She took a deep breath and exhaled. "I want you, Louis. . . . I want to feel you in me, holding me and caressing me as I'm caressing you."

Looking up at the ceiling, Louis groaned, "Why are you putting me under this great trial? That isn't fair. It's too much for me to take. . . !"

Taking her hands he placed them against his chest. " . . . Do you understand how I really feel for you? You're every breath that I take. For the past year, I prayed to God for an obedient heart, to do well by you . . . I'm learning, Julie. This path is new to me, and I'm afraid. I don't want to do anything to hurt you. So please, no more testing for now. . . ."

As he was explaining his feelings to Julie, he looked at her face and saw she wasn't joking. He lifted her face and looking in her eyes said, " . . . I too feel the same way. I want you, Julie."

Holding her face with both of his hands, he kissed her on the forehead. " . . . I will not let you do something that goes against your principles. You told me you believe sex should only be in a marriage and I promised that I would not touch you until we get married. I'm not going back on my word. I love you too much to take that away from you. . . ."

Kneeling before her, he wrapped his arms around her and laid his head against her stomach and begged, " . . . Please, Julie, marry me tonight."

Julie was not expecting him to say that. Pressing her hands on his head, she lifted his face to look at her, wondering if she was hearing things.

" . . . All I want to do is to make you happy," Louis said and repeated, "Marry me tonight."

Trembling with excitement, she asked, "Is that possible?"

Getting back on his feet, he stepped back halfway down the stairs. Louis shouted, "Patrick!"

Patrick was on his way to the back of the house but at hearing Louis shout, he came running and said, "I never heard you shout before, Louis. Is there anything wrong?"

Louis was going like a fool. "Julie and I want to get married," he burst out excitedly.

Extending his hand, Patrick came forward to congratulate them. "Great! May I be the first one to congratulate you two?"

"Tonight! We want to get married *tonight.* I need a license and a priest," Louis demanded urgently.

Breathless, Julie interrupted him, "No."

"No, don't you want to get married tonight?" Louis asked with a dangerous glint in his eyes, hopping from one foot to another.

Julie hurriedly clarified her statement. "Yes, but a judge would be faster."

"That's even better," Louis said, turning back with a sign of relief. He started naming off the things he would need one by one to Patrick. "Get Judge Thomas and a marriage license or a certificate, and two witnesses."

Laughing, Patrick pointed. "You'll get plenty of witnesses."

"Do we have food and drinks?" Louis continued as his mind ran a mile a minute.

"More than enough," Patrick said.

"Good," Louis said joyfully. "Invite everyone on the plantation. How long will it take you to get everything ready?"

Patrick looked at his watch and said, "Give me an hour and a half."

"It's now six o'clock." Turning to go, Louis said, "So I'll see you at seven-thirty. If you see Henry, send him to my room."

His mind cluttered with plans, Patrick was already halfway down the stairs.

"All right," Patrick acknowledged absently. He ran to the den and Julie and Louis continued going up the stairs. At her door, Julie said, "See you later."

Blowing her a kiss, he continued on to his room. "I'll be there."

Upon hearing the news, Viviane sprang into action. With one breath she instructed Maxine, "Go up to my room. In the closet you'll find four boxes. Take them to Julie, help her get dressed and dress yourself. . . . Nicole please help fix the ballroom. You too, Loziane. Bring the flowers from Julie's room down to the ballroom."

George spoke up, "I'll take care of all the food and beverages." He left the room to instruct the rest of the servants.

"Everyone, hurry," Viviane continued. "There's a wedding tonight and Bill," speaking to the toddler in her arms, "you're the ring boy, so let's go get ready."

The ranch became a beehive of activity. Everyone was on the move. In less than an hour everything was ready. Julie was quickly washing herself. Maxine brought the boxes in and laid the gown on the bed. When Julie came out of the bathroom, she found Maxine was laying a gown on her bed.

"Where did you get this wedding dress?" she asked in amazement.

"Aunt Viviane," Maxine smiled and replied. "I love that woman. She doesn't play with time."

Julie walked over to the bed and tenderly stroked the satin ivory gown, with tears glistering in her eyes. She looked up and laughed. "My mother is always prepared. She must have got it in New York when Louis first proposed to me. The following day Louis wanted to spend the whole day with his son alone."

Putting her hands across her bosoms, Maxine smiled in relief. "Yes, *his* son."

"I said it didn't I?" She smiled back and repeated, "*Our* son. Boy, do I have a tale to tell my grandchildren. . . !"

Maxine nodded her head in agreement as Julie continued, " . . . And since the following day William was not with us. I took Mother to Chinatown for Chinese food. Then we took a nice stroll around town to Little Italy. I remember I was admiring this wedding gown on the mannequin in the window. I thought it was simple, but elegant. I didn't tell her about it. I guess she was reading my mind."

With Maxine's help, she put on her undergarments and did her hair. The gown was an off-white that formed her shape her well and the small matching hat had a short veil that only covered her eyes. There were also matching shoes.

Maxine stood back in awe. "Julie, look at you! You look so beautiful and oriental. Louis will fall in love with you all over again."

Maxine put on the other dress that was in the box, a beautiful sky blue gown with matching gloves and shoes. Likewise, she looked beautiful. She put her hair up with little bang-tails around to decorate her hairstyle.

Julie couldn't stop looking at herself in the dressing table mirror. "I never thought I was going to have a complicated life at all. But the minute I met Saul, my life became a roller coaster ride, from one adventure to another. That man had kept my feet off the ground the minute I met him. He impregnated me with a boy I dreamt of as a child, which happened to be his best friend, then fixed us together before he took off. Did I summarize it well?"

Maxine rhymed, "Very well! The stranger in black in your dream came back. And you two are so madly in love with each other, even more than before. That is one dream come true. What more can a woman ask than to be loved by two men. Your life story will be more than just a fascinating story to tell. It puts Romeo and Juliet's story to shame."

Julie replied, "He was always in black."

"I guess it was because he was always surrounded with death, and plus that is his style. He can't help it. I finally saw a smile on Louis's face. You bring life into his life, Julie."

"I feel like I'm walking on air. Louis makes me feel like an angel. Is this for real, Max? Am I really getting married again, with Louis Janvier? Am I dreaming this?" she asked out loud with a hint of unbelief in her voice. Maxine pinched her. "Ouch," she exclaimed.

"No, you're not." Maxine hugged her, reassuring her with admonishment. "Now stop thinking. You deserve your happiness. . . ."

Julie breathed in and out to calm herself down. She was getting anxious. Maxine wanted to make her laugh. She noticed that Julie was getting cold feet. " . . . Don't start the crying now, child. Save the shivering and the moaning for Louis tonight. You'll need all your energy. That wild man has not been with any other woman since the last time I opened my big mouth to squeal on him. Remember the pool table? That was more than a year ago. For a man like Louis, that was a castration, a death sentence. . . ."

Julie smiled and called her crazy. She listened to Maxine talk. " . . . I know for a fact many women would love to be in your shoes and you know it, too. Louis loves you with all his being and everything he has. . . . I will stop talking if you could picture any other man who could walk in Saul's shoes beside Louis. Then I would tell you don't get married tonight. . . . Louis has no doubts. He loves you, Julie, and I saw the hunger, the thirst, the craziness that is raging through your very soul right now. You want him, too." She held Julie's hands. "The family you dream to have is now in your grip. This is what the good Lord provides, so grab it with both hands and be happy, you and Bill."

A knock came at the door. Maxine called, "Who's there?"

A voice behind it answered, "It's Henry. . . ."

Opening the door slightly as she poked her head out, Henry handed her some documents with a pen and said, "Julie needs to sign these documents."

Julie took them from Maxine to sign them. Watching her signing the papers, Maxine got nervous, thinking that Julie didn't know what she was putting her signature on. She asked, "What are these papers and why are you signing them now?"

Julie explained to her she was supposed to sign them before she got married. Henry stood outside the door, while she signed the papers and handed them to Maxine to give to Henry. These were things from her previous marriage. Louis wanted to make sure she had everything that belonged to her and that no one could take them without her permission. She had read them all previously that afternoon. Julie reassured Maxine she knew what she was doing.

Henry brought the papers to Louis while he was getting dressed. "Julie signed them."

"Great." Louis smiled. "Everything is set."

"No," Henry replied as he pulled some documents out of his briefcase. "I will feel more at ease if you had her sign these papers, too."

"What papers are those.. . . ?

He handed them to him. Feeling dismay Louis was asked, "What is the meaning of this?"

Henry started to explain, "I had the feeling you were going to ask her to marry you, the way you were going. I didn't think you were thinking straight, so I took the liberty of drawing up this prenuptial agreement for you. I didn't give her to sign them yet, until I showed it to you. It's going to take less than five minutes to sign these papers and have her sign them."

"I'm glad you didn't show these foolish papers to her, because I don't need a prenuptial agreement."

He insisted, "Fuji, every wealthy couple has one."

Louis replied, "We're getting married, not divorced. . . . Believe me when I tell you this—only death will us part. And I don't believe Julie and I would ever die."

Henry ignored Louis's statement. He smiled. "It's a form of protection of your assets from one mate to another, and I'm sure Julie would agree to sign it."

"Since when did I need you to tell me what Julie would agree and not agree to. . . ?"

Henry didn't reply. Louis said, "Do yourself a favor—remove these documents out of my sight and never mention this to me again or even whisper this to Julie."

Henry was persisting. He questioned, "Fuji, are you sure she's the one you've been waiting for?"

Angered by Henry's question, Louis banged his hand on the dresser. "This will be the last time you'll ever ask me that question, and I'm going to answer it for you once and for all. I've never been more sure. Now pass me my tie, and never doubt her and me again. You're my best man. Act like it and be happy for me."

"I am happy for you, Louis," Henry rushed. "I just don't want to see you heartbroken, that's all."

"You worry too much, Henry," Louis said impatiently.

For a moment Henry didn't say anything, then he took the papers and tore them and threw them inside his briefcase. He stood there looking at Louis, then smiled. "You two are going to make a good team, a very good couple!"

Putting his arm around Henry's shoulder, Louis said, "Don't worry, you will find a good mate someday."

Downstairs, everyone was waiting and everything was almost ready. The judge and his wife were glad to assist and all the rest of the farmers were present with their wives. Everyone was dressed in their best clothing. No one wanted to miss that big event. They had all been waiting for this. Some had never been invited to such a special event. This was the first time, and they were not going to miss Louis Janvier's wedding for anything.

Before returning downstairs, Viviane went to her daughter's room to congratulate her with her joy and happiness. She also went to Louis's room to ask him for the rings so Bill could carry them.

Louis said, "I'm so excited, I almost forgot the rings. I have had the rings since the night you invited me to the cook-out. I knew she was my wife to be. Mother, is that strange?"

Tenderly she touched his face. "No, Louis, not at all. You chose a good woman and Bill will make a fine son. Go and make my daughter yours. Make her happy."

She kissed him on his cheek, picked up the rings, and left the room.

Nadine Janvier had just arrived. As she greeted Viviane, Nadine asked, "What's going on here?"

She noticed everyone was dressed up and all the hustle and bustle that was going on. Viviane replied, pulling her into the room with the rest of them, "A wedding."

"Whose?" Nadine asked in surprise.

Viviane replied enthusiastically, "Julie and Louis's."

Nadine answered as she glanced from Viviane to Nicole, "And they didn't invite me?"

Brian walked in wearing a tux. He was just happy to see Nadine.

Viviane hastened to tell her, "No one knew till an hour ago."

Henry and Louis looked sharp in their black tuxedoes as they descended the stairs. Nadine walked over to meet them, stuck out her hands to Louis, and said, "Congratulations, cousin. I was on my way here for hours. Traffic was terrible."

Pulling her close, Louis hugged her joyfully. "I'm glad you're here Nadine, Brian."

Brian and Louis shook hands as they hugged. Brian congratulated him, then Louis turned to Nadine and hugged her again and said, "I was afraid you were going to miss my big day."

Laughing with exhilaration, she asked, "Who else knows about this?"

Henry responded, "The farmers and us—no one else."

Nadine was relieved. "Great. I'm glad there's no reporters here."

Patrick called everyone's attention, "The ceremony is about to begin. Places. Places! Louis, Henry, your position is over here, the small table here is where you and your future wife will sign the license, and the judge will stand here."

While Patrick was busy arranging with Aunt Viviane, the judge said to Louis, "I never thought I'd live to see this day."

Louis shook his hand gratefully. "I'm glad you could make it, Judge Thomas."

"*Merci*," Judge Thomas said, "for remembering me as a judge."

"The pleasure is all mine. *Merci*."

Patrick was still instructing, "Aunt Viviane, you and Nicole will sit right here with Bill. . . . Oh, give the rings to Henry, and Henry, you'll pass the rings to Louis and Julie. You all got it?"

Everyone chorused, "*Oui!*"

Brian played a love song as they filed to their places. Viviane walked in with Bill, and Maxine followed behind once everyone was in place. They stood up as Julie walked in. All eyes were on her. Louis stood there with his breath caught in his throat, thinking, *I must be dreaming. If I am, let me stay in my dream world, I don't want to wake up. She looks so radiant and elegant as usual. My, she's beautiful. Can you hear me, Julie. I love you so much, Julie. Can you see what I'm feeling, what's inside me right now?*

Jean walked beside Julie proudly. He was asked to give her away. He stood tall in one of Brian's black suit with a warm smile as they walked across the floor to where Louis was standing.

Julie looked at Louis's sparkling eyes smiling at her. She could hear his soft, gentle voice calling to her. She mouthed silently, *I love you.*

Jean kissed her on both cheeks and placed her hand in Louis's. Louis lifted the little veil from her face so he could see. He wanted to kiss her and she wanted to do the same. It was a fast ceremony; the vows were said, the license signed, and before you know it, they were husband and wife. They kissed, and everyone applauded. Patrick took their picture. Everyone came forward to congratulate them.

Louis and Julie only had eyes for each other, each looking forward to the rest of the evening when they could be together in private. Viviane came forward. "It's time for you to dance, my children."

Louis took his bride by both hands, then moved backward to the dance floor. He thought as he took her in his arms, *I wish my parents could have seen this moment, especially my mother. They would have been so happy.* He whispered, "I love you, Julie, for always."

Placing his left arm around her waist, he placed her hands on his chest and cradled the back of her head with his right arm. Slowly they danced to the music. Bill's eyes were on them as they danced. Everyone was happy for them. He lifted her in his arms like he claimed his prize.

Turning with her, Louis kissed her and headed for the door. He forgot about everyone and everything until there was more applause. He stopped to look where all that noise was coming from. Calming his raging emotions he gently let her down, but Julie felt like she was being teased because she wanted him so bad.

Enjoying the activities, Henry Claude was trying to converse with Nicole. "I'm happy to see you here tonight, Nicole. Will you dance with me?"

Nicole responded, "You're always happy to see me whenever it serves your purpose!"

Ignored her comment, again he asked, "Can I have a dance?"

Conscious of her eye injury, she was hesitant to dance with him. She was trying hard to avoid eye contact with him. He misunderstood and felt like she was trying to avoid him. Feeling peeved at her treatment he asked, "Why won't you talk to me? It's been a month now since we have seen each other. You hang up the phone in my face. Are you angry about something? I miss you, Nicole." He tried to touch her, but she pulled away. "Why are you turning your face from me? Does my breath stink?"

Nicole didn't want to dance with Henry, but not for the reason he mentioned, and she told him so. "I have many reasons not to like you, Henry, but the reasons you mentioned aren't part of it."

She turned and walked away to the side doors to the patio. He followed her and demanded, "You know I don't like being ignored, and you've been avoiding me enough. If you don't like me, tell me now!"

"You're right. I don't like you, Henry. You're really bad. I thought you and I had something special going on, but I was just a toy for you to play with. You're a user, Henry."

"Why would you think something like that? You know I have great affection for you."

"Great affection for me? You really think I'm stupid, don't you, Henry? You slept with Carine. I knew you were going around, but I thought you wouldn't do something like that to me. My sister! I know you really want to help Louis, but I don't think he told you to sleep with her. You hurt me, Henry, and I'm not going to let you do it again."

Henry couldn't deny what he had been accused of. He said, "What happened between Carine and me was an accident. We were drunk. I helped her to her room and one thing led to another. That will never happen again."

"Definitely it will not happen again," she replied, "because I will not be part of your harem."

"Give me another chance," Henry pleaded.

Nicole sneered, "You have got to be joking!"

"Please look at me."

She slowly turned to face him and removed her glasses. Henry's drink almost dropped out of his hand when he saw her eye. His shocking gasp was a testament to the way she looked.

"My God," he exclaimed, "what happened?"

He felt like his heart was breaking as tears filled his eyes. He felt an overpowering rage. He pulled her toward him and demanded to know, "Who did this to you?"

"This was a wake-up call," she said, pointing her finger at her wounded eye. "What you have done to me hurts me more than the bruise on my face. . . . You see, eventually this mark will disappear, so it does not matter."

Henry pulled her toward him and exclaimed, "Yes, it does matter! Jacque did this to you."

Pulling away she snapped, "The injury has already happened." She placed her shades on her face. "It's over, just as you and I."

She walked outside in the yard, crying. He followed her, apologizing. "I'm sorry, I did not mean to make you cry. I'm so sorry."

Henry held her in his arms and let her cry, murmuring soothing words till she calmed herself, while he thought of a thousand ways to hurt Jacque.

He didn't press on for a second chance, because he knew he wasn't ready to settle down at the moment and he had a lot to work on, not just with her but with himself. They talked about the wedding, how beautiful it was, and in such a short time.

Nicole smiled and said, "This is the fastest wedding ever, but it turned out to be quite a success."

Inside, the reception was in full swing. Louis and Julie were about to depart for the rest of their special night. Saying goodnight to everyone while they were standing on top of the stairs, they disappeared into the darkness. One by one, the people left for their homes.

Julie stood in front of Louis's bedroom. She had not seen his country house bedroom. But Louis had told her how he had decorated it. . . . It was stationed away from all the other bedrooms, the whole top floor of his three-story ranch house. The room was very huge, masculine, with beautiful designer woodwork. From his bedroom, one could see all around his plantation and even further away. His bedroom was surrounded by windows, with a balcony built all around. At each window stood a telescope, which enabled him to see all over his property. There were two sliding glass doors, one that led to the terrace and the other one to his whirlpool room, big enough for six people to fit in. Inside, where he slept, laid a complete imperial designed bedroom set for a very tall man, and the bed was covered with a light blue satin spread with gold trim and several pillows on top. Near one of the windows stood a round table with two fancy imperial armchairs that matched the table under it. The table was fixed for two, and beside it stood a crystal ice bucket, inside of which sat an expensive bottle of champagne for them to drink. On the high ceiling hung a stunning chandelier. The room was well designed with passion. It was romantic.

Suddenly, Julie was swung high as he lifted her and kissed her hungrily. Not breaking his kiss he shouldered the door open and carried her in, kicking the door shut behind him. Slowly he laid her on his bed. He looked at her like a hunter who was about to enjoy his kill and satisfy his hunger.

Louis tore off his vest and removed his tie and unbuttoned his shirt as he undressed himself. Gradually, he moved toward her. Julie lay there as he removed her shoes and stockings and kissed her feet, caressing her body as he kissed his way up to her lips. That was something Louis wanted to do since the first time he was introduced to her. He slowly moved his hand over her body as if trying to memorize all the planes and hollows. Kissing her, he unzipped her dress. Before she knew it, they were both naked.

Passion filled the air. This was the first time Julie felt free to express her feelings to Louis, the boy she dreamt of since she was a child. Now he was a man, loving the woman she had become. She ran her hands over him, caressing his fine-cut body. She was lost in his arms as he took her. They were completely absorbed in each other.

I never had something this good, Louis thought and confessed, "My God! Julie, you're sweeter than I had ever imagined."

Words could not express the bliss he was having. He sank his lips on her neck, her body lay pliant under his powerful shape. . . . He eased up on his elbows, not wanting to put all his weight on her, afraid he might hurt her. Julie was eager for complete fulfillment. She pulled him on her so she could feel his complete hard shape. She realized he was holding himself back because of her. "Don't be afraid. You will not hurt me, my love. I've wanted your touch since my first night here in Haiti. . . . Yes," she confessed, "feel me, make me yours now and forever."

Her voice was ringing like music in his ears. Louis gave up. "Yes, my darling, now and forever."

Louis sank deep into her very being and with rhythmic movements sought to give them both what they craved. He exhaled as she grabbed his back tighter and tighter, he was enjoying the way she was expressing her feelings to him. "Give your soul to me, my Julie."

Julie felt everything around her shattered as he took her beyond the realms of reality, where there were only feelings and touches. Never did she think making love could be so sweet. Louis knew every corner and uncovered feelings she had been hiding. Places she didn't think she had feelings had surfaced. Her soul came to life. He set her mind on fire, and as for her part, she wanted to give him the same. All he ever wanted from a woman, tonight she was going to be all woman for him. Together they both reached their destiny. He kissed her and turned with her in his arms. He touched her stomach tenderly and said, "I think you're pregnant."

She smiled dreamily because she remembered the second time Louis and she went riding and he told her about the married woman he was in love with and how he wanted to really make love to her.

"Really . . . Fuji?"

They made love and talked all night till she slowly fell asleep in his arms. He whispered in her ears, "I love you, my wife."

Likewise he drifted off to sleep.

The next morning Richard and Jean went for a ride around the plantation. Jean wanted to get acquainted with him. Maxine and Nadine were sitting in the den talking. Maxine said, "Last night, we witnessed Julie Bertrand and Louis Janvier's marriage. That was one night no one will ever forget. Louis Janvier truly found his perfect mate."

Nadine said, "If I was not here to see it with my own two eyes, I would never have believed it if someone else had told me my cousin Fuji got married."

Nicole walked in just then. "Good morning, everyone. How was the night?"

Maxine looked at her. This was a different Nicole from last night. "Fine. . . . You seem happier this morning. What's the glow?"

316

Trying to look nonchalant, she said, "I look like I'm glowing?"

Nadine looked at her. "Yes, you are. What's your secret, girl?"

Nicole said, "I guess when one has a good conscious, you don't worry about too much. So last night I slept well. It has been a long time since I had a good night sleep."

Maxine cautioned, "Don't tell Jacque or Carine that Julie and Louis got married."

"Never," Nicole assured her. "I'm not going back, Max. I advise you not to go there either till we have everything straightened out with those monsters, Jacque and Carine."

Maxine protested, "I have to go home. I can't impose on Julie and Louis, Nicole. They just got married, plus Aunt Viviane would be there."

"Not for long, Max. She might decide to go to New York tomorrow, and where would that leave us."

Nadine interrupted, "You don't have to, stay with me. I have two extra bedrooms in my house. It will be just like the old school days."

"Thanks, Nadine," Maxine and Nicole readily accepted.

They hugged each other and continued their conversation.

Upstairs, Julie and Louis were just waking up. Last night was a long night. It was spent discovering a lot about each other. Louis lay on his side looking at his wife lying beside him. Looking at her size and height, he wondered, *How did she manage to flip me across?*

He smiled to himself, thinking, *I have a lot to learn about my new wife, the cactus lady, with a short temper,* and kissed her.

"Good morning, Mrs. Janvier."

She tried to get up from the bed, but Louis held her back by trapping her with his arm and a leg flung over her. "Where do you think you're going?"

Laughing, she said, "I'm starving for food. I smell strawberries."

Rubbing his face across hers, he said, "I was eating strawberries."

He reached over to the nightstand and took one from the bowl and popped it in her mouth, saying, "Breakfast is on the way now."

There was a knock on the door. He covered her body with the blanket and pressed a button that was on the side of the bed. The door opened and Ninot wheeled in a table laden with breakfast, greeting them with a broad smile. "*Bonjour, Madame et Monsieur Janvier.* Your breakfast."

Louis thanked her. "Good, we're hungry. Just leave it there. We'll let you know if we need anything else."

Checking to see that everything was in place, she bowed and left the room. "*Oui, Monsieur.*"

They got out of bed to eat. Julie put on his shirt that he had tossed across the room. Louis put her underwear over his head and around his neck. Julie dissolved in laughter when she saw what he did. "It looks nice on you. Beige becomes you."

She couldn't help admiring his shape. She thought how well her husband was made and remembered the first night she saw him. She thought she was seeing a Greek god in the flesh. Now here he was standing before her, and he was all hers. He stood here letting her paint his body with her eyes, into her mind. She saw why many women wanted her husband. He was desirable. He was a woman's fantasy. She thought, *This is the first time I'm seeing a beautiful man.*

Louis was beautiful from the crown of his head to the soles of his feet, with a sexy voice to go along with it. Her longing was no longer for breakfast. She slowly moved toward him, hooking her fingers in the underwear that was around his neck. She pulled him toward her as she showed her perfect smile and growled, "I'm hungry."

"Then I shall feed you," he vowed as they both toppled backwards on the bed.

He pulled her close to him and saw her arms wrapped around his neck. He lifted her up to him so he could drink the honey of from her lips. She wrapped her legs around his waist. Passion flared, the kisses, the touch, knowing she cared, was making him want her more. His hunger rose rampant and he must be filled. He was thirty, and he had to quench his thirst now. The one he was longing for was finally his. He held on to her as she softly pronounced his name, "Louis. . . . "

Julie felt all her strength and power were under his control. The heat of electricity she was feeling was going through her body like bolts of lightning. It made her shiver.

He knelt and looked up at her, watching the effect his skillful fingers were invoking. He spoke to her, telling her how she was his complement, the one he'd long searched for. He ached for her, his Julie. She was his dream come true. He gathered her to him and held her tighter as she whispered, " . . . Fuji, my love."

Louis had been marked by her love. Very softly he said, "I yearned to hold you like this in my arms, to love you."

With burning desire he kissed her. Sweat ran down all over their entwined bodies.

Julie's eyes were closed, consuming all the feeling she was receiving from Louis. He whispered, "Look at me, Julie."

As if she was dreaming, she opened her marble brown eyes and looked directly into his eyes, burning with a passion so intense there was no need for words at this moment between them. His emerald green eyes were full of love, rampant with emotion for her and her only. A tremulous sound came out of his mouth as he whispered, "Let me breathe into your mouth . . . let me breathe inside you."

She opened her mouth, readily breathing, "Yes."

He sealed her lips with his and breathed softly into her. It felt so good. Julie felt like crystal glass that would shatter into tiny pieces at any time. She was like a sheep that was being guided by her shepherd. The feeling was too much for her to handle. Tears ran from the corners of her eyes. He opened his eyes to look at her, concerned that he had done something to make her cry. "Am I hurting you, my love?"

Smiling tearfully, she reassured him, "No, my darling, I never felt better."

She held him tighter as she thought of her dream, how he had made love to her, and the reality was even better. He kissed away the tears from her eyes and whispered, "I love you."

The fire raged and traveled like a bolt of lightning through their entwined bodies that left them both gasping for breath and shaken. When it was over, Julie held his face between her hands, catching her breath. She softly spoke, "I felt like an erupting volcano and you were the ocean to calm me down."

Feeling totally satiated, he nibbled her ears and neck as he rolled off her. He turned on his side and pulled her into his arms. Kissing the honey of her lips, he vowed, "I love you so much."

Yawning widely, Julie replied, "I love you too, Louis. I'm so hot. Is the cooling system down? I need a shower."

Checking the knobs on the panel above the bed, Louis said, "The cooling system is not down."

He got up out of the bed and turned the knob to make the room cooler. She tried to get up but she was unable to. Concerned, Louis asked, "Are you all right?"

Grimacing at the sticky feeling, she said, "I'm trying to get up. I feel weak."

Laughing at her expression, he came to her aid. He picked her up in his arms, then went and sat on an armchair with her in his arms. He pulled the tray of food close to him. "You need food, my darling."

Uncovering the warming dishes that held an array of food, he picked up the fork to take some of the food to feed her. Spearing a piece of bacon, he instructed, "Say Aaahh!"

Julie was too tired to even open her mouth. He begged and cajoled her as one would a small child, "Please, darling, open your mouth for me. Eat something."

Julie refused to open her mouth. She buried her head on his chest and closed her eyes. "I'm too weak to chew."

"Then you leave me no choice. I'll have to chew and you'll just have to swallow."

She opened her eyes to look at him, thinking he was insane. He had a big smile on his face, looking at her, waiting for her answer. Reluctantly she opened her mouth and took the piece of meat on the tip of the fork, chewing slowly. "Good girl."

She passed her hand over his shoulder to enjoy the feel of his body when she came to a sudden stop to look at the marks that were on Louis's shoulder. She stared at them with sorrow in her eyes when she saw her teeth marks on his shoulder. She couldn't believe she was that savage toward the man she was so madly in love with. With tears in her eyes she kissed the marks she had given him and apologized to him for her cruelty. Kissing her cheeks he let her know that he wasn't upset about the teeth marks she had put on him.

"These marks," he glanced over his shoulder, "are your brand to identify your stallion."

She couldn't help but to smile as he kissed the tears away from her face. Then they finished breakfast and went to take their shower and meet the rest of the world as Mr. and Mrs. Janvier.

Chapter Seventeen

Weekend's Over for Some, Back to Work on Tuesday

Jean and Nicole were on their way to work. He looked at Nicole and commented, "I can't wait to see the wedding pictures. I must say, I didn't expect to have such a good weekend. It turned out to be quite a success."

Nicole rested her head against the car seat and smiled contentedly. "Julie is truly kind. Her ways motivate anyone who is around her. I was so afraid of our big brother, I overlooked her kindness toward me. She gave us all an opportunity to make something of ourselves, to have our own, but for my part, I took her kindness for granted."

"You're not the only one, Nicole," Jean sighed. "I blew up every opportunity she handed out to me. Saul had handed me his firm to help Julie run it, but instead I suggested Jacque would be better for the job. I was a coward, afraid to take chances, blind with anger, which caused me to be weak. But not anymore. I'm not going to let Jacque destroy the confidence Julie has in us."

Closing her eyes Nicole, took a long deep breath and exhaled in an expression of sorrow as she nodded her head in relief. "We could definitely say we are blessed. We would have been homeless for what Jacque is planning to do. Julie had a big impact on Louis. He's giving us a chance to make amends to Julie. He seems so different when you get to know him. The things I heard about him, I thought he was just a good-looking, skillful, deceptive monster. Now I'm having second thoughts. He didn't seem mean or ruthless at all. He's always very respectful whenever I meet him. And for the type of girl Julie is, she would not fall in love with a ruthless man."

Jean nodded. "Like Maxine said, only if you challenge him. Tell you the truth, I never heard his associates put him down, besides Jacque and Carine. He wants to be everything Louis stands for. I always knew Julie was a smart woman. I'm so happy for her. I hope Louis will bring her the happiness she truly deserves. She is a gem."

Meanwhile at the old house, Maxine was talking to Julie. She was very concerned because Julie was going to be with Jacque by herself in the mansion. Aunt Viviane had gone to Jacmel with William and Loziane. And Marie was no longer an employee. She tried to reason with Julie. "Do you think it's safe to be there alone without Louis or a bodyguard? Lately Jacque is going crazy, you know."

"Don't worry, Max. Jacque and I are only going over some papers, and all I have to do is sign them. I can handle Jacque, we'll be all right."

"Well, to be on the safe side, I've asked Richard to be here with us."

"You did what?" Julie was disappointed. "Jacque is mad about something and I want to get to the bottom of it. I don't want Richard to get involved. He's only going to agitate Jacque more and make matters worse. Call Richard back."

"It's too late," Maxine said. "He is outside waiting for us."

"No, Max!" Turning, she picked up her glasses from the table. "I'm leaving now."

Julie perched her shades on her nose and left the old house with Maxine. They met Richard at the side of the house.

"Richard, I need you to leave now," Julie said as she walked past by him.

Looking at Maxine, Richard hesitated and walked after them. "I want to take you ladies over there, Mrs. Janvier."

She was adamant. "Nonsense. Right now I have business to take care of. And don't follow us, you hear me?" she commanded. "Oh, and by the way, please call me Julie. . . . Let's go, Max."

Julie continued on her way. Maxine kissed Richard and sighed. She ran after Julie to catch up with her.

Julie and Maxine were walking up the terrace steps of the mansion. Carine was looking out of the window when she saw them coming up the field and called, "Jacque, they're here! Julie's here."

Jacque told her to calm herself. Pasting a welcoming smile on her face, she slowly walked outside to meet them. As Julie and Maxine neared the house, she held out her hands in greeting. "Sisters, welcome home. When did you guys arrive from your weekend?"

"Late last night," Julie replied.

Carine embraced them and kissed both of their cheeks, saying, "Since you arrived from New York, this will be the first time we'll be able to spent some real time."

Turning to Maxine, she asked, "Did you see Jean, Max?"

Snobbishly Maxine replied, "Since when did Jean and I look for each other?"

They walked into the house to the family room. Jacque got up from the chair he was sitting in and greeted them enthusiastically.

"Julie!" He brought both of her hands to hip lips and kissed them. "I'm so glad to see you. Max, how are you baby sister?" He gave her kiss on her cheek. "How was your weekend? Did you see Nicole and Jean?"

"Oh please!" she snapped. "Give me a break here. I had a wonderful weekend; don't spoil it. They would have been the last two people on earth I would want to see." She smiled. "Boy! I had so much fun. I'm going up to change to something more comfortable." Turning to Julie, she invited, "Come up when you're finish talking to Jacque."

"Okay," Julie promised. Fanning herself she said, "It's a little hot in here."

Jacque replied, "I just turned the air conditioner on. Soon it will be cool in here. . . . I was having some lemonade. Care to join me in a glass?"

Pouring her glass of lemonade, Julie asked, "Why wasn't Marie at my place when I returned last night?"

Immediately Jacque answered, "She quit."

"She quit!" Julie exclaimed. "I was very fond of her."

"I know." Jacque gave a sad smiled. "I'll send someone to your place now. Please call Roy, Carine."

Carine left the room to call the butler.

"How's Aunt Viviane?" inquired Jacque, putting is arm across Julie's shoulders and smiling into her eyes. "And Bill, a nice little fellow."

Sidestepping his arm discreetly, she gave him a smile. "They're fine. From the ranch Mother decided to go directly to Jacmel, but before we start to talk, let's do the first things first, shall we? The documents! I want to get them out of the way. I'm going for a long ride later on."

Trying to hide his gleeful expression, he replied, "Oh yes . . . it almost slipped my mind. Let's go to the library, it's more comfortable for business. . . . And after, I'll take you for a very long ride."

"Sorry," she smiled. "Louis already volunteered."

Suddenly Jacque pulled Julie toward him. He was displeased. "Call him and cancel. You spent the whole weekend with him. I think you two have seen enough of each other. What do I have to do to get you to understand? Do I have to be bad, a player, have a lot of women for you to notice me?"

Looking at Jacque's hands on her shoulders, shaking her, as if to make her to come to her senses, she calmly breathed, "Jacque! Are you okay? I think you should let me go. I don't want to break your fingers."

Grasping at what she said, Jacque realized he was holding on to her and quickly let her go. He apologized, "I'm sorry, I didn't know I was holding on to you so tight. Did I hurt you?"

"Next time you put your hands on me like that again, I'll hurt you. Do you understand?" she replied as he softly passed his hands over her shoulders to soothe her. She thought, *If Louis finds out that Jacque put his hands on me like that, God help him. The world would be too small for Jacque to hide.* She commented, "I think you are losing it. I don't want my favorite brother to lose his head. Lucky I'm not a person who bruises easily."

He thought as she counseled him, *Julie thinks because she's my boss she can do whatever she wants to. She'll be surprised.* Jacque smiled. "You're right, I'm so sorry."

He felt he better keep calm till Julie finished signing those documents. They walked to the library. Jacque closed the door behind him and Julie sat on the chair in front of the desk. He walked behind the desk and took out the documents he had prepared for her to sign. She made a pretense of examining them carefully, so carefully that Jacque was beginning to get edgy. He asked anxiously, "Is there a problem?"

"No," she stated, not taking her eyes off the documents in her hand, "but it's always good to read what you're about to sign. This concerns my future and I don't want to sign my entire fortune over to anyone."

Relaxing visibly, Jacque agreed with her. "Of course not."

She was hoping that Jacque would come clean. That what Louis told her and showed her it was just a misunderstanding. She took a quick glance at him. He was looking at her, so she asked, "Is anything wrong?"

"Nothing, just admiring your beauty," he answered.

She smiled at his response and looked at the documents. She prayed he would have said, "*No, Julie, don't sign these papers. I don't want to be one of those men who had deceived you. I'm sorry. Please forgive me.*" But he did no such confession.

Carine entered the room just then with a drink for Julie. Julie stopped reading accepted the drink, and invited Carine to read the documents. "Good, you're here, Cat. Come here and read these documents."

Carine looked at Jacque, who signaled his okay with a nod of his head. Julie continued talking, pretending she hadn't seen what had taken place between them. "You know my French is not that good. I need someone to explain a few things to me."

"You're quite right," Jacque agreed. He smiled smugly as Carine read the documents. "But don't you trust me, Julie?"

She looked at Jacque and said, "With all my belongings."

Jacque looked at Carine as she pointed out a few things to Julie. "Well the first part explains the location of the land and how big it is. The second part is where you sign your name that you acknowledge your property. Voilà! Do you understand?"

There was a knock on the door. Jacque called, "Come in."

The butler announced, "I brought some refreshments, sir."

"Put it there on the coffee table, Roy."

Julie took the papers and placed them carefully on the desk. She smiled at Carine's explanation, because she was not surprised at her interpretation, and continued her conversation with Carine, to Jacque's annoyance. She purposely wanted Jacque to send Carine out of the room.

She asked, "Carine, what are your plans for tonight?"

"Julie, the papers," Jacque interrupted.

Waving away his protests, she admonished, "We have plenty of time, Jacque. I'm not in any hurry. Well, Carine," she continued, "what are you doing later?"

Carine glanced at Jacque furtively. "I planned to invite a few friends over tonight to celebrate."

"What's the occasion?" Julie asked with interest.

Jacque recovered quickly. "We were very happy, so we invited a few good friends to join in our happiness. It was supposed to be a surprise for you, to cheer you up. Now Carine blew it."

Pretending surprise, Carine said, "Oops! Now I have to change a few minor details."

Opening the door she called out, "Roy, Roy, the party is no longer a surprise, so no need to rush."

Sidling out into the hallway, she closed the door behind her. Jacque continued his conversation with Julie. "Where were we?"

Turning to Jacque with a smile on her face, Julie asked, "Can you fix me a drink, Jacque?"

Jacque hurried to do as she requested with a smile on his face. "Sure, my love."

He got up from his seat and went by the coffee table to fix her a drink. From the corner of his eye he watched how she was reading the documents. He hurried up and poured a glass of brandy for her. When he finished, he handed her the glass and thought, *Now is a better opportunity for me, she might get drunk.*

He fixed himself a glass, then went and stood by the window. Julie sat back on the chair pretending she was reading the documents as she signed them. She looked up and saw Jacque staring at her. Again she asked, "What's wrong?"

"Nothing." He nodded his head. "I was wondering, how did you spend your weekend?"

"It was great," she said and continued signing.

I guess sleeping with Louis was a great time, Jacque thought, *and you have no shame to express it. You'll regret that, Julie. You'll wish you never met with Louis Janvier when I'm through with you. You've giving me more strength. . . . I will not have any regret.*

She finished signing them, then she handed them to him, saying, "Good, I finished signing the papers."

He quickly put the glass in his hands down on the coffee table to accept them with eager fingers as he arrogantly announced, "I'm going to take good care of you, Julie."

"Thank you," she said demurely.

She tasted her drink and cautioned Jacque, when she saw him closely examining the papers, "Be careful, you might smear the ink where I just signed my signature."

"You're right. How thoughtless of me. . . . Thank you."

He folded them carefully so as not to smear the writing. He walked behind his desk and placed them in a drawer, saying, "Tomorrow I'll bring them to the archive. Let's go to the family room. It's more comfortable to talk about pleasure."

At the same time, at the hospital, Louis was in his office talking to Henry as he was going over some patient charts. Remembering the bruise on Nicole's face, Henry was concerned. "You think Julie will be okay by being alone with Jacque?"

"You don't know my wife like I do," Louis reassured. "She'll be more than okay."

Henry was wondering how so but he didn't ask. Louis smiled. "She could kick your butt without even trying hard. The very first time we were at the ranch, the following morning I was in my meditating room. . . ."

Henry cut in, "You had showed it to her!"

"No, she found it while I was in there practicing." Louis was joyfully excited as he explained. "I thought I was going to have some fun with her, so I put on my mask to scare her away. . . . Before I knew it, I found myself flying across the room."

"What did she do?" Henry asked anxiously.

"She had no problem flipping me." Henry laughed as he listened to Louis. "She didn't give me any time to talk. I was defending myself from her, trying to block away her blows. The girl has superb skills! Her techniques are masterful. She was kicking my butt."

"You let her hit you?"

"It not a matter of *letting* her hit me." Louis laughed. "She *was* hitting me. I thought she was going to hit like a little girl. Boy, was I surprised! You should have seen her short legs doing the flying kick across my chest. They were like thunder kicking me, and a strong right hand and a left to back her up at punching my face. When I wouldn't identify myself, she picked up my katana. It was amazing! I almost lost my head, if I didn't identify myself to her. She was able to counter a lot of my steps. Everything she did was well calculated. She set my mind on fire. . . . Remember what she did to me when she found out I impregnated her without her permission."

"Yes." Henry sighed, then exclaimed, "Wow! You should have captured her on camera."

"I did," Louis smiled. "That morning I turned on the cameras to record my moves. I wanted to examine my fencing technique. I was happy that I did. She knows how to use the sword very well. . . . Saul taught her the technique. . . ."

They chorus a laugh. Henry said, "She almost killed you!"

"Almost decapitated," he said while he held his neck. "I had to back away like a mouse running for his life."

"I want to see the tape," Henry replied. "She looks so innocent."

"That's just a camouflage." Louis shook his head as he pushed back his chair to open his desk drawer. Pulling out the videotape, he handed it to Henry and said, "Watch it now when I leave the office . . . I was fooled by her also. She looks like she can't even open a soda bottle without help of a man. Then again, she never really hid who she really is. . . . She's the cactus lady." He smiled. "I just didn't believe it till I saw what she really is, for myself . . . and Jacque doesn't know how dangerous my wife is. He'll be very surprised if he tries anything or pulls one of his stunts with her. . . . And the truth is I'm counting on it."

Louis broke the pen he was holding. Henry didn't have to ask what was he counting on, because he felt the same way, too. Finishing going over the patient charts, Louis left his office to make rounds on his patients before he went to the board meeting he had called. He opened the door just as Richard was about to knock on the door. Absently, Louis acknowledged, "Richard."

"Fuji," he began urgently, "I want to tell you something."

Impatiently holding up a hand, Louis said, "Tell Henry about it."

He hurried out of the room, leaving Richard with an open-mouthed expression on his face at Louis's abrupt departure.

Back at the mansion, Julie put down her barely tasted drink on the desk. She was very disappointed. Never in her life would she have thought that Jacque would be dishonest with her. Together they walked into the family room. Peering at Jacque, she thought, Louis was right; she helped Jacque too much.

Tears almost ran out of her eyes as Jacque continued talking to her as if he had done nothing wrong.

While all this drama was going on, Carine went up to Maxine's bedroom. She waltzed in hugging herself and boasting, "By tomorrow, I'm going to be so rich, baby brat sister."

Maxine looked at her with disgust. "You sound so happy. Which dog did you have this time?"

Ignoring the crude remark, she replied, "The only man I ever want is Louis."

"Why are you lying to yourself," Maxine calmly said as she looked at her with pity. "You were dating Brian, his cousin, for five years then were engaged for two. You and Louis never dated . . . he never wanted you then. What is possessing you to think that Louis would want you now?"

"I'm a beautiful woman, Maxine," she replied as she looked at herself in the dresser mirror.

"Yes, you are," Maxine agreed, "but you'll need more than just beauty to get a good man. Something that's called talent. How to be a woman of value, because in time beauty fades."

"I'll have money to back me up," she smiled. "I'll be able to have anyone I desire, and Louis is the man."

Maxine expounded, "Even if you have all the money in the world, there are some man you can never have, and Louis is one of them."

She laughed scathingly. "That's where you're wrong, my dear baby sister. You forget who Louis is—he's a material man. . . . Now that I have so much money, Louis will give me the attention I require from him"

"His refusal for you was never about money, Carine," she reminded her. "He never loved you. And plus he wouldn't hurt his cousin for you. . . . Stop bothering him. Eventually he'll really hurt you. Stop humiliating yourself. This is your last warning."

"No," Carine lashed at her, "this is your last warning! I see your game, Maxine. You're pretending to date Richard so you could throw everybody off track, especially Julie. I saw what's going on between you and Louis. All the nights you were sneaking out to meet him, going to his house. You thought I wouldn't catch on . . . Louis pretending he came here just to see Julie. You three have become so close these days. Since when was Louis so sociable, inviting you along every time he invited Julie over to his ranch? Richard is just a cover-up, isn't he, Maxine. You and Julie are sharing the same man, Louis."

Maxine was appalled. "If Julie wasn't here at the mansion, I would have slapped these words out of your dirty mouth. You're the most disgusting person I've ever known. What you're saying is very hurtful. This is the way you are. It's your dirt you're putting on our backs. You would love for us to be like you, so you wouldn't feel alone. . . . You have no excuse, you are just a mean nasty person. You really are stupid! No, more than stupid, you are totally an idiot, repulsive. . . . You're sick!"

"What happened, Max!" she laughed. "Did I cause you to bleed? You see, Louis is my destiny. We were meant to be together since we were teenagers. Eventually, he'll realize that I am his perfect mate. And I will do anything to make him happy. You better not stand in my way."

Maxine exclaimed as she repeated an incident that took place years ago, "He's not looking for a puppet. I wish you had removed that crazy idea out of your twisted mind. You're still letting what that witch lady foretold lead your life. And you're listening to Jacque, helping him with his own crazy ideas, thinking one day Julie and him would be like husband and wife. You two are fools to believe in lies!"

"What are you talking about?" Carine asked.

Nodding her head Maxine said, "I'm sure you remember, because you are trying to live up to that life. We had just moved from Cité Delmas to the mansion after the death of our parents. He had come to our house once with Jean because they were on the same soccer team. He thought we were all cute, but you were a beauty. Aunt Viviane was inside talking to some old friends, and we were in the yard playing. You slipped him a little note in his pocket when he was leaving. I was the only one who saw what you did. He called you a day later to ask you out. The following day, you told Aunt Viviane you were going to see your so-called girl friend Michelle, who wasn't living too far from us. You and her were going to study, then go to the movie. You were invited to spend the weekend over at her house. You two were going to have a wonderful time. Aunt Viviane trusted you, so she let you stay over at Michelle's place for the weekend. But what she didn't know was you two were going to spent the weekend with Louis and his good friend Henry. . . . I remember it so well . . . you gave him your virginity because he was a very good-looking, wealthy boy, and he was a great soccer player."

"So you were a spy since then," Carine mockingly said.

"I was not trying to spy on you, Carine. I was surprised the others didn't see what you did. I regret I never told Aunt Viviane on you. . . . I saw you and Michelle meet them down the road, where you two got in their car. Henry was driving and Louis was sitting in the back. He got out to let you and Michelle in. You sat in the back by Louis and Michelle sat in the front with Henry. Two days later you returned as if nothing happened, you did nothing. . . . A month later, I overheard you talking on the telephone with Louis, and I was listening on the other end. You said, 'I'm afraid I might be pregnant'. But he reassured you that his condoms didn't pop. So there was no way you could have gotten pregnant by him and to rest your mind at peace, he said, if you were he would pay for the abortion because he was only fifteen years old and not ready to be a daddy. He noticed you wanted money, so he gave you a couple of thousands of dollars out of his allowance he was saving. . . . You saved that money well. You acted like it was the money Aunt Viviane was giving you that you had saved. Aunt Viviane was so proud of you. . . ."

Maxine laughed as she continued, " . . . You were such a liar, making everyone feel bad that you knew how to save money and the others didn't. I was the only one who didn't care because I knew how you got that money. . . . I just kept my mouth shut. I was ten years old when that happened. Then a week later, Julie returned with dad from New York. You tried everything to get her to go to Michelle's house, but she wouldn't. She wanted to stay home to play with me and her animals. A week later, Jacque took us to one of the neighbor's back yard party, and there was a crazy lady who was reading everybody's hands. All of our hands were read except for

Julie's. She didn't want that lady to tell her anything. She felt that was unchristian. The party we were invited to was a voodoo ceremony, and she was right. You thought she was a stupid little girl who was afraid to know the unknown. Everything you have read and learned from Aunt Viviane was gone in an instant. But Julie was strong. You were not able to convince her to let the woman read her future like you did to everybody. . . ."

Maxine paused for few seconds staring at her. " . . . And you hated her since then. You realized she was one person you could not persuade to do what you want them to do. I admired her more ever since then, because you were not able to change her way of thinking and the values she was brought up with and taught. You believed the witch lady more than the woman who raised us . . . when she told you the boy you gave your virginity to was a player, and he was very dangerous. He will kill you if you cross him. You felt embarrassed when she revealed your secret before everyone. You denied that ever happened, but you displayed your hatred toward Julie, who had nothing to do with that."

Carine snapped, "She sat there listening to that woman reading everyone's future, including mine, read out, except for hers!"

"Julie was shocked when she heard what that witch accused you of doing. She thought the woman was lying about you. You wouldn't have sex before marriage. You were so religious. . . . She didn't even want to stay. She was leaving when Jacque threatened her that she better wait and listen to him because he was the one who brought her there so she better sit and wait for everyone. She didn't care. She was willing to walk home alone, which she did . . . when Jacque realized she was gone, he drove the rest of us home. We got there before Julie. . . . Aunt Viviane asked why wasn't she with us. Jacque said she was being stubborn, she didn't want to listen to him. She almost got in trouble, if it wasn't for me. I told Aunt Viviane what had happened. . . . So when the witch revealed your secrets to everyone, you wanted to know about Julie, but little Julie didn't care about any boys at that age. . . .

"You're the one who started to accuse Julie of being better than you, wanting everything she had and worked hard for. . . . You used to tease her, but Julie never had low self-esteem. She never paid you any mind. Louis never gave a damn about you. He didn't care whether you dated his cousin or not. He spent a year screwing both you and Michelle. He didn't care for you. Two years later, when Louis's father passed away, you were convinced that what the witch foretold was true and you did the right choice by becoming good friends with Brian. You thought he was going to inherit everything. He was going to run the family business. Everything you ever dreamed of, you would have in life. But you did! Brian Bravé was good for you! And you didn't want Louis then. You concentrated on having Brian. . . . You thought it was Brian who was going to inherit the dynasty. . . ."

Maxine gasped as she continued, " . . . You would have hurt anyone who stood in your way, then you dumped him cruelly. Right before Louis, who was happy to be his cousin's best man. . . . Everyone who was present at your wedding rehearsal was happy for you, till you opened your greedy mouth and told Louis he was the one you were in love with all that time, when you found out he was the big guy, not Brian. You forget that Brian had potential, but all you were concerned about was money, and you wanted it at that moment, but you still don't have it . . . and whatever you're going to get, you're going to deserve every bit of it."

Carine laughed. "I remember it better than you. You've forgotten the most important detail the witch had mentioned. She also said with my beauty I could get whoever I wanted, and Louis is what I want. . . . And by the way," she turned to go, "we're having a celebration tonight."

Not one thing Maxine spoke about she noted or cared. Maxine asked, "What's the occasion?"

"The return of Mrs. Saul Philip the Third." She laughed over her shoulder as she left, slamming the door behind her. Maxine's mind troubled her when she remembered what Constant told her. "If Julie signs the documents over to Jacque, he is home free."

Maxine wondered if she gave Louis the duplicate documents and gave Jacque the original ones. She was confused and afraid she might have helped Jacque deceive Julie, that Julie trusted them so much, she wouldn't bother reading the documents and unknowingly sign her wealth over to Jacque and Carine.

Leaving her room, Maxine ran down the stairs. Bursting into the library room, she didn't find them there. She became frantic and ran to the family room, where she found them laughing and joking like old friends.

"Julie, did you sign any papers for Jacque?" she asked without preamble.

Jacque choked and almost dropped the drink he had in his hand. Maxine continued, "They are trying to steal from you. Carine was just in my room boasting about how she's struck it rich."

Jacque tried to shut her up. "What are you talking about?"

Maxine ignored him while she pleaded with Julie, "Julie, it's true. Jacque and Carine are thieves."

Julie tried to calm Maxine's outburst and hoped that Jacque came clean and confessed to what Maxine was accusing him of. "Take it easy, Max. No one is stealing from me, least of all Jacque and Carine. Jacque always tries to help me. He's my confidant. That's a nasty thing to say about him. I would appreciate it if you'd apologize to him."

By saying that, she was hoping that Jacque would feel embarrassed and come clean. Maxine desperately wanted Julie to believe her. "But, Julie, don't be naïve. It's true."

Amidst the talking, Carine walked in inquiring, "What's going on? Why is Max talking so loud?"

Jacque informed her, "We've been accused by our dear sister here that we are thieves."

Carine looked at Maxine in shocked disbelief. "How could you, Max?" She pretended she was about to cry. "How can you say that about your family?"

Maxine was almost in tears. "Most of us are not like them. Julie, don't believe her. She was just in my room boasting how she just struck it rich!"

"Enough, Max. Stop now and apologize to them!" Julie ordered.

Maxine hesitated, but Julie insisted and yelled at her sternly, "Apologize to your brother and sister! And I never want to hear you say that about them."

Looking at Jacque, Julie almost cried when she saw how his eyes opened wide with joy while she spoke. He smiled coldly at Maxine, who was crying openly. "Your friendship means more to me than anything in this world, Julie. I'm sorry. I didn't mean to make you angry, I just don't want them to do something like that to you when you have helped us so much. Everything we own, everything we have. . . ."

"Enough," Julie interrupted. "I heard enough, Max. Apologize now."

Reluctantly and with tears streaming down her face, Maxine turned to Carine and Jacque. "I'm sorry for accusing you two as thieves."

Jacque recovered quickly enough. "It's just a misunderstanding, right, Carine?"

"All is forgiven," Carine agreed, grinning at Maxine. Walking toward Maxine she hugged and kissed her on her cheeks to show Julie that she didn't take what Maxine said to heart. Maxine whirled and left the room quickly. She ran to her room and grabbing a suitcase from the closet, she threw it on the bed and began to throw clothes in helter-skelter, talking to herself under her breath, "I've got to get away from here."

Feeling so nervous, she didn't feel she was able to drive. She called Nadine to ask her if she could pick her up as soon as possible. Hanging up the phone she locked the suitcases, carried them down the stairs, and placed them on the porch. Then she walked back to the house. Looking around carefully to see if anyone was about, she said to herself, "If Julie will not believe me, I just have to help her. I'll give her proof."

She slipped into the library and closed the door softly behind her, walking behind the bar, where she knew Jacque hid some important papers which belonged to Julie. She put them all in her underwear and closed the secret compartment Jacque had, then she went to the desk and opened it and took out the papers Julie had signed over to Jacque. She read and reread them, just to make sure she wasn't seeing things. She smiled because they weren't the original papers, and thank God that she had given Louis the documents without any further delay. Taking a deep breath of relief, she thought, *My word! I almost blew it.*

She smiled joyously as she placed them back inside the desk just as she found them. She quickly walked away from the desk, looking around to see if she had left everything intact. Softly she opened the library door.

Julie was about to walk out from the family room when she saw Maxine coming out of the library. She pushed Jacque and Carine who were behind her back inside the family room and closed the door to say, "Oh, Jacque, I almost forgot, what time is the party tonight?"

Recognizing what Julie did, Maxine quickly made her escape up to her room to finish packing the rest of her things. She then went into Nicole's room and packed a few things for her. She ran back down and found Julie, Jacque, and Carine in the lobby. Carine looked at the bag over Maxine's shoulder and asked in surprise, "Where are you going in such hurry?"

Trying to go around her to get to the door, Maxine replied, "None of your business."

Carine tried to grab the bag. Jacque got it first. "What's inside this bag of yours?"

He took it from her and opened it to see what was in it. Closing it, he handed it back. "Oh, its just make-up!"

Trembling, Maxine grabbed her bag from him. "I'm not coming back here."

She rushed out the door. Jacque was about to go after her but Julie held him back. "Don't! Let her go. I'll talk to her."

Julie turned and ran after Maxine. Jacque and Carine looked at each other. Jacque put his arm around Carine's shoulders and squeezed to reassure her that everything was fine. Julie found Nadine outside waiting for her.

"You're here. Good, Nadine." Turning to Maxine she said, "Max, I'll talk to you later."

Maxine apologized, "Julie, I'm sorry, I didn't know."

"I know." Gently she touched her face and softly told her, "Now go."

Jacque and Carine had just arrived on the front porch. They stood there watching from a distance, waving goodbye to their sister. They did not suspect anything. Julie moved from the car and walked back to Carine and Jacque.

As she was heading toward them, Jacque thought, *I'm going to marry you, Julie.*

He was feeling strong, believing he had power over Julie. He thought Julie had good connections, her public relations, and her reputation to uphold. He wanted her. At the moment he felt she would do anything he wanted her to do if he was tough with her. She would need him to raise her son. And he knew Julie wanted to have a good reputation before her son.

Julie walked up the steps toward them, as he said to Carine, "Will you excuse me? I want to talk to Julie."

Without any protest Carine replied, "Well, Julie. I'll see you later. The party starts at seven. I was hoping Aunt Viviane was going to be here."

She kissed Julie on her cheek and went inside. Turning to Julie, Jacque said, "We have many things to discuss."

Looking at him in surprise she asked, "What do we have to discuss?"

"There's a very big question I want to ask you," he said smugly, "but I'll save it for tonight. It's one of the surprises. But I also want to let you know that, in the future, you're going to need my help even more, concerning your son. He's going to need a good guardian and financial support."

"A good guardian." Julie gave a sound between a snort and a laugh before she could control herself. "Whatever gave you the idea I'm going to need financial support?"

"Well," he continued, "I don't know how much money you have in America. But I know one thing—your husband did not leave you much in Haiti, and I know for a fact he had made some bad investments and he gambled the rest. If you plan to live in Haiti, your son will need a good education and you'll need someone like me to help you bring him up. I know a woman like you wants to uphold her dignity, so you'll need me."

Julie could not believe her ears. "What do you mean?"

"I used to think you were a woman who loves to have her own," he shrugged, "but I guess a certain man could make a woman like you lose her mind. You have become senseless. And your mother is not paying attention to what is really happening around her. She's also hypnotized by that man, too."

She thought Jacque had lost his mind. He pushed, " . . . Your mother helped when we were in need. Now I feel it's right for me to give back something for all the help she gave me and my family."

"And what kind of help do you think I'm going to need from you?"

"Helping you get back your senses," Jacque answered.

Jacque has no character, Julie thought. She said sarcastically, "You're so kind, Jacque."

"Indeed I am." He was oblivious to the tone in her voice, "Because I choose you over Debbie."

She sneered, "Don't do me any favor, Jacque. Debbie needs you more than I'll ever need you."

"That's where you're wrong, Julie . . . I'm thinking of your future, even though I know you don't love me. I'm willing to sacrifice everything I have to make you happy. You think I'm going to stand there, watching how you're throwing your life away. . . ."

Julie felt he had really gone out of his mind.

" . . . I could tell you wanted to have Louis. You see, a man like him is not cut out to be a husband. He will mess with your mind then he'll leave you with enough to kill yourself. That's the kind of man Louis is. He isn't cut out to be a family man." Jacque went relentlessly, telling her that Louis was a man like Saul, even worse. He exclaimed, "Louis would never marry you. . . !"

He wanted her to open her eyes, for her not to be blind over Louis and fall for him like she did with her late husband. He went on to say that Louis treated every new face who came to town like he was doing to her: " . . . I know you slept with Louis Janvier, or should I say Fuji, the running player.

I can't believe you slept with him, not me. I would have concealed your reputation. He's dragging you like a dog in the streets of Haiti. . . ."

Julie stared at him as he talked, trying to hide her rage and disgust. She didn't say a word. She shook her head with disbelief as he continued, " . . . So you see my dear, be smart, like I took you for, because Louis will use you and hurt you in a heartbeat. He'll treat you worse than garbage when he's through with you. . . . Look at the way he treated Carine. She gave her virginity to that man, then later he seduced Maxine. I wouldn't be surprised if he slept with Nicole, too. That's his style; one woman could never satisfy him. I couldn't believe you went back to his ranch after what he did to you the last time."

Gasping for some air, Julie breathed, "What do you know of that, Jacque?"

"He tried to have you both, Maxine and you at the same time."

Julie almost slapped him, but she held her hands against her chest. "Where did you hear that?"

"No one has to tell me, Julie my dear." He brought her face up to look at him. "I know the type of a man Louis Janvier is. He's still involved with Carine. Why do you think she had a fit whenever she saw the way he was looking at you? He ruined her life. She doesn't want him to do the same thing to you. Don't be fooled by his good looks and the expensive gifts he's sending you. Who knows who he robbed to give you the jewelry he's been giving you. . . . He caused many girls to commit suicide over him. I wouldn't want that to happen to you. I saw you heading in that direction."

Julie couldn't believe that Jacque would stoop that low to get his way by defaming another person to make himself look good. He continued to degrade Louis and her judgment. " . . . You cannot spend a day without seeing him. Louis is good for that, making a person attracted to him. He is a master player. Did you not notice the way he looked at your mother, Aunt Viviane, the way he touched her face. Right before your eyes Julie, he's trying to get involved with her. . . . I could understand if Aunt Viviane got involved with him . . . she's lonely. You have no excuse, because you have me for you. . . !"

As Jacque was talking, Julie never blinked. She couldn't believe her ears, although she heard the voice talking to her. She thought, *Was that really the Jacque she grew up with?*

She crossed her arms in front of her, listening to every word that came out of his mouth. Jacque spoke without mercy, " . . . The man is debauched. I thought you were a smart woman, Julie. I can't believe you of all people were taken in by that man, Louis, of all people. You allowed him to put his filthy hands on you. He'll cater to you like you were the only person in the world till another good-looking face appears. He'll do you worse than Saul, use you then dump you. Like I told you before, I do business with him because that's the only thing he's decent at. Even with that I have to watch myself with him. Marry me, Julie!"

Holding on to her, Jacque pulled her toward him, smelling her hair and rubbing his nose on her forehead as if to caress her with his lips. Her scent enticed him.

"Let go of me, Jacque! She pushed him away from her, disgusted by him.

"Oh, Julie, please, love me," he pleaded as he tried to hold her back. "Forget about Louis. Let's raise William together. Wherever you want to live and start a new beginning, I'm willing to follow. Here or in America, anywhere you want. Give me your answer tonight. Help me humiliate that bastard Louis for humiliating you."

Julie's palms were itching, and she knew at any moment she was going to let him have it. She was saved from doing something damaging by the arrival of Brian. Hurrying to get away, Julie called over her shoulders to Jacque, "I'll never forget your kindness to me."

She ran in the mansion as fast as she could to calm herself down as Jacque hurried up to meet Brian with a welcoming smile. "Mr. Bravé, just in time!"

"I had so much to do for Louis," Brian said as he watched Julie storming in the house. "Did I come at a bad time?"

"No, let's go inside," Jacque invited as they walked into the library. He tapped him on his back and asked, "How did you manage to keep it away from him?"

"It wasn't easy." Brian grimaced. Carine was in the library waiting for them. When she saw Brian, she pretended she was going to leave. Noticing the way she was looking at him, Brian deliberately went on to say, as if Louis was out of his mind, "All he was thinking of was Viviane. You know, Julie's mother, taking Julie horse back riding, playing big daddy with Julie. But I had many papers that needed to be signed so he just signed everything. Well, where's my commission?" he inquired.

Carine walked toward the sofa, then sat. She pulled out a briefcase from under the coffee table beside her and laid it on the table. With a flick of her wrist she opened it and said, "Forty thousand. It's all here."

Jacque said, "Do you want to count it?"

Brian pulled over the suitcase, looked at the money, closed the lid, and picked it up, saying, "I trust you. I did my part and you did yours."

Jacque offered him a drink. "Would you like a drink?"

Looking at his watch, Brian refused. "No, I have to go. There's a few things I have to do for Louis and his new family."

Jacque informed him, "Soon, I'm going to need more help. How about working for me? Louis is an idiot. He doesn't appreciate good talent. Whatever he's paying you, I'm willing to double it."

"I'll let you know." He smiled as he looked at Carine, heading for the door. "Now I really have to go. I don't want to arouse any suspicions."

"You're right," Jacque agreed. "We'll talk later."

Later in the afternoon, Jacque was talking on the telephone with Louis. "Tomorrow afternoon around two. . . . Okay, after lunch. Better yet, let's have lunch together at the Quest Restaurant. . . . Then one o'clock it shall be. Great! Oh yes! I will be there. Give Henry my regards. See you. . . ."

Jacque hung up the phone and smiled. He was quite pleased with himself. "Everything is settled. Tomorrow is the beginning of my new life. Julie, prepare yourself for your new master. And Louis Janvier, move aside because there's a new man in town."

He sat there meditating on the relationship between Brian and Louis. He felt Brian and Patrick would never be close with Louis. And Brian had more reasons for disliking Louis. Not only had Louis taken everything from him and his brother, but he also took Brian's woman away from him. Louis left him with nothing. He even took away his dignity. He was nothing to Louis except a messenger boy. He was not even using his agricultural skill to help Louis developing his lands.

The real reason Jacque thought Brian was working for Louis was to take vengeance for the death of his parents and for the loss of Carine, his fiancée. Jacque thought of the old saying "Keep your friends close, but your enemies closer." He thought that was precisely what Brian was doing, keeping close to Louis.

Roy walked in and asked, "Sir, do you need anything?"

"Come here, and fix me my favorite drink," he commanded.

Roy brought him a brandy. Jacque tasted the drink, swore, and spit the drink back out in the glass. "Don't you know my favorite drink? I should fire you for that. Cognac . . . cognac is my drink! Now do you remember! And no more brandy! This drink could cause you to have heartburn."

Taking the glass from Jacque, he placed it on the tray. "Yes, sir."

Confused Roy hastened to prepare the cognac drink and brought it to him. He smelled and tasted it, licking his lips in pleasure. Jacque continued talking, "Maybe I should change my name. What do you think, Roy? What about Sir Jacque Bassine the First? Don't you think that suit a man of my wealth and means?" he mused, stroking his chin.

Looking at his master strangely, Roy answered worried, "Yes, sir, that names suits you."

Imitating Louis, Jacque stretched himself the way Louis usually did, pushing his hair back away from his face, and asked in a low and mild tone of voice, "Roy, are you getting everything ready for tonight?"

Roy was stunned by the transformation. He thought Jacque had really flipped this time. "Yes, Monsieur Bassine, the staff and I have everything prepared and ready for tonight."

Roy gazed at him, wondering what was wrong with his boss. For a minute he thought that Louis Janvier was here with him talking or that Jacque was possessed, because Jacque did not talk calmly to anyone. Jacque continued, "Please pass me the phone, Roy."

Wondering, Roy handed him the phone and Jacque dialed.

"*Oui.* Can you put Dr. Janvier on the phone please," he said to the other person in the line.

He waited for a few seconds and said, "Oh yes, Fuji, I almost forgot. Tonight I'm giving a small celebration for Julie. Please do come. I'll be very happy if you could. And I'm sure Julie will especially be thrilled, too! Oh please don't make me beg. . . . Julie already knows about it. It's for her return, you understand. . . . Good! It's at seven! Thanks again. . . . See you then."

He hung up the phone and took a sip of his cognac; he thought, *Yes, I know he would be very happy to see Julie. He hasn't got enough of her. . . . Louis Janvier, make yourself happy . . . you can love her tonight. You can start warming up that cold fish for me, she'll like that. . . .*

Then Jacque flashed back on an incident that took place earlier this morning between him and Debbie. Smilingly he tasted her drink as if he could see her before him.

Didn't you hear what I said? It's over between you and me. Because of you, Julie didn't take me seriously. I need to get her complete trust and her attention. With you in the picture I can't do that. You messed things up the night of Nadine hang out. You deliberately wanted to talk that night when you damn well knew you were going to have an abortion. Then you tried to tell her right at the party, I could have wrung you neck for that. You came that close to getting your behind kicked that night."

"*That was over a year ago," Debbie brusquely replied. "You're totally out of your mind! Maybe you didn't see the king of the town was prowling around her that night, and he still is. You think a beggar like you will ever have a chance?"*

She laughed in Jacque's face to make him agitated. He grinned. "Now let go of the door and get out of my way!"

Debbie refused to move out of his way. He moved a few feet away from her. She yelled, "You think you can just come in and out of my life when ever it suits you? But not this time, Jacque. I can play the game, too. If you think you're going to walk out of my life and dump me like garbage, that's pure bullcrap, because I'm not going to make it that simple for you. You played with me too much, and I say enough."

"*Enough!" Jacque gruff. "I decided when it enough here, you get that!"*

"*Oh really," she exclaimed as she shook her head, then blurted, "I'm not one of your sisters you could just bully me around. . . . How long you and I have been together? Since I was nineteen. If we were married, we would have been together for over fourteen years, Jacque. You're still waiting for Julie to come to her senses, who grew up with you, was married to another man. And now running with Louis Janvier, who will hurt you if you stand in his way. I invested too much time on you, Jacque, to let you walk out of my life like that. I'm going to tell Julie everything, your plans and your stupid dream of getting wealthy off her back. And when I'm through, you will not have a face anywhere in town. Everyone will know what kind of scum you really are!"*

Slowly Jacque walked toward Debbie and said, "What did you say?" as he grabbed her by her face.

Debbie screamed, "Let go of me, Jacque! All I want to know is why have you treated me that way? All I ever did is love you. After all these years, I was always here for you, and this is how you thank me, you plan to marry Julie, not me? You're a bastard (She slapped him as she cried) Why?"

He grabbed her. "I heard you, but I don't want to hurt you, Debbie, get out of my way. I will hurt you if you ever threaten me again!"

He pushed her face away. She tried to ward him off with her hands, but Jacque caught her hands. She screamed as he pushed her away from him and she fell on the sofa. She picked up the vase that was on the table and viciously threw it at him and hit him on the head. He walked back to her and grabbed her when he saw blood was coming out of his head. He got on top of her and screamed in her face like a demented man, as his blood dripped on her face, "I could just kill you!"

Her face was covered with his blood. She whispered, "I guess you're really going to have to kill me because I'm not going to have an abortion again."

Shocked by her answer, Jacque quickly removed his body off her. "You're pregnant again?"

"Immaculately." She smiled.

"When were you going to tell me?" Jacque got up and said.

Pulling her up, he lifted her into his arms and carried her to her bedroom. He laid her on the bed, trying to reason with her. "Debbie, don't think I don't love you. I'm doing all this not for me only but also for you. We're going to need money, and the only person I know who could give me cash without asking too many questions is Julie. I need money. We will need money to raise our baby, understand! I don't want to leave you. But I need you to stay out of sight for the moment till I finish getting what we'll need from her. I will come to you. I don't want you coming around the mansion when she's around. Do you understand where I'm coming from?"

"I'm listening." Debbie frowned.

"My plan will benefit and profit both of us, and our unborn child." He touched her stomach. "Just be patient. Don't I always take good care of you?"

"Yes." She nodded her head. "But don't ever tell me you're leaving me."

"You're right." He gave her a kiss on the mouth. "I don't want to leave you."

He continued kissing her as he kept giving her his options. Then he removed his clothing. Taking a towel from her linen closet and wetting it in the sink in the bathroom he used it to wipe some of the blood off him. He looked at himself in the mirror on her bed headboard while he was murmuring, "Look what you did to me. You hurt me. Why must you act like a savage animal and talk back to me? You think Louis Janvier would be so rich if he had allowed his women to keep him down?"

Snatching the towel out of his hand, she gloated, "You're not Louis Janvier."

She went to the sink and rinsed the towel and wiped the rest of the blood off his body. He kissed her stomach gently as she wiped the blood off him. She whispered soothingly, "There, I'll make you feel better. I'll make you feel good all over again. . . ."

She removed her clothes and had sex with him. "You see, I'm can be very good when you're a nice guy."

Lying back on the bed with her, she smiled as he mentioned the things he was going to give her. "I'm going to give you money, jewelry, take you to fancy clubs and restaurants. We'll travel around the world. And you'll have this gorgeous body any time you want. Except, of course, if I'm dealing with business. Then sex comes later. . . . I'll make you happy."

After the moment of passion, Jacque kissed her lips as he moaned, "I have to go. Julie will be there soon. I wouldn't want my future wife to wait. If it were you, you wouldn't want me to have you waiting, would you?"

"Don't push it, Jacque," she replied, helping him get dressed and sending him on his way.

Deep in thought, the phone rang, jerking him back to the present. He picked up the phone. "Hello? This is he . . . I almost did not recognize your voice. Who's not coming home tonight. . . . I don't want them to come anyway. They might mess things up and I don't want any conflicts. Maxine almost messed things up today. I'll deal with her and her stupid boyfriend later. . . . Okay, see you later, Carine. . . ."

During that very time, back at the hospital, Louis was in a board meeting with all the chief doctors and heads of staff. He had just dropped his bombshell: "I would like to give my position to a new, talented surgeon–Richard Landers."

There was absolute silence, then one of the doctors spoke up, "But Dr. Janvier, why?"

"I'm resigning from this point. I want more time for my family, my wife and my son."

Another doctor asked, "Who are your wife and son? Do we know her"

"In time," he answered. "I'll introduce her to you all soon. But at the moment, please, no more questions."

The third doctor present said, "You've been with us for over seven years. It will be hard not seeing you around, but if this is your wish, I'm personally happy for you. I wish you all the best."

Another doctor agreed, "I, too, feel the same. It's about time you settled down."

One of the older doctors got up and shook his hand. "Congratulations, a wife and a son." He slapped Louis on the back, hugging him. "Do you think Dr. Landers is qualified for the position like you?"

Louis assured them, "I think he's even better than me. I'll give you three months, then he'll take over. Of course, with your permission."

"Fine," they all agreed.

Louis cautioned, "Don't tell Dr. Landers anything, it's a surprise. . . ."

It was four o'clock, the rush hour in Port-au-Prince. One has to know exactly where he or she is going so as to get out of this mess. Louis couldn't wait to get home to his wife. He thought to himself, *I can't live here, too many people in the city. The country will be better for us. Bill will have space to run. I don't want to repeat the same mistakes my parents did with me.*

Louis thought of Bill's education, how he hated the idea of children sitting in classrooms. He believed in hands-on training, traveling to the places or things he wanted to know. Seeing it, living it, touching it, and practicing it, that was the best way to learn. . . . He glanced in his rearview mirror and smiled as he thought of Julie. *I'm almost home.*

He stopped by the florist. The man brought him a large bouquet of flowers. He put it in the back seat of his car. Louis said, "Now I'm set."

Up, up into the mountain, toward his estate. You could smell the difference in the air of his domain. French hybrid lilac, jasmine, sweet shrub, and the double mock orange fragrance, and the mint plants were competing with the rose garden, surrounded by well-manicured grass. It was cooler tonight. At the entrance to the estate, the security guards were in the little house. One of them came forward eagerly to open the gate, greeting him, "*Bonsoir, Monsieur,*" as he drove through.

When he reached the door of his mansion, another security guard opened the door of his car. Louis handed him the keys to put away the car. He instructed, "I'll need the Jeep tonight. Bring it around seven."

Taking the keys from Louis, the man bowed, "Yes, sir."

The front door opened. Francois was already there, waiting with a drink. Suddenly Louis remember the flowers. Turning to the man he waved and called, "Wait."

Before the man could drive away, he opened the back door of the car and took the flowers out, walking toward the entrance of the house with eager steps. He took the drink from Francois, he tasted it, and placed it back on the tray, then asked, "Where's my wife?"

Then he saw her, standing like a beacon on the steps leading into the hall waiting for him. She came toward him, gliding across the floor. She flung herself into his arms, almost toppling them both over backward. He caught her and held her by one hand, while the other hand held the flowers he brought her. She plastered her lips to his like a drowning woman catching air, kissing him. They stood like that for a while, till gasping for air they both stepped back as Julie asked breathlessly, "How was your day?"

He handed her the flowers as they walked up the stairs. She kissed him to thank him. Heading for their room, Julie lay the flowers on the dresser and then proceeded to help Louis get more comfortable. She removed his jacket and his tie and unbuttoned his shirt. She told him to sit down so she could remove his shoes. He looked at her while she knelt and undid his laces, then he pulled her up to him and kissed her.

Louis asked, "Did Jacque tell you about tonight?"

She nodded to say yes. Louis continued, "Well, he invited me to his place tonight. He is having a party for you. He thinks I'm playing with you. . . . And by the way, everything was taken care of. Maxine gave me the deed to your mansion. You have all your original documents that Saul and your father left both you and your mother. This Jacque is something else. I thought I was bad, but that man doesn't know when someone's trying to help him. . . . If it wasn't for the deep affection you have for him, I would have hurt him to the core!"

She held on to her stomach like she actually felt pain. Noticing the way Julie reacted, Louis tried to comfort her, "I'm sorry, my darling. Did I frighten you?"

"No, you didn't." Julie sighed mournfully. "It's so hard for me to swallow that Jacque of all people would have done that to me. If it wasn't for you I would have signed all the papers he had handed to me without thinking. I trusted him with everything that I have and he did that to me. He hurts me. Jacque thinks I'm soft and stupid."

"Jacque definitely is blind," he replied, "if he thinks that you are."

"I'm hoping the party he's having tonight," Julie said, "is to come clean and he will apologize for his deceptive act."

Louis knew she wouldn't get that kind of apology from Jacque. He stayed quiet for a moment, looking at Julie while he finished removing the rest of his clothes. She was very disappointed at the fact that Jacque did this to her. Louis was feeling regret for letting her know what was Jacque up to. He thought he should have taken care of the situation himself without letting her know.

Julie took a glance at Louis. "What's wrong?"

He didn't answer. Louis's eyes looked dead. She continued on to talk, "Your silence told me that you're worrying for me. Well don't! There are certain things I need to know, even if it's hard for me to get over. You must tell me or otherwise our relationship won't survive. I don't want to repeat history. I want to learn from it and do better. We wouldn't be a team if you have kept what Jacque was doing a secret from me."

Louis could hear the sorrow in her voice as she spoke to him and how angry she was when she mentioned Jacque's name.

"Believe me," Julie continued, "I'm happy to know, even if it hurts. What Jacque did wasn't something I would have just swallowed and gone on with my life. I grew up with him, you know. He was the big brother I knew and grew to love dearly. I trusted him. . . . that should have been enough for him to think back to how we used to play. He was my confidant. Jacque was one man I thought who would never do anything to humiliate me, but he did. And without mercy he was going to con me out of everything I have helped establish and work hard for. I never want you to think of keeping me out of your plans, because if you do, we have nothing! We are husband and wife, and we are also partners in business and in everything we do now. I want to share everything with you, the good and the bad. Don't you ever forget that. Please, Fuji, don't get soft on me or think of leaving me out of the things that may be troubling you or me."

Louis sat back on the armchair, listening to what she was saying. Julie came and knelt before him. She looked up at him as she continued to talk,

"Jacque wants to hurt us, and I'm not going to have that. He wants to play games, and I'm not a toy for him to think that he could do whatever he wants to do with me. I never did and I'm not about to start. I don't know where he got his ideas that he could treat me like that, but he will be so wrong."

Passing his hands over her cheeks, Louis said, "Jacque probably thinks you're weak and you can't defend yourself."

"He is mistaking my kindness and my affection for him for my weakness." Looking him straight in the eyes she said, "He never met the other woman in me who can teach him a thing or two."

He chucked at her expression. "You think the other woman in you can teach this monster a lesson, Julie?"

Smiling innocently, she replied, "I don't know, but right now I feel I could teach this naughty man a lesson or two."

He pulled her up close to him as he stood up. He twirled around with her playfully till he tumbled with her on the bed, with her pinned between him and the bed.

"So you want to learn," she threatened playfully. She shifted beneath his weight. He groaned, "Are you going to teach me how you climb a coconut tree?"

Nodding her head. "Ooh! Fuji."

She brought her legs up around his waist, moving her body under him, holding him tighter with her legs as she made the movement as if to climb him like a coconut tree. Consumed with passion, Louis made no attempt to hide his arousal. "Oh yes! This is a lesson you're going to have to take your time teaching this naughty, horny monster. I really want to learn, and I'm a slow learner. . . ."

▣   ▣   ▣

The clock was ticking and the celebration time was here. It was early evening. Jacque and Carine's friends were arriving. Jacque was dressed all in black. From the back one could actually have mistaken him for Louis. Carine, coming into the room, was taken aback. "Jacque, for a minute I thought you were Louis. You even have his elusive scent. How much money did you spent to carry this one off?"

Jacque waved his hand with a flourish. "Right now money is no object. If you got it, flaunt it."

Admiring his appearance she replied, "My, you do look so handsome. . . . For a moment, if you were not my brother, I would marry you myself." Jacque smiled smugly to himself. She looked around the room at the gathering of people and asked, "Where's your guest of honor? She wasn't at the old house?

Jacque replied, "She went horse back riding with Louis. She'll be here soon. Speaking of the devil, they're here."

343

Jacque waved as Louis and Julie appeared through the door. He walked toward them, shaking Louis's hand and kissing Julie's hand. "Welcome to my home."

Carine and Michelle (whom she met at Nadine's place the second night she was in Haiti) also walked over to them. Carine extended her hands in a welcoming gesture. "Hello Louis, Julie. . . . How was the ride?"

"It was great." Julie gleefully smiled, looking at Louis.

"I bet it was," Jacque said. "Tomorrow, Julie, I'll take you for run around town."

Taking hold of Julie's arm, Jacque called out, "Let me introduce you to the guest of honor." He turned to Julie. "This is Julie. Some of you have already met her. I brought you all here for a special occasion. I want to let everyone know, especially Fuji," he pointed to Louis, "my good friend, how much I love Julie. . . ."

Louis and Julie stared at each other, trying hard not to laugh as he continued to talk. Louis almost smiled but he managed to keep a straight face. " . . . I want you to give me your answer now!" he demanded of Julie. "Will you be my wife?"

Managing not to show any expression, Julie said, "I thought you were going to confess something else. You have me speechless, Jacque."

Everyone stood there looking at them, shocked by Jacque's proposal. It was the one thing no one expected of Jacque, asking a woman to be his wife. Michelle and every other friend of Jacque's was surprised. They wondered what happened to Debbie.

Some remembered the time Carine was about to get married and how it turned out, and now this. What was going on with Jacque and Carine?

Carine knew Louis was not the marrying type and Julie was old-fashioned. She would need a man to help her bring up her son, and as Jacque knew her longer. He would know what she want. She felt that Jacque had a better chance than Louis. . . . Julie would not be able to handle Louis alone, because he was a freaky man. . . . How would Julie answer?

Looking around to avoid Jacque's eyes, Julie remarked, "Boy, am I thirsty."

Signaling to the help, Jacque quickly instructed, "Yes, please bring out some champagne."

Julie, Louis, and everyone present took a glass of champagne that the servants handed out. Jacque raised his glass, took a sip, and said, "Well, Julie . . . what will be your answer? My companions are waiting."

Everyone was still in shock. The atmosphere was tense. All eyes were on Julie. Some were eyeing Louis, who was staring at Julie, wondering what he was thinking. Julie took another sip of champagne and commented, "Mm, good champagne!" She licked her lips, looking at Louis with a lusty desire, causing some of the guests to murmur in shock at her gesture. Without looking at Jacque she said, "I'll think about it, big brother."

She made Louis and everyone along with him laugh at his request. The tense silence was broken as Jacque looked at both of them in frustration, saying roughly, "This is not the answer, ma belle."

Turning, Julie put down her glass. "I'm sorry, big brother. I must think about it, or I'll respectfully decline, like I've been telling you since I returned to Haiti."

She walked by Louis and spanked him on the buttock. She growled at Carine and Michelle, who had stationed themselves by Louis, "His butt is mine! So, girls, don't get too close!"

She made Jacque's proposal turn out to be a big joke to everyone. Jacque was looking at the way everyone was laughing at him. He felt like the world had fallen on top of his head. He watched as Julie twirled and blew a kiss at Louis as she walked away from the gathering and down to the terrace, leaving Jacque's guests laughing behind her. Jacque followed her, rage in all the vibes of his being. Louis was watching out of the corner of his eye as Jacque followed her. Michelle and Carine ignored Julie's warning. They were trying their best to entertain Louis, hoping tonight they could get a piece of that man. They tried to block his view of Julie.

Jacque stood behind her with blazing anger and said, "You think Louis is going to make an honest woman out of you." Julie glanced at Louis while Jacque spoke. "Yes, Julie, look at him standing by Carine and Michelle. I wouldn't be surprised if he's asking them to go to bed with him tonight. I was giving you the chance to humiliate him for running you around like one of his whores, and this is the way you repaid me!"

"You like to humiliate people, Jacque," Julie said calmly. "How did it feel on your part tonight, when you were wearing the shoes. You think you are the only one who could play that game, but I bet tonight you were surprised to know that I know how to play too if one pushes the right button. Don't you ever dare put me on a spot like that again. Get it through your thick cruel skull that I will never marry you."

"You haven't seen cruelty, Julie my dear," Jacque hastily breathed. "Because you are going to realize that soon you are going to need me. And the next time you think of pulling a stunt like that you'll think twice. You're going to pay dearly, my beloved Julie, for the embarrassment you caused me. How dare you humiliate me in front of all those people, and talk to me the way you did!"

"You humiliated yourself, not me." Shrugging, Julie glanced at him over her shoulder. "I thought you were going to apologize for your conduct toward me, but you didn't. I have all the right to dare to talk to you the way I did. You disgust me!"

Angered at Julie's response, Jacque lost his temper and grabbed her. Taking a firm grip of Jacque's hand, Julie reminded him, "Didn't I warn you this morning about putting your hands on me!

Louis saw Julie's hands go up and knew what was about to happen, murmuring to the people he was talking to, "Oh no. . . ."

Sidestepping the girls, he started running toward Julie, who had already lost control. In a split second she flipped Jacque flat on the ground. Jacque didn't know what hit him. Louis reached them just as Jacque was trying to get up. Louis wanted to hurt him, but Julie held him back.

"Louis, no." Shaking her head as she held him back, she pleaded urgently, "No more scenes."

Louis looked at her with such gentleness and wonderment as he asked tenderly, "Are you all right?"

"I slipped," Jacque mumbled as if Louis was talking to him. He was trying to get to his feet and figure out what had hit him. Louis looked down at Jacque without pity and said, "If you ever put your hands on Julie like that again, I'll kill you. Julie wouldn't be able to stop me from doing so."

Tears were shimmering in her eyes. She couldn't look at Jacque. She closed her eyes and asked Louis to take her home. Louis put his arm around Julie's shoulders, looked at Jacque halfway on the floor, shook his head at him, and turned with Julie and walked toward the parking lot.

Carine and Michelle ran toward Jacque. "What happened?" they asked in shock.

Jacque lied, "I slipped and I fell down."

Carine looked at Julie and Louis retreating back and asked petulantly, "And where are they going?"

Jacque replied, "Julie's not feeling well so I asked Louis to take her to the hospital."

"To the hospital?" Carine looked ready to kill. "Do you think that was a good idea? He's taking her over to his place."

Jacque lost his control and snapped, "Do you think I care! He's had every woman in town, why not her, too? And whether she wants me or not, she'll be my wife. She will come to her senses sooner or later, when Louis finishes using her."

Chapter Eighteen

My True Friend,
There'll Never Be Another

In some parts of Haiti, things could turn out to be a routine, and routine was something some folks tried to avoid. Julie was one of those individuals. Like Louis, she was awake before dawn.

Julie learned she had a lot in common with Louis. They loved to exercise. But most of all, they liked to work on their lands, taking care of their animals (they both were farmers at heart). Like that, they were able to unwind. Louis usually practiced alone; now, he had a partner to practice with. Julie had known martial arts for quite some time. She was good. She wanted Louis to practice with her, but he was holding back, afraid he might hurt her.

Julie noticed and taunted him, "What's wrong with you? Are you afraid you might hurt me?"

Louis did not respond because she was right. Julie emphasized, "If you will not practice with me, how am I going to get better? I know you're good. No man was able to bind me the way you did." She sneaked pleading kisses against his lips. "Please, please help me, Fuji."

Louis got up from the floor reluctantly. "All right, show me what you know. Let's rumble."

He spanked her on her buttocks. She put all of her strength out, trying to defeat her husband. But he was fast on his feet. Every now and then, Louis swatted her. Her behind was getting sore, and Louis was getting all

347

excited. He was trying not to smile, but Julie could see his eyes smiling like an idiot. He requested, "Oh, baby! Why do I have to do all the spanking? I like to get spanked, too."

Julie got upset at his remark. She lashed out with a trick move that she had been taught. Before Louis realized what had hit him, he was flat on the floor. She quickly sat on him and trapped him. Julie used her legs to pin him as she sat on his back, swatting him. "So you like to get spanked?'

"Now you done did it," he exclaimed as he rolled over to remove himself from under her. Standing up he said, "Now, let me show you some of my techniques."

Louis stood a few feet away from her, jumping up and down, loosening his body muscles. She ran toward him and threw a punch at him, but he spun out of her reach and grabbed a handful of clothing. He removed her top, saying, "I'm going to strip you limb by limb."

He did it so fast she did not notice her top was on the floor. She was standing there in her brassiere till he said, "I don't want to make you feel uncomfortable."

Stepping back, he removed his top. Dropping it on the floor, he invited, "Come and get me."

Shaking her head, she objected, "I don't think so. You come and get me."

"Then I shall come and get you."

As he was coming toward her, she spun around and threw a kick at him. He held her legs with his hand to prevent her from falling. He pulled her toward him and held her close to him. She realized she couldn't prevail under his grip and he undressed her. She pleaded softly, "Louis, Fuji. . . ."

She tried desperately to free herself from his powerful grip. Louis was superior in strength, skill, and size. He started to kiss her on her neck while he removed her brassiere. She surrendered under his touch of love. He let her go and gently lowered her to the mat, not taking his eyes off her as he kissed and caressed her. He made love to her on the mat.

He softly said, "You have filled my emptiness. You're all that I need in life."

As Louis made love to her, he thanked God for rescuing him. She was his darling. A precious gift she was to him. She was his strength, his way to freedom to life. She was everything he'd hoped for. He was finally complete. He gathered her into his arms and whispered, "Bone of my bone."

His words filled her soul as he breathed the last sentence into her mouth, kissing her like there was no tomorrow. Drowning in the sensations enveloping both her mind and body, she whispered his name.

"*Oui, mon amour* (Yes, my love)," he answered as he requested to hear her voice. "Let me know how you feel."

With love in her eyes she looked at him. She caressed and framed his face with her hands as she softly spoke to him. Louis's eyes were like stars in the heavens that were guiding her. He had brought meaning to her life.

The day Julie finally met him, she knew there was a God somewhere, because he was real. All her life, God had been guiding her to Louis. She dreamed of him when she was a child. She knew him before she even met him. Louis was her dream come true. She was his helper, a complement by his side. She was created to be for him. She concluded, "I love you so much."

"*Je t'aime, ma chérie* (I love you, my darling), Julie," Louis emphasized as he placed his arms under her body and turned her over on top of him. She lay on top of him, trying to catch her breath. "What technique was that?"

He laughed. "Julie turns Louis on."

She laughed too and sighed, "Oh no! It's Louis turns Julie on."

They were both laughing at each other's comments, then he said, "Are you ready for round two?"

She stared at him, wondering, as he maneuvered her again so that she was lying beneath him. He murmured, "I feel untamed. . . . Subdue me, Julie."

Julie smiled at his request, wondering at the power she had over this man. "Who are you, my husband, Louis Janvier, Fuji, or should I call you Tempest?"

He chuckled with a sinister glow in his eyes. "Yes," He slowly moved on her, "The beast within." She laughed softly at his description of himself. "Efficient and explosive. I'm destructive."

He captured her interest. She gave her last fighting words as she became lost in his arms. "Let go of me . . . Louis."

He parted her mouth with his and whispered, "It's futile. I will not let you go." He kissed her deeply.

She smiled as he consumed her once more.

Later that morning, Louis was all dressed up for work. He looked good in his beige suit. Viviane had returned from Jacmel last night. Julie was standing with Bill in her arms, admiring her husband, who was sitting in the study room reading his newspaper. He looked up at the sound of her voice saying, "Look at Daddy, William."

Bill was waving at him with a wide smile on his face. He put the paper down and opened his arms. Julie walked over and as William ran into Louis's arms, he sat Bill on his lap and kissed him. Louis tickled him saying, "Good morning, my son. How was your night? And you," he turned to Julie, "how is your morning, my heart?"

"I'm exhausted," she replied with wide yawn.

Looking up at her innocently he asked with interest, "How come?"

She replied, "I had to fight this six-nine foot man off me."

"Did you win?" he asked with mocked innocence.

"No, he made me beg for mercy."

Louis considered the matter. "I have to talk with this man on that matter."

He rubbed his chin, his eyes twinkling. She bent over and kissed him. "Please do. . . . I'm going over at Nadine's, honey. I want to spend the day with the Bassine girls with Bill."

"Then I'll call you there," he said, getting ready to leave. He hesitated. "Do you want me to drop you there. . . ?"

Loziane came in with the baby bag and all the necessities. Francois also walked in and greeted them, "Good morning, Madame, Monsieur Janvier. Your car is waiting for you, sir."

"Thank you," Louis replied, taking up his briefcase and going toward the door. "Are you ready, my love?" he inquired of his wife.

"Yes," she replied, turning to Loziane. "Do you have everything we need?"

Loziane checked again. "*Oui, Madame.*"

"Then we are ready, darling." Julie walked beside Louis with the toddler in his arm to where the Jeep was waiting outside. Loziane walked behind them. Louis saw them all secured and comfortable, then he got in and drove off.

At the mansion, Jacque and Carine were having a good breakfast. Carine asked, "Are you ready for today?"

Jacque replied smugly, "More than ever. Today is the day my name will make history. Of course, yours too! At one o'clock I'll be sitting with Louis Janvier and signing the deal of a lifetime with him. Then I'll overthrow him, too. My name is going to be feared in the world of business. And Julie will regret that she didn't accept my proposal."

"I thought she had more common sense," Carine stated, "but I was wrong."

"She became stupid since she started to hang around Louis," he banged his hand on the table. "Damn Louis really messed up her mind. What does he have that I don't have? Every woman seems to be charmed by him so easily."

"Money, my dear brother." She touched his face. "You already have the look. . . . And you need to practice your charm. . . ."

Jacque smiled as he kissed her hand to thank her. Carine continued. "And I think she was trying to embarrass you last night, but she made a fool of herself by leaving with Louis. . . . Everyone knows what the outcome would be."

"Embarrass wasn't the word," he exclaimed. "I was humiliated, but today will make up for the misery she's been causing me. She still didn't get what kind of a person that lazy, materialistic, and bully of a man Louis is . . . he has his coming. He thinks he's all that. What gave him the right to move in on my territory? But I'm going to play the game well with him. When he gets hit right in the middle of is face, he won't know what hit him." He noticed she was dressed for outdoors. "Are you going somewhere today?"

Carine finished her breakfast and prepared to leave. "I'm dropping by Nadine's to talk with our sisters, to talk some sense in them. I'm kind of lonely here."

Jacque waved her off with a pat of her shoulder. "Go then, and give them a word of warning. Tell them what happens to those who don't listen to me, and those who turn against me. . . ."

At Nadine's, Julie had just arrived. Nadine came out to meet the car. She took Bill from his seat as she greeted Louis. "Hello, Fuji. *Bonjour.*"

She reached into the window of the car and kissed his cheek, then turned to go with the baby into the house. Loziane and Nadine walked up the steps and inside the house, giving Julie and Louis time to share a goodbye kiss. Maxine ran out of the house to pull Julie off Louis.

"Help, someone!" she called playfully when she couldn't pull them apart.

Nicole ran out to help her. Julie and Louis were laughing like two kids who've been caught doing something they shouldn't be doing. Eventually, Maxine and Nicole managed to tear them away from each other. They were throwing kisses at each other.

Maxine pulled Julie toward the house. She instructed, "Say bye-bye, Louis."

They were still throwing kisses at each other as he slowly drove away. Julie breathed in deeply, smiling like the cat that got the cream. "I'm all right now."

"Are you sure?" Maxine laughed.

"I need to cool down." Julie nodded, fanning herself with her hands.

They walked into the cool house. Julie was dressed in black. Indeed, she did need to cool down. It was beginning to get hot outside. Her hair was shining like a sleek golden bronze mane. Nadine directed them to the guestroom where they could put away their things. Then they went to the den. Loziane had Bill in her arms, sitting on a comfortable chair, a short distance outside to play with Bill.

Julie called her over to the group, "Loziane, don't let him go in Nadine's rose garden and don't let him run too far."

"Yes, madame," Loziane replied and left the room.

Maxine was browsing through a wedding book, looking for the wedding dress she wanted to wear for her wedding. She found one and showed it to Julie. "Julie, this is what I want to wear for my wedding."

Julie took a look at the picture. "This is nice. How many bridesmaids you plan to have?"

"Six girls and boys," Maxine said dreamily.

Nicole piped up impatiently, "Well Julie, how was it with Louis?"

"Oh my word!" Laughing Julie said, "None of your business!"

The others chimed in, "Yeah, Julie, how was it?"

Julie blushed and smiled. "I'm glad my mother did not come with me." She laughed and put her hands to her chest and sighed. "I felt like I had never been touched before." They laughed as she closed her eyes to say, "Yes. Now I understand why so many women wanted him."

Nadine asked, "What made you two get married that night?"

"I wanted him so badly." She sighed. "And he was going crazy, too."

"No," Nadine cut in, "I want the beginning of the story, all the juicy parts that lead to the marriage."

Everyone agreed they all wanted to know the secret of how she was able to capture the unyielding man. Smiling, Julie said, "Oh, well, girls, get your popcorn and a tall glass of cold water."

They all chorused, "Why?"

"Because I don't want you girls getting crazy like I did."

Nicole said, "We have no popcorn, but we have plenty of ice water and lemonade."

"Then we're all set." Again Julie closed her eyes and exhaled. "The night I returned from New York, Louis invited us for dinner. It was pouring that night so we all got wet. Louis and the others took us to change our clothes in the guestrooms so we could dry off. He had Bill in his arms. He took Billy and I to his room and Richard took my mother to another room. I thought he had left the room so I removed all my clothes."

"*All* your clothes?" Maxine teased.

"Everything! Then he walked in with two shirts in his hands, talking to Bill. It was so embarrassing. I just stood there frozen and he just stood as if turned to stone. Then he turned his head away. . . ."

Nadine was surprised. "Fuji turned his head? Unbelievable! I guess he did not want to scare you."

Julie continued her story, "He changed Bill's clothes while I put on the other shirt that was in his hand. Then when the time came to feed Bill, he asked if I was going to breast feed him. I told him I had stopped. You wouldn't believe what he said."

Nadine was eager. "Go on, girl!"

"Well," Julie said, "he said if he was my baby he would not want to stop breast feeding."

Maxine was stunned. "Oh, my God!"

Everyone laughed. Nicole asked, "Where was Aunt Viviane?"

"In another room." Julie said. "Then he went and put on a robe, too."

"Why?" asked Maxine.

"He said he wouldn't feel comfortable if he didn't because everyone had robes on."

"Then it turned into a slumber party!" said Maxine gleefully.

"You could say that," Julie answered. "After dinner we talked for a little while but my mother was very tired and she went to her room to sleep. I made to follow my mom, but he held my hand like he didn't want me to go. I went up with my mother anyway."

Everyone said, "Uh! Poor Louis."

"After I finished putting Bill to bed, I met him down in the lounge. . . ."

Nadine cut in with excitement, "There! You two made wild and passionate love in the lounge."

Julie laughed and shook her head as she exclaimed, "No . . . nothing like that. We played pool and then he took me for a tour around the mansion. But there was one door he kept on skipping that he didn't show me. I asked him what was behind those golden doors. He said if he showed me, I would have to marry him."

"Smooth . . . that's my cousin." Nadine laughed, and she went on to say, "You remember the first time we met?"

Julie answered, "In the restaurant on Bissantnaire."

"Yes," she replied. "When Louis heard Jacque mentioned his name. That was the first time I saw my cousin turn to look at a woman and get nervous. Henry got scared when he noticed that. . . . You know those guys, they still want to stay macho. I didn't give Louis's reaction much thought till you arrived that night at the hang-out. The way he held your hands and how he looked at you. Then he insisted for you to give him the definition of your desert plant. Why would a beautiful woman like you be a desert plant! He was intrigued, everyone was. Louis, who barely talked, was speaking, asking questions, volunteered in the conversation, and actually forced Jacque to issue an invitation for lunch."

"I thought he was a bold and arrogant man," Julie said.

Nadine continued, "That he is. But that was a surprise to everyone there that night. You caused a lot of jealousy. Some of the women were happy to see you leave. You made my cousin thirsty, the way he breathed when he looked at you. You aroused his appetite. I was afraid for you."

"You were?" Julie asked. "Why?"

"Because I noticed he made you nervous," Nadine replied. "You couldn't breath, too. It was amazing! Since that night, I felt you two were going to be lovers, but I kept silent. He kept on questioning you. He couldn't keep his eyes off you. I was happy to see you were able to keep my cousin interested. He became alive that night, he was talking so much. And when you left, he went home, too."

"Yeah!" Julie retorted. "To a hot date!"

"How did you know?" Nadine replied, and looked at Maxine. "Maxine!"

They all laughed as Nadine threw a pillow at Maxine. Glancing at Nadine, Julie said, "Saul was also there, too."

Nadine was surprised that she knew. "He didn't want you to know that he was there."

Noticing that Nadine was beginning to feel strained, so did Maxine and Nicole by her revelation, because they knew Julie was tempered, Julie smiled to put everyone at ease. "He wanted to make room for Louis."

They all laughed in relief, then Nadine said, "I never thought my cousin was the marrying type."

"Well my sister here," pointing her finger at Julie, Maxine laughed, "was able to melt the man of steel." She looked at Julie and asked eagerly, "So what was behind the doors?"

"The ballroom!"

Everyone laughed. Nicole urged, "What happened then?"

"I started to dance and waltz by myself," Julie replied. She got up from her seat, hugging herself and simulating a waltz.

"That was a seduction dance," Maxine laughed. "The Salome dance! Works all the time, because the king granted you his head."

Maxine got everyone to laugh. Julie smiled. "I was not trying to seduce him. I was just being playful. You know, like a kitten. . . . I danced around him as I was about to waltz away from him. He held me back, pulled me close to him, and kissed me deeply and hungrily. I almost fainted, so he had to carry me to his room."

Nadine gave her thumbs up signal and crowed, "Home run for my cousin!"

They all sat there in anticipation, big smiles on their face, waiting for Julie's next words. "He laid me on his bed, removed his shirt off me, and stood and removed his robe and everything off him. Girls! I thought I had died and gone to heaven! I was seeing a Greek god in the flesh. . . . I begged him to have mercy on me."

Nicole asked breathlessly, "Did he?"

Julie closed her eyes at the memory. "Yes, he did. He did not touch me. He was confused about what I was asking, I explained to him my values on sex and marriage."

"What value is that?" Nicole asked surprised. On hearing what Nicole asked, Maxine looked at her and burst to laughter. She exclaimed, "You're such a tramp! If Aunt Viviane heard you say something like that, she'd have a heart attack. And ask you if she ever taught you self-worth."

Looking at Nicole, Julie said impatiently, "I believe sex should only be in marriage."

"He accepted that?" Nadine asked skeptically.

"Not only did he accept it," Julie replied, "he also promised me he wouldn't touch me until we got married. So when we returned to the ranch, I wanted him so badly, and he wanted me, too. But he had made a promise that he wouldn't touch me unless we got married. And before I knew it, I agreed, so here we are. *Voilà* (That's all)!"

Nadine said, "You're so smart. . . . One smart woman, you're going to have to teach me how to be a cactus."

"You, a cactus!" Maxine laughed. "You don't even know how to boil an egg or how to hold on to a broom. You're a rose, my dear. The sun would scorch you. You better find a shady ground to stand on or do like most of the islanders do, walk with an umbrella. Otherwise, you would not survive."

Nadine threw a piece of folding paper at Maxine. The bell rang. She was surprised. She was not expecting any visitors. "Who else knew we were going to be here?"

The maid came in and told her, "Miss Carine Bassine is here, Miss Janvier."

Carine walked in, looked at the group, and remarked, "Oh, you're having a party here!"

Maxine continued complimenting Julie, "You two make a very handsome couple."

Julie opened the French door to call Loziane to bring her son in to her. Picking up the toddler Julie remarked, "It's getting hotter, let me have him, Loziane. . . ."

She handed Bill over. Julie asked, "Could you get his water for him, please?"

Loziane went to the back to get his cup. Nadine said, "What brings you here, Carine?"

Nicole asked petulantly, "What do you want?"

Looking around for some where to sit, Carine insisted, "You girls are having a party and I was not invited?"

Again Nadine replied, "There's no party, just us girls chatting."

Carine walked over to Julie and sat in the empty chair by her. "Can I hold him?"

She stretched out her hand and tried to take the toddler but he wouldn't let her, and he started to cry. Maxine said, "Look what you've done. Bill knows the witch that you are."

Maxine came and took Bill from Julie. He stopped crying. "There, there," she crooned. "Did she scare you?"

Nicole asked again, "What brings you here?"

Carine looked at her. "I miss you girls. So I dropped by to see how you were doing."

Loziane came in with the water for the baby. "Here is the bottle, Mrs. Janvier."

Carine choked on her own saliva when she heard what the maid called Julie. Nadine smirked. "Are you all right, Carine?"

Everyone stayed quiet for few seconds, trying not to laugh, while Carine sat back on the chair trying to catch her breath. She asked breathlessly, "Can I have a glass of water, please?"

Nicole went to the back to get her the water.

Meanwhile, Jacque had just arrived at the restaurant for his appointment with Louis. Louis, Henry, and Brian were already there. Jacque, with his briefcase in his hand, was directed to where they were sitting.

"Sorry I'm late," Jacque apologized.

Louis looked at him. "You're not late. We're early. Sit down, Jacque," Louis invited, indicating the chair. He was sitting at the head of table with Henry to his right and Brian sitting across the table facing Louis, leaving the left seat next to Louis for Jacque. The waiter came over and offered the menu to Jacque. Louis, Henry, and Brian had already ordered. Without looking at the menu, Jacque said, "Whatever Monsieur Janvier is having, I'll have, too."

"*Oui, Monsieur.*" The waiter bowed and left the table.

Louis turned to Jacque. "Let's get right to the point. Where are the papers you wanted to show me?"

"I have them here," he replied, picking up his briefcase and setting it on the chair next to him.

Opening it, he handed them to Louis, who read them one by one, taking his time. The waiter returned with Jacque's drink and placed it in front of him. Jacque tasted it and said, "It's water."

It was mixed water with a twist of lime. Jacque said, "I wanted a cognac."

The waiter looked at him in dismay. "I am sorry, monsieur, I thought you want the same thing Monsieur Janvier was having. I shall bring you your cognac, or is it brandy?"

Jacque waved him away. He didn't want to cause a scene at this point. "It's okay . . . I'll drink this."

The waiter left the table and went about his business. Louis finished reading the papers and handed them to Henry. He picked up his glass, tasted his drink, and looked Jacque straight in his eyes and said, "I already invested in those plantations, Jacque."

"What do you mean, Fuji?" Jacque was beginning to feel nervous. "I have all my documents here. And I know you are a man of your word."

"What you're showing is already mine," Louis said as he sat back to listen to his explanation to him.

Jacque said agitatedly, "You mean half of the plantation. The other half belongs to me. She had signed everything over to me. And I have learned . . . you own the other half and the procedure should make it even easier to complete, and I don't see any problem when it comes for you to do your part. I have all the papers here to conclude the closure as you promised."

Henry looked the documents over and passed them to Brian. "These are not the original papers. These are copies."

Jacque grabbed the papers from Henry. He looked at them in disbelief. "That's impossible. No one else had the originals but me, and she signed them over to me."

Louis replied, "I already invested with the rightful owner."

Jacque pushed them before Louis. "Look! Her signature. These are the real papers. . . . How can you have signed these papers when you need the other party. . . . Under his breath he said, "Maxine! When did she invest?"

Louis heard him. He pushed his hair back to calm down as he made himself more comfortable. "That is none of your concern. And that's not even her name."

Jacque slid the paper before him and studied the name on it. The signature read "Julie Philip III." He wondered what was Louis talking about, this was her name. He insisted, "Carine and I saw her sign the documents, and Brian, you saw her leaving my house yesterday," trying to tell Louis that Brian was involved in his scheme.

"To be more precise, Brian chuckled, "I saw her going into the mansion. I thought that was her home. She lives there."

Jacque didn't know what to say. He rubbed his hands over his head, he was so angry. He wanted to scream. "How can she . . . aarrgghhh. . . ." He cut himself off.

"So," Louis said, "you seem to find it hard to believe that the rightful owner had already had them, Jacque. You're right, I am a man of my word and I've helped you to be the same. That was what you were supposed to do, I presumed, hand those documents to Henry so he could take care of them. I assumed that was what Saul wanted you to do. He trusted you to do that. So I've helped you keep your part of the bargain. You could get yourself into serious trouble for counterfeit. . . ."

Louis's voice got softer, because right now he had never been angrier in his life. " . . . Do you know when you took something that belongs to Julie without her permission, you disrespected me? Are you trying to steal from me, Jacque? You know my reputation better than anyone in Haiti. Taking something that belongs to me without my permission or trying to double-cross me. I don't take hostages."

Jacque was blustering, "I was not trying to double-cross you, Fuji. There has got to be a mistake."

"Consider yourself blessed." Louis looked at him in contempt. "Lately I've been in a good mood. I'll let you slide this time. . . . You're a special man, Jacque! Julie loves you very much and your family. She wouldn't be happy to hear that I dismembered you, but let me give you a word of advice . . . don't ever cross my wife again. I'll hurt you if you ever try to hurt her or anyone my eyes had come in contact with, and that is your last warning. . . ."

Jacque tried to explain, "Fuji, I wasn't trying to steal from you. I. . . ."

Louis grabbed Jacque's hand while applying pressure on Jacque's neck, causing him pain. He stopped Jacque from speaking. The way he was sitting next to Jacque, one would think they were the best of friends.

"Don't insult my intelligence," Louis said. "I could still hurt you, Jacque! How's your breathing. . . ?"

Jacque couldn't answer because Louis was using a pressure point that caused him to be short of breath.

" . . . You're walking on thin ice, Jacque. You betrayed her and you had committed treason. You have no honor or loyalty. You hurt the woman I love. You went against Julie, but in reality you went against yourself. And since you didn't appreciate her kindness, you're not going to freeload on her anymore. I haven't forgotten about last night, and the time you put on your talent show on the day of Julie's conference. You embarrassed her and me with your theatricals. I haven't gotten over that yet." Louis released his hand. "What happened today is just a little taste of what your future holds if you don't change your ways. You actually thought I couldn't hurt you, but you were wrong. . . .

"Next time you try to stand in my way, I'll break your legs." He let go of Jacque's neck. "You're a fool, Jacque. You should have continued being the brother Julie needs, maybe you would have had suckered her husband. You and Debbie have something very special on the way. Be a good example for your unborn child. Don't let your child grow up to know his father was a thief, a deceiver, who stole money from a woman who helped him out all his life and this is how he thanked her. That wouldn't look good in your resume, before your child, would it?"

Jacque shook his head no. Louis carried on to say, "You owe Julie a very big apology because she's hurt by you. I swear, if you do not help her get over the wrongdoing you caused her, I will inflict great harm upon you. I'll make sure you never recover when I'm through with you, so I suggest you make amends to her and very fast, because I'm running out of patience, and I easily get bored, so I'm always looking for something new to do. Do I make myself clear. . . ?"

Jacque nodded his head in understanding as he took a quick glance at Henry who was staring at him. Louis concluded, "I never talk that long with anyone besides Julie. My!" Louis looked at his watch. "I usually do all the listening. I spent some valuable time talking to you. I would hate to know that I have wasted my precious time talking to you. Therefore, I would advise you to stay out of Julie's business affairs for now on. And one more thing . . . you have not earned the respect of my friendship for you to call me Fuji. The next time you call me Fuji, I will rip your tongue out of your mouth and make you eat it. Now remove yourself from my sight before I personally remove you."

Jacque felt humiliated and angry at the same time, but still he had never heard Louis talk that much. He quickly picked up his briefcase and the papers and rushed out to his car. He couldn't understand the situation. He opened the door of his car and threw the briefcase in. He was thinking out loud. "I spent over a year plotting getting these papers together, and this is how the deal ended. No! She couldn't have the original papers. Who told her about the lands and of my plans? Saul, her husband? No, he's dead.

Constant . . . he had to tell her. Julie acted like she didn't know anything. She's more malicious than I thought!"

He drove like a madman to Constant's office. Constant had just finished with a client. Jacque walked into his office, past Constant's secretary before she could stop him.

Constant looked up as Jacque burst in. "Oh, Jacque, I didn't see you."

Jacque slammed the door behind him. He was furious. He pushed the chair he was sitting in over and knocked him down. Grabbing Constant, he screamed, "You weasel . . . you double-crossed me! I'm going to kill you!"

Constant was struggling to get out of Jacque's hold. "What are you talking about?"

Jacque yelled, "You told her . . . you told Julie about the lands, you pig!"

Constant yelled back, "Nonsense! You were here when I spoke to her. When did I have time to tell her things?"

Jacque moved closer to him and punched him in his face and tried to choke him. Constant tried to push him off, but Jacque was too strong in his consuming rage. Constant tried to yell, "Get off me!"

"I'm sure you told somebody," Jacque said through his teeth, putting pressure around Constant's throat.

Constant feared Jacque was really going to kill him, but he managed to get a breath out. "You're mad! Help! Help somebody!" he yelled.

Luckily there were many people in the outer office and they came to his aid. They pulled Jacque off him. Constant shouted, "Take him out of here . . . you crazy bastard! Get out, and don't ever come back here again, you thief!"

Constant was pretty shaken. Jacque stomped out to his car. He knew Constant did not tell Julie. He thought of his sisters. *Maxine! She was the one I sent to get the documents for me. She gave me the wrong papers and gave the real thing to Julie. Wait till I get my hands on you.* Jacque thought in his clamoring rage. *No one will recognize her when I'm through with her!*

He made a U-turn and almost ran over a merchant who was sitting on the street of Bourdon. Then he thought of what Louis had said earlier. "*Don't ever cross my wife." That idiot . . . he had really screwed with her mind. No wonder she is hooked on him. He's playing husband and wife with her. That man is really evil. He has all that money and he wanted Julie's properties, too. He's not giving anyone a chance to make it rich. . . .*

He hit the steering wheel with his hands over and over. "It's impossible for Julie to have those papers. Some other thief beat me to it. Maxine or Jean, they must have given them to Louis. And that thief Brian set me up and robbed me. I can't believe he did that to me when I was trying to help him to settle the score with that bastard Louis. What is the world coming to?"

A man was passing by Jacque's car. He lowered his head down to the front window of the passenger side of the car and said with concern, "Hey, mister, are you okay? Do you need help?"

Jacque cursed the man, "*Vou-zant monche* (The hell with you)!"

The man responded, "*Pitit chien, cochon* (Son of a dog, pig)."

Jacque almost ran the man off the road. He screamed, "Damn! I'm short of a lot of money. I owe more than I'll ever have. I'm broke!" He gave a crying smile. "Julie is an understanding woman. But how can I get her trust back? She has so much money and her mother. Damn! I should have gone after her mother instead of her. She looks nice for an old hag. She would have appreciated me more than her daughter. Louis had her over at his place. I'll call her. I'll ask her for a date. She can't refuse me. I'm young and good looking, I'm a stud, and I'm sure she'll like that."

Jacque had really gone out of his mind for him to think the woman who helped raised them would become his lover. Not once did he stop to think to calm himself down. All he could see was the money he wanted, and he was going to do anything to get what he wanted even if he had to marry Aunt Viviane. He drove through the yard of the mansion like a madman and stopped in front of the door. He ran to the library to check on the other documents he was hiding from Julie. Everything was gone. Jacque screamed like a tormented man!

Roy, who was heading to the library, ran in to see what was going on. He found the library was in total chaos. There were papers and books all over the room. He saw Jacque at his desk talking on the phone. "Can I speak to Mrs. Bertrand?"

On the other end Francois told him, "I'm sorry, sir, she went out of town."

He asked urgently, "Do you know where she went? It's very important that I contact her?"

"I'm sorry," Francois answered. "I don't know where you can reach her."

Jacque hung up and went totally out of control. He rushed by Roy out of the mansion and got in his car. Remembering what Brian stated yesterday afternoon at the library, how Viviane was always on Louis's mind. "Louis is really a dog, one sick dog. He married her mother. Now I understand why she's over at his estate. They secretly got married. This is one greedy man. All that time he had me thinking he's after Julie and he was working on Aunt Viviane. No wonder she's always tired, too tired to talk to me. How did he manage to trick me? Now he's playing daddy and grandpa. Now I understand why he was so overprotective of her. He has them both under his spell!"

Jacque didn't want to believe that Louis was speaking of Julie when he said "my wife." So it had to be Aunt Viviane, because Louis said it would have been better for him if he had continued playing Julie's big brother and forgot about the part he could have suckered her husband. His mind was racing over and over, spinning out of control.

Throughout the time that was taking place, Richard had joined the girls for lunch. They had a big meal because Julie claimed she could eat a horse.

She would need all the energy she could take in, because she was having a sexual appetite. After they finished watching Julie eat like she was starving, they all trouped back to the living room to continue their conversation.

Maxine touched her stomach. "Where did all that go, Julie?"

They all laughed as Julie stretched her body and said, "All over!"

Carine was still shaking from the previous news. She sat by the corner window, wondering when Julie and Louis got married. She noticed the gem on top of Julie's left wedding finger. She thought, *Damn that must have cost a fortune!*

But still she felt they were putting on an act. Maxine was always teasing her, and Nicole was now helping her because she let Jacque hurt her. She stared at the baby's hands . . . that was the doll Julie received the night of her slumber party. . . . She slowly and cautiously moved over to Loziane, who was holding Bill, thinking, *That's lot of money William is holding in his hand.*

She said, "Can I see your doll, Bill?"

Trying to take it from him, the toddler screamed. Before Julie could say anything, Loziane snapped at her, "Will you please remove your hand from him? Don't you see you're frightening the child? Move away from him. . . ."

"Realizing what she just said, she turned to Julie. "Oh Madame, I'm very sorry."

Julie took Bill from Loziane and dismissed her out of the room. Carine replied, "*Bonne sa frekan* (This maid is fresh). Look at the way she spoke to me. Hey Julie! You need to train your maid."

Julie was surprised by Loziane outburst. She looked at her as she was leaving the room. She thought, *Well I don't have to worry too much when I'm not around, she'll make sure no one messes with my son.* "She is not a maid, she is William's sitter, and you heard what she said."

Carine contemptuously replied, "Whatever . . . maid, sitter, they're all the same to me. All I want is to look at the doll."

Carine was still trying to take the doll from William. Julie snapped, "My son is playing with it. Now leave him alone before I lose my temper."

Carine replied sarcastically, "*Oh, oui, Madame Janvier.*"

"That's right," Julie shot back. "And don't you ever forget that I am Mrs. Louis Janvier."

There was a knock on the front door. Richard went to answer it. Nadine was surprised. "The gate was closed. How did that person get in without ringing the bell?"

Suddenly Maxine said, "Richard, don't open the door!"

But it was too late, he already did. Jacque walked in. "So, you girls were not going to open the door for me."

Nicole said, "We don't want any guys in here. As you can see, it's only us girls."

Jacque pointed at Richard with a sneer. "Then who the hell is this, Rachelle?"

Maxine asked, "What do you want?"

He smiled coldly. "I came to take you and Nicole home so you two can stop associating with low lifes."

Maxine looked at the others, then back at him and said, "The only low life that's here is you."

He tried to grab her but she ran behind Richard. Nadine intervened, "Jacque, this is my house. I don't want you to start any trouble here."

He smiled at her and looked back at his sisters, "I don't want any problems either. Give me my sisters, and I'll be on my way home."

Nicole turned to Carine. "Well, Carine, get the hell out of here. You're not needed here." She turned to Jacque. "She is the only thing you have here."

Jacque looked at her in spiteful amazement. "My, you grew spikes, Nicky. I'll talk to you when we get home. Now get your bags and let's go!" he ordered.

Maxine spoke up, "We are not children that you could just waltz in here and order around. We're not going anywhere with you."

"You heard them," Richard backed her word. "They're not leaving with you. Now go."

Richard pointed to the direction of the door. Jacque looked him up and down contemptuously and sneered, "So you're Marie's boy. You think you are big enough to make me leave?"

Turning his back on Richard, he moved toward Julie, gave a wolfish smile, and said, "So I see you're here with the rest, and how's my future son doing?"

He tried to pat Bill's head. Pulling the baby out of his reach, Julie replied, "Keep on dreaming, and you heard what Richard said. Get out before I lose my temper!"

Maxine moved toward Julie to stand by her. Richard turned to Jacque. "Let's go."

He walked ahead of Jacque to open the door. Suddenly Jacque picked up a vase from the table nearby and hit Richard over the head with it. Maxine screamed as she watched her fiancée crumple to the floor. She ran toward him, trying to revive him.

"You bastard!" Maxine shouted at Jacque. "You're a coward!"

Turning to Julie with pure venom in his voice, Jacque said. "Now let me hear you talk the way you did before, Julie. Daddy Louis is not around to protect you like last night."

Julie didn't move. She handed her son to Nadine as she kept her eyes on Jacque. "Nadine, move from here with my baby. . . !"

Taking William out of Julie's hands, Nadine moved out of her way and Jacque's.

"Are you out of your mind, Jacque?" Nicole cried out. "You will be killed for what you're doing here!" She thought that Jacque had gone mad, as she pleaded, "Louis will kill you if you even think of hurting her, Jacque. Stop." She tried to hold him back. "Get away from her, Jacque. . . . We'll go with you, right, Max!"

With tears running down her face, Maxine nodded her head to say yes, knowing that was the only way to prevent their brother from being killed.

"You're not going anywhere with this maniac," Julie, still standing, rigidly instructed. "Move, Nicole."

Nicole reluctantly moved away from him. Carine was still sitting by the window, watching the scene.

Julie continued, "I've been putting up with you and Carine for a very long time. You borrowed money from me, and you never say when you're going to pay me back. I say friendship is better than money. You lied to me. I say everyone lies sometimes to make themselves look good, so who am I to judge you two? I know there'll never be anything between you and I. Then you and Carine tried to steal from me, but you two didn't succeed. So I thought, let's forget it because of Max, Nicole, and Jean. So what's next, Jacque? You're going to beat me to make me obey you? I don't think so." She made a gesture with her hand.

Jacque said spitefully, "Spicy little thing aren't you, Julie? Or should say Miss Cactus, who let Louis turn her into a slut."

He acted like he was going to leave, then suddenly he turned to grab her. She was swift and took a hold of his hand and punched him in his face, then flipped him like she did last night. Jacque was trying to get up, but Julie restrained him. One of her feet was on the back of his head, pushing his face against the floor, while she held one of his arms twisted it and said, "I warned you before about grabbing me. Didn't I tell you I would break your arm if you ever did that again? I don't want to hurt you, Jacque. Behave yourself. If Louis found out what you did here today, he will hurt you, and I will let him, because he has his right to do so."

Nicole yelled, "Behind you, Julie!"

Julie grabbed Carine's arm with her other hand and pushed her against the wall beside her. Richard was just regaining consciousness. Everyone stood in astonishment. Maxine was kneeling beside him rubbing her hands over his head. Richard couldn't believe that Jacque hit him on the head. He was angry. He removed himself from the floor heading for Jacque.

Julie said, "No, Richard! Move away from him."

She was still holding on to Jacque. She asked, "Please, everyone, can you all leave the room. I want to talk to Jacque and Carine alone."

Maxine hesitated. "You want us to leave you with them!"

"Please!" Julie enforced. "I want to be alone with them."

Without any further back talk, everyone left the room. Noticing he was not resisting, Julie slowly let him go. Removing himself from the floor he said, "So you know karate." He rubbed his face and stomach.

She asked them to sit to talk. She wanted an explanation from them. "What did I do to you two that you guys dislike me so much and wanted to hurt me like that? Why, Jacque?"

Putting his head down, he replied, "You never took me seriously, even when I poured my heart out to you. Always big brother, nothing more. What I want to know is why you never loved me like you did Saul and Louis?"

Jacque's words brought grief to her heart. Julie looked at him and sighed. "Even though you and Jean were not my biological brothers or related to me, I grew up loving you guys as if you were. I was hoping that you would have felt the same way, too. Love me like I was one of your little sisters. I never thought you were looking at me in such a way. The thought of you thinking about me that way makes me feel dirty."

"Why wouldn't you look at me more like a man than just a brother," Jacque cried out softly. "I would have done anything for you."

"I couldn't help loving you like my brother," Julie replied. "You are my family, the oldest brother I've grown to love dearly."

"No!" Jacque shouted. "I was nothing in your eyes, just a caretaker of your properties. A butler!"

The name angered him. Julie couldn't believe what Jacque just said. She repeated, "Just a caretaker, a butler!"

"Yes," Jacque uttered out at her. "That's how you make me feel. Your parents took care of us when we were children, and now you are doing the same thing. I feel like I was one of your pets that you put in a nice home, taking care of it. Not once was I really able to do for my family, Julie. . . ."

Julie couldn't believe what she heard. "I stopped you from doing what?"

"You were always the one to pay for everything we needed," Jacque yelped, "even though we were working, Julie. Still you gave us an allowance."

"You have to be kidding," Julie cut in. "I never heard anyone complain. I never forced you or any of you to take anything from me."

"True, you never did," Jacque replied. "But you never asked for payment. We kept on asking and you kept on giving. You always want to be in control."

"Why not," Julie answered. "I work hard for every penny that I have. Everyone had their own."

He shook his head. "I learned no matter how hard I work, I could never surpass you. You were good in dealing business, and you married a very wealthy man who was able to cater to your needs and all your desires. I was not qualified to be your man. Another word, you were above me, never your equal."

Taking a deep breath to force the tears back, Julie replied, "I never put anyone before you guys, not even myself. I would have done anything for you, except that, to love you intimately. I thought we were family . . . I couldn't love you any other way."

"I felt," Jacque replied, "it's because I was not wealthy enough for you. I would have done anything to see that happen."

"I never thought money was an issue between you and I," Julie retorted. "I entrusted you with all my belongings, everything except my body. I guess that wasn't enough for you. You had to have me, too. I see. Where do you leave Debbie and your unborn child, Jacque?"

He was stunned, because she was not supposed to know about that.

Looking at his reaction Julie said, "Don't be surprised, Jacque. The very first time I saw her again, I knew she was pregnant by you. It showed all around her face. One had to be blind not to see that. It was a shame that she aborted her innocent child so you could work on how to have me. You thought I wouldn't find out what you had her do. When you told me you were going to Jacmel to get the place ready for me, the real reason for your sudden departure was to have her kill your baby. You took her to the Dominican Republic to butcher your baby. Do you know how many people would love to be able to conceive a child and there you went, killing an innocent. There are so many ways and so many birth controls one could take not to commit such a crime. I just hope she doesn't let you convince her to repeat the same mistake again. That was very cruel of you. . . . And yet you have the nerve to call Louis a killer when you are a murderer."

"Is that what is worrying you, Julie? Jacque said. "She might be pregnant? That's the reason you don't want me? You can put your mind to rest. She's not pregnant."

"I see." Julie sighed and gasped in frustration, "She's not pregnant. You are planning to kill this child, too. You must think that I'm stupid or blind not see the run-around you are doing to Debbie and the sacrifice she's willing to do to satisfy your sick project. You resented me more than I thought. You wanted to bring me down. You wanted to control me, like you did with all the members of your family. . . . So that was your plan, to take what I have and put me under your submission, so that's the price your beloved Julie should pay, taking over her life. You disrespected me and humiliated me and it wasn't enough for you. Please don't kill this baby on my behalf again. My soul cannot bare the burden of you murdering your unborn child for money that I have. So it is money you want, Jacque, so you could feel power over me. . . ."

Julie picked up her purse as she continued on to talk, "How much! Consider yourself lucky that Louis listened to me and he didn't swallow your head like the devil you took him for. You jeopardized all your assets by trying to steal from me. You once told me Louis is a man who plays fair. He would not ask for what he doesn't deserve. What is it now? Did Saul take something that was yours, and you feel you have the right for retribution? Since I was his wife, tell me how much is it, Jacque? So I may redeem what he had done to you. I want to settle this matter before Louis returns to pick me up."

Jacque growled at her, "What does Louis have to do with our discussion? For the past year, all you've been doing is running around with that maniac! You've become sick like all the women he had been screwing! What's going on between you two?"

"Louis has all the right to interfere with what is going on in my life," Julie stated, "because that maniac is now my husband!"

Shocked by her last statement, Jacque staggered back on the chair, remembering what it was that Louis told him at the restaurant. He startled. "Husband?"

"Yes," Julie verified by displaying her left hand to him, "my husband! He didn't treat me like the slut you said he would. . . . We got married over the weekend at his ranch."

Looking at her, Jacque frowned. "You mean you two were already married when you guys were over at the mansion last night?"

Crossing her arms Julie nodded her head and replied, "Yes!"

"Why didn't you tell me?" Shaking his head, Jacque chuckled. "Why the game?"

"You're the one who started the game." Julie laughed. "And you know Louis loves a good challenge. What Saul didn't let you know was that Louis and he were very good friends. He had entrusted Louis with everything. I know you knew you were dealing with Louis. You knew he was the unknown buyer. You told me Saul had asked you to hand Henry Claude all the documents of his business to him. Instead you chose to keep them, trying to trick me into signing my assets to you and a marriage certificate without knowing that I married you. You were willing to pay off a judge and a lawyer to accomplish your dreams by taking over my life. How does it feel to be fooled, Jacque, when your deal of your lifetime with Louis had slapped you in your face?"

Jacque couldn't answer her. That wasn't the plan he had in mind. He thought he had a perfect plan. And what had possessed him to do something like this to her? She had already trusted him enough. What was wrong with him? And why didn't he listen to reason? Not once did Julie show him she didn't appreciate him. She was always grateful for everything he did for her. How was he going to earn her respect again? All those thoughts were going through his mind while Julie was talking to him.

"All that time when I was signing those fake documents, I was hoping you would have come clean. When Max revealed your plans, by your reaction I knew you weren't going to confess, so I made Max apologize to you two. The glow of victory was written all over your face. I was hurt. Even at the last moment I sincerely believed you could come clean at the party.

Instead you wanted to humiliate me some more. Yesterday you thought you have succeeded when you started to tell me your plans and my role in them. And today you would have come here and beaten the crap out of me if I didn't know how to defend myself."

"You should have told me you were married to him," Jacque cried out, covering his face with his hands.

"You wouldn't want to hear it," Julie responded. "All you were concerned about was how to cheat me, to bring down my spirit, and to take over my life, as if you have the right. You felt underpaid, and like I have robbed you two out of your fortune."

She took out her checkbook from her purse and a pen. She yelled, "How much, because if it's money that made you two act that way, I'm willing to give you what you wanted."

Jacque didn't answer. He started to cry. Tears were flowing out of his eyes and it just couldn't stop pouring as he was coming to his senses. "I'm sorry, Julie. I was just jealous of you, everything about you. You were right, I just wanted to possess you, because you were a strong woman. I feel like an incompetent when I'm around you. You intimidate me! When I couldn't have you, I didn't want any other man to have you. I felt like a servant to you, never your equal."

"Did I ever treat you guys like that?"

Carine replied, "You didn't have to. You're good in everything you do. You can even sing. You are perfect."

"Perfect!" Feeling peeved, Julie laughed and cried, "You are blind if you think I was good in everything. I work hard. I keep myself busy so as not to go crazy. And when I'm too tired I'll lay down and fall right to sleep. This is how I live my life every day. I never take the easy way."

"You never pushed us," Carine answered.

Julie couldn't believe what Carine had suggested she should have done. "You guys are not children that I have to take your hands to direct you on the right course. I encourage. I never pushed because I was never forced to do anything I didn't want. I treated you guys the same. I study hard to be good at the things I do. Nothing was handed to me on a silver platter. And all of you know that."

Carine responded, "You're the one with all the luck."

"Don't even go there," Julie pressed. "I didn't take my blessings for granted. I worked hard to keep what was mine. I don't put my faith in luck."

She scoffed, "Here you are, you decided to move to Haiti to start fresh, and not even a year later, you're married to one of the most handsome available men in Haiti, who happens to be very wealthy. If this is not luck then what is it? For a person who doesn't believe in luck, twice you married, both times to a very wealthy man."

"Maybe it's because I wasn't looking for a wealthy man," she sneered at Carine, "or believed in some crazy witch who didn't know her own future. She had you believe that you two could get anything without working hard, but you two forget the most important thing about the real meaning of life. . . ."

Mockingly Carine replied, "And what is that, Julie?"

"Love, Carine," she soothingly replied. "Love, the very four letter word you don't want to acknowledge. This is something you'll never know if you continue the way you are going. You're a senseless person. On top of it you're insensitive. Many times, I turned my eyes away from the cruel things you did to me, Carine. I kept on hoping one day you would come to your senses. Instead you got worse, and Jacque, yes, big brother Jacque, who didn't want to be my brother, encouraged you to do what is bad for his own interest. But not anymore. You guys better shape up or get out of my life for good. Since I returned, I have to finish what Saul started to do at the mansion and at the plantation. Not once did you come and volunteer to help with the work, but lived large in my expense."

Jacque was still shaking by Julie's revelation. He couldn't believe that Julie and Louis were married. He sat there shaking, trying to get a grip on himself. Turning to Jacque, Julie said, "Well, Jacque, what else do you have to say to this slut? I never thought for one moment you would have thought of me in such a way. Again I judge you wrong. You were trying to take advantage of me, when I was in my most vulnerable stage in life. I trusted you. I would have laid down my life for you, all of you."

Julie closed her eyes as she breathed in and out to calm herself down, then looked at him and said, "All those years you were showing me you care, and in reality, your friendship was only based on possessions, sex, and money. I'm waiting. I'm running out of patience. I may never have all the answers to what really happened between us. But know one thing, you disappoint me, Jacque. I was wrong to think that you were a brother to me. I thought you would have been the last person who would have hurt me the way you did. Like I said before, how much money do you two need so I can get rid of you?"

Getting up from the seat, Jacque walked and stood before her and said, "I was blind, and very stupid, greedy, and abusive. You gave us money and many opportunities to get our lives together, and because of you, I was able to have my own hotel. I failed to realize my blessings, even when death is facing me. I kept on agitating the situation. I owe you enough, it's time for me to pay back what I owe."

He took her hands and held them against his chest. Jacque pleaded, "You were right. It is my fault that Carine was acting the way she was. I talked her into doing these things when I found out that Saul had sold half of everything to Louis. I felt left out and my jealousy overtook me. I became thoughtless and so selfish, that I forget everything, even our friendship. I wanted to ruin everything that your parents, you, and your late husband had worked hard for. Julie, I'm so sorry that I caused you so much pain. Please forgive me."

Julie was reluctant. She pulled her hands away. She didn't want to look at him. Jacque pleaded again to her, "I know there's a lot of cleaning up for me to do. I couldn't bear to lose your friendship. I let my jealousy and anger overtake me. We're family, you are my baby sister, I love you. I will never look at you that way again. Please forgive me. I'm going to do everything in my power to make things right between us. Please, Julie, don't turn your back on me."

She took a glance at him as he continued to beg. Jacque knelt down with his hands together, "Please forgive me."

She moved a few steps away from him, leaving him kneeling on the floor. Jacque bent his head, covering his face with his hands, crying.

Julie said, "I don't know if that is genuine or a show you are putting on for me. I don't trust you anymore, Jacque."

"You have your reasons," he sobbed. "Please forgive me."

Carine sat back, reflecting about her past. She, too, was crying. She spoke up, "I'm sorry too, Julie. I've been hurting myself and everyone around me for so long. I could have said no to Jacque like everybody, but my greed for money made me lose out in a lot of things in life, even a good man. I don't know how to get out of the situation that I'm in. I'm lost . . . I need help."

Julie went and sat for a few minutes. She didn't say anything. She stared at them for a while, studying them. She put her hands over her face, passing them away from her face, then looked at Jacque, who was still on his knees crying. She removed herself from the seat and helped Jacque up. "Yes, I forgive you both. But you two are going to work real hard to gain my trust again. And as for you, Carine, the first help I'm going to give is a little advice. . . . If you ever put your hands on my man as if to entice him to sexual activity, I'll break your fingers, understand? And if you don't take me seriously let me demonstrate something that I could do to you and big brother Jacque. . . ."

She raised her hands then yelled as she hit her hand against Nadine's heavy wooden coffee table and split it in two. Jacque and Carine jumped in fear. Julie snarled, "Do I make myself clear?"

Carine quickly nodded her head in understanding and walked to Julie and gave her a hug and a kiss on her cheek as she replied, "Yes, I understand . . . and I'm sorry."

Jacque stood there looking at her in shock, then chuckled and thought, *She doesn't think she intimidates me.* He smiled and said, "There's a lot I don't know about you, Julie. You look so fragile and innocent."

"Oh, one more thing, Jacque," Julie said and caused him to fumble. "The next time I hear you hit the girls, I'll cripple you for life and you owe Nadine an apology for entering her house without her permission. Everyone, and especially Nicole, Maxine, and Richard."

"Yes ma'am!" Jacque replied with a salute as he once used to say when he agreed with her with something. After they finished settling their argument, they hugged each other, then thanked Julie for her compassion.

Julie walked to the door to let everyone in and found all their heads were leaning against the door listening. As she opened the door they all fell down inside the room. Shaking her head at them, they all acted like they had something fallen on the floor and they were looking for it. Julie stood there looking at them crawling on the floor, shaking her head as she stared at them and laughed. Everyone else followed with their laughter.

Julie said sadly, "Nadine, I'm sorry about your coffee table. I owe you one."

"Don't worry about it," she said. "I wanted to change that table for very long time."

Jacque walked to Richard and apologized to him and to everyone after they removed the broken table and the broken vase out of the living room. When they finished fixing up the room, they all trouped into the den. With all the laughing going on in the room, no one heard the bell. Louis and Henry walked inside the house into the den. Jacque was sitting by Julie. As soon as he saw Louis he quickly got up and caused Julie to turn.

Slowly they moved toward each other. Louis gently pulled her in his arms and kissed her, then turned to look at Jacque and said, "I'm glad to see you and my wife getting along again."

Jean had also arrived at the same time with Viviane. Jean looked around at the den, looked at Jacque, and asked, "What happened here?"

They all came and embraced Viviane, who was standing by Jean.

Jacque walked toward Jean and gave him a hug to apologize. Jean was stupefied. His eyes bulged out from the socket. He didn't know whether to push Jacque or hug him. He stood there with a dumb big smile on his face, which made him look like a clown, causing everyone to laugh. Nicole rushed over to his side to hug him, saying, "Boy! You'll never believe it. I'll tell you all about it another time."

Jacque took Viviane's hands. He also apologized to her and promised her that she was going to see a new Jacque, a very respectful man.

Maxine looked in amazement at Julie. Lifting Julie's hands to look, she said, "You never told me you could do that."

"Come on, girl," Julie said and reminded her, "remember how I used to crack the almond seeds. You used to tell me 'you're going to hurt your hands,' to use the rock you gave me to break the nuts. And I also remember telling you that these hands could chop wood and bricks. You were not paying attention."

"Yes you did," she smiled and whispered, "but I thought it was Louis. . . . You've got to show me some of those moves."

"Yeah," chorused the rest of the girls.

Nadine turned to Julie. "You're truly a Ms. Cactus. I want to learn that technique, Mrs. Janvier."

Michelle had walked in with Patrick beside her with a box of cake in her hand and smiled. "What's happening here?"

"Everything is fine," replied Nadine.

Handing Nadine the box of cake, Michelle was looking from Julie to Louis standing with their arms wrapped around each other, wondering what was going on between them. She whispered to Nadine, "When did those two become a couple? Or should I ask if he's screwing her now?"

"Let me let you in on a little secret," Nadine whispered back with glee. "They're married."

Michelle looked at Louis's left hand and saw a wedding band in his wedding finger and at Nadine to see if she was joking. "I don't believe you . . . you're not joking."

Michelle shook her head wondering, shocked at the news she had just received. She moaned in despair.

Richard was looking at Julie in awe. "Oh, Julie, you have to teach me how to fight."

Julie looked at him and said, "I don't really know how to fight. . . ." Louis looked at her and gave her a kiss on the lips as she grimaced. "I just hate violence."

"You do," he replied tenderly, "but you're so good at it."

"Louis," Julie reprimanded, "I'm not."

Everyone chorused a laugh at Louis's comment.

"I love you," Louis said to her and gave a kiss on her nose, which made everyone blush as they looked at him holding Julie tight in his arms to kiss her again.

Carine walked up to them and said, "I haven't had a chance to congratulate you two . . . I'm sincerely happy for you, Julie."

She gave Julie a kiss on both her cheeks then kissed Louis on his and said, "Welcome to the family, big brother."

Louis couldn't help but smile and thanked her. Jacque came by and did the same. He shook Louis's hand and said, "Thank you."

Louis didn't respond but his actions told Jacque he was welcome, because he tapped him on his shoulder. Turning to Nadine, Louis said, "Well, Nadine, we're heading home."

Nadine looked at Julie with a broad smile and said, "Julie, I was happy to have you here with me. Your presence always bring joy and excitement to me. Again thank you."

Loziane came in with William and handed him to his father, then she went and placed everything in the car.

That was an evening Julie and her friends would never forget. But time does heal all wounds. Brian continued working for Louis as his chief executive for his plantations. As for the forty thousand dollars, he gave it back to Jacque.

Jacque was very happy and grateful. He was working hard to make things right between Julie, her husband, and himself. He apologized to Debbie for the way he had been treating her. He recognized that he had a lot of lost time to make up for. Like Louis, he married Debbie a month later. Nothing big, just the family.

Carine finally had courage to apologize to Brian. She hoped one day he would find it in his heart to forgive her for all the wrong and pains she had caused him for the last few years.

<u>Chapter Nineteen</u>

Love That Binds

When you are in love time stands still. You don't go wandering about. Sunshine is always in the air. You yearn for a stormy night, so you can hug and kiss the one you love. Then you'll make love all night long. This was true in the case of Mr. and Mrs. Janvier. Last night was a special night. Julie and Louis were celebrating their third month anniversary and his retirement from the hospital. Only a few of their closest friends did they let participate in their enjoyment. Then they disappeared for the rest of the night. They made love half of the night on the bed then in the shower. Louis was still feeling he was dreaming her, he felt so good touching her. As he took her, Julie felt she was making love to a god. Louis knew her very being. In her arms he was refined, pretentious. He never wanted to stop having that affectedly grand he was feeling.

"Oh, Julie," Louis conferred, as he watched her trembling in his arms. He gathered her closer toward him as he deeply entering the depth of her being. She consumed every stroke and movement from him. She moaned and breathed out his name in pleasure as she released. They were romantic. They were authentic. In each other's arms, time and space did stand still because their love was real. After finishing wiping her, Louis carried her back to bed so she could rest for the remainder of the night. If you are searching for a couple that was made in heaven, you can definitely pick them. They shared everything.

Julie stretched herself and turned over in the bed. She reached over and passed her hand on the side where her husband slept and encountered empty space. Uh oh! Louis was not there. She opened her eyes, got out of bed, put on her robe, and went to look for her man. Then she noticed the light was on in the bathroom. She smiled as she walked toward the light. She opened the door, and she saw Louis kneeling on the floor in front of the toilet, vomiting. She pulled the towel from the rack, wet it at the sink, and bent over his asking, "Are you all right, honey?"

She dabbed at his forehead and went to get him some water so he could rinse his mouth and wash his face. Then she helped him get up and took him back to the bed and tucked him in under the blanket. He grimaced and made a face at her. "Hopefully in a week I'll be over this morning sickness. I had the same problem, when you were pregnant with Bill. I just hope it's not as bad."

He placed his hand on her stomach as she lowered her head to kiss him. Julie's stomach didn't show. She was only two and a half months. Today was a big day for her best friend Maxine. Jacque was to give her away to Richard and Louis was Richard's best man. Julie was her maid of honor. Time was ticking and Maxine was nervous. Someone was knocking on the door. Julie got up off the bed and went to open the door. It was Maxine.

Julie whispered, "Why are you up so early?"

She walked out of the bedroom, quietly pulling the door shut behind her so as not to disturb Louis. Maxine said, "I can't sleep."

They walked downstairs into the ballroom which was decorated for the festivities later on. They checked around. Julie placed her arm around Maxine and they started to waltz with each other. They laughed and giggled as they turned on the dance floor.

"How's Louis?" Maxine asked.

Julie said somberly, "He hasn't got over his morning sickness."

Maxine laughed as Julie reprimanded, "Max!" But she was laughing too. "That's not funny."

Maxine was in hysterics. "Who would have thought Louis Janvier would get morning sickness, Mr. Macho? You have to admit, Julie, he would be the last person I would think of something like this happening too."

Julie put her hand over her stomach, "I feel for him."

Maxine stepped back and held her at arm's length. "And look at you, not even a little nauseous. All you're doing is carrying the baby. I like that, it's romantic!"

They continued dancing to no music. Julie said, "I had better stop. I don't want to get tired, I want to enjoy tonight. Don't worry, Max, everything will be fine. The ballroom only needs flowers and the caterers will make sure everything is done the way you want. I'll see you later. Let's go back to our beds."

They walked back up stairs arm in arm.

Everything was going well for Julie. Her dreams had become a reality and her loneliness was over. She didn't mind not knowing where she was heading, as long as she was at Louis's side. His love was like the river pouring in her life. She knew she was holding her well for this slow dance. They would have a history to pass on for generation to come. And she knew wherever Louis would go, he would take her with him, because he felt the same way she did. They both found what they were searching for, their soul mates.

Maxine and her husband Richard were to go to New York for their honeymoon. This would be Richard Landers's first time in the U.S. Louis and Julie were to accompany them to the Big Apple along with their son William and Julie's mother. Bill was to stay with his grandmother Viviane, since this was their honeymoon, too.

Maxine looked at her seat belt to see if it was fastened. Then she looked across her seat on the plane, and saw Louis was kissing and caressing Julie's stomach. She overheard him say, "*Je besoin ton chaleur* (I need your warmth)."

Maxine smiled and thought, *I think those two should be left in private now.* She turned to look at Richard and whispered to him, "I think we're taking them to their honeymoon."

Smiling, Richard pulled her toward him embraced her and kissed her too, as the plane was landing. . . .

THE TURNING POINT OF OUR LIFE

I was hers, but I didn't know it until I was at her gate.
I didn't know—I smiled when I saw her face—
that my prayers had been heard, and that God had set his eyes on me.

****

She opened my eyes with four single words:
"Hello, come on in!"
She caused me to be humble with her gentleness.
She calmed my heart with her love; I would serve her with rejoicing,
not knowing that I was going to make myself happy.
The softness of her hands were like cotton against my shaved face,
but yet they could crush.
She was powerful, and I didn't know it until she had me
whispering in her ear that I loved her.
From that moment, I was reaching out for her, wanting to hold her and
kiss her in the morning before the sunset.
I wanted to inhale the essence of her body
while I held her in my arms for a few moments longer
and kissed her as she whispered back, "I love you too."
And as I drink in the fountain of her mouth,
I blessed God's name with my soul
so I would not forget who had brought me out of She'ol
and forgave all my transgressions.
And I thanked You.

CHAPTER ONE

BITTERSWEET MEMORIES

A young man was standing barefooted and shirtless on the balcony of his penthouse looking at the city view. He yawned while he stretched his arms backward, clicked his neck twice from side to side, and then rotated his shoulder forward and backward. He took a deep breath in and out of his lungs to relax his muscles.

Afterward, he leaned against the beige marble wall of the balcony listening to how the water in the pool, which was facing him, was bubbling. He was wearing a pair of white boxers that revealed his masculinity very nicely. His sun-tanned body was unblemished. His square chin showed his nice-sized pink lips, which were well pronounced and cut evenly on his face. His nose was straight, not overlapping, which brought out his long eyelashes on his bright, gentle aqua eyes and his thick, neatly shaped eyebrows on his oval face well. He walked a few feet toward the railing of the balcony to look at the city view.

He looked up at the dark, cloudy sky, enjoying the cool air that just ran through his reddish, light-brownish, soft, straight hair, which was trimmed down to the back of his neck. His physique was built like that of a mighty man. If one was searching for a beautiful man in the world, one to be praised so much . . . here was one who was so handsome from the sole of his foot to the crown of his head. He proved to have no defect on him.

Tonight, the sky was clear with a few stars sparkling above. By the way the air was blowing, cool, he could feel a storm was heading his way. He closed his eyes calling out to God, to whom he had not prayed for a very long time. He tried to clear out the bad thoughts in his mind to bring in some positive thoughts. He was trying to understand why his mind had been troubled all those years, why God had never given him a clue as to why he was having loving and sexual feelings for a woman he had never met and never even known where she really was.

Again he looked up, and through about how he was to solve the problem he had been facing through those years, which now haunted him more than ever. He took a deep breath and let out a long, deep audible exhale to express his sorrow, while he ran his hands through his thick, shining hair, pushing it back away from his face.

At the moment, he was feeling anguish because rage was taking over his heart. He was feeling empty. He whispered God's name as he tried to control the madness that was befalling him. He had reckoned that he would never have peace if he failed to find the missing essence of his life. Nor would there ever be peace between him and his brother if he couldn't find the solution to both of their problems. He had enough calamities, and he wanted to set his heart free, to love, and to share his deepest desire with only one, the woman of his dreams. Resentment was coursing through his soul because of what he was thinking.

He muttered, "Why am I constantly thinking about a woman who doesn't even know that I exist? Why have I allowed Him to keep her concealed from me?"

For a moment, he closed his eyes, trying to reason with himself as he spoke to God. A few drops of tears rolled down his face. He quickly dried them as they came out. He made a promise to God. He swore if He gave him what he wanted he would remain loyal to her. He was in deep thought when he took a quick glance through the sliding door of his bedroom and saw his phone was flashing silently on the night table.

Quietly, he walked in to pick it up and went back out on the balcony, closing the glass doors behind him to continue looking at the clear, dark sky.

"Reginald," he said shaking his head. "It's bad timing."

Knowing his caller ID wouldn't pick up his cell phone number, the caller replied at the other end, "William Lordsteel Janvier." He sarcastically replied as he laughed, "How did you know it was me calling you, when I'm not using my home phone?"

"Who else would have dared call me at this particular hour and while I have a woman here with me?"

The building Reginald was living in was across the street from the building where he was living, not too far from Central Park. Likewise he couldn't sleep. He was standing on his balcony looking out. Reginald laughed, "I was out looking at the scenery of the park, when I noticed your light was on. So I decided to check on you through my binoculars. . . ."

William nodded his head while he listened to Reginald running his mouth. Reginald continued on laughing. " . . . that was some wild sex-er-cise you were engaging her into. Were you possessed so that you were in need to exorcise the demons out of you . . . I was starting to wonder what you were on. You definitely deserved two thumbs up. I thought you were going skinny dipping to cool down the hellfire that was burning in you. . . ."

Again William nodded at Reginald's sarcastic remark.

" . . . you've been standing there for quite some time. You should be sleeping, restoring back your strength, for someone who had been engaged on that long, totally excruciating workout. But no, you're still looking out in the sky at the polluted air of New York. What's up, big brother?"

William was happy to hear the gleeful sounds in his brother's voice. He gave a little laugh. "I'm glad I was able to give you a good show, but didn't Father tell you to stop being a Peeping Tom? It's not polite."

"You have got to put blinds or curtains on your windows or get rid of the glass doors," Reginald laughed. "You gave too much easy access."

"What I will do is take away your binoculars," William laughed. "I understand why Father had all those far-sights around his ranch bedroom windows in Haiti, but you used yours to pick on my bedroom. Are you looking for pointers?"

"Speaking like an expert. You have a lot to teach, big brother."

"I could teach you a lot more, Reginald, beside sex," William responded. "Beside being a Peeping Tom, what are you up to, Reginald?"

"I'm getting ready to go to Texas right now!"

William's smile got brighter. He exclaimed, "Great!"

"I knew you would have gotten a kick our of that, but that's not the reason I'm heading that way. Since you're my boss, you have compelled me to head in that direction . . . so here I am going there, hoping no one will see me while I'm in Texas having a family outing with our parents, doing what you have forced me to do since you're my boss."

"I'm glad you know I'm your boss, but still, I'm giving you the choice. You don't have to go, Reginald. Send someone else, like you've been doing for over five years. I'm not forcing you to go. It is still your choice."

"I know, William," Reginald said. "You have a way of making people do things and having them think they made the choice."

William did not object. He replied, "I hope you have a wonderful time with the family Reginald."

"Yeah, yeah? I'll give Grandmother, Mother, Aunt Maxine, and Father your regard too. . . . And brother," he laughed, "take mercy on Diana."

Annoyed by his brother's remark, William turned and glanced at the woman lying down on his bed sleeping. As he said good-bye to his brother and hung up the phone, he was thinking, *This is just another booty call.*

He didn't feel any love for this woman he just had sex with. He looked at her like she was a plaything that he had just enjoyed. Now it was over and soon he was going to put her away. *God, help me!* He thought and whispered, "I'm damned!" He growled under his breath, "Why can't I have what I want?"

CHAPTER TWO

REMINISCENCE

William stretched as he went in through the sliding door that had opened to him automatically to fix himself a drink. He glanced at his bed and noticed that Diana wasn't asleep. But she closed her eyes so he would think that she was. He stared at her as he fixed his cognac. He noticed by the way she was lying down that she was waiting for his attention.

At the moment, William didn't want to be bothered with her. He left his room and went to his living room to sit for a moment. He placed his glass down by a flat package on the coffee table that was about two to three feet in width and length. Picking up the package, he tore the white glossy paper wrapped around it and pulled out a painting he had brought from an art gallery he went to a few days ago with Diana. He sat it on his sofa to look at it. He wondered what the artist was thinking when he painted that portrait.

The picture reminded him of spring. Looking at the portrait, he saw people smiling as they were riding their bikes in the park on a clear, sunny day while a couple of people were sitting on benches: some were playing chess and others were listening to a man playing his guitar. There were children lined up ready to buy ice cream from an ice cream truck stationed in front of the entrance to the park. However, William's attention was on the loving couple sitting under a tree having a picnic, how the man was smiling looking upon the woman, as she let him take a bite of her apple.

The painting made William feel gloomy. He wondered what was on his mind when he chose to buy this painting. Looking at it made him feel even lonelier than ever. He turned the painting so he wouldn't look at it, because he was getting agitated. He picked up his cognac, then tasted it.

Afterward, he walked up and down to every room around his luxurious penthouse as if he were searching for something. He went back and stood by the steps that led to the upper floor. While looking up, he thought he saw the woman of his dreams looking and smiling down at him; then her vision disappeared. He knew he was definitely going mad. At the moment, there wasn't anything he wanted that was here with him.

William walked back to his room. He stood by his bed looking down at Diana, whom he knew wasn't asleep. He wondered what she was hoping to happen between them. At the moment, he wanted her out of his room. He made ready to shake her to tell her to go home, but he hesitated when he came to realize what he was about to do. He didn't want to be cruel to her . . . it wasn't her fault that she couldn't give him what he was looking for . . . in his heart he apologized to her as he quietly moved back away from his bed. Then he went right back on the balcony to meditate.

William sat on the rail of the balustrade with a drink between his right fingers and continued looking up at the dark sky. He reflected on his life, thinking back on his childhood: he was more than a handful. He always seemed to be in trouble. His mind took him back to when he was the age of thirteen, fourteen years ago. . . .

It was early September; William's weekend had just ended. It was late in the afternoon when William was in his room sitting on the balcony playing on his laptop computer while his mother was talking on the phone in the library.

"William!" Reginald called out as he rushed into his room. He relayed to William everything he had heard their mother discussing with a woman named Mrs. Henderson.

"Is that true, Bill," Reginald asked excitedly, "what Mrs. Henderson is accusing you of?"

William didn't answer. Reginald smiled with enthusiasm and requested, "Would you tell me later how it all happened, William? Mother is going to be very angry," he laughed. And if you want me to lie for you, I would. I'll tell her that you were with me all the time . . . I got your back, big brother.

William didn't reply. After listening to Reginald, he closed the laptop, removing himself from the edge of the balcony on which he was sitting. He walked into his room and put down his laptop on the desk that was near the window. He walked a few feet away from his desk to lie down on his bed while his brother was telling him what to say. William thought as he listened to Reginald running his mouth. I can't believe she called on me.

There was a knocking on the door. Reginald went to open it. It was Loziane, their personal servant. She let them know that their mother was waiting for William in the study room.

William rolled off the bed and put his shoes on. He breathed in and out of his mouth to keep calm while he headed for the library room. He quietly walked in and stood in front of the desk at which his mother was sitting.

Putting the book down, she walked around the desk and stood before him. She couldn't look at him face-to-face because he was already much taller that her; she had to look up at him. She asked him to sit on the chair before her desk. She sat on top of the desk to talk to him.

She took a deep breath, exhaled, and said, "I was talking to Mrs. Henderson, Cindrale's mother, the young woman who was one of the bridesmaids at Steward's wedding . . . a man who happens to be a friend of your father. I believe you were the usher who walked beside her. Louis told me that you were too young to be an usher. But I thought it would be a good opportunity for you to socialize with some of the youths that were participating in the wedding, a chance to make new friends. I've given you the benefit of the doubt that you would make the right decision because you seem to have a lot of understanding about the facts of life. But today, Mrs. Henderson called and told me to tell you to keep your dirty hands off her daughter . . . what do you have to say for yourself?"

William didn't answer. He was thinking, Why didn't Gloria Henderson tell my mother the whole truth that she was jealous? *He stared at his mother and then looked away.*

Julie stated, "Not that I care what her mother has to say, but I do care for you. And I want to know the truth. Your silence is not going to help you, Bill."

Hearing the disappointment in his mother's voice toward him, he responded, "I'm sorry . . . I'll keep away from her."

"That's all you have to say? 'I'll keep away from her'? I want an explanation, boy. Just because you're taller than me doesn't make you a man. You're only thirteen, and when I ask you a question, I want an answer. Do you understand, boy?"

"Yes," he replied.

"I'm listening!"

William stood up to look down at his mother as he shoved his hands in his pants pockets, then stared down at her. He said, "I feel like there is certain information best for parents not to know."

"And what is it that I shouldn't know, Mr. William Lordsteel Janvier?"

He knew his mother was angry because she called him "Mr." He didn't want her to be upset.

"I was sleeping with her," William said in a low tone voice. He was upset. "Now you know."

"Her mother called and told me that she had caught you doing her seventeen-year-old daughter whom I know is twenty. I feel that I should have her daughter prosecuted for that kind of behavior."

"Then if you knew that," he stated with an attitude, "why did you make me say it? It's personal what we have done together; it's not polite for anyone to invade my privacy!"

"Are you out of your mind?" his mother replied even angrier for the way he had responded to her. She snapped, "The only privacy you should have is when you're using the toilet. I'm filing charges against her."

"I'll deny it," he calmly replied.

"William, you're only thirteen. In a court of law what she did to you was statutory rape!"

"I do know my age," he cut her short. "And I know how my body feels. I don't need you or Father to tell me that I'm too young . . . I do use protection."

Julie's hands trembled, feeling the want to slap him and bring him to his senses. But she kept her cool. She listened to how he spoke to her as if he was a man. She calmed herself down so she could reason with him. She wanted him to understand the importance of preservation and respect for oneself, the damage he had caused his flesh, and the danger of having sexual intercourse without being married. She told him how Louis, his father, and she waited until they were properly wed.

She told him about the transmitted diseases that were out there, preying on those who had no self-control. She understood how he felt, she said because she was once that age too. It was nothing new, the way he was feeling, but he needed to hold back, using the "principles" that he had been brought up with. She wanted him to wait until he was grown and married to a woman that he was truly in love with.

She punished him after her speech for a whole month. Later on, when his father came home, he emphasized her punishment by telling him that he couldn't leave the territory of their home.

Later that evening, William went to the library to read. He was lying down on the sofa upstairs, on the second level reading area when Julie and Louis came in to relax. Thinking that they were all alone, Louis and Julie started conversing with each other while they were enjoying their cognac. William, however, overheard his mother talking to his father.